W9-BVM-243

S

Visit Tyndale's exciting Web site at www.tyndale.com

TYNDALE is a registered trademark of Tyndale House Publishers, Inc.

Tyndale's quill logo is a trademark of Tyndale House Publishers, Inc.

Flee the Night

Edited by Lorie Popp

Designed by Cathy Bergstrom

Scripture quotations are taken from the *Holy Bible*, New Living Translation, copyright © 1996. Used by permission of Tyndale House Publishers, Inc., Wheaton, Illinois 60189. All rights reserved.

Scripture quotations are taken from the *Holy Bible*, New International Version®. NIV®. Copyright © 1973, 1978, 1984 by International Bible Society. Used by permission of Zondervan Publishing House. All rights reserved.

This novel is a work of fiction. Names, characters, places, and incidents are either the product of the author's imagination or are used fictitiously. Any resemblance to actual events, locales, organizations, or persons, living or dead, is entirely coincidental and beyond the intent of either the author or publisher.

Library of Congress Cataloging-in-Publication Data

Warren, Susan, date
  Flee the night / Susan May Warren.
    p. cm.
  ISBN 1-4143-0086-7 (sc)
  I. Title.
PS3623.A865F58 2005
813'.6—dc22   2004023139

Printed in the United States of America

09 08 07 06 05
7   6   5   4   3   2   1

FOR YOUR GLORY, LORD.

Acknowledgments

God again gifted me with the blessing of co-laborers to see this project come to fruition. My deepest gratitude goes to the following people.

Doug Satterly, a generous soldier whom I met on the plane to Kalispell. Thank you for letting me quiz you for two-plus hours, for your candidness and your advice. Your insights into the men of the Special Forces helped me craft Micah and Conner. May God keep you safe.

Olaf Growald, rescuer extraordinaire, in so many ways. Thank you for looking at these SAR scenes and helping me get them right. Any mistakes I made were mine alone. Thank you for always being "on His shift."

David Lund, for your thorough descriptions of Internet security and for making them understandable to a nontechie. Again, any mistakes I made were mine alone.

Tracey Bateman, for your stellar critiques and insights into Missouri. Beyond that, thank you for being iron on iron. For the times you don't take me seriously . . . and the times you do. I'm proud to know you and Rusty.

Anne Goldsmith, for knowing how to help me craft a story—you say, "Fix this" in the nicest way! And for liking Jim Micah and the entire Team Hope cast. You help make dreams come true.

Lorie Popp, for smoothing out this story into a seamless, polished piece. You have the touch! Thank you especially for helping me rename my 1980s calculator.

Andrew Warren, for poking holes in my plots, then helping me restitch them. You're my Jim Micah, and I'm so glad I waited for you.

David Warren, for the day you sat in my office and astounded me with your spiritual insights into Isaiah 61. The metaphor of the dungeon belongs to you. Thank you also for making me lunch. I might starve without you.

Then they cried to the Lord in their trouble, and he saved them from their distress. He brought them out of darkness and the deepest gloom and broke away their chains.

PSALM 107:13-14, NIV

Chapter 1

THE PAST COULDN'T have picked a worse time to find her.

Trapped in seat 15A on an Amtrak Texas Eagle chugging through the Ozarks at four on a Sunday morning, Lacey . . . Galloway . . . Montgomery—what was her current last name?—tightened her leg lock around the computer bag at her feet. She dug her fingers through the cotton knit of her daughter's sweater as she watched the newest passenger to their car find his seat. Lanky, with olive skin and dark eyes framed in wire-rimmed glasses, it had to be Syrian assassin Ishmael Shavik who sat down, fidgeted with his leather jacket, then impaled her with a dark glance.

She couldn't stifle the shiver that rattled clear to her toes. Why hadn't she listened to divine wisdom fifteen-some years ago and stayed at home instead of running after adventure? Lacey forced breath through her constricting chest. She hadn't hoped to outrun her mistakes forever, but why today with Emily watching?

Lacey pried her fingers out of Emily's sweater and laced her hands together in her lap, cringing at her weakness. She'd been taught not to give away emotions, liabilities, secrets. But she'd die before she'd let them harm a hair on Em's head.

If only she'd possessed such an impulse seven years ago.

Tightening her jaw, she stared out the window. The Amtrak hustled north in the murky dawn, the Missouri oak, red buckeye, and hickory trees flanking the tracks—gray, silent sentries to her ill fate.

Oh, please, not here. Not now. She and Emily were so close to finding peace. Now that the Ex-6 program had met National Security Agency (NSA) approval, the nightmare seemed to be over. After this little time-out and escape with her daughter to Chicago, Lacey would fine-tune the encryption/decryption program, then hand it over with a sigh of relief and the sense that she'd finally found a way to atone for her mistakes. Never again would the field agents be without a way to secure their communications. No more ambushes due to intercepted messages. No more corrupted information.

Lives—and national secrets—safe.

And finally, too, a safe home for Emily. *Please.*

She didn't know to whom she might be addressing her plea. God in heaven hadn't looked her way for over a decade—not that she blamed Him. She was wretchedly on her own.

Around her, innocents slept—families, singles, the petite bourgeoisie voyaging to Chicago or beyond. Wealthy romantics above her were in compartments, perhaps for nostalgia or novelty. Lacey didn't have a romantic bone left in her body, despite the aroma of a dining car, the charisma of faux leather seats, or even the hypnotic locomotive pulse. She didn't have the energy or time for it, even if the errant inclination to be held in a man's arms haunted her in the lonely hours of the predawn. Then again, it wasn't just any man's embrace that haunted her.

Lacey rubbed her forehead and considered her options. It hadn't been so long ago that she'd memorized the exits and the players of every room she entered, but hope had smudged her reflexes. Ishmael sat two seats away, smack-dab in the middle of the car, blocking a desperate sprint down the aisle. The forest hurtled by at breakneck speed, discouraging a flying dismount.

Lacey stuck her hand in her pocket to rifle for her switch-blade and brushed against Emily's worn Beanie bear and only confidant that she named Boppy. Lacey had sent the child the Beanie Baby from Seattle—she still remembered the neon lights striping her hotel room, mocking her as she wrote a note to her toddler daughter, secreted in Aunt Janie's care.

Life wasn't fair.

She found the knife and tucked it under her thigh as she stole another glance at her killer. It sent a decade-old threat through her head: *You can't run from me.*

She blew out a breath and fought her climbing pulse as she clung to her training. Surprise. Focus. Determination. These things would help her flee, keep her alive.

What about Em? She longed to run her fingers across her daughter's face, over the smattering of freckles on her high cheekbones, then through the short curly blonde hair that, like John's, simply refused to obey a brush or a comb. Emily smelled of the fabric softener her aunt Janie used in the laundry and of soap from her predeparture bath. Curled into the fetal position, the six-year-old leaned her head against the dark pane, drooling on the pillow tucked under her shoulder. Her breathing seemed shallow, uneven, as if she were caught in the throes of a night-mare. But it was only the consequences of a desperate and fatal mistake—one for which Lacey could never, ever forgive herself.

Forgiveness wouldn't help her now, anyway. Not when her murderer stared at her like a slit-eyed wolf.

The air felt weighted with the slumber of passengers—some stirring, others in full collapse. The quiet pressed Lacey into her seat, made her heartbeat thunder in her ears. Fatigue played with her fear, pitting it against hope. Perhaps the man who had boarded this train wasn't the same one who had threatened to slit her throat from ear to ear. Frank Hillman's long arm of revenge.

Lacey *had* been careful. So careful she'd lost herself years ago in the torrent of aliases and the blur of constant movement. She often wondered if she would ever, even if the nightmare ended, find her way home.

Who was she kidding? She couldn't go home when her mistakes branded her like an ugly, festering *T* for *traitor* on her forehead. But if she somehow escaped the stigma of being an accused murderer, she might return to the family farm, a place that still held secrets and hopes. She'd start over with Emily and build a new life. A peaceful life. An absolved life.

Yeah, right. If she kept supposing, she might as well dream that she hadn't derailed her life seven years ago on a similar Sunday morning in an armpit country south of Russia . . . hadn't ignored the urgings of God or whatever impulse had made her pause briefly in the hotel as John loaded his Ruger pistol.

"I want you to stay here," he'd said. "And trust no one." John Montgomery always had the bluest eyes, even in memory. Ocean blue, with flecks of pure sunshine that melted her into a senseless puddle. She'd fallen for those magnetic eyes first and his idealism second.

"No," she'd said, shaking free of the hesitation, propelled by that same naive zeal that made the couple famous in the company. John and Lacey Montgomery, dynamic duo, spies of the spectacular new era when industrial espionage reigned in the vacuum of cold-war intrigues. "I'm coming with you."

He hadn't argued; she often blamed him for that omission. It seemed easier somehow. *Why didn't you stop me?*

There were moments, ethereal seconds, when she imagined spinning back in time, past the mistakes in Kazakhstan, past the choices in Iraq, the years at MIT, past even the wedding of the century in Ashleyville, Kentucky. It reeled back to an October day in high school twenty-two years ago, when she'd tripped off the football bleachers, clarinet in her grip, and fell into the oh-so-ample embrace of the wide receiver for the Ashleyville Eagles.

Jim Micah.

In those seconds when her future loomed blank and glorious before her, life scrolled differently. She chose more wisely, with her heart instead of her adrenaline. In this future, she stayed in Micah's arms. She clung to his steadiness, his rock-solid emotions that seemed firm footing in the face of danger. She would learn to read the emotions in his eyes and take a chance on heartbreak. And she'd never, ever let another man woo her away with the tease of a tastier, more vivid life.

Then the nano-dreams would vanish and she'd return to whatever bus, train, or airplane she'd landed on, head bumping against the seat, wondering how long it would take for the NSA to advance her a few more bucks.

She swept her attention casually across the travelers opposite the aisle. Asians. A family of overseas tourists, judging by the way they clutched their bags to their chests and eyed the other passengers. She connected with an elderly man, his gray hair in high-and-tight spikes around his round wrinkled face. He looked at her with such disdain, she wondered if he could see through her to her ugly past and abhor her for her mistakes.

He wouldn't be the only one.

Ishmael chose that moment to clear his throat, as if hoping to arrest her attention.

Lacey stiffened and forced her gaze to the carpeted floor.

Maybe she should throw her body over Emily and beg for their lives in Arabic. Or grab Ex-6—the one thing that could redeem her lost soul—tuck Emily under her arm, and bolt.

Instead, what if she left Emily in the safe hands of the gentleman sitting across from her? No one but Lacey knew that the little girl belonged to her. With the fake name on Em's ticket not even remotely similar to her real name, the six-year-old blonde could be anyone's daughter. The man appeared to care for her daughter, the way his eyes darted to her, a worried knot in his wide brow, as if he were some sort of private body-guard. He'd even purchased Emily an ice-cream cone at the station in Little Rock. Still, with the crazies out there on the prowl for innocents like Emily, it might be safer to attempt a flying leap into the forest with the train going 50 mph. Suddenly the ice-cream-cone treat felt downright . . . creepy.

What about a conductor? She could give him Emily's backpack, along with Janie's address and telephone number. Then Janie would become Mama again—a thousand times better than any mama Lacey had ever been.

Lacey winced. She was a horrible mother to be plotting her daughter's abandonment. Bitterness lined her throat at the injustice of having to relive her mistakes in a million private sacrifices. But Emily would be better off alive and in the arms of Lacey's sister than watching her mother be murdered. Or dying as a victim in the tussle. Lacey would do anything to make sure she didn't cost any more lives.

She always knew she'd lose Emily to pay penance for her foolishness. Somehow it seemed heart-wrenchingly fair.

If only Micah were here. That thought drilled a hole so deep through Lacey's chest she nearly gasped. Yeah, right. He'd be lining up behind Ishmael for kill rights.

Movement, a sigh from the nemesis in seat 13D.

Lacey's heart lodged in her throat as she fingered the six-inch blade hidden under her leg. Habit dictated its presence. The metal handle pinched the bunched flesh of her fingers.

Ishmael rose, glanced past her, as if trying to mentally distance himself from his prey, then staggered down the aisle. Lacey's other hand clenched the armrest.

Ishmael had filled out in presence, if not in girth, and added gusto to his swagger. His gaunt face betrayed more lines, his eyes harder as he stared forward, as if he didn't recognize the woman he'd framed for murder. Lacey froze, her instincts draining from her body.

He bumped down the aisle. . . .

She eased the knife out, hid it in her palm. Held her breath.

He passed by her without even a nod.

Her breath drained, her heart crammed between her ribs. So maybe she'd been imagining—

The train shuddered, a ripple of pain along the body of steel, then a gut-twisting squeal of metal on metal. Lacey grabbed the seat rests. The passageway lights strobed and died. "What—!"

Her heart bucked as the car lurched, jumped. She reached for Emily but snared thin air as momentum yanked Lacey from her seat. Her body wrestled with gravity and a visceral scream. The computer bag walloped her on the chin. Blood filled her mouth.

"Em!" She slammed against bodies, hitting her hip hard, arms flailing. "Em!" Around her, terror-filled voices competed for significance. Explosions pummeled the compartment. Lacey instinctively covered her head. "Emily!"

Metal screeched against forest or perhaps rail. Smoke. As she pitched through the twisting carriage, Lacey groped for purchase on anything—an armrest, a seat cushion, her daughter.

She landed with a bone-jarring slap. Hot pain exploded up her arm and into her brain. She sprawled broken, breathless, cocooned in bodies. "Emily." The stench of fear filled her nose, choking her. Her breath came like fire.

Then darkness.

"You have to trust me, Brian. I promise I won't drop you." If anything, Jim Micah kept his promises. They'd have to pry his rigor-mortised grip from the kid before he would let him fall, even if every muscle in his body begged for reprieve.

So maybe Micah wasn't 100 percent recovered from the scalpel and loss of a few organs. He wasn't going to let his battle with the six-letter silent killer—cancer—cause him to endanger this kid's life. Not while he still had breath in his scarred lungs.

"Hold on to my neck," he said, and Brian's scrawny arms tightened around him. Micah felt the panic-driven heartbeat of a twelve-year-old pound against his chest. "Hey, buddy, calm down. Slow your breathing. You're going to be fine."

Buried deep in the Pit—a wild, uncharted cave redolent of clammy basement and bat guano, sunk in the hills of eastern Tennessee—Micah tried to believe his own words. But Brian and his two fellow campers had been trapped here for the better part of twelve hours with nothing more than T-shirts and shorts and a fifty-five degree hypothermic slumber. As the darkness ate the flimsy light from their lithium-lit helmets and turned time into knots, Micah didn't want to guess which side might be winning.

Sarah Nation, a tall NYC paramedic, worked silently beside him, fixing the splint on Brian's leg where the fifteen-foot fall had resulted in an ugly landing. Micah cringed at Brian's scream when Sarah moved the limb to immobilize it.

On a ledge above them, Alaskan climber and helicopter pilot Andee MacLeod worked to warm the two other spelunkers. She'd layered the boy in every blanket and extra stitch of clothing she could find. Right now, she huddled in a sleeping bag and wrapped the girl in a 98.6-degree clench.

"Help me move him, Micah." Sarah grabbed the Sked litter, an inflatable cot designed for cave rescue. It wrapped around a patient's body, providing a smooth sled to maneuver through the cave's labyrinth. She'd already snapped on a C-collar, checked for a head injury, and strapped him onto a waist board.

They slid Brian onto the Sked. Sarah inflated and secured the litter while Micah affixed the Gibbs ascenders to the rope.

"I'll climb to the top, then haul him up while you follow and steady him," Micah said.

As Micah climbed, he grieved the loss these kids would have at enjoying the subterranean world. He'd wager his next meal that they would never set foot in a cave again. They'd miss out on so many treasures—calcite straws dangling like teardrops from the ceiling; stalactites, drips of rock frozen in time; snow-white, selenite crystals blooming like ferns; egg-sized cave pearls; and pools of clear water that reflected like mirrors. All because their camp counselor—now warm and safe in the company of Micah's search and rescue (SAR) compatriots—decided to lead with his sense of adventure instead of his common sense.

A memory scurried across Micah's mind—nearly translucent so as to deny its presence but real enough to make him flinch. *"C'mon, it'll be fun."* John Montgomery had said as his curiosity led them into a deserted Kentucky coal mine. Adventure, *right.* In the end, adventure had been John's demise.

Adventure and his unlucky Penny. Micah didn't know what was worse—that he'd introduced his best friend to the woman who took his life, or that he, Jim Micah, had loved her first. If love was blind, he'd also been knocked deaf, dumb, and brainless the day Lacey Galloway literally fell from the bleachers into his outstretched arms. Her chagrined smile snared him, and right then a bittersweet love/hate affair birthed. One that had yet to die.

How quickly his "Penny" invaded his head—her lips against his, light, laughing, tasting of cherry punch; her copper hair, as unruly as her spirit, twining between his fingers. He'd spent too many lonely nights wondering if their children would have had her infectious smile or been cursed with his impatience and bullheadedness.

Micah swallowed a choke hold of grief. A smart man would expunge her the second she started tunneling through the soft tissue of his emotions. Thankfully, his brain wasn't nearly as fickle as his heart.

He'd been praying for righteous justice for seven years, and if it was up to him, he'd figure out a way to send Lacey Galloway to the slammer for life and the hereafter if he got her in his sights again. That was a promise.

Micah reached the ledge, checked on Andee and the two kids fighting sleep, and rigged the Sked's ascent. Brian cried the fifteen feet to the top, too exhausted to feign courage. His screams echoed against the rutted limestone.

The crawl out of the Pit took eight hours, twice the time it had taken to locate the cavers. Micah dragged the Sked through Amoeba Alley and hauled it over Pouter's Lip; then he and Sarah ferried it through Popcorn Cavern, dodging stalagmites and calcite formations on the wall that resembled the late-night movie snack. Micah kept Brian awake, telling him unclassified stories of adventure overseas, originated from his years of clandestine missions as a Green Beret. Missions that just might be old history if he didn't figure out a way to get himself reinstated to the active duty list.

Please, God, one more miracle? According to his latest blood work, his cancer had vanished. He hoped God was paying attention. Time to go back to work. Even with Senator Ramey plugging for him, Micah knew he'd need God's intervention if he hoped to join his Special Forces team anytime soon. He'd spent serious time on his knees over the past year, hoping that God had bigger plans for him than just a swift discharge and a floundering plunge into the private sector.

Thankfully, his medical-leave status gave him the opportunity to hang out with the few outdoor athletes he'd befriended over the years—Conner, Sarah, Andee, and occasionally Dannette, Andee's former roommate. They'd met more than a few weekends over the past year and volunteered their skills to the local SAR teams on opportune occasions. He'd discovered that the hope of finding lost souls ignited his adrenaline in a way that his years as a warrior never had.

Micah chose not to dwell on that realization. Explorations into his feelings usually ended up breaching old wounds and laying bare his mistakes. There was a reason he was called Iceman, and right now he needed all the ice he could get to keep memories from burning a hole in his heart.

So he stuck to the Gulf War stories, especially when Brian asked, "What war?"

Micah groaned when the kid couldn't name the presidents before Reagan. Glancing at Sarah, he gave her a look that asked, "What do they teach kids these days in school?"

She shrugged, and the fact that she could smile through the grime streaking her face made him realize how lucky they all were to be laughing at Brian's bewilderment. Behind them, Andee was tethered to the two youngsters. She kept them going with horrendous renditions of "Fried Ham," a camp song without end. Micah finally bartered a year's worth of ice cream for silence.

They reached the twilight zone, the near exit to the cave where lichen and moss grew, hinting at life and sunlight. The hint of real air fumigated the smell of subterranean mud and dirt. Micah made out spotlights, heard the crackle of radios, and braced himself. *Media.* He lumped them with the liars and connivers, with people like Lacey. And he hated them most when they exploited kids.

He stopped, turned, and smiled at Brian. "You okay, kid?"

When Brian nodded, relief poured through Micah. For the first time in twelve hours he felt the coil of dread around his chest begin to loosen. Fighting the burn of emotion, he breathed deeply, composed himself, and stepped out into the circus.

Mission completed without casualty. This time.

Chapter 2

SHEER PANIC SHOT Lacey to the surface of consciousness. Light assaulted, so bright her eyes teared. The repugnant odor of antiseptic swilled her brain. She gulped a cleansing breath, then groaned, feeling as if she inhaled through a web of nettles. "Where . . . ?"

Reaching to rub her eyes, a stinging and pull in her hand made her wince. She blinked away the prick of tears and stared in horror at an IV taped to her skin. *A hospital?*

Twilight poured into the room, mottling the dark confusion that permeated her mind. Lacey felt stiff on her left side. She realized with another chest-ripping gasp that her arm had been plastered to her chest in an immovable sling. She wiggled her fingers and, with a rush of relief, felt pain slice up her arm and into her neck. At least she was still intact. The silence was fractured only by the hiss of an oxygen machine as she scrounged through memory, unconsciousness to—

Ishmael Shavik.

Explosions.

Falling!

A train crash?

Her chest thickened, breaths forced. *Emily!*

Lacey forced herself to move, searching for the nurse's call button. She held the box to her plastered chest and squeezed her thumb into it. Obviously she'd pushed a little hard because the nurse barreled in, wearing a definite non–Florence Nightingale expression, and ripped it from Lacey's embrace.

"Where's my daughter?" Lacey's voice rattled through her parched throat. "Emily Montgomery."

The nurse, obviously dog tired judging from her fuzzy halo of brown hair and her forehead etched into a frown, sighed and reached for Lacey's chart in a file holder above the bed. She flipped through it. "Nope. Nothing here about a daughter." Her Southern smugness, rife with nasal twang, razed Lacey's barely knitted calm.

"Yes, okay. No, I think she was traveling as . . . uh—" Lacey fingered the air, grabbing for mental purchase—"Janie Simmons. Yes."

The nurse had rough hands, and when she pushed Lacey back into the folds of the bed, she didn't spare her the full brunt. Lacey had sudden images of Stephen King's psychotic Nurse Wilkes. "Sorry. Your chart lists you as traveling single."

"No!" Lacey grabbed the nurse's wrist in a death grip. "I have a daughter. Six years old, blonde hair. She's wearing a sweater and her jammies." Thoughts of Emily—crying, alone, bewildered, or worse, trapped in the smoking remains of the Amtrak car—pinched Lacey's voice to a squeak. "Is there someone in charge of the crash I can talk to?"

Nurse I-Am-Misery Wilkes yanked her wrist from Lacey's grasp, glared at her, and stalked out.

Lacey dropped onto her pillow, feeling like she'd been dragged a thousand miles through the Texas landscape. Of course, the hospital—or Amtrak for that matter—wouldn't have Emily listed as her daughter or even her traveling companion.

She'd purchased her ticket under an assumed name for safety purposes—so people like Ishmael Shavik couldn't . . .

Lacey grabbed the nurse's call button again.

This time Nurse Wilkes spared her no mercy. "You're already in enough trouble." She kicked the call box on the floor, where Lacey would have to dive over the side of the bed to snare it.

Lacey ignored her. "Do you have a patient here, a Middle Eastern man? His real name is Ishmael Shavik, but he could be traveling under an alias. He's tall, thin, dark hair—"

"Thank you for calling us, Maggie." The baritone accompanied a tall man, grim and stoic in a navy suit, with a crew cut, and the face and girth of a prizefighter.

Lacey swallowed her words as Maggie Wilkes smiled, not sweetly, and abandoned her into the hands of . . . ?

"Agent Michael Brower. FBI." He flipped out his credentials as if she could actually read them from six feet away. He closed the door behind Maggie. "And you're Lacey Montgomery."

Her heart stopped. Actually lurched in her chest and froze, midflight in her throat. She didn't nod, didn't blink.

"You're under arrest."

With an agonizing jerk, her pulse restarted and took off like a shot. "What?"

"For the murder of NSA Agent Brad Mitchell." His dark eyes betrayed no tease, but rather painful shards of malice.

"Murder?"

"Murder."

Lacey reached for the bed rail, ignoring the pull in her hand. "I didn't kill anyone." Well, at least not directly. She flinched, hoping he thought it was from the pain of her injury—which, at this point, she still wasn't sure what that was.

"Your prints were all over the knife that neatly dissected his aorta."

My prints? "I don't even know a Brad Mitchell." She stared hard at him. "And I certainly didn't kill him. How could I when I was unconscious?"

Fury gathered on the man's clean-shaven, squared-off face. He had a nose that looked like it had met up with a few uncooperative suspects. "Tell it to your attorney."

Lacey took a deep breath. "Who is Brad Mitchell?" she asked, forcing her voice to be calm and scrolling through her list of contacts, afraid that she'd inadvertently added another enemy. But certainly she would remember killing a man. She hadn't been able to dodge the memory of *nearly* killing a man, regardless of her attempts.

"Your NSA bodyguard," Brower answered. He looked disgusted, arranging his chiseled features in a glare. "Tall man, built like a linebacker, brown hair?"

She let his sarcasm bounce off her, closed her eyes, and tried to pluck the description out of her memory. It came to her in a painful flash. The burly ice-cream buyer from the train. "He was my bodyguard?" A chill started at her toes and ended in her hands gripped on the bed. "Murdered?"

"Do you want me to spell it out?"

Fighting the mental image of springing from the bed and knocking the snide smile from his face, she glared back and said clearly, just in case he didn't get it, "I. Didn't. Murder. Him."

Agent Brower smirked and picked up her chart. "We're going to let you sit here for another twenty-four hours. Let that dislocation heal. But now that you're awake . . ." He slipped the chart back into the file holder and stepped toward her. She could have sworn the man actually enjoyed pulling out a pair of handcuffs and locking her good hand, IV and all, to the bed rail.

She stared at the handcuff. The cold radiated up her arm as he Mirandized her, finishing with, "Do you want to make a telephone call?"

"Telephone call?" she echoed like a sick parrot. She shook her head. Who could she call? Never in her life had her she felt so bitterly alone, even when she lay in a grungy warehouse in Almaty, Kazakhstan. And even then she'd known that Micah would find her.

But any hope she had of her hometown hero locating her today while she died of desperation in a Missouri hospital had vanished years ago when she started collecting aliases like shoes.

Traitorous tears bit her eyes. "Listen, I really don't care what you accuse me of. But I have a daughter. Six years old. I was traveling with her. Can you please, please find her?"

The agent drove despair into her heart with a single look and left the room.

Lacey trembled from head to toe, twisting the metal against her wrist, wondering how she'd managed to be accused of murder—again.

Who would have thought that the girl voted "most likely never to leave Ashleyville" in high school would find herself, twenty years later, running from an international thug, living under an array of assumed identities, and shackled to a hospital bed? Then again, if Micah had chosen her, perhaps she would have never left.

"Hey, Lucky Penny." The memory of Micah's voice swept over her as if he'd yelled across the hospital room, reviving the smells of decaying autumn leaves, the taste of youth, the ebullient sensation of hope. She bit her tongue, fighting the image of Jim Micah waving his helmet as he ran across the football field in his modern-day warrior regalia. He'd looked every inch

the ruddy senior, with a spackling of five-o'clock shadow along his chin, and wide, wide-receiver hands that could grip a pigskin or catch a girl falling at his feet. Built like a power-house, Micah plowed through opponents like matchsticks and took her heart away with his rapscallion grin.

"A bunch of us are going out after the game—hangin' at Shakey's Pizza. Come along?" So it hadn't been an invitation to the homecoming dance. She hadn't dared hope that Jim Micah might actually see her as more than a tagalong, someone who had nearly dug a hole of humiliation in the dirt at his feet. But since that moment when she'd fallen at his feet—a split second of sheer embarrassment, followed by unutterable joy at his impressive game-winning thirty-yard catch—he'd called her his "lucky penny." And, well, it fertilized all the dangerous daydreams she'd entertained about the six-foot-two senior.

Daydreams that turned into full-fledged regrets now as Lacey glanced at the handcuff tethering her to her dark future. She wished she could wipe away the tears that blinded her. No, Jim Micah hadn't loved her. Despite her attempts to get his attention. Attempts that had not only failed miserably but caused him to despise her.

She balled her fist in the shackles, despair rising to choke her. "Oh, God, what now? Please . . . help." The tinny words escaped her lips before she could bite them back. She had no right to approach God after her years on the lam. But lately, foxhole prayers had bubbled from some well of desperation in her soul. She let the prayer rise and hover near the ceiling, even lifted her head as if hoping He might swoop down and snatch it up.

Nothing. She'd run so far from God the doors to heaven had been permanently locked. "Okay, fine. I'll save her on my own," she mumbled.

Night blanketed the windows and she stared at her own miserable reflection. Matted, tangled copper red hair, puffy eyes, gaunt face. Unable to face the hollow, despairing woman in the window, she turned away and craned her body over the side of the bed, enduring a wash of sheer torture to haul up the nurse's call box with her slung arm. She somehow finagled the television power button at the top and prayed for news about the train crash. Maybe a reporter would tell her Emily was safe and looking for her mother in a local hospital. Then at least Lacey wouldn't need a sedative to sleep tonight.

She flicked through the channels. Reality shows, sitcoms. Her heart sank. But—oh, thank you!—they had CNN. She read the headlines ticking across the bottom. Something about the Middle East and the latest verbal boxing. A pretty brunette with caramel-colored skin mouthed news. Where was the volume? Lacey fiddled with the buttons and managed to add sound . . .

"—just emerged from a cave ominously called the Pit, where a group of local cavers rescued campers Jenny Davis, Brian Cummings, and Levi Schumann. The three had disappeared early yesterday morning when they hiked off with a counselor from Camp Break Point." The picture panned to a handful of grimy rescuers climbing out of a slit in the earth's crust. A slight drizzle blanketed the crew, adding to their grim, muddy appearance.

Lacey pumped up the volume.

"SAR-trained spelunkers exploring in the area volunteered to hike into the cave early this morning after receiving the missing person bulletin." The on-scene reporter, a skinny woman with stringy brown hair, barely hiding a scowl, poked her microphone at the bunch. "Can you tell us how you found them, sir?"

Lacey sat stone still, watching one of the rescuers turn.

Face nearly blackened with dirt as if he'd spent a year buried to his neck, the man gave the camera a death look.

She knew that look. Her breath caught and saliva pooled in her mouth. Yes, it had to be him. Lacey recognized the scar on his chin, showing as white as a laser against his filthy beard, and she'd never—not in a thousand lifetimes—forget those gray green eyes, the color of stones glistening in a flowing creek. Her eyes watered as Jim Micah, in all his dirty, rumpled, man-sized glory, growled, "Yeah. The counselor was pretty disoriented when he finally made it out for help. I'd have to say that God was the one who found them. We just kept searching 'til He showed us where they were."

"And where did you find them?" The reporter shivered in the cold, but Micah stood stoic, as if untouched by the elements.

"Around Tiptoe Ledge, a pathway along the inner cavern of the Pit. One of the campers had fallen about fifteen feet off the ledge." Micah kept glancing back at the boy he'd hauled out on some kind of inflatable stretcher. If Lacey didn't know Micah better, she could have sworn she saw his face twitch to hold back a wave of emotions.

Then he turned back to the camera. "Praise God we found them when we did because they were all pretty near hypothermia."

The reporter nodded and faced the camera for the close of the segment.

Lacey focused on Micah. While her breath froze in her chest, she saw him wipe his cheek. Yes, the man *had* sprouted tears. For a second, doubt slivered her confidence. The Jim Micah she knew had cried only once in his life, and even then he'd done it privately. Or thought he had.

As the camera panned over to the huddle of victims,

Micah grinned at them, a look of pure warmth and genuine kindness.

It nearly swept Lacey's heart right out of her chest. Oh yeah, that was Micah. And if anyone would help her find Emily, it was Jim Micah—Green Beret and the best friend of Emily's father, John Montgomery. Lacey glanced at the ceiling, as if expecting to see a crack in those heavenly doors, and pushed the nurse's call button.

Maybe she would make a call after all.

Had he made it clear that lives hung in the balance? It seemed fitting that he'd taken to calling himself Nero even during his off-line time. Powerful, but surrounded by incompetents. No wonder the Roman ruler had turned slightly deranged. He threw his cell phone against the wall. It fell to the floor with an unsatisfying thump next to the television remote.

Silent images came from the muted television. He recognized the news of the Amtrak wreck and saw the reporter's mouth move as she most likely described the snarl of machinery that littered the track. Nero's gut churned. Where was the Ex-6 program?

Ishmael was dead. Confirmed by none other than the wolves tracking his every move. Nero felt a stab of pain, inconvenience mostly. He'd spent a good decade relying on the man. It would take another decade to find another assassin with Ishmael's skills, someone who shared his goals and who looked beyond morals and ethics to the potential the current political climate stirred up. With the attention of the world focused on the Middle East and the consequential panic for oil, millions of greenbacks waited for the swift and astute.

Thanks to careful planning and Lacey's recent advances in cryptology, he was both. He had been wise, as usual, to keep the former CIA whiz under his wing. He didn't fight a smirk as he stepped up to the mirror and righted his appearance. The thin ivory tie, the matching dress shirt, the black silk suit. No need to betray the panic that iced his veins.

Perhaps he should trek down to Poplar Bluff and get eye to eye with the people who should be mopping up this mess. Just call him Mr. Inspiration.

He had lives at stake after all.

Besides, wouldn't it be nice to glimpse Lacey, handcuffed to her bed, surprise and terror on that beautiful face? The past, returning to offer him retribution.

He glanced at his watch, and his stomach reacted to the time by climbing up his throat. Retrieving his cell phone, he tucked it into his suit pocket, grabbed his key, and hefted the garment bag over his shoulder.

Two hundred and forty-three miles to Poplar Bluff. Five hours. That left him forty-eight more to find the Ex-6 program and save his neck.

One o'clock in the morning and the lady at the hospital admissions desk sounded as weary as he felt when she refused to tell him how the three kids were doing. Micah dropped the receiver onto the cradle and scowled at the telephone. Bureaucracy.

He combed his hand through his wet hair, feeling chilled clear to his soul. Some animal had climbed inside his gullet and growled demands for food. But after standing in the shower for thirty minutes, watching grime and guano pool at his feet, Micah could barely drag his bone-weary body to the hotel bed, let alone muster the vigor to hustle it to the local IHOP. The animal would have to wait until morning to be appeased.

Dressed in a pair of cargo shorts, Micah flopped against the pillows and dug around for the remote. He scanned through the channels, found the obligatory CNN feed, and caught the tail end of himself being interviewed. Oh, he looked lovely in a filthy yellow helmet and blue jumpsuit, dirt blackening his face. He barely recognized his voice, so flattened was his Southern drawl. Twenty years in the army had nearly obliterated his Southern good-ole-boy distinction. He sounded like a Yankee with a bad cold.

When the stranger on the screen wiped his face, as if clearing a tear, he turned off the set, disgusted. He could just imagine fellow rescuer and ex–Green Beret buddy Conner Young sitting off to the side, holding his gut laughing, or worse, writing to Micah's former cohorts from the 10th Special Forces somewhere in war-torn Eastern Europe. *News flash: Jim Micah has feelings! And they're dripping all over national TV.*

He cringed at the thought. Iceman, they'd called him, and he'd had no problem living up to that reputation. Emotions were—and always had been—a liability. The last time he'd actually let something akin to his real feelings show, he'd ended up embarrassing himself, his best friend, and losing the only woman he'd ever loved.

"You're *marrying* her?" Even now, more than a decade later, the memory of his own voice pitched into incredulity made him wince.

John Montgomery had frowned, as if confused by Micah's question. "Of course. She's perfect for me."

Not, *I love her.* Not, *she's the one I've wanted since you introduced me to her our senior year*, but, *she's perfect for me.*

As in, *she'll fit* my *life,* my *goals.* Micah had wanted to grab his best friend by the throat.

"But . . ." Panic had laced Micah's throat, and his emotions gurgled out. "Does she—?" He bit off his words.

John laughed. "Wait, are you still thinking she loves you? C'mon, Micah. She's been my girl since high school. She was over you the day you introduced us at Shakey's Pizza."

Micah felt sick, remembering Lacey's wide eyes, silver and precious, twinkling as Micah wrestled his best friend through the packed pizza joint to meet the girl who felt like laughter and sunshine to his soul. "You're the quarterback," she'd said, awe in her sweet voice.

Micah had watched with a sinking heart, somehow holding on to his smile as John took Lacey's hand, and with one swift, senior move, stole Micah's girl.

"Well, yeah, sweetheart. Someone has to win for the Eagles." Then John winked at her, exuding 120 percent Southern male charisma. Couldn't she see the guy was all glitter? He didn't have a serious bone in his body. John Montgomery loved the moment and poured his heart and smile into it.

Sometimes Micah actually hated his best friend.

Especially when, seven years later, Micah had stuffed down his last hopes, apologized, and slapped his friend on the back, congratulating John on his nuptials. Then he slinked away like a hound to lick his wounds.

No, emotions only led to painful admissions, regrets, and what-ifs. Besides, today he wasn't fraying at the seams; he'd just been relieved that the kids were safe. Micah's sudden flux of emotions had absolutely nothing to do with the fact that he could never have a son like Brian, a kid who reminded him of his nephew, complete with mischievous brown eyes and questions on overdrive. Since his cancer, that it had become a physical impossibility.

Muting the television, Micah tossed the remote onto the bed. Silence blanketed the room. Outside the cheesy hotel—there wasn't another one closer than thirty miles on this lonely strip of back-mountain highway—a half-lit neon light turned the dingy carpet bloodred. The room reeked of embedded cigarette smoke and dust. He'd constructed a trail of towels across the moldy bathroom floor to his bed, pretty sure the Centers for Disease Control could find a few new biological weapons ringing the shower drain or breeding in the grout.

Rolling to the center of the lumpy mattress, Micah flung the bedspread over himself and crammed the pillow under his head. He wondered if Andee and Sarah had returned from their quest for a convenience store. Conner had found shelter in his pickup at a local campground. Never one to leave his computer gear unattended, Conner actually got chest pains at the thought of leaving his wizardry alone for the night. The former communications whiz personified the new wave of adventurer, equipped with a four-wheel-drive Chevy, over-the-bed topper, satellite television, and Internet hookup. Conner strapped on his cell phone like a six-gun before he even climbed out of bed. He'd been showing off his latest acquisition—a palm computer with cell phone capabilities—when they'd received the alert for the missing children.

The call had interrupted a precious caving weekend. With Andee and Sarah trekking down from New York, it wasn't often the group carved out time to cave together. At least Micah and Conner had spent a couple of relaxing days at Micah's condo in Ashleyville before heading out to east Tennessee to meet up with Sarah and Andee. Conner mentioned looping over the mountains and wandering up the coast while he frittered away his vacation. With his latest gadgets, he could run his information technology company from anywhere as long as he was available for consulting.

Now *there* was a life in which Micah might be interested. No ties and flexing his brain for his bucks instead of throwing his body in the line of fire. He couldn't even guess where his old unit slept tonight, but he'd put money on the assumption that it wasn't in a bed or even in a place marked legibly on a map. Then again, how much worse could it get than being rolled up like a burrito in a polyester bedspread, the back of his stomach rubbing against the front in hunger?

He'd thought when he'd signed up for glory in the Green Berets, he might find eternal purpose. Instead he discovered that serving in the military played out like any other job, one long day after another. As years spooled out and he climbed the ranks, it became more and more difficult to roll out of the bunker and see light threading down from heaven.

Micah's unexpected battle with cancer had allowed him to step back, regroup, and take a fresh look at his life verse: "The Lord has already told you what is good, and this is what he requires: to do what is right, to love mercy, and to walk humbly with your God." By embracing the Green Beret motto—to free the oppressed—he thought he might accomplish Micah 6:8 all in one swoop. He longed to be God's man, had thought he was on the inside lane toward finishing well. Then why did his soul sometimes feel like a rock sitting hard and cold in the middle of his chest?

Micah slammed a fist into his pillow—roughly the thickness of that IHOP special he kept dreaming of—and tried not to think about his bleak future.

Settling into the magic between REM sleep and consciousness, Micah envisioned Lacey, backlit by the bathroom light. "Hi there, hero," she said. At first she seemed a shadow. Then she smiled, and he smiled back, settling into the comfort of his dream.

"I missed you." She came toward him, wearing an old football jersey and a pair of jeans. The pants dragged on the carpet, her painted toenails teasing from under the cuffs. "Rough night?"

He tucked one arm under his head, watching her. Her eyes glowed, the love in them twisting his heart enough to make him gasp. "Yeah," he heard himself say. "A couple more hours and we would have lost the kids."

She reached out and lightly ran two fingers along the scar on his stomach, the one that extended under his arm and around his back. "Does it still hurt?"

"Sometimes," he said, suddenly wanting to hide the way he still fought for breath during a long run or the weakness that often rushed over him, knocking him to his knees.

Tears filled her eyes, glistening in the lamplight. "I'm sorry, Micah. So sorry." She moved her hand up to his cheek. He turned his face into its softness, fighting the burn in his throat.

Headlights blared across the room into Micah's eyes. He blinked, and Lacey's image died, leaving only the silhouette of the ethereal moment traced on his heart.

Micah stared at the ceiling, gritting his teeth, furious that in sleep she came to him, mocking the contempt he wanted to feel. He pushed himself off the bed and padded to the window. The drizzle had turned frenetic and splattered the ground like machine-gun fire. He leaned his forehead on the cold pane, watching the car that had awakened him obliterate a puddle. His pickup parked across the lot looked dark and lonely. Andee and Sarah had either not returned from their expedition, had parked down the row, or—with their combined brainpower and verve, this wasn't unlikely—decided to hightail it to the nearest city and find a real hotel, complete with room service and spa.

Only the raindrops and his regrets lingered to keep him company. He put his hand to his chest, feeling cold and hollow. *Lord, please drive this woman from my mind. I'm only human and these desires aren't right, let alone healthy. Please free me from this grip she has on me.*

Micah followed the towel path to the bathroom, got a drink, washed his face again, then returned to the bed and thoroughly tangled the bedsheets, wrestling with his insomnia and the enduring outline of Lacey on his subconscious.

He had finally found a comfortable position, a place where every muscle didn't retort with malice, when his cell phone jangled. Clawing his way out of the swaddle of sheets, he lunged for it, digging it out of his backpack on the fourth ring, a second before it switched over to voice mail. "What?"

"Hello?"

The voice scraped off the final vestiges of sleep and dragged him down the tunnels of time. "Hello?" he asked, sure his ears deceived him. He knew his heart did because it stuck in his ribs, glued there by bittersweet joy. It was completely unfair that after nearly seven years of not hearing her voice it still turned his insides to mush. Hadn't God heard his desperation?

"Micah, is that you?"

Despite the fact that he'd been called by his last name since his junior high football days, only one person used it as if it were a sweet song, with a soft catch of hope in her voice. Only one person knew he'd wanted to be everything that name embodied.

"Yeah, Lacey," he said, fighting to keep his tone flat, "you found me."

Chapter 3

LIGHTNING FLASHED, CRACKING the dark pane of night and illuminating the bowing hickory and oak trees. The winds picked up the loam and decaying leaves and strewed them across the road. Few knew this route like he did, but still, Nero eased up on the gas. A painful plummet into the gulley flanking the road didn't fit into his short-term goals. His headlights carved out a mournful path through Mark Twain National Forest as the thunder now groaned its misdeeds.

He'd do well to hole up and wait until morning. It wouldn't help the situation if he showed up at Baptist Hospital in the middle of the night, drenched, bone weary, and furious. Not if he wanted the NSA boys to keep their distance. One whiff of trouble and they'd put Lacey in custody so tight he'd never wheedle the truth out of her constricted throat. No, he wanted to be the one to tighten the noose, thank you. He owed her. He deserved the honor.

Lightning strobed again, two long flashes, and this time Nero made out a figure huddled in the opposite lane. A deer? Nero hit his brakes, not wanting the animal to flee into his bumper. He slowed and his lights skimmed it.

Not an animal.

A child.

He stomped his brakes and a screech pierced the air. The child stood up, eyes wide, arms out, screaming. A snapshot of pure fear. Then she turned and ran into the forest.

Nero slammed the car into park and barreled out. "Stop!" Could luck have finally dealt his card? After searching and planning and waiting, could fate have dropped in his lap the one collateral that guaranteed his success?

"Wait, little girl!" *Emily?*

Crashing, screams. He dived into the forest, his eyes making out only hulking trees, the web of brush as it scraped his face, his hands. "Emily! I'm a friend of your mommy!"

More screams. He followed the sound, stopped, and listened to his own heartbeat. Branches caught his suit coat, blackened his shirt. His feet felt soggy and cold. The wind found his ears and drilled them with the humid breath of early fall. "Emily! I'm here to help you!"

A whimper. He plunged through the dark, holding his breath, and nearly fell on her. She crouched between the thigh-thick roots of a tree, her legs drawn up, her skinny arms around her knees, her head tucked into her body.

"No, sweetie, I'm here." He sat down and forced away the image of another little girl, crying, *"Daddy, don't leave!"* He touched the little girl's arm.

She jerked, looked up at him, and howled.

The sound churned a hole through his soul. Overhead, the lightning crackled, and he glimpsed her terrified face. "It's okay," he said, trying to recall how his voice should sound. "I'm here to help. Your mommy sent me."

She looked at him again, a black outline against the night, but she didn't scream. He slid his arms behind her, under her legs, lifted her, and held her close. She tensed, but as the lightning scraped the sky, she dug her hands into his shirt.

"That's right. Just relax," he soothed as he wrestled her out of the forest, back to the road, and into his car. He settled her in the backseat, dragging out a coat from his suitcase. He tucked it around her, wiping her wet face with his hand. "There, there. Don't worry. You'll be just fine."

Oh yes, fate had been kind.

Lacey dreamed of her escape. Because no one else was going to look for her daughter.

Micah's incredulous snort still echoed in her mind. The conversation started ugly and mutated fast. She knew she shouldn't have called the second he said hello. His voice still sent a rumble of warmth to the center of her body. Thick. Salving. Quintessential Micah. How she longed to hear him laugh.

"It's me, Lacey," she'd said, as if he hadn't just recognized her. Even now, the fact that he'd known her after all this time made her tingle. Her voice had trembled. "I need your help."

Then he *had* laughed. A short burst of disbelief. It felt like a knife sliced through her chest.

"I've been arrested."

"Finally."

Tears lashed her eyes. "They've accused me of murder, but I didn't do it."

He sighed. "Is there a point to this conversation, or are you just calling me up to prove that cats can't change their stripes?"

She flinched. "I know what you think. But I'm innocent. Again." She swallowed, wishing she could spill out the story, wishing history wasn't classified. Tears ran down her chapped face. Her voice dropped to a desperate whisper. "Listen, Micah. I was in a train wreck. In Missouri. I'm in the hospital and my little girl is missing. Please, please I need your help."

Silence. She could imagine him rubbing his temples with his thumb and forefinger, looking like he had the night she told him she was moving to Massachusetts to attend MIT. He handled it par for Micah—passionless, like he didn't care in the least that she was walking out of his life and slamming the door.

He'd blown out a breath, pursed his lips, and nodded. No "Please don't go." No outcry of frustration. Not even a wince that he might never see her again. Just a nod. Sometimes that nod, in memory, made her want to slap him hard.

Other times, memory seduced her to grab him by the lapels and kiss him, freeing the emotions that swirled in her chest. He'd looked beautiful that evening—nearly regal in his army dress uniform. To think she'd actually dreamed of that night for weeks, not caring in the least that John was off risking his neck while his best friend, Micah, took her to senior prom.

She'd hoped that seeing her in the blue chiffon gown would suddenly alert him to the fact that she wasn't the fifteen-year-old fan that had tripped into his arms, but a grown-up lady, with a grown-up mind to match. She'd hoped it would shatter the frozen Jim Micah facade and release a man of passion, of emotion. A man who loved her more than a friend.

Just like she'd loved him. Regardless of her feelings for John Montgomery, Micah had been her friend through her darkest hours. He'd been the one to whom she'd wanted to give her heart.

Oh, the foolish, romantic fantasies of a teenager. Instead of taking her back in his arms, running his wide, strong hands through her hair, and kissing her with the same emotions she thought she'd glimpsed in his eyes, he'd nodded. Iceman. Wasn't that his new nickname? He'd earned it.

He obviously hadn't shaken it in twenty-some years either. "Why should I help you?" he asked.

Her breath caught, as she chose to hear hope instead of disdain. "Because you were John's best friend. And because my little girl is John's daughter."

She could hear him swallow, absorbing the information across two states. "And," she said, her voice tremulous, "deep down inside, you know I'm innocent. You know I could never kill anyone."

Silence again, and in it Lacey's optimism mushroomed. *He believed her.* He had to know that she could never—would never—kill the man to whom she pledged her life. She'd nearly died trying to save John. Even if Micah couldn't be privy to the private files of the CIA, he knew her better than anyone. Knew that she spoke the truth. She bit her lip, tasting salt, feeling nearly buoyant.

"No, Lacey. I don't know that. In fact, I'm pretty sure you're lying to me right now. I can't believe you actually had the nerve to mention John." His voice shook. "Please don't ever call me again."

"No—!"

The telephone droned in her ear.

She began to shake as she cradled the receiver to her chest. The night pressed against the windows, sweeping despair into the room. She stared into the darkness, seeing her wretched self in the reflection, imagining a six-year-old huddled against the elements, terrified, abandoned . . . dead. A moan started in the pit of Lacey's stomach and emerged in a feral cry that frightened her. She let the receiver drop, pulled the cotton sheet up to her nose, and wept.

The agent had stomped into the room at the noise, then skulked out. Nothing but the sound of her hopes shredding, piece by piece, remained.

She must have succumbed to the grasp of exhaustion because the sound of a food cart rattling down the hall woke her like the ghost of Christmas Future. She lifted her head, dazed, and scrambled for comprehension.

Nighttime had surrendered to the sun, and it trumpeted into the room like pure oxygen, reviving and full of joy. Lacey felt hollow and raw in the face of such brilliance. She went to scrub her face and her arm caught.

Handcuffs. Oh yeah. She closed her eyes, longing for the oblivion of unconsciousness, even as her brain wrapped around ideas for escape. Micah may have deserted her, but she was going to go down kicking. And they'd have to catch her first. She examined the cuffs.

She hadn't forgotten all of her training.

A knock at the door. She turned away, her back to the food service. The last thing she needed was prying eyes on her pain. Besides, anything she put in her stomach would return in an ugly rush.

The door clicked open. "I'm not hungry," she said in a voice she hoped barked, "get out."

"That's good, because I don't have any food."

Even as she turned, disbelief washed over her, dislodged her heart, and swept it clear away.

Jim Micah stood in the doorway, appearing big and bold and fierce, the cutting edge of handsome in a leather jacket, a gray shirt, and black jeans that doubled his stun power. Even from six feet away, she could feel a seductive power in his presence, one that made her feel at once both weak and uncannily safe. The materialization of her every dream.

Except for the fact that he looked about as happy to see her as he might his executioner. His gray green eyes drilled through her, and the grim set of his mouth held no welcome.

She dredged up a smile. "Hi."

"You'd better not be lying to me or so help me, Lacey, I'll find a way to convict you and see that you hang myself."

Nope, not thrilled to see her. But he'd shown up, hadn't he? Lacey couldn't help but smile.

Micah still didn't believe her. He resolved that to himself as he stared at her, feeling his heart rip from its moorings just a little. She looked . . . awful. Her penny red hair in stringy ringlets, her face red-streaked from the coarse pillow. Her left arm had been slung tight to her thin body. The other was shackled to the bed. It twisted his gut to see it, even if she deserved it.

Believing that part still took his breath away. He ground his feelings to a nub and gave her a hard look, hoping to match his voice to it. "I mean it, Lacey. If you're lying—" he shook his head—"what am I talking about? I know you are."

"You don't believe that." Her gunmetal gray eyes held the texture of hope, and he knew he'd just made a serious mistake. Either that or the fatigue of hopping in his car and flooring it eight-plus hours from Tennessee to Missouri had left him with his defenses on idle.

"I do," he managed.

"Then why are you here?" Her smile could still knock him to his knees, and she wielded it now with painful accuracy.

"Because . . . well . . ." *Okay, yes, I want to believe that you have been telling me the truth.* "If you're on the level, then I owe John."

Her voice dropped, devastatingly soft. "Deep inside, you know I could never lie to you."

He stalked to the window, where he looked out at the parking lot. The sun glinted against pools of rainwater. "I don't have time for your games. If you want my help, you have about five minutes to convince me before your bodyguard returns from the little boys' room."

He heard her sigh, as if giving up on their past, and for a moment, he longed to let her run her litany by him again, just once, to see if there was something in it he could grab on to. Some shred of unturned evidence that might help him unravel the truth. He ached to believe something other than what he'd seen with his own eyes.

"I was pregnant with John's baby in Kazakhstan," Lacey said. "I didn't tell anyone, and I begged the CIA to keep it hushed."

"Obviously." Micah turned, clenched his jaw against rising emotions. Pregnant. With John Montgomery's child. A child who should have been his. "And just how did this mythical child survive your wounds?" He looked pointedly at her stomach, from where he'd extracted a six-inch knife. As clear as if it were yesterday, he remembered her groans, smelled the blood caking his hands and fatigues, and tasted the fear lacing the back of his throat as he raced her to the nearest international hospital. He again tried to deny what he'd seen, but the image of John's corpse sprawled on the warehouse floor saturated his mind.

"She was born three months premature. If it weren't for you . . ." She looked away, and he saw her fight a tremor in her jaw.

Oh, boy, this was a bad idea. He should have known it from the way his heart had leaped from its grave and pounced on his cell phone callback button, connecting him to the switchboard at Baptist Hospital in Poplar Bluff, Missouri. He should have done the smart thing—sat down and waited for his heart, along with his common sense, to come crawling back. Instead he let it lead the way out to his pickup and across the state line. Evidently, she still had the power to make him think with his emotions, not his brain.

"C'mon, Lacey, I was there. I saw your injuries. I saw you. You didn't look any more pregnant than I do."

She gave him a look that could take out ten men. "I hid it. From you. From John. From the company. I have to live with my mistakes, but I'm not going to fabricate a daughter just to get you to help me."

Micah took two steps closer and clamped his hand over her mouth. "Shh. I don't need the cavalry interrupting us."

She shook herself free and shot a look at the door. "Something you want to tell me?"

"No." The last thing he needed, besides having the NSA arrive and mar his return to active duty through a suspicious liaison, was Lacey Montgomery's sympathy. "Let's skip ahead. Assuming that you're not lying—" he held up a warning finger at her flush of color—"tell me when you last saw her."

She swallowed hard, corralling the look of curiosity in her eyes. "Okay. On the train. We were taking the Eagle to Chicago, and it derailed last night. I have no idea where I am, because no one will give me any information. I don't know if she's dead, wandering around the forest, or safe in the hospital somewhere." Her voice fell at the end. "Please, Micah. You're my only hope."

He closed his eyes and turned away. He didn't need to hear that. *Lord, give me wisdom here. Don't let me be duped by my longings or her wiles.* "What's her name?"

"Emily."

"My mother's name." He winced at the way his tone betrayed him.

Lacey stayed silent.

He turned and met her gaze. In it, he saw the woman she'd been. His Lucky Penny—the clarinet player, the homecoming queen, his prom date, the MIT graduate, and master spy. *Please,* her eyes cried. "How old is she?"

"Six. Blonde curly hair, John's blue eyes. She's probably still in her jammies."

He broke her gaze. "I'll see what I can turn up." He made to leave, but she grabbed his shirt with her hand, stretching out her slung arm. A flash of pain across her face made him flinch. He hadn't wanted her to see that her pain could needle him right in the heart.

"Thank you, Micah. I'll make it up to you."

"You can pay me back by forgetting my name," he said harshly, then strode out before she could see him totter over the fine precipice of control.

Chapter 4

"LACEY, THIS CAN be easy or difficult. It's up to you."

How she wished those words might be coming from the doctor, the one who'd x-rayed her arm thirty minutes ago. Her shoulder still ached from the way they'd twisted it, hoping to get a good angle. She might have picked easy, given the choice.

But, no. The question came from NSA Deputy Director Roland Berg, a fifty-three-year-old relic who she had always assumed was on her side despite her wild ideas.

Agent Michael Brower stood behind him, and his demeanor hadn't stepped down from the lynch-mob posture. If anything, the gray hues under his eyes only gave him the appearance of a street thug.

Maybe they were serious about this murder charge. She moved her wrist inside the cuff. It rasped against the metal of her bed rail. "You know we're on the same side here, Director."

"At the moment, Lacey, you're going to have to convince me. Did you know you had an NSA agent shadowing you?"

She stared at the men without blinking as Roland turned a chair around and straddled it. He looked tired himself in a rumpled suit, as if he'd slept hard on the plane.

"Of course not," she said. "And if I did, I certainly wouldn't have sliced open his chest." Berg narrowed his eyes at her. She didn't look at Agent Brower. "Think about it. If I was trying to kill Agent Mitchell, I wouldn't have used my own knife to do it."

"That's the unclear part. Your behavior over the years has been iffy at best, but we tolerated this cloak-and-dagger routine because of your paranoia—"

"Paranoia? My father was run off the road in broad daylight, my brother attacked on our farm in Kentucky, and my arm broken in Seattle during a mugging. He would have broken more if I hadn't scared him." Lacey's mind traced the shadows that followed her, the feeling of her fine hairs rising many times when she was being tracked. "Shavik has been after me since Kazakhstan."

"So you say."

"You can't seriously believe that his being on the train was a coincidence."

"We haven't found Ishmael Shavik or anyone matching his description." Agent Brower seemed to relish delivering this bit of gut-wrenching news.

Lacey gave him a hard stare. "I didn't dream it. I saw him."

Roland stood up, walked over to the door, opened it, and left.

Lacey watched him go with a sinking heart. A short interrogation meant he was only warming up. She swallowed and turned her attention back to Agent Brower. He shifted his weight, his eyes boring into hers. "I had nothing to do with any murder."

"Shut up."

She looked out the window. The sky was turning gray again, low clouds obscuring the sun. Leaves skittered across the window view, flung into oblivion by the breeze. She knew how that might feel.

Her daughter was out there. Shivering in the cold rain. Or worse, wounded. Afraid, for sure. The thought grabbed Lacey around the throat and threatened to cut off her breath. Don't. Fall. Apart. Now.

Micah, please find her.

The memory of Micah, his dark eyes tinged with just the finest edging of sympathy had kept her from dissolving into a pile of despair. She felt brittle. And on the fine edge of shattering into a million pieces. Never in her worst nightmares did they include her daughter lost, herself in custody and accused of murder. She had to get out of the hospital, retrieve Ex-6, and clear her name.

Funny how time repeated itself. She stared back at Agent Brower, pretty sure that she had seen him before. At least she'd seen his type. Narrow-minded. Angry.

Oh yeah, that was *Micah*.

Only Micah had driven across two states for her, hadn't he? Hope stirred her heart. She shot another glance at heaven. Strange how God answered sometimes. Then again, He'd been silent for so long, she shouldn't start jumping to conclusions.

For now, despite Micah's—and God's—apparent intervention, she should still assume she was on her own.

Situation normal. She felt the acrid edge of despair fill her throat and fought it. Now wasn't the time to let fatigue blur her common sense.

The door opened. Director Berg returned with a newspaper. He tossed it onto her bed, the front top headline screaming: Sixteen Dead in Train Derailment.

"Ouch," Lacey said and gave the paper a nudge with her knee.

"Tell me that you didn't plan the entire thing. That you're

not planning to steal Ex-6 and sell it to the highest bidder," Berg said.

Lacey was hardly able to digest his words.

"Here's the deal," Berg continued as if he hadn't just accused her of industrial treason, the very crime she was trying to prevent. "You hand over the Ex-6 program now, we'll finish it, and we'll make sure you're sentenced to minimum security instead of lost in the labyrinth of DOJ maximum security dungeons."

Lacey looked at his hazel eyes, at any traces of duplicity found there, and scrambled to make sense of his request. Where was her laptop? Surely it survived the crash. Where was the Ex-6 program? The thought of it in Shavik's hands sent a chill into her belly.

"I know you were nearly finished. Did you fix the glitches that still remained—like encrypting the transmission signal?" Berg's question sliced through the scenarios of terrorism waging through her brain.

"The fact that I'm even answering this question should give you some pause as to my traitorous plans," Lacey said, unflinching. "Yes. I just need to test it with the hardware a final time; then it will be ready for production."

Director Berg nodded like all this wasn't completely over his head. But developing the Department of Defense's most advanced on-field encryption/decryption system pushed even Lacey's PhD in mathematics to the limit. "Then faking its destruction now would be advantageous to your selling it into enemy hands."

"Hardly. I've never hidden my agenda from you, Berg. I want nothing more than to put this program in the hands of our field agents and retire quietly with my daughter in some safe place, with a nice white-picket fence and a pack of Dobermans.

Selling Ex-6 would betray everything John and I fought for and everything he died for. How dare you accuse me of treason after everything I've given to you and my country." She started to shake.

Was that a smirk on Brower's face? How she longed for two minutes alone with the creep, even if she had only one good arm.

"I am not a traitor," she told Berg. "I have full intentions of handing over the program to the NSA as soon as it is finished. Just like I promised."

"Then I trust you have a copy?" The deputy director's voice held the urgency that should have been reserved for younger, less experienced men.

Lacey studied him. Berg understood as well as she the importance of Ex-6. Hadn't he looked at her with the same gleam when she'd come to him shortly after Em's birth, with the plans for a quantum-based encryption system? He knew the price she'd paid in Kazakhstan seven years ago, the price too many agents paid in the age of electronic communication. She'd felt his excitement burn behind her heart. Maybe she wasn't quite as vulnerable as it might seem.

She gathered her courage and produced an even, flat voice. "Yes, I have a copy." She took a breath. "You'll get the encryption system when I find my daughter."

She would have gotten less of a response if she'd slapped him. How he'd ever been John's handler baffled her. Even she had a better game face. She remembered when Omar Al-Akim had stood toe to toe with her and told her that he would some-day send her home to Kentucky, one body part at a time. She hadn't even flinched.

"You're not in a position to bargain with us, Lacey. You hardly have a stellar reputation for loyalty. A few well-placed suggestions in the right ear and you won't just serve time for murder; you'll be walking the green mile for high treason."

Lacey didn't respond. The fact that Berg waved her past before her eyes like a red flag should have had her swallowing, blinking back ugly scenarios, and protesting. But Emily was still out there, and past experience told her that her best ally was her own wits.

Except . . . well, maybe now she also had Jim Micah. Still, he hadn't exactly jumped for joy at seeing her. He might be on the telephone right now, ordering out pizza and hightailing it to the nearest Marriott, wishing he'd never answered his cell phone.

Somehow, however, she didn't think so. Micah may believe her a traitor, but he was a man of his word. He kept his promises. At whatever cost.

"Think about your daughter. We're the only ones who know about her. You'd hate for her to get picked up and placed in the foster-care system." Berg shook his head, and suddenly Lacey knew why he was in his position. He may not be a field agent, but he delivered ultimatums like a one-two punch right to the kisser.

He pursed his lips as if he might actually care and pulled back for his final jab. "She might be lost forever or adopted out—she is still at that sweet, tender age when a loving family might want her." He smiled, jackal-like. "And you, well, you really don't know if we haven't already done that, do you?"

Lacey fought a betraying expression. No. If they had Emily, they would have told her. It would have been Berg's first line of offense.

Still, she could use this threat. Perhaps it was time to remember just how this game was played.

Until she figured out what Ishmael had been doing on that

train and what had happened to Ex-6, and until she proved her innocence again and Emily was in her arms, she'd be the woman they thought she was. Broken. Afraid. Guilty.

Cooperative.

"Okay, yes. I'll give you the copy. But promise me that you will take care of Emily. You'll return her to Janie's ranch." She didn't have to fabricate the desperation that laced her voice.

"Of course." Berg frowned.

And, yes, that was a smile on Agent Brower's face. Made him look like a wolf—all teeth and lots of bite.

Lacey enacted a sigh. "You'll find a copy in Chicago in a safe-deposit box at First National Bank." She motioned for a pencil.

Berg took her scribbled information, stood, and patted her blanketed legs. "Good girl, Lacey. You get better now. See how easy that was?"

Easy? Easy was her dreams—living on the farm, mothering Emily, teaching her to ride. Easy was falling for the memory of Jim Micah in her arms, dancing under a canopy of brilliance strewn across the Kentucky sky. Easy had nothing to do with sewing together the tattered remains of her shattered life, always looking over her shoulder. Or trying to prove to a man who hated her that she wasn't a woman with murder in her past.

No, there was nothing easy about tomorrow. There was only one way she was going to get better. Get free. Get Em.

And run.

Micah paced the parking lot of the Baptist Hospital, staring at the late-afternoon sky and clenching his cell phone. What he wanted to do was hurl it across the parking lot or maybe do about a thousand laps at the high school track down the road.

Lord, I thought You were on my side.

One telephone call and he'd come running back to her like a lovesick puppy. So much for ripping her out of his heart. She had tentacles that reached through time and space and knew how to make a man gasp. Especially when she looked at him with those slightly needy, oh-Micah-you're-the-only-one-who-can-help-me eyes.

But he was starting to return to his senses, and the first glaring reality facing him was the fact that by hanging around Lacey Montgomery he was jeopardizing his military future. Again.

"Hello?"

Micah drew a stiff breath lest he bark into the telephone and permanently damage Conner Young's ear. Conner was probably at the helm of his pickup, listening with an earphone, or hiking along the Blue Ridge Mountains on one of his mysterious walkabouts. Conner had definitely gone on some sort of life expedition over the past year since he left the commandos, as if searching for something just out of his reach. Most days, Micah knew how he felt.

"Conner, where are you?"

"Where were you this morning? There I was, sitting at the Southern Restaurant all by my lonesome. I had to finish the pile of grits I ordered for you."

"I'm in Missouri."

Pause . . . then, "Actually, I know that. I'm about three hours due east. I logged your cell phone frequency into the GPS system I designed and . . . well, my curiosity was piqued when Andee called me, looking for Dannette's telephone number."

After spending the afternoon picking around the train crash site, searching the hospital, and chatting surreptitiously with local law enforcement, Micah had returned to the hospital. He peeked into Lacey's room from across the hallway and saw her watching the window, a wan look of grief on her face.

It was then he decided to give it a smidgen more effort. Two hours later, a visit to the Mark Twain National Forest ranger's office had netted him exactly nil in the area of a joint search. But Ranger Hank Billings did offer to drive through the back roads of the forest for a look-see.

Micah had no doubt his look-see would end at sundown. Just about the time the night hours began to wrap a six-year-old child in a hypothermic clench.

He'd called Andee on his way to the local SAR office. It hadn't taken more than two calls to convince Dannette Lundeen, Andee's former roommate and SAR canine specialist, to load up her dog, Sherlock, and head east. Thankfully, she was wrapping up a search in Oklahoma. Micah expected her within the hour.

"How's Brian?" Micah asked Conner. The image of the kid he'd rescued, streaked with dirt and shivering, did nothing to assuage Micah's nerves. The sky overhead let loose with a low groan.

"Good. They set his leg. Said he'll be playing soccer by fall."
Thank You, God. Now, how about another one?

"Wanna tell me why you're in Missouri when you're supposed to be caving with me? Or, at the very least, fending off the local hero-starved population? I had to sign your autographs today at the hospital."

Micah glanced heavenward as he spoke to Conner. "I'm trying to find a little girl . . . six years old. She's lost. And the pressure is dropping. I think we're in for a storm."

"What is the local SAR team doing? Have they had a call-out?"

Micah sighed and ran a hand over his head right where it was beginning to ache. "They have their hands full at the moment, trying to clean up a train wreck. They're still hauling in the injured and searching for survivors. They don't have time to helm another search."

"Train wreck?"

"Long story. But the little girl was on the train." Although she's not listed as a passenger. He was just about to march back into Lacey's room with that little item of information and watch her squirm. The sick fear that she was playing him coiled deep in his gut like a rattler. "I picked up some topographical maps, did a rundown on our victim, the terrain, and the weather, then divided the section where the train crashed into a workable grid. When Dannette arrives, we'll start fanning out. See what we can find before the storm washes away any scent."

"You've been busy." Micah heard curiosity in Conner's voice. "Andee and Sarah are on their way. They called me from Nashville."

"I know." They'd worked together on search-and-rescue ops before—twice on a mountain rescue in Washington state last summer and once in Iowa at Dannette's request. The last operation had unearthed the body of a college coed. Micah still remembered the defeat that flushed Dannette's face. "I hate to drag you guys all the way out here."

Conner was silent for a moment. "Something you're not telling me? Like, why aren't you more worried about this kid? Six years old, out in the rain and cold?"

Micah stepped out of the way as an SUV rolled past him, splashing water onto his jeans. Great. Hungry, tired, and now wet. He wondered how Emily might feel right about now.

"You're right. Hurry, Conner. It's getting colder. I don't know how long this little girl can last."

He hung up and stalked toward the hospital entrance.

Nero spied the guard, sitting like a zombie outside her room. His eyelids drooped and Nero smiled. They were all a little tired, most of all Lacey. This move felt a little like taking candy from a child. Especially with his insurance sound asleep in the backseat of his car. Warm. Secure.

He straightened his tie and walked up to the man. "Take a break, pal." He gave his best professional smile, the one he reserved for his employees. The agent sat up, stared at him, and frowned. "I want to peek in on her." Nero smiled again as the agent relinquished his post and trotted down the hall.

Nero turned, aiming for her room. He just wanted one glimpse. Wanted to surprise her, maybe catch her distraught and defeated when she didn't have her defenses on DEFCON 1.

He took a step toward her door when he saw him, striding down the hall, fire in his dark eyes. Nero stifled a curse. Captain Jim Micah didn't look any more friendly than the last time he'd seen him, even without his war paint, M-16, and BDUs. Obviously he hadn't received the not-so-subtle hint seven years ago to back off . . . and stay there.

Nero turned his back to the door and shuffled down the hall. What was Micah doing here? Hadn't he learned his lesson once? Then again, Micah didn't know the truth, did he? A smile pushed up Nero's face, despite his frustration. No, only five people really knew what happened in that Kazakhstani warehouse, and two of them were dead.

Jim Micah didn't even stop to check for guards. As if he knew they wouldn't stop him. He plowed into her room.

Nero scooted back, listening. He could have stood in Canada and still heard the conversation.

"She's not on the passenger manifest. Did you know that?"

Nero smiled. No, of course not. Lacey wasn't that stupid. Never had been.

"She is, but you wouldn't know it. She's traveling under an alias."

Ah, Lacey. Still feisty. Still determined to hide her most precious treasures from the world. He wondered if she still hoped to prove the truth also. Good luck.

Silence. He could imagine them glaring at one another. If Nero hadn't done his homework, he might be missing the significance of this exchange. But he hadn't been tracking his prey since Kazakhstan without learning her vices and regrets. Jim Micah, the man she let get away, the man who saw her murder her husband. This moment had special irony. Micah was searching for the daughter who might have been his, had he had the guts to stick by her. Nero nearly laughed aloud.

"I called a few friends. They've agreed to come look. But it's getting cold and rainy out there, and I'd better not be tromping around in the dark for no reason. Do not lie to me. Again."

"I'm not. I swear, Micah. Listen, she has a teddy bear. Last thing I remember, I put it in my pocket. Get my clothes; see if it's in there. Maybe it'll help you find her."

Lacey's voice sounded strained. *Good*, Nero thought. Maybe she would feel what it's like to watch your daughter's life ebb out, helpless to stop it.

Nero whirled away from the door, suddenly angry. And just in time, for Micah charged out, nearly running him over.

Thankfully, he had already started to amble down the hall in the opposite direction.

Nero peeked back over his shoulder, watched the former Green Beret stalk away, and smiled. It would be a long, cold night for Jim Micah and his merry band.

He couldn't wait to hear Lacey howl when they returned empty-handed.

Then she'd know what it meant to be afraid.

Chapter 5

"IF SHERLOCK WEREN'T a trailing dog, we'd be in big trouble." Dannette Lundeen leaned over the hood of Micah's pickup, her flashlight trailing over the topographical map he'd scrounged up from the local Forest Service. "With the air saturated with human scent and the wind picking up, Missy wouldn't have a bug's chance in July of finding this little one."

Micah looked up from where he was stuffing his survival pack. "Where is Missy, by the way?" Dannette's air-scent dog, proficient in searching for human presence in an otherwise uncontaminated grid, was his favorite of her two canines. Or maybe he was just partial to a dog that didn't look like it might break into tears at any moment, its jowls dripping with saliva. One look at Sherlock and Micah wanted to lunge for a rag . . . or keep the bloodhound at a safe and cleanly distance. However, Missy, part golden retriever and part German shepherd, had keen intelligence, warmth, and enough charm to make him miss Gracie, his yellow Lab.

"She's in Iowa with my grandmother. I didn't have time to go get her."

Micah would have to call his own family—namely his brother—and inform him of his delay in returning home. He still didn't know how long of a delay it might be. A huge part of him—the common sense part—wanted to throw his survival pack, MREs, space blanket, and tarp into the back of the truck and floor it east. Away from Lacey and her lies.

But today when Micah had accused her of lying again, desperation lined her eyes. The same desperation that had been etched on her face as she had begged his Green Beret team to save John's life. Then again, he wasn't so sure she wasn't lying then either.

Still, he *wanted* to believe her. The thought lanced open a low, throbbing wound deep inside. If she wasn't lying about Emily, just what other truths might she be telling?

"We don't have much daylight left." Dannette folded up the map. "And maybe less time before the rain starts. We need to get going." She attached the lead to Sherlock's collar. He already wore his shabrack, the orange SAR vest that identified him as a working K-9. She grabbed her water bottle, his collapsible bowl, and his Frisbee.

Micah motioned for his team to huddle. "Since there is only one canine unit, we'll have only one search crew. Andee, you run with Dannette, keep her charted as best you can. If you find Emily and she's in more trouble than we can handle, we'll need to know how to tell the EMS to locate you. Conner, do you have your new ELT?"

Mark Twain National Forest could get dicey, especially at twilight, and he didn't want anyone to fall into a chert opening or wind up in Lake Wappapello. An Emergency Locator Transmitter would at least give the rest of the team their position should one of the searchers get lost.

"I'll go with the team," Micah continued. "Sarah, you stay here and keep track of us on the grid as Andee radios in our position. Hopefully we won't need your EMT skills when we find her, but if we do, you'll have to come in with the EMS team."

He'd run enough missions to know to fuel hope into the task. They needed to believe that little Emily was out there, despite the wind, the damp breath of fall on their necks and wheedling through their jackets, and the darkening grip of the oak, elm, and willow.

Dannette handed the map to Andee, who pocketed it inside her Gore-Tex rain suit, and pulled on her hood. Although they'd been roommates in college, Andee and Dannette couldn't be more different. Andee with her petite climber's frame, short curly black hair, and dark complexion, was spunky and bright. She put the adrenaline into the team and added the spark of hope.

Dannette, however, was pure Swede—tall, lanky, with short-cropped straw blonde hair that poked out of her orange hood. Conservative and quiet, her hazel eyes radiated concern. Something about her arrival had pounded grim reality into Micah's bones.

Most of the searches Dannette was called in for involved police medical examiners and body bags. *Please, Lord, not today.*

He'd met Andee and Sarah on Service Road 80, just north of the crash site. While they waited for Dannette and Conner to arrive, they had done a sound sweep search, angling toward the Last Known Position (LKP), using whistles and Emily's name. As they approached the train wreck, the voices and noises of machinery told them that their labors would prove fruitless. By the time they returned to their haphazard staging area, Conner was unloading his GPS equipment and checking the batteries on their Motorola radios.

Dannette pulled in moments later, already geared up for the search. Micah briefed them, omitting most of his dark history with the victim's mother, and pressed the teddy bear, now in a Ziploc, into Dannette's grip. The fact that Micah had found it in Lacey's jacket had given him the final push to even drag his team out here this late without a formal call-out.

"I'm going to work our way to the LKP and then let Sherlock start trailing." Dannette squatted next to her bloodhound, running a hand under his muzzle. "Hang in there, buddy. Just a little bit longer, okay?"

Micah had once asked Dannette how she fell into the business of search-and-rescue dog handling. Besides working with her own two dogs, she trained police dogs for the Iowa Sheriff's Department and sometimes contracted out to train K-9s in their elements around the tristate area. That she had a touch with animals seemed obvious, but the long hours, the physical demands from heat to extreme cold, the hunger, and raw frustration of finding victims already perished . . . well, the SAR life certainly didn't possess the ingredients of an easy hobby or a lifetime of fun.

Dannette hadn't answered his question. Not long on words anyway, she was the one member of his private SAR team who didn't seem to want to buddy up and who didn't spend decompression time hanging with the team, playing speed Monopoly or pickup soccer.

Which made her smiles, when earned, that much more powerful. And her practical jokes—especially the time she'd changed the sugar for the salt and he'd poured it over his Wheaties—that much sweeter.

Micah liked Dannette, despite her driven personality and her secrets. Secrets that he'd agreed to leave alone.

Dannette flicked on her flashlight, and they ran a final radio check. Conner had tapped into the local Poplar County SAR team's frequency so he could track their progress. Micah had his team set on a different channel. Hopefully one that wouldn't attract too much attention.

"Okay, guys, huddle up."

Sarah's blue eyes met Micah's a moment longer than necessary. It was because of her that they'd even begun these missions. She'd dubbed them Team Hope, and the name wedged in Micah's mind enough to make him pause before the launch of every search and pray.

A crack of thunder overhead nearly obliterated his voice. "Lord, we need Your help here, as usual. Give us wisdom, safety, and success. Help us find Emily before this storm breaks wide open."

The team broke with Micah's mumbled amen, but it hit him like a fresh slap that Lacey's—no, John's—child just might be out there, huddled against a tree, crying, terrified. Or worse. A child who might have John's blond hair and blue eyes, but hopefully had Lacey's guts and determination.

A child he should have been protecting long before this moment.

If it hadn't been for his inability to face his mistakes, his stubborn pride, and even his blindingly loyal friendship with John, maybe Emily Montgomery would be home inside her mother's embrace, her Boppy bear under her arm.

No. If it hadn't been for his fear, the type that locked his emotions inside his chest, maybe the little girl would be named Emily *Micah*, and her home would include a mother *and* a father.

The wind twisted under his collar, sending a trickle of cold down his spine. The air smelled of decaying loam and moisture and held a trace of doom. The finest coil of desperation wound around his heart and squeezed.

"Stay on your toes, gang," he said and followed Dannette into the tangle of forest.

✚ ✚ ✚

Twilight hadn't lingered as it swept across Lacey's room. The gray pallor of night pushed against her hospital window, fractured only by a few courageous lights skimming the wet parking lot. Lacey drew the thin cotton blanket up to her chin with her still-slung arm. *Where are you, Emily?*

The look on Micah's face when he'd accused Lacey of lying—again—sent a shudder through her. But maybe he'd found the teddy bear. And that meant that he could be out there. . . .

She stared out the window, conjuring up the image of Jim Micah foraging through the woods, calling Emily's name. He'd looked more capable than she remembered—and she remembered well the feel of his arms locked around her, the take-no-prisoners expression in his eyes.

Please, please find her, Micah.

The handcuff on her arm burned into her wrist. They'd cinched it down too tight, and already it had rubbed a raw swath into her skin. Or maybe that was from her constant twisting, an unconscious rebellion against her bonds.

Prison was something she should be getting used to. She'd been in bondage, in one form or another, for seven years. No, if she were to be honest, probably closer to twenty—since the day she'd met John Montgomery and eventually surrendered to his charisma and decided to chase after adventure as his wife and a CIA operative.

That had been a prison sentence, of sorts. The thrill had died after her first real assignment, and she longed to rewind time and choose peace, stability, honesty. However, since she'd taken the oath to preserve her country's secrets, she'd been shackled to lies, to a double life, and then to a life on the lam.

It seemed fitting that she should end her career in very real shackles. Their cold bite gave reality to the feelings in her soul.

She swallowed a knot in her throat. Her stomach growled—she'd refused lunch, too frustrated to put anything in her stomach. But that had been about the time the NSA agents had returned with the news that they'd found the safe-deposit box and the disk. The precious hours she'd purchased with that half lie would grind down to nothing when they returned and asked her to run the program. Then she'd really be in trouble.

Maybe she should run.

Oh yeah, that would convince the entire world of her innocence. If she had a prayer of getting Emily back, of maybe someday, somehow, starting a real life with her daughter instead of one comprised of clandestine holidays or surreptitious visits to Janie's ranch, then she'd better stay put and take her hits. Truth would prevail.

Right?

Lacey clenched her teeth before despair sucked her under. The truth wasn't something she was at liberty to profess. Not yet, at least.

Not with Frank Hillman still stalking her every move.

Her old boss was behind this. She could feel him, like an icy hand moving just over her skin. She still hadn't convinced the CIA of his scheming in John's murder, but she knew it. And she didn't believe for an instant the stories of his daughter being kidnapped, his cooperation being fueled by extortion.

The man had too much money at stake. In her soul, she knew Hillman had set John up, helmed the double cross in Kazakhstan that took his life, and now trailed her, plotting his revenge.

If only she could prove it. But she'd dismissed the dream years ago when CIA Deputy Director Berg glued her case shut and filed it in the bowels of the Pentagon. Well, she'd *consciously* dismissed it. But it haunted her like an old war wound.

The wind moaned outside her window and her stomach echoed. Feeling empty and brittle, she slid down on the bed and curled into a ball.

Please, please, find her, Micah.

She couldn't consider the fact that he might have packed up his truck, or whatever he drove, and floored it out of her life. The thought made her eyes sting. Without Micah, she had no one.

Not that she had Micah either, really. Even if he found Emily, he'd egress her life so fast she might just get windburn.

As if to emphasize that point, even the NSA had left her room. The agent on duty had suddenly decided to sit with her for most of the afternoon, as if she had intentions of sneaking out of the huge picture window, dropping two stories, and making a break for it.

She refused to admit how often she'd mulled over that scenario. Just in case.

But by evening, he'd dropped the magazine he was reading onto the little table and marched out. To let her face the darkness alone. It had left her feeling raw, as if someone had drilled a hole through her heart. Somehow it felt easier to ignore the hollow roaring of her soul by listening to the anger. The injustice of false accusation.

She heard the door open. Soft footfalls and the jangle of a cart. She turned and in the shadows saw an orderly bringing in her dinner. He stopped at the foot of her bed. Dressed in scrubs, the huge Asian man with a wide face, graying hair, and dark eyes looked out of sorts in his role. "Suppertime," he said as he grabbed a tray and placed it on her bedside table..

She sat up. "Thanks."

He moved the table over her bed, within reach of her slung arm. "Bon appétit," he said and pushed his cart out.

She lifted the lid. Under the cover, where her food should be—maybe slices of roast beef with mashed potatoes, Jell-O, or broth—lay a . . . cell phone.

It trilled.

Lacey startled. Stared at it.

It rang again.

She shot a look toward the door, where her NSA Doberman probably sat in the hall, and snatched up the Nokia. "Hello?"

A little girl's mournful cry rent the line, a loud shrill of terror, maybe even pain. It punched Lacey's breath from her chest. "Emily?" she gasped. *Please, no!*

"Mommy!" The cry repeated again and the sound clicked off.

"Emily!" Lacey stared at the screen, her hand shaking. "Emily, where are you?"

The telephone beeped a warning: *Incoming text message.* Lacey watched, horror cutting off her heartbeat as the message filled the screen.

```
HELLO, LACEY. I HAVE EMILY.
WILL EXCHANGE FOR EX-6.
NO TRICKS, NO NSA.
NO JIM MICAH.
WILL CONTACT IN 24 HOURS.
```

Lacey saved the message, then tried to redial the contact. A mechanical voice, high and piercing, came on the line and informed her that the number was out of service.

Of course.

Her hand greased with sweat as she tucked the telephone behind her back, her brain now replaying Emily's scream. She clamped her mouth shut against a wail. Staring out into the darkness, into the night where her Emily cried, she felt herself beginning to shatter. Whoever had her not only knew about Ex-6 but also knew she'd called Micah and asked him to find her little girl.

Which meant he was watching her. Or listening.

Her throat burned. Micah might be walking into his own murder. As if she were replaying time, she'd put another man she loved in danger. She should never have called him. Never have dreamed of starting over.

Never have dreamed of escape.

She'd never flee the nightmares. The mistakes. The roaring through her empty soul.

No Jim Micah.

Oh, please, God, no.

But God wasn't in this. No. She deserved this punishment so He wasn't about to reach out of heaven and save her. Why would He? After years of running from Him and making mistakes, she could barely look at her own dark, barren soul. She couldn't imagine that He would consider it.

She was alone.

No NSA.

No Jim Micah.

So much for the truth.

I'm sorry, Micah, she thought as she studied her handcuff.

✦ ✦ ✦

"He's lost the trail, Micah." Dannette crouched beside her bloodhound, who nuzzled her, then ran away, nose in the air.

Sherlock's frustrated loops along this lonely stretch of road—the way he ran down one length, turned, and ran the other—had Micah's nerves stretched to pinging. "The scent cone is diminishing with the wind and time. I'm sorry. Either she's not here or her trail's been compromised."

Micah blew out a frustrated breath, then called Emily's name, just in case. The sound died in the bitter wind. "I thought for sure we'd find her."

In fact he'd been riding on hope from the minute Dannette had presented the teddy bear to Sherlock at the LKP site and the sniffer had picked up the trail almost immediately. Through bramble and shrubbery and across felled trees, they'd zigzagged through the forest until the dog stopped at a trampled well between the thick roots of a hickory tree. He'd circled the area until Dannette caught up. Micah wasn't more than two steps behind, but when he'd found only the matted outline of a little person's presence, his heart took a dive to his gut.

It had stayed there for the better part of the last hour. "It's like she vanished." He tore off his hood, letting the breeze soothe the sweat on his brow. "Andee, do you have a fix on our location yet?"

Andee had struggled to keep them oriented as they slogged through the forest—no easy task in the darkness under direction of flashlight. At best, she had them in a five-hundred-yard radius of her guesstimation. The advent of the highway lent some indication of their position. At least it was marked on the topo map.

"I think so," she answered and knelt on the road.

The ELS and GPS systems that logged the position of the base camp would reel the team back in. But Micah wanted to move faster. The body posture of the dog—perked ears, tail up—told Micah that Sherlock had been after someone—Emily or another human. Micah didn't want to waste time finding the ranger or the local, exhausted SAR team and talking them into an official call-out.

He toggled the radio. "SAR-1 to Base."

"Base, SAR-1. Go ahead." Sarah's voice over the radio sounded tight, as if she were dealing with her own frustrations and not well.

"Our POS is negative. We need a CERT team. We're 10-19 but need a pickup."

"10-4, SAR-1. What's your 10-20?"

Micah handed the radio to Andee, who rattled off their estimated position.

"What's your ETA?" Sarah asked.

"Give us twenty minutes," Andee responded.

"And tell Micah that we have a 10-14."

Micah frowned at Andee. Sarah had someone on her tail? He motioned for the radio. "Come again, Base."

"Local ranger type. Wants to talk to you."

Micah remembered his conversation with Ranger Hank Billings that ended with, "I'll take a look around, but I don't want you tromping through the woods, ending up another casualty." Obviously Ranger Billings hadn't decided to head for the local pub after work. Maybe Micah had acquiesced too quickly for the man to be fooled.

He made a face. "Copy that." It was probably time to get the locals involved anyway.

Dannette gathered in Sherlock and attached him to his lead while they waited for Conner and Sarah to pick them up. An overhead cluster of thunderheads, still jockeying for position, obscured the moon and released a miserable, fine drizzle. Micah couldn't pry the image of Emily—dirty, scared, and nearly hypothermic—from his mind. He stomped along the ditch, wanting to hit something hard.

Micah didn't know what made it worse—that Lacey had had a daughter all these years and he hadn't known it or that he had stood at the foot of her bed and called her a liar.

What part, exactly, of the last seven years was fiction . . . or fact?

Conner pulled up first, followed by Sarah in Dannette's truck. Dannette loaded Sherlock into the dog carrier in the back—a long box filled with straw, food, and water—while Sarah trudged up to Micah, murder in her expression.

The woman was from New York City, a paramedic who didn't rattle easily. Micah had seen her stare down a frantic gang of townspeople bent on running into the woods after a missing teenager—and becoming victims themselves—without flinching. Someone had shaken Sarah off her moorings.

"Get this guy off my back," Sarah growled as she met him.

Micah raised his eyebrows and looked past her. "Hank Billings?"

"Yeah. Says the park closes at dusk. Says we're breaking the law."

Hank Billings at night didn't look at all like the clean-cut, uniformed, glassy-eyed ranger Micah had met earlier in the day at Ranger HQ. Billings swaggered when he walked, and with his black jacket and cowboy hat, he looked like someone out of a Kevin Costner Western. "I didn't say that."

"You did." Sarah turned and Micah thought he saw smoke in her eyes. "You said, 'What you folks are doing might be called going over the line.'"

"Right." Ranger Billings stared at her. "You're jumping to the wrong conclusions, missy. I was inferring that you might be going overboard with your search. I put in a call to the local

SAR team, and they said there was no one left at the wreck, that all the survivors had been brought in. You should be checking the local hospital, folks."

"I was there. Emily wasn't." Micah's own tone—terse and on the don't-push-me side of angry—startled even himself. He hadn't realized he'd invested so many emotions into this search. Micah sighed. "We have reason to believe there is a six-year-old girl out here in her pajamas, freezing and lost. We were just headed into town to talk to the CERT and see if we could get them to do a call-out. I appreciate your checking up on us, but we're fine. And all done here."

Hank Billings must have done time in the army. He stood six-foot-something and didn't so much as take his eyes off Micah, let alone flinch. "Okay. Contrary to popular belief, I wasn't checking up on—"

"Hounding us is more like it," Sarah said, and both Micah and Hank stared at her as if she were a rattler reared back to strike. "You deliberately stood outside my truck and listened to me . . . my . . ." She swallowed and turned away, her arms across her chest.

A smile quirked up Micah's face. "You were singing, weren't you?"

Sarah had few cracks, but when they opened, she had only one fix—singing.

"I like 'Jesus Loves Me.' Reminds me of my mama." Hank shrugged, as if he had no idea he'd just seen inside Sarah's heart.

Micah slipped an arm around Sarah. What Hank Billings couldn't know is that singing had saved her life once upon a time. "We could use some singing right now. A little girl's trail has vanished. And only Jesus knows where she is," Micah said gently.

Hank looked at him, a frown on his face. "I'll follow you into town. You might need some backup. Our team is pretty tired after the last two days."

Maybe Micah had misjudged the man.

As Sarah stalked away, Hank's gaze followed her. "I made her mad."

"Yeah. She'll be okay. Doesn't like people to see her soft side."

"She has a soft side?" Hank cracked a lopsided smile as he sauntered back to his truck.

Micah watched him go, wondering if they'd have to shake him, or if he'd come in handy.

"What's the weather say?" Micah asked when climbed into the truck next to Conner.

He was on the Internet, working his palm PC. "It's going to get down to the thirties tonight." Conner's expression gave no hint of hope.

Micah felt his chest knot while they drove back to their hastily set-up base camp.

Fifteen minutes later, he got out of Conner's truck, climbed into his own. "I reserved us rooms at the Tree-Line Motel. I'll meet you there later. I need to swing by the hospital first." The thought of Lacey's eyes emptying of all hope in front of him punched a burning hole in his gut.

Hospital visiting hours were obviously long over. The parking lot glistened under the glare of lights. The rain misted in their rays, evidence of the gloom beyond. Micah shoved his hands in his pockets and headed toward the doors, feeling his failures like Freon in his veins.

He walked past Lacey's guard, preparing to do some fancy maneuvering, but the man didn't stir. Sunken in sleep, he looked like he no longer felt Lacey was a threat.

The guard obviously didn't know her like Micah did.

Or did he? In fact, there was so little Micah knew about this woman that the questions suddenly felt alive, burrowing through his chest. Like, why, exactly, did the NSA think she had murdered someone? Why had her daughter been traveling under a different name? Or even, why had it taken her seven years to call him?

Actually he could answer that last question. Pride. Hurt. Betrayal. Only whose betrayal? Hers or his?

He stood at the foot of her bed, watching her sleep, her head lolled to one side. His lucky penny. Her red hair was tangled, matted against the pillow, and in the darkness, she looked so peaceful. So unlike the woman he'd seen in Kazakhstan, blood dripping from her hands. Her voice rushed back to him as it had so many times, and he remembered the way she grabbed him by the shirt, eyes ferocious on his. "Help John."

But it had been too late. John's aorta had been severed. His life flooded on the floor, his blue eyes glassy. Micah nearly lost ten years of composure right there in the middle of the gutted warehouse.

He'd held together long enough to scoop Lacey into his arms and race through the Almaty streets toward the hospital. Long enough for her to moan, her hands curled around her body, "Oh, it's all my fault. My fault. I killed him."

He stared at her now, his throat thick, those words pinging in his head, and for the first time he wondered if maybe he should have stuck around long enough to decipher the meaning of those words.

Maybe there were a lot of things he should have stuck around to do. He trudged to the window, scraped a hand over his hair, and stared out into the darkness. Regrets seemed to line every conversation he had with Lacey over the years.

"Micah?" Her voice, soft, full of hope, made him wince. He heard her shift, then a quick intake of breath as she sat up.

He turned, stared at his feet. He couldn't look into those gray eyes. "Lacey, I . . . we found her trail and followed it." He closed his eyes, feeling sick. "We lost it. I don't know. We have a dog and he just lost it. I'm so sorry."

She stayed silent. No moan. No mourning cry. Nothing. Then again, Lacey was a spy . . . or had been. She could mask the truth like a Shakespearean actor. Although her eyes were hard and still, the way she swallowed once, then twice, sparked something deep in his gut.

"You're not . . . very surprised by this information."

When she looked away from him, the feeling in his gut blazed to an inferno. *Oh no, what if* . . . "Lacey . . . they haven't . . . found her, have they?" The idea of Lacey's—John's— daughter down in the hospital morgue made him reach out for the back of the chair.

She shook her head.

"She's not dead?" he asked in a thin voice.

Lacey closed her eyes, as if the answer pained her.

He sat down, emptied. He heard only the thumping of his heart and the soft swish of rain outside the window. "Lacey, what is it?"

"Micah, I have to ask you to leave. I'm sorry, but I have to . . . handle this on my own."

"What's going on?" He heard the rush of anger in his voice, shocked that he could race from sympathy to fury so quickly. Lacey had always had the uncanny ability to light a match under his emotions. Still, he'd douse them to cinders before he let them get out of hand. He hadn't earned the nickname Iceman because of his propensity to let himself unravel.

"She's . . . I think she's okay. For now." Lacey was fisting the covers in her hand, her slung arm clutched tightly to her body. He noticed her wrist, a reddened mark where the cuffs had been. "Thank you for coming to help me." She didn't look at him, but he heard the tremor in her voice. "I . . . appreciate it."

"Appreciate it?" His voice rose and he fought to stifle it. "I haul my body across two states and spend part of the day and night tromping about the forest and you *appreciate* it? What do you think I am, the cavalry? The local national guard? Honey, you're going to have to do better than that." He pounced to his feet, a thousand questions screaming in his brain.

The wide-eyed look she gave him froze him on the spot. As if she were . . . afraid of him. As if she thought he might mean something else by his words.

Micah had no idea what had happened to her since that ugly night in the dingy warehouse, but he had a feeling it wasn't good. He sat again on the chair, his body shaking. "I'm sorry. I . . . just meant that you can't kick me out of your life again that easily."

"I thought you'd be relieved," she said in a whisper-thin voice. "I thought . . . well, that you wanted me to erase your name from my mind."

Oh yeah, he had said that. Now he felt like a class-A, prizewinning jerk. "Maybe I just want to help."

She stared at him, and he noticed the faint glistening of tears film her eyes. She licked her lips and opened her mouth, but no words emerged. When she closed it, she swallowed and looked away. "You've done more than I could ever expect. Get away from me, Micah. I'll only cause you trouble."

Now what was that supposed to mean? But it was his own words that startled him. His voice softened, and if he wasn't mistaken, he said, "I'm a big boy, Lacey. And I'm not afraid of a little trouble."

But he was in trouble. Big, big trouble. And looking at her, a single tear streaming down her cheek, he knew that he was a liar.

He was very, very afraid.

Chapter 6

"LACEY'S UP TO something. I know it." Micah paced the motel room, worry knotting his thoughts. "I saw it in her eyes."

"Sit down. You're making me dizzy. I can't think with you prowling." Conner lay on one of the two double beds, a pillow crunched behind his neck, legs crossed at the ankles. Micah had caught him in his room, surfing CNN and FOX News. "She just told you to leave?"

Micah stopped, glanced at his reflection in the mirror, and shuddered. He looked like he'd done a two-day tango with the Tasmanian Devil, whiskers bedraggling his face, his hair in spikes from where he'd raked it one too many times. No wonder she'd asked him to leave. Only . . . he couldn't dodge the niggle that she'd been lying about Emily's being safe. Throwing him off the case for his own good. The haunted look in her eyes called out to him and followed him like a moan to the motel.

"Something happened today while we were out searching. I returned with this horrific news that her daughter had been out there and we didn't find her, but Lacey was completely calm. As if she already knew that our trail had gone cold." Micah turned away from the ghastly person in the mirror and leaned his hip against the dresser, crossing his arms over his chest. "I think someone has her daughter."

"Like social services?"

"No, like . . . someone snatched her. I think Emily is still in danger and Lacey is going to do something about it. Something that is going to get her into more trouble than she's in now."

Conner took a sip of his Mountain Dew. How the guy could drink that stuff at midnight baffled Micah. In a convoluted way, however, it helped Conner unwind, slowing his perpetual autobahn pace. "What is it with you and this woman, Micah? She's got some kind of power over you like I've never seen. Wasn't she the one who came after you in Iraq? I don't recall you two being big pals after that op."

Time rushed Micah back to post–Persian Gulf War Iraq, to Operation Ground Truth and the three weeks he and Conner and another Green Beret had spent as POWs of Caucasian rebels. Lacey and John had hunted them down and saved their lives.

The memory of Lacey could still sweep the breath from his chest. She'd snuck into camp, dressed like a gypsy, and surprised them all with her savvy thinking and guts. But instead of telling her the truth—that he loved her—he'd let his fears overpower him, and he'd all but shoved her onto the first transport back to the States. Of course, she'd been oh-so-thrilled by his chivalry. While he'd locked the right words safely in his chest, he'd watched her choose John and a life of espionage. Micah had spent the last thirteen years fighting the many sides of regret birthed in that moment.

Micah shook his head, agreeing to Conner's words. "I haven't talked to her since John was killed."

"Yet you're acting like that time we were in Bosnia and

that little girl got hurt. Desperate. If I remember correctly, you went berserk."

"She was dying in my arms. I had to get her help."

"You were crying, man. As if your chest had exploded." Conner took another sip. "You really freaked us out. I thought you were going to get yourself—and the rest of us—killed."

"Thanks, Conner. I so appreciate your dredging up that memory for me." Micah sat down on his bed and stared at his car keys lying on the nightstand. "The fact is, Lacey and I have a history that goes way past the mission in Iraq. She was my best friend in high school. The first girl I ever kissed, the first girl I prayed out loud with."

"Whoa. You prayed out loud with her?" Conner wore a teasing grin.

"Yeah, well, I've come a long way. Back then, it felt like I was tearing open my chest for her to get a good peek. And she didn't even flinch."

"Sounds like she still has a hold on you."

Micah picked up the car keys and twirled them around his finger. "It's just memory, nothing more. To cut to the chase, I wanted to tell her I loved her—that I wanted to marry her—but I blew it." He nearly cringed at how it hurt to say that aloud.

The silence from Conner's side of the room made him glance over at his friend. Conner had his can of soda halfway to his mouth, eyes wide. "She's the girl who got away?"

Micah gave a wry shrug. "She might not say that. She never knew how I felt. She married my best friend without me making a peep."

"Ouch."

"Yeah, well, in the end, I was the lucky one," Micah responded. "She murdered the guy."

"What?" Conner put down his soda, then scooted over to

the side of his bed, arms on his knees. "Back up. She killed her husband? Who was your best friend? And you're out here hunting for her daughter? I think I need a few more dots connected."

Micah got up, tossed his keys onto the bureau, and walked over to the sink. He ran the water and wet a washcloth. Conner said nothing as Micah scrubbed his face. The white washcloth came away dirty. Micah tossed it, wadded, into the sink and braced his arms on the counter, staring at Conner in the mirror. "Okay, here's how it is, but you have to promise to never breathe a word. I'm only telling you because you had clearance, okay?"

Conner nodded.

"Remember when we were in Kazakhstan, working with the Khanate tribe? It must have been your first year in the Green Berets."

"I remember. We were tracking Iraqi and Afghani transmissions to Pakistan."

"Right. Well, we got a call to back up one of our operatives in Almaty. Rumor was he was compromised and needed extraction. I led the team in and got there three steps too late. The bottom line is, the subject was my buddy John, and I found Lacey holding the knife. No one else was around."

Conner made a face. "You know better than I do that there had to be more to it."

Micah toweled off his face, turned, and stalked back to the bed. "I thought so too. But the look of guilt on Lacey's face and her own words indicted her for the crime. Besides, I was on assignment. When I returned eighteen months later, Lacey had dropped out of sight, and the CIA wouldn't let me near the file. The best information I got was that John had been on a mission of some sort, and Lacey had somehow been a part of a double cross. I hit roadblocks everywhere I went until one night I got a call."

"A call?"

"Yeah. On my cell phone. The voice on the other end—which had been distorted—told me that Lacey was trouble and if I had half a brain, I would keep away from her."

"And that didn't make you more suspicious?"

Micah grabbed a pillow and shoved it under his neck. "I was shipping out for another tour, and I had other things on my mind. And life took a nosedive after that, as you know."

"Right." Conner was one of the few Micah had allowed into his hospital room, into his secrets. The man nodded and folded his arms across his chest. "So there could probably be more to this story than 'what you see is what you get.'"

"Probably. But the bottom line is, Lacey killed John. And that's something I can't forget."

"How about forgive?"

Conner's question felt like a saber plunged to the hilt, right in the center of Micah's throat. He didn't answer.

"I don't think it's just memories tethering you to this woman, Iceman. You still have feelings for her. I'd even label it regret."

Micah closed his eyes. Lacey's image filled his mind, the adventure behind her laughter, the intelligence in her eyes. *Deep down inside, you know I'm innocent. You know I could never kill anyone.*

Did he still have feelings for Lacey? If he let himself sink into memory, he could smile at the picture of her in her band uniform, tooting her little clarinet. Or enjoy her sweet little grunts as she'd tried to arm-wrestle him, both hands around his fist. Or find a place of peace inside the times they'd spent riding on her family's farm. Lacey had been innocent, with just enough tomboy to make her exhilarating, just enough princess to make her untouchable. He'd lost his heart a thousand times over the night he'd taken her to her senior prom.

But that Lacey had vanished the day she said "I do" to another man. And especially the moment in Kazakhstan when she'd stared at Micah, white faced, and whispered, "It's all my fault." No, the Lacey he knew was a double-crossing, lying traitor. The Lacey in his dreams was only a haunting apparition. As for regret, he should be thanking God for intervening and keeping him out of her Medusa clutches all these years.

"No. I don't have feelings for her. She's history. I just want to help her find her daughter. For John."

Conner nodded, but his eyes held suspicion.

"Really. She's nothing to me." But Micah couldn't ignore the sharp pain in the center of his chest when he said it.

"Well, then, Mr. She's Nothing. Try and get some sleep. She'll be there in the morning. She's not going anywhere with her dislocated shoulder. Besides she's under guard and handcuffed to the bed—"

Micah winced. "Oh no." He wanted to bang his head against the wall hard to jostle his brains into action. "The hand-cuffs. They were off when I was talking to her. I remember seeing the red rash on her wrist."

Conner made a face. "Uh-oh."

"She *is* up to something." Micah rushed over to his jacket and snatched it up. "Stay by the telephone."

"Hello? I want to sleep. In my *truck.* "

"Keep your cell on, then. Because I have a feeling this night isn't going to end pretty."

"Just don't get into any troub—"

Micah closed the door behind him.

✦ ✦ ✦

Lacey listened from just inside her door. No rattle of carts, no buzzing from the nearby nurses' station. Nothing but her thundering pulse. She took a breath and steeled herself for the possibility of a very alert Rambo-type outside the door, hating the fact that she was only armed with a now-deformed fork.

Then again, she'd given a significant warning with just a spoon to an overly friendly waiter one night after he'd followed her to her hotel room. She still wasn't sure he hadn't been one of Shavik's zealots. She clenched the fork and cracked the door open.

Someone was smiling over her because Mr. Menace was asleep, slouched over in his chair. The NSA had put their confidence in flimsy handcuffs, which she'd picked open easily, and the belief that she trusted the system.

Yeah, right. She'd been down that road. And she wasn't going to stick around watching the NSA play with her daughter's life.

She had no doubt that whoever had Emily meant business. The prize they were after told her that if she didn't take them seriously, she'd be crying over her daughter's grave next to John's in Arlington.

She stole down the hall, stopped briefly before she got to the nurses' station, waited until she saw it empty, then let herself into a linen supply room. She ditched the sling and pulled a pair of scrubs on, including the little shoe guards. She'd have to find decent footwear between here and Kentucky.

Striding out of the closet, holding a sheet and towels, she beelined for the far exit.

"Ma'am, can you help me?"

She froze, grimaced, turned.

An elderly man, his frail body gripping a portable IV stand, stood in the middle of the hall, his eyes blinking in confusion. "Can you tell me where I am?"

Her heart tugged. "Um . . . you're in the hospital, sir." She gazed past him, toward her room and the agent stationed in the hall, who had stirred at the sound of voices.

"Do you know my daughter? Where is she?"

She advanced toward him. "No. But you need to get back in bed, sir."

"No!"

She winced, then stepped closer, one eye on her guard. "Okay, listen. I'll call your daughter. But you need to return to your room." *Before you get me killed.* "Please?"

He stared at her, and something like fear edged his eyes. "Where am I? Do you know my daughter?"

She tried not to groan. She crept up to him, turned him slowly toward his room. "You're in the hospital. Do you remember why you're here?"

"Am I sick? I don't feel sick," he mumbled as he shuffled to his room.

Lacey glanced toward her end of the hall and saw that her guard had awakened and was on his feet. She lowered her eyes. "You might be sick. I don't know. But you have to get in bed." She opened the door and helped him inside his private room.

Her heartbeat thundered when the door clicked behind her. She wanted to scream in frustration as she helped the man into his bed. She forced her movements to remain steady, gentle.

"Where am I?" he asked, his voice laced with panic.

She sighed. "I dunno. But you're going to be okay."

She tucked the covers over him, straining to hear voices, footsteps running down the hall, maybe a siren. She was about to turn when the old man grabbed her arm. Frail as he was, his bony fingers ground into her muscles and stopped her.

"It's so dark, you know? I'm afraid."

She frowned. But he wasn't looking at her; his eyes were fixed past her.

Icy fingers ran up her spine. "I'm sorry, sir, but I have to go." She swallowed, then backed way from him.

His eyes focused on her. In the wan light, he looked like a prisoner of war attached to life support, bony and weak. "Run."

Her eyes widened; then she turned and gripped the door handle. She heard him groan as she opened the door and peeked outside.

Her NSA guard had just run past the door. She watched, her heart in her throat, as he flung open the door at the end of the hall and ran down the stairs.

Lacey glanced back at the old man. He lay, eyes open, staring at something. Was he breathing? Running toward his bed, she hit the code blue button on the wall, spun around, and raced out the door. She ducked into a room opposite the man's room before it filled with nurses and on-call doctors. Then she walked briskly down the hall and out the opposite exit door. Taking the stairs two at a time, she hit the outside exit and picked up her pace.

The cool, moist night air hit her face, her lungs with the taste of freedom. She ran through the parking lot into the street and began a stiff walk. The drizzle slicked her hair to her skin, and the shoe protectors on her feet did little to shield her from the wet gravel. She finally kicked them off.

On a side street, shadowed by a giant, creaking elm, she found an unlocked, mideighties Volkswagen Rabbit. The door creaked open with the accumulated rust, and she mumbled apologies to the owner as she crept into the driver's seat.

In less than two minutes she had connected the wires and popped the car into drive. She roared off, cringing at the noise, and pushed the pedal to the floor.

She'd find the real copy of the nearly finished program in Ashleyville. If the U.S. government thought she'd sacrifice her daughter's life for the key to the nation's secrets, it hadn't learned anything from Kazakhstan. She'd spent the last seven years running.

If she had to, she'd do it for the rest of her life.

Micah knew it. Just knew it. Still, the sight of a group of NSA regulars swarming around the hospital and Lacey's room made him a little sick.

She'd run. Fled the sanity of organized help for some hysteria-based mission to find her daughter. Or maybe it was more than hysteria. Maybe someone would discover she was lying about the entire daughter thing in the first place.

That thought made him find a bench in a deserted hallway, sit down, and cradle his head in his hands. He listened to his pounding heartbeat. *Lacey, what have you done? Where are you?*

Conner's voice returned to him. *"Do you still have feelings for her?"*

A smart man would get up, go back to the motel, and force himself to sleep. And in the morning, apologize to his friends and drive back in disgrace to Ashleyville and . . .

Ashleyville.

The Galloway farm, where Sam Galloway, Lacey's brother, still bred Thoroughbreds. Lacey hadn't been back there in years . . . according to Sam. But if there was one place Lacey wanted to hide something, Micah knew where it would be.

SUSAN MAY WARREN

He stood, walked away from the convention of cops and toward the emergency exit.

"Jim Micah, what are you doing here?"

He whirled and nearly died on the spot when he saw Deputy Director Berg stride toward him. Berg's eyes were cracked with red and his suit looked rumpled, as if he'd slept in it. Although Micah hadn't seen him since right after John's murder, Berg looked painfully similar to the last time they'd chatted—wrung out and furious, gripping his last fraying thread of nerves. Of course, then Micah had been hovering over Berg's desk, talking in a low, dangerous tone, suggesting that Berg should elaborate on Lacey's disappearance.

Now Micah was on the side of information. He wasn't so sure Berg wouldn't get the same answer he'd received from Lacey . . . nada.

"I thought I told you long ago to stay out of the Montgomery case," Berg said, without greeting.

Micah bit back a retort and mustered up a blank demeanor. Okay, so he'd also bypass niceties. "Did I miss a memo? I don't recall ever being a part of the Montgomery case. I nearly got a nosebleed when you slammed the door in my face seven years ago. Sorry, pal, I'm here with my SAR team, looking for a lost child."

Director Berg narrowed his eyes. "Emily Montgomery, maybe?"

The name hit Jim in the soft tissue of his heart and nearly made him flinch. The final confirmation of Lacey's honesty. He swallowed and kept his face stoic. "Emily Montgomery?"

"Oh, please. Like Lacey didn't tell you about John's daughter. We don't miss much, you know."

Micah hid a smirk. "Nope. You guys are pretty smart. So what happened? Did Lacey give you the slip?"

83

Fury gathered in Berg's eyes, and he poked a finger into Micah's chest. "You'd be smart to put mileage between you and Lacey Montgomery. Besides, she's trouble. If you have half a brain, you'd turn around and go back to whatever region of the world you're saving at the moment."

Micah stared at him, a sick feeling in his gut, recalling a certain telephone call that had full-stopped his inquiries.

"Besides, you don't want news to get back to the army that you've been helping a fugitive, right? That might make it difficult to get reinstated," Berg sneered. "Unless you're looking to do a tour or two in Leavenworth."

Micah gauged the director's height and weight and whether he'd fit into the trash can beside the front doors. "No, sir. Like I said, I'm just here with my SAR team. I'm not looking for trouble." *Yet.*

"Good boy." Berg turned and walked away.

Nope, the man wouldn't have fit into the can . . . his head was too huge.

What did Lacey have that NSA poured over the hospital grounds like cockroaches looking for? If they were truly after Lacey, then they'd have a team on their way to Kentucky.

Unless they were already there.

The sick feeling in his gut turned into a full-out burn as he stalked out to his pickup.

Chapter 7

LACEY PRIED HERSELF out of the rattletrap Rabbit, wanting to throw it into the next county. No, the next state. Instead she kicked the beater. Pain spiked up to her knee. She bit back a cry, glad that the hurt swept her feelings away from horror, if only for a second. She needed shoes, clothes, a decent meal, and sleep.

No, she just needed Emily. Emily's voice had burned into her brain and kept her foot to the floorboard for the past three hours, through the fog and drizzle, along the deserted Missouri back roads, to the Kentucky state line.

It seemed some sort of divine retribution that her stolen car should die within sight of the Kentucky Welcome sign.

Thankfully, the rain had stopped and only the coolness of early morning remained. She crossed her arms against the prickle of her skin and began to trudge along the ditch. Her feet would harden in an hour or two. Or maybe she'd find a nice person to pick her up before then. Good thing she still had her fork.

The dawn had dented the eastern horizon, a simmer of rose and lavender that hinted at a warm and hopeful day. She cast it a glance and was reminded of the sunrise over the Rockies. For a time she'd been holed up in a cabin nestled in the pine and birch of Glacier National Park working on Ex-6. One morning, lost in the tangle of programming language and loneliness, she'd ventured out to greet the dawn. Perched on a rock, she watched the light glide over the mountains, gilding the trees, turning each rock to gemstone. Out of the darkness emerged detail, color, blemish, and beauty. When the sun broke free of the horizon, it warmed Lacey's face like a long-awaited kiss.

"The people walking in darkness have seen a great light; on those living in the land of the shadow of death a light has dawned." The verse echoed through time in the voice of her father. She blinked and behind her eyes she saw Gerald Galloway holding his weathered Bible and reading the book of Isaiah. She swallowed a ball of grief before it lodged in her throat and threatened to cut off her air. Her father had been the voice of reason, the calm behind her storms. How many times had he told her, as if he were the prophet Isaiah, that she was heading into darkness if she ran after John? As if he could see the future.

She swiped away tears, or maybe it was just dew on her face. Still, her chest clenched as her mistakes ran rampant through her mind. She was living in the shadow of death. But no light was about to dawn for her. Now or ever. She'd lived in the shadowlands far too long to turn toward the light. The illumination would decimate her from the inside out, like the sweep of a laser, burning a trail across her heart. She knew her sins. She didn't need to pour light on them for God or anyone else to examine.

She balled her fists and ignored the throb of her cold feet as she passed the Welcome to Kentucky sign. The sound of a truck engine behind her made her turn. Headlights pushed against the waning vestiges of night. Hope lit inside her as she held out her hand, waving.

The vehicle slowed. With the sun glaring on the windshield, she couldn't make out the driver. She hoped he might be elderly, perhaps a farmer. But the pickup looked too new, despite the layer of dirt and grime. The truck crunched to a halt next to her. She reached behind her, where she'd shoved her fork into her waistband.

The window rolled down. "Would you like a ride?"

Oh no. She made a wry face. "No. I guess I don't."

"Get in, Lacey." Micah didn't look any happier to see her than she was to see him. Weariness etched his dark eyes, and his hair looked like it had gone through a baler. Dark whiskers layered his chin, giving him a renegade look.

Then again, he'd come after her. Just like some kind of rebel. Or hero.

"What are you doing here?" She took a step away from the truck.

No Jim Micah. Her heart plummeted. After all she'd done to ditch him, and here he was, as if she had a GPS system strapped to her that linked directly to his brain. Hadn't he received her message loud and clear in the hospital? Or did he need army speak to hear and obey? She went cold at that thought. Maybe he'd been sent by the NSA. Micah was red, white, and blue to the bone. He believed in the system. Had given a good chunk of his life to support it.

She took another step back. "Go away."

"I want to help." His tone tugged at her defenses, rattled them. He sounded genuine.

No, Micah, don't make me believe you. Don't play with my heart. "You've already helped. I have to do the rest on my own."

He hit the steering wheel with his palm. "Good grief, Lacey! Get in the truck! It's cold out, and you're freezing. I promise you, I want to help."

"Oh, sure you do. Just about as much as you believe I didn't kill John. C'mon, Micah, I'm not stupid. You'd love to see me in jail for a small eternity."

He winced, and she swallowed hard. She had only voiced her theory, but the look of shame on his face solidified all her suspicions into a hard ball. She turned and stalked down the road.

"Lacey! Stop!"

She strode ahead, her fists closed.

The door slammed and boots scuffed on the gravel, rushing up behind her. She broke into a run. But she was barefoot, and he not only was fully dressed but hadn't recently dislocated his shoulder.

He caught up easily, then spun her around by her good arm. "Stop it!"

"Get away from me!" She pushed him and swung around to kick him. He caught her foot and she went down.

"What's the matter with you, woman?" He scooped her up as if she were a small child.

"Micah, put me down."

"No." He started for the truck.

Her bad shoulder was crunched into his chest and screamed with agony. "You're hurting me."

"The feeling is mutual, honey." By the whitened look on his face, she wondered at his words.

She stopped struggling when he set her down beside the passenger door. He was breathing just a little too quickly for a man who had spent the better part of his life with a rigorous PT schedule. She glared at him.

"Get in."

"Why? So you can take me back and the NSA can arrest me? No." She put a hand on his chest, meaning to push him away, and felt his heart pumping, his chest rising and falling with effort. Her heart hiccuped. "Are you okay?"

"I'm fine." But he wasn't fine. She could tell by his heaving breathing and the look in his eyes. He looked . . . wounded.

Her anger died in a snap. "What's wrong?"

He stared at her. For a second she saw something akin to fear rise in his eyes, something she'd seen only once before on the night John died and she'd been stabbed by Ishmael Shavik and left to die. It spiraled her back to the very real terror on Micah's face when he'd gathered her in his arms and raced through the streets toward the hospital. He hadn't been winded then. At least not until she told him she'd killed John.

The past vanished as she remembered the look of hatred in his eyes. She'd wanted to cry then. Now it only made her moan. Micah couldn't be a casualty here. She'd made enough mistakes. "Please, Micah. Let me go. Before you get hurt."

He opened the passenger door, pointed at the seat. "I'm already hurt. Get in. I'm sure the NSA is on my tail, and if you have any hope of getting to the farm without being caught, you're going to need me."

Micah wondered if fatigue had melted his brain cells, stopped his synapses from firing. It was the only reason he could scrounge up for sitting in his pickup with a known fugitive, a murderer, the one woman who could pry his heart out of its hiding place with a smile . . . or a glare.

At the moment, she wore a death-ray look that could deep-fry him if she turned it in his direction. Thankfully, she had crossed her arms over her chest and stared straight ahead, glaring as daylight swept over the Kentucky meadows.

What was he doing here? A guy who had spent a good part of his life figuring out tactics and learning how to negotiate with hostiles in their own territory should be able to untangle his motives in tracking down a national fugitive. But other than reverting back to his reset mode—save Lacey—he couldn't account for why he'd raced across the Missouri countryside, praying he might find the woman who could cost him his career.

It was Emily. *Of course.* His insides turned into hard knots when he thought of her in the hands of . . . whom?

Or maybe this was all a big game, cooked up by Lacey to make her look less guilty. To make him believe she might have a reason for fleeing NSA custody.

He slammed the brakes, made a U-turn, and took off for Poplar Bluff going seventy.

"What are you doing?" Lacey yelled.

"Coming to my senses."

"Turn this truck around right now." Lacey's voice held a sharp, low edge.

"No. You're going to get yourself killed."

"Jim Micah, you turn this truck around or you're going to regret it for the rest of your life."

"Believe me, I already do." Acid pooled in the back of his throat as he said it.

She sucked a quick breath.

Better angry and alive than dead. Well, maybe, he thought. A live person could call him up, torment him with requests, a smile, a pleading voice. Then again, a dead person could haunt him with regrets.

At least putting Lacey in custody could give him time to figure out why his heart took a leap and tumble every time he looked at her and why he'd run to her aid in Missouri in the first place.

"I said turn the truck around." The sound of her dangerously calm voice was accompanied by a sharp prick at the base of his neck, at his jugular.

He stiffened. "Is that my knife?"

She pushed hard; he felt heat. "I said turn it around."

He kept driving. "Were you this cold-blooded when you killed John?"

"Jim Micah, if you care anything about John's daughter, you'll turn this truck around or at least stop it and let me out." Her voice softened. "Please."

He clenched his jaw but applied the brakes. The pickup skidded to a halt. Sudden silence saturated the truck, fractured only by the thunder of his heartbeat. He finally ground up words. "This is a bad idea, Lacey. You can't run from the law. You know they'll find you."

"I'll find Emily first." She inched toward the door.

"Are you going to run all the way to Ashleyville in your bare feet?"

"I would have been closer ten minutes ago, if you hadn't lied to me."

He whirled, made a grab for her left hand. She hit him with her right, a chops-ringing blow for someone who had just dislocated her shoulder. Still, he didn't even grunt as he hung on. "You attacked me with a *fork*?"

She launched herself back and kicked him hard in the chest. He gasped, let go. She was out the door and running across the weedy ditch before he caught his breath.

He hurtled out of the pickup. "Lacey, stop! Okay, you win!"

She ran down the road, unfazed. She never had been one to listen to him. Not that he'd spoken up much. No wonder she fled from him like he might be the grim reaper. He certainly hadn't given her reason to think otherwise.

He stifled a word of fury, dived back into the truck, turned it around, and floored it. He cranked down his window. "Lacey. Fine. You win. I'll take you to Ashleyville."

She didn't even look in his direction. She kept running, long strides that had to cut her feet. But her face was stoic.

Seeing her tore a hole in his heart. Maybe her daughter really was in danger. "Please get in the truck and I'll listen. I won't turn you in."

"You're lying."

"No." He bit back a retort that suggested he wasn't the liar, but suddenly his words, his posture felt . . . abusive. As if he'd been the one doing the hurting. "No, I'm not. I promise on my letter jacket that I'll take you back to Ashleyville. If that's what you want."

She slowed, glanced in his direction. The sun hovered above the horizon, and in the dim light she looked tired. Wan. As if she'd just emerged from a long illness, a walk through the corridors of despair.

Well, he knew what that felt like. He stopped the pickup and got out. "Let me help you, okay?" Had he really said that with so much pleading in his voice? She too must have wondered, because she stared at him, those beautiful, intelligent eyes wide and desperate.

With a hard jolt, he realized that he meant it.

The thought froze him as she rounded the truck, opened his door, and dug around in his glove compartment. She surfaced with a Night Force folding knife. She held it up, her eyes fiery with warning, then climbed into the pickup and closed the door.

Sliding back in, Micah felt tentacles of dread coil around his chest. Something had happened, seriously happened, to Lacey's very real daughter. Enough to make Lacey break a thousand laws and risk any hint of friendship that might have pulsed between them.

Lacey looked out the window. Amazing how little she'd changed, despite the seven years since he'd seen her up close, at least without blood on her hands and tears striping her face. Her red hair with highlights of gold now tangled past her shoulders, unruly as her character. She still had freckles, but they'd faded to a fine wisp along her nose and cheeks. She even bore the same wild, smart, even sassy demeanor.

Not that he was noticing. He forced his gaze to the road but not before he caught sight of her feet. Cracked, with a trickle of blood on her left heel.

He shouldn't be surprised. Before the incident in Kazakhstan, he'd heard rumors, his ears pricked for any whisper of her, and knew she'd earned her keep as an asset in the post–cold war games. John and Lacey had made a striking duo . . . John with his charisma and boldness, Lacey with her creativity and courage.

Okay, yes, Micah had fought the beast of jealousy on more than a few occasions. But he'd beat it to a pulp and won. At least he'd thought so.

"We can't go all the way into Ashleyville," she said. "It would be best if you got off at the Mars Hollow exit. The road runs northeast, and it'll hook up with Stony Bend. Take that to County 38—"

"I know." He shot a glance at her. "I still live here, you know."

"You should let me off at Mahoney's Grill. I know a short-cut—"

"What's this all about?" Micah exited the highway, onto County Road 320. Gravel picked at the truck. Leaves ground under his wheels, the litter of a recent storm. He cracked his window, letting in the smell of loam and field. He needed the fresh air to stay awake.

"I can't tell you." She still hadn't turned his direction and instead spoke to the windshield.

"Does it have to do with John and his death?"

He saw her flinch and suddenly he felt like a jerk. His harsh accusation rose in his memory, his voice hot: *"How could you, Lacey? You killed your husband. What kind of traitor are you?"* He let silence throb between them, wishing he could somehow ease the scars.

"I can't talk about it."

He blew out a hot breath of frustration. "You want to get off at Mahoney's?" He hit the brakes and they skidded to a stop sideways in the road. "Well, guess what? We don't move another inch until you tell me what's going on."

She faced him and the look in her eyes made him wince. Regret. He glanced at the knife she held open in her lap. But she made no move to raise it. Her voice dropped to a strained whisper. "I can't. Please believe me when I say that I'm only trying to keep you safe."

He blinked at her. "Safe? I'm a big boy, remember?" He suddenly noticed that she was shivering. She should be, dressed in short-sleeved, paper-thin scrubs. He pulled off his jacket and, even as she protested, draped it over her shoulders. They needed to get her different clothes as well as shoes.

"Yeah, I remember." She shook her head. "I shouldn't have called you. I should have known better." Except she reached up and pulled the jacket just a little tighter over her pale arms. "I was just . . . desperate. I didn't know where Emily was—"

"And now you do?"

She looked away, her jaw tight.

"Has she been kidnapped?"

She swallowed and closed her eyes.

"Lacey!" He wanted to shake her. He grabbed the steering wheel in both hands and touched his head to it, relishing the coolness against his forehead. "I can't help you if I don't know what's going on. The NSA is hunting you. And you can bet they'll have a posse at the farm. You'll never get in there undetected. And how are you going to help Emily if you're in maximum security?

"Listen, I have a friend. A senator. He's a good man, and he'll listen to you. Let's call him. I'll bet he can get the NSA to back off or at least let you have some maneuver room—"

"It's all about Ex-6." Sighing, she twisted her fingers in her lap. "It's a quantum encryption program I've been working on for the past few years."

"Quantum encryption?" The theory had been batted about for years, and some of the best professors and research facilities in the nation had their hottest minds trying to decipher it. Quantum physics took the on-off binary code used in standard encryption and multiplied it by exponent 6. A code that was created by quantum encryption was virtually unbreakable by today's code crackers. But it also meant that quantum decryption could crack today's algorithmic codes in a mere blink.

How could Lacey . . . well, she had graduated from Massachusetts Institute of Technology with a PhD in physics and mathematics and could do advanced calculus in her head. Moreover, she'd mentored with the best tech minds in the company before launching out onto the field with John. Still . . .

"It's the next level of encryption." Her voice had dropped, and she glanced out the windshield, then back to her hands, always away from his gaze. "The current encryption systems are based on very advanced algorithms and symmetric key encryptions. Basically, when a message is transmitted, it is encrypted with a symmetric key, in code, that unlocks the secret code in which the message is written. To open the message, the recipient must use the key code.

"Right now, we use a combination of private and public keys—one key is embedded in the code and its information is sent to the recipient. The other key is embedded in the recipient's computer. For example, when you go to an online source, you download the key codes for the information you hope to unlock. And you have to have the right password to download the codes. The system is fairly secure—against the average hacker. But the NSA isn't afraid of average hackers."

"They're worried about terrorists intercepting our messages and using them to steal industrial secrets." Micah had heard about this in various briefings. The idea that a terrorist group could gain key codes and infiltrate public utilities—water, power, air travel—had the government working overtime on encryption techniques.

"Yes. But every code can be broken if there's enough time. More important is knowing whether a message or system has been compromised or tampered with. How do we know someone is listening? We need not only a fail-proof system, which is nearly impossible to create, but also a way to detect if it has been tapped."

Lacey looked animated, vibrant, the hours of exhaustion erased from her face. "I was able to use the basic principle of quantum physics to create hardware and software to protect our current encryption systems."

Micah's face tightened into a frown as he processed her words.

She took a deep breath and continued. "Quantum encryption uses photons—particles of light—to transfer data between computers. I figured out a way to take our current algorithm encryption, attach photon interference hardware, and then create white noise in the transmission. Basically, we can make static in our transmissions so the messages we send are unbreakable because the information can't be parceled out. Like a massive party line, only the static and myriad conversations come from one source.

"I also developed a program to filter out the white noise and decrypt the message. But the most important part isn't the encryption or decryptions. It's the fact that if a would-be eavesdropper taps the line or diverts the transmission, the signal is contaminated. We know we've been compromised." She took another breath, and grief filled her face. "And maybe lives are saved."

"So what you're saying is that you figured out a way to transmit encrypted information and then detect if it has been tampered with?"

"Yes. And I created a corresponding decryption program that can unravel the information."

"So you made a modern-day enigma machine."

"It has its glitches, and it's not wireless, but . . . yeah." She managed a slight smile.

Micah gaped at her, processing the information in slow microbytes. "When my unit was in Afghanistan, we were sent a message from HQ, coordinates for a group of suspected al Qaeda terrorists. It was one of my last missions." He remembered Conner listening on the radio then, heard the static over the line. "The message lost its integrity, but we had the go-ahead and decided to run the op." He ran a finger over his dashboard. "We were ambushed en route. They knew our every tiptoe."

Lacey closed her eyes and shook her head, as if the story had strummed her deepest fears. "That's why Ex-6 is so valuable. With the war on terror expanding, we need a way to communicate safely. You can see it's important that the wrong people don't get ahold of it."

She looked at him finally, and tears hung from her lashes. "Ex-6 is why Emily's life is in danger. And why you have to let me go. No one else is going to die because of me."

Those words felt like a line drive right to his chest. *It's all my fault.* He blinked at her. "This is about John."

She gave him a hard look. "No. It's about Emily. And it's about my getting her back, no matter what happens to me. And it's about your dropping me off outside town so I can get a decent pair of shoes and some jeans before I try and get the only copy of Ex-6 out of hiding."

"From your father's vault in his office in the barn." He raised one eyebrow when she shot a frown at him. "Of course I know, Lacey. Remember you hid John's collection of Elvis records there when he left for West Point? I was with you."

He saw memory streak behind her gaze, and for a moment, the small smile she gave him whisked him back in time to the bittersweet smell of hay, the whinny of horses, the laughter of that Saturday afternoon, the sweet taste of anticipation. He'd felt slightly guilty that he'd spent the morning enjoying her friendship to the extent he had. He'd been entrusted to watchdog her for his buddy, not fall head-over-heels for her smile. Lacey had grown up to pure woman in the two years Micah had been away at basic training and special ops school, and when she met him at the bus for that weekend, the sight of her in a cotton tank top, Guess? jeans, riding boots, and her hair a long, curly mane had nearly knocked the breath right out of him.

At the time, he could hardly believe that he was the lucky guy who would take her to her senior prom in John's stead. His mouth dried, in memory, just thinking of her in his arms.

He swallowed, forcing himself back to the present. "Are you planning to exchange Ex-6 for Emily?"

The blood drained from her face. "I'm getting out here." She reached for the door handle.

"No." He touched her arm, painfully aware that something like panic had rushed into his throat. "Let's get you some clothes." He glanced at her feet. "And a pair of boots."

When she just stared at him, he could almost see her weighing his words with his actions, reaching for faith, and yanking herself back before the flames of betrayal. She looked at the knife in her hand, then back at him.

He didn't realize he'd been holding his breath until she nodded.

"But don't get any bright ideas, Soldier Boy. You're not going to get between Emily and Ex-6. Nothing is more important to me than my daughter." Her expression held more than warning, maybe . . . desperation? "Nothing."

He ignored her threat, rattled more by the use of her nickname for him. Wow, he'd forgotten how good that name on her lips made him feel. Dangerously good. Somehow he found a smile. "Let me buy you breakfast, and then we'll talk about your sneaking onto the farm with—or without—me."

Chapter 8

"I THINK THIS would look outstanding on you." Micah stood in the women's section of Wal-Mart, holding up a pink, padded bathrobe.

Lacey sent him a half glare and turned her back to him, excruciatingly aware of his presence behind her. What was he doing here? Not in the women's section of the store, but *here*, in her air space. Why had he run her down . . . only to drive her to the Wal-Mart in Hermantown, as if he not only believed her but wanted to help her?

He was up to something. But if she didn't untangle herself from his brain-tingling charisma in about three-point-two seconds, she'd be telling herself she didn't care that he might be plotting to blindside her and drag her back into NSA clutches. The way he teased her with his ridiculous shopping advice, not to mention the fact that he'd wrapped his jacket around her, which left his masculine smell lingering on her when she returned it . . . well, it churned up her deepest longings. He looked twenty years old, devastatingly handsome, and way too dangerous for her heart as he leaned on a rack of black dress pants, his hair mussed, a two-day growth on his face, and a smile in his smoky gray green eyes.

She focused on the rack of jeans and found a pair of low-rise Levi's. "How about finding me a jacket?"

"No, I'll just . . . stay here."

She heard hesitation in his voice, despite his efforts to mask it. She swallowed and hid the realization that he fully expected her to . . . ditch him?

She wanted to wince at how heart-wrenchingly close to the truth that hit. She flung the jeans over her shoulder, manufactured a smile, and faced him. "Okay, I need a T-shirt."

He followed her to a bin of Ts, where she dug out a lime green, scoop-neck shirt. As she pushed her cart to the shoe section, she picked up some undergarments and a lined jean jacket.

Jim Micah walked beside her, like a husband might walk beside his wife, ambling, a half grin on his face. Was he enjoying this little time-out in Wal-Mart? "You never asked me how I found you," she asked.

"How *did* you find me, Penny?" He laced his voice with a drawl that sent a ripple to her toes. She wouldn't even think about his use of her nickname.

"I saw you on CNN. You rescued a bunch of kids from a cave?"

His smile dimmed. "Yeah. Their brain-dead camp counselor led them on an expedition into a cave that almost got them all killed. One of them fell and fractured his leg. They nearly died from exposure." Emotion flickered across his face.

"You do that a lot? Rescue people?" She stopped the cart in the shoe section, wandered toward the size eights.

Micah stood at the end of the row, hands in his coat pockets. He shrugged. "Sometimes. A bunch of friends and I do some part-time SAR work when we're in the area and there's a need and we're called upon."

She picked up a pair of tennis shoes. "Are these the same folks who went to look for Emily?"

He said nothing.

She glanced at him. "Thank you, by the way. I know you think I used you, but the truth is, I didn't lie to you. When I called you, I thought she was wandering in the woods, alone and scared and hurt." Her voice dropped as emotion clogged it. She turned away before tears could betray her, put the tennis shoes down, and reached for a pair of hiking boots.

"I believed you," he said softly. She felt him close in on her. He picked up the box of boots. "Sit down. You should try these on."

She sat on a bench, unable to look at him as he snatched a bag of socks from a nearby bin, crouched before her, took out the right boot, and laced it. He opened the bag, took her foot, and put a sock on. "We'll keep the wrapper and pay for it at checkout," he said, as if she thought he might steal them.

She couldn't find words when he fitted the boot on her foot. He tied it carefully. Sweetly.

The image of this powerful man, her once-dearest friend, on his knees before her, attending to her feet, knotted every errant emotion in her chest. She didn't know what to think about Micah. Was he on her side? Or was he about to betray her and wrench her heart out between her ribs?

"How does it fit?" He pushed his thumb into the space between her toes and the end of the boot.

"Good."

"Stand up, walk around." He scooted back and didn't meet her eyes. As if he, too, felt the vulnerability of the moment.

Lacey stood up and lumped around on one booted foot. "It fits." She sat down and bent over to unlace the boot . . . and conked heads with Micah.

"Ouch," he said, but his grin spoke forgiveness. "You okay?"

She rubbed her forehead. "I think I'll live."

He began lacing the other boot. "You can't walk out of here barefoot."

There were a lot of things that she couldn't—or shouldn't—do, and running around barefoot was the least of her issues. But she smiled as she submitted her other foot.

He tied the laces, backed away, and stood up. "Okay, what's next on the list?"

Lacey stared at him, suddenly seeing the man who'd been the best athlete in school, the most handsome fella at prom, and the man she'd seen bow his head and ask God to let him be His man. He deserved more than this. Better than this. A good woman, a family, children. "Micah, I should have asked . . . are you married?"

His mouth opened slightly, and he reddened. Looked away.

She'd made him blush. She tried not to enjoy that, but somehow that fact only made her bolder. He hadn't married. Please, *please* let that have something to do with her. "How about a girlfriend?" Okay, she'd just treaded onto sensitive territory.

He turned and stalked away, then grabbed their shopping cart as if for balance or support.

"It's just a question."

"No. There's your answer."

O-*kay*. She sidled up to him. Yes, those boots were comfortable. And in them she just might be able to outrun him. But at the moment ditching him was the last thing on her mind. He didn't have a girlfriend? "Why not?"

Micah looked at her then, a swift glance that revealed all his emotions, right there in his eyes. His jaw clenched. "Maybe I just never found anyone worth surrendering my life for."

So it *was* about her. Like, John had given his life, and she hadn't been worth it. "Oh," she squawked.

Lacey walked beside him, the silence thick and prickled with his accusation. The pain throbbing in her heart should be one of many good reasons to keep her mouth shut, to dodge any moment of fond recollection of a warm and fuzzy friendship with this man. Their future had as much chance as a snowball in Jamaica, and every synapse in her brain screamed at her to run. Besides, Jim Micah had nothing but contempt, with perhaps a smidgen of sympathy, for her.

"Are you hungry?" Micah veered into the chip-and-soda aisle. He reached for a jar of peanuts.

"Pork rinds." Lacey trolleyed down to the end of the row and chose a bag of barbeque-flavored pork rinds.

Micah made a face. He'd forgotten her affinity for them, a fondness he never could figure out. "You can't be serious. I thought that was a phase."

She tossed them into the cart. "Some habits are hard to break. Even if I wanted to, which I don't." Like the habit of wishing Jim Micah might forgive her someday. She muscled past a wave of sorrow and grabbed a Diet Coke with lime. "I love this new stuff." She also loaded in a box of Fruit Roll-Ups. "Emily eats these all the time. She dangles them out of her mouth like a tongue."

Micah smirked.

Lacey wheeled to the cosmetics section, picked up some mascara, lipstick, a hairbrush, a ponytail holder, and panty hose. "So I take it you're on leave or something?"

"Or something," Micah said.

She glanced at him. "You're still with the commandos, right?"

He nodded but didn't meet her eyes.

Something felt . . . wrong. She remembered the way he'd carried her . . . and the strain in his eyes. "You weren't . . . I mean, you're not . . . were you wounded?" She fought the mental image of him pushing papers, filing, or even analyzing missions. But he wore a strange—no . . . *unsettling*—look. As if he had his own secrets.

He gave a harsh chuckle. "No."

Somehow that made her feel better. She pushed the cart toward the shampoo aisle. "I always thought you were a lifer, just like John. You both had this patriotic zeal in your eyes at graduation." Micah had also let her peek inside his soul for a good glimpse at his real reasons. Honest, just, biblical reasons that should make an accused killer like herself turn tail and flee.

"Yeah," he said softly, "I'm a lifer." But she heard the strangest tinge in his voice. And when she turned, the look in his eyes sent a flash of heat to the center of her chest.

She made a quick escape toward a display of sunglasses.

Jim Micah, get ahold of yourself. *Right now.*

Micah clenched his jaw in an effort to lasso his emotions. Three hours with this woman and he felt like he'd been in a firefight for three days and was on his last clip. He tightened his fists in his pockets and followed her to the sunglasses display.

Married, indeed. As if he could ever get married when he was still in love with—

No, not in love. He had a career. And that was enough. As soon as he figured out a way to wrestle Lacey back into the truck and surrender, he'd run, full out, back to that career and never look over his shoulder to this moment when she so neatly ambushed him with the question, *"Are you married?"*

Never. Not when it cost his best friend his life. Not that Micah was against marriage—to the right woman. He recognized plenty of good marriages in his midst—like his parents and his brother Joey to Becky. But stacking his plate with one mission then another left little time for Micah to meet someone who might dig through his layers, someone for whom he might crack open his heart and let inside.

Not that he'd ever tried. All desire for marriage died the day he saw the only woman he'd ever loved say "I do" to his best friend. And when she killed him . . . well, case closed.

Micah walked behind Lacey through the accessories section, watching her pick out a bevy of interesting items. Ten minutes later, he paid for them with his credit card.

She disappeared into the bathroom while he paced. Somehow he needed to negotiate her into surrendering. The last thing she needed was another charge on her list of allegations. Senator Ramey was an honest man, someone who would listen. He'd written Micah's recommendation for reinstatement, and if Micah could get Lacey to listen, maybe . . .

Who was he kidding? Micah had barely talked himself into listening to her. Even now, he had a gut feeling that she was hiding enough secrets to get them both shot on sight. Perfect. Just what he needed to bolster the review committee's opinion of him.

He ran a hand through his hair, feeling even more greasy and disgusting than he had the night before. And with the smell he was emanating, he might just pass for roadkill.

Lacey, on the other hand, despite her rather at-loose-ends attire, could still turn a man to knots with her curly red hair, silver eyes so full of energy, and her smile that seemed to blindside him and elevate his heartbeat. He hadn't expected her questions or her soft concern about his health. *Were you wounded?*

Yeah, a sniper bullet straight to his heart about twenty years ago. Status—critical.

He ground his molars, placed his arms across his chest. *"I always thought you were a lifer. . . ."*

She'd meant in the army. She had no idea that she'd zeroed in on his biggest problem—the fact that he'd never flushed her from his system. Never exorcised the memory of Lacey Galloway from what was left of his bleeding heart. But he'd spent years shoving his feelings into compartments, eating tactics, breathing duty, knowing that if he ever let his feelings out of the box, they might devour him.

And he wasn't about to let Lacey Galloway interfere with twenty years of training. He'd waited—no, *prayed*—for this day. Hadn't he?

If he hoped to be God's man, he had to do what was right. He had to haul her back to the National Security Agency. Kicking and screaming, if need dictated.

A woman exited the bathroom. Her blonde hair bobbed just below her chin, and her face glowed with fresh makeup. She wore a pair of jeans and a lime green T-shirt short enough to hint at skin, and she clutched a jean jacket thrown over her shoulder. She strode by him and left in her wake a fragrance that could awaken an army of dead.

Micah caught her by the arm. "Good try."

When she whirled and quirked an eyebrow, all his wounds reopened with a single slash. Oh, this woman could tangle his brains and sweep the breath out of him with a smile. "So, what do you think?" she asked.

"I think that the NSA better be on their toes or you'll walk away with the nation's secrets *and* the key to Fort Knox."

Or maybe what was left of his heart.

Chapter 9

"OKAY, I KNEW you were hungry, but c'mon, three orders of pancakes *and* an omelette?" Micah stared at Lacey over the menu, his face partially hidden, but she saw the smile in his eyes.

She'd called herself a fool a thousand times during the past three hours since their stopover at Wal-Mart, but she couldn't get past her personal name-calling to actually ditching this man who had so completely come to her rescue . . . again.

It was a habit she'd have to kick if she hoped to keep him out of this mess—and alive. *No Jim Micah.* That meant that whoever had Emily knew Lacey's past and her heroes.

Micah did look like a hero in the full, late-morning light. A man-sized, slightly rumpled, dark, frowsy-haired, whiskered, smoky-green-eyes-etched-with-concern hero.

"Okay, maybe you're right. But definitely the Denver omelet and at least one order of cakes to start. I need the carbo load." She felt ravenous, despite the bag of pork rinds and half a bottle of Diet Coke. She smiled at the waitress, a barely updated version of Aunt Bee, who nodded approvingly.

Micah closed his menu and handed it to Bee. "I'll have a bowl of grits, lots of butter, a cup of coffee, and a piece of whole-wheat bread with honey."

"Yuck."

He smiled. "Yeah, well, I'm not trying to eat for a small nation."

"I don't know when I'll eat again," Lacey mumbled. The reality of her situation loomed like a guillotine, despite the uplift from a change of clothing. She had tied her hair up with the panty hose in the Wal-Mart bathroom and shoved on a blonde wig, picked up at the accessory counter. It felt hot and itchy on her head. Now she just needed to use her new toothbrush and she might be able to live with herself for another twenty-four hours.

Then again, if she didn't have Emily back in her arms—and soon—she might never be able to live with herself again. She already flinched every time she looked in the mirror. How had she gone from sophomore clarinet player and choir member to fugitive with a record?

One bad choice at a time. Until she'd gotten so far down the road, so far from God and the memories of faith, she couldn't find her way back.

She couldn't scrape from her mind the split-second look of admiration on Micah's face when she came out of the Wal-Mart dressing room. She knew she'd almost fooled him when she walked quickly past him, which meant she might also be able to ditch him. Probably another bad choice, but again, she'd backed herself into a corner with her abysmal decisions.

She turned over the fork and studied it, remembering how she'd screwed one like it into Micah's neck. As if he couldn't have sent her sprawling onto the pavement.

Only he hadn't.

In fact, he'd been . . . kind. She swallowed against a rising tide of longings. It would do her—and Emily—no good to remember his friendship and how she'd wished for nothing but his protective presence in her life. Desperation had made her call him . . . and that same desperation would send him packing.

The small-town café near Ashleyville smelled of frying bacon and buzzed with the early morning chitchat of patrons. The bell over the door clanged every few moments, and Micah eyed each person as they entered or left, like some sort of PI.

"So, you know how I found you . . . how did you find *me?*" Lacey asked.

He glanced at her. "I haven't forgotten your tricks. I figured you'd head to the safest place you know. Remember the time you and John got in that fight—what was it about?"

She smirked. "Theology. Probably our usual fight—God's plan versus our free will."

His eyes held sweet amusement. "Oh yeah, you were so angry, I thought you were going to wallop him."

"I should have. He was always so smug. So right. It drove me crazy." She felt a real smile tug her face. "I ran home, got on Sugah, and rode to the caves. You scared me nearly out of my skin when you crept up like a cougar."

"I didn't want to get hit either." He grinned, obviously remembering her sitting in the dark, huddled against the chilly summer night, fury sizzling in her bones.

"Well, I eventually came over to his point of view. He believed in choices, said that without them, we were puppets and our salvation didn't bring any glory to God." The words in her mouth felt dry, raw. It seemed as if she had done nothing but make God cringe for over a decade.

"But that's the mystery," Micah said. "Without God completely in charge, foreknowing, we are left with a handcuffed God. Someone who isn't in charge of circumstances, who has to go with the flow, at the mercy of our whims." Micah leaned back for the waitress to place his coffee before him. "Decaf, right?"

She gave him a Southern glare and waddled away.

"Micah, you were always so cerebral in your faith. You believe God is in control, but you don't think with your heart. How could God be in control of tragedy? of heartache? If He sees what will happen, He can change it and keep us from—" she rubbed her finger around the rim of her cup—"making mistakes that will destroy lives."

"You're precluding the fact that He doesn't want it to happen," Micah said, concern in his eyes.

She felt slapped. "I can't believe that God would want John to be killed in cold blood. He was a good man. Idealistic maybe and sometimes too reckless, but a good man." She turned back to Micah, barely able to form words. "No, it was my choices that caused that. Not God's."

Micah moved his hand, as if he might touch her. Except he stopped, let it rest in the middle of the table. "Yeah. Well, then again, there's the mystery. I believe God knew it would happen. Why He didn't stop it? I don't know." His voice was steady, unfazed by her confession. Iceman, even in the face of his friend's death.

Micah picked up his spoon, turned it between his fingers. "When my pop was working the streets, he'd come home from the night shift wrung out and grieving the victims. I remember the nights he caught the occasional drug dealer. He'd meet Joey and me at breakfast before we left for school, and you know what we'd do?"

Lacey dredged up a picture of Micah's father, so much like his son, broad, bold, and brave in his sheriff's uniform. "What?"

"We'd pray for them. He'd thank God for letting him nab

them, then ask God to use the darkness to show them the light. He'd ask for their redemption." Micah shook his head, and in that action she saw him as a boy, the one she'd admired from three pews behind in church. Micah's sensible, rock-solid faith had always centered her, like a bulwark against life's tempest. And now, staring at him, she felt the tingle of old feelings, old longings.

"I remember the day I challenged my dad," Micah continued. "I asked him the very questions with which you and John wrestled. Is God in control? What about the horrible things that happen to people?" He looked her in the eye. "Do you remember that night I found you after your fight with John?"

She shrugged, but she remembered well the smell of him as he led her horse home. Remembered how she felt safe in his shadow, how she'd leaned into his friendship. The memory made her ache.

"Do you remember the moon?" Micah persisted, unaware that he'd yanked her back to her regrets. "It was full and trailed a path home."

"Yeah, I remember." *Mostly because your eyes glowed in the moonlight, and I couldn't unsnarl the feelings in my heart.* "You said something about darkness illuminating light."

He grinned, and for the first time since she'd called him and he'd barged into her hospital room with ultimatum in his eyes, she saw genuine friendship. The old friendship, filled with equality. With grace. "That's right. Light without darkness isn't remarkable. We take it for granted most of the time. It's all around us; it helps us live our lives. But put us in a dark room and suddenly the light is all that we long for. It gives us hope. It shows us how to be saved."

"You're saying that God let those drug dealers fall into trouble so they'd see . . . what, salvation?"

"Sometimes we have to see darkness to understand the light."

She leaned back as the waitress brought her omelette; then she moved her glass of water to make room for the plate of pancakes. The smell of blueberry syrup tugged at her stomach. "Sorry, Micah, that's a great theory, but the fact is, no one is going to be better off because they're doomed." She should know. She'd grown up with the light, and it still didn't hold a flicker against the darkness permeating her soul. "Let's eat."

"Let's pray."

"No. You pray if you want." She picked up her fork, refusing to look at him as he bent his head, fixed to his ideals. She didn't buy this idea that somehow God might be at the helm of the mistakes she'd made. Because if He was, then maybe, instead of God being helpless and just disappointed in her, it turned God . . . mean.

Her eyes filled. No, thanks. She liked John's way of thinking. Free will. Her unforgivable mistakes. Because if the mistakes weren't hers, and God was in charge, then . . . she'd have to forgive *Him*, right?

She blinked the tears back before Micah could see. He said amen and began to wolf down his grits. Obviously the man was as hungry as she.

"Thanks for the clothes, Micah. I'll pay you back."

He looked at her, raised his eyebrows. "Okay. Pay me back by turning yourself in. If your encryption program is so important and someone wants it, you have leverage. You can do this, Lacey. I promise I'll do what I can to make sure Emily is safe." He reached out with a look of pure, one-hundred-watt concern.

Lacey turned away. "You don't understand. I don't trust the NSA either."

✦ ✦ ✦

"Good girl. Sleep." Nero pulled up the cotton blanket and tucked it over Emily's shoulder. A puddle of drool pooled under her lips, and her blonde hair slicked to her grimy face. It hadn't been hard to get her to scream. He'd simply tape-recorded one of her many nightmares. How he wished he could have seen Lacey's face when she heard that.

He knew too well how Lacey might feel. The sweaty palms, the kick in the gut, the low moan that emanated from the chest and never fully died. Oh yes, he was well aware of the kind of pain one suffered when a loved one screamed.

Leaning back in his chair, he flicked on the morning edition of CNN. Nothing about the train wreck. Which was good, he supposed. Old news. He thought of Lacey on the run again.

He'd give her another four hours, then call and check on her progress. He had no doubt she'd have good news for him. If anyone could do the impossible, it was his favorite spy.

He took a sip of Pepto-Bismol. He hated the stuff, how it coated his gut. But it made the pain subside, at least for an hour or two.

The little girl stirred, yawned, shifted on her pillow. Nero glanced at her, and the image of his own daughter hit him broadside, nearly knocking the wind out of him. Stacy. Blonde, a sweet smile. Innocent.

Grief welled in his throat. She would have been in her early twenties by now. He took another swig of the Pepto.

Lacey would pay. Even if she found Ex-6 and handed it over, she would pay. He owed his wife. He owed himself.

He owed Stacy.

Micah finished the last of his coffee slowly, watching Lacey sop up her syrup with her final bite of pancake. The woman had the appetite of a horse, just like he'd remembered. The comparison made him grin. She was as stubborn and wild as any of her family's Thoroughbreds. "Why don't you trust the NSA? Aren't you on their team?" The questions nagged at him like a burr under his skin.

She looked up at him and made a face. "Let's just say that I find it particularly suspicious that I'm bushwhacked within weeks of finishing the program. They had a guard on me. Then they offered to take Ex-6 off my hands . . . in exchange for keeping Emily out of the foster-care system." Her jaw tightened as she said it, and he saw fury in her eyes. "Like they think I might make off with it and sell it to the highest bidder."

Micah thumbed the handle of his cup. "The highest bidder?"

Lacey wiped her mouth, then took a sip of her coffee. He noticed she still liked it like candy—two sugars and a packet of creamer. "Other countries. Obviously America has a huge advantage with Ex-6. Not only can they encrypt their information and detect interceptions of their transmissions, but also decrypt other messages."

"The skeleton key to any regime."

"Well, in the right hands." Lacey sat back. Her blonde wig outlined her high cheekbones. And that lime green shirt did distracting things to her silver eyes. But he'd been wrong about her not having changed much. He saw hardness in her expression. Combined with an etched sorrow, it made him want to reach out and pull her into his arms.

That thought made him freeze, and little sirens blared in

the back of his head. Danger, *danger!* Then again, he already knew that. Still, all this grown-up toughness pinched him deep in his soul, where he'd buried all his feelings, all his hopes.

Lacey had changed. And he'd had the power to stop it.

He harbored no illusions that if she hadn't been handcuffed to her bed, nursing a dislocated shoulder, she would have been tromping about the woods alone . . . probably still would be. With a pang, he realized what it had cost her to call on him for help.

And he'd called her a liar.

He winced. "I need to call Conner." He reached into his pocket and pulled out his Nokia. The screen was black. "I have to plug it in to recharge. I'll have to call him from the truck."

"Who's Conner?"

"One of my search-and-rescue buddies. He and our team are back in Poplar Bluff. Probably waiting for me to return from the hospital."

She tweaked a one-sided, rueful smile. "Sorry. You should turn around, Micah. Go back to them."

He set the phone on the table. "So the NSA is after you because they want Ex-6?"

"I don't know. I'm probably a bit jumpy." She gave a self-deprecating shrug. "They're probably after me because they think I killed my bodyguard." She sighed and looked out the window at the dirt parking lot.

"Did you?" He didn't know what he believed, but suddenly he didn't want to know the truth. He held up his hand. "Don't answer that."

"Of course I didn't kill him—" she frowned—"at least I don't think so." She looked at Micah, and he saw vulnerability wash through her expression. "They said I was holding the knife. The last thing I remember was flying through the air during the train crash, landing hard, and blacking out. I remember screaming Emily's name. And I remember the guy sitting across from us. Big guy. He bought Emily an ice-cream cone in the Little Rock station. He was supposedly my bodyguard. Maybe . . . I landed on him. I remember I was holding the knife just before we derailed." She frowned again as if trying to untangle her memory.

"Back up. You were holding a knife? Why?"

She opened her mouth, as if she'd just been caught saying too much, and then made a pained face. "I thought I saw Ishmael Shavik."

The name nudged something in the back of his mind, but he couldn't get a fix on it.

"The man who killed John." Lacey didn't break his gaze as she said it, but a second later she looked down. "I shouldn't have told you that."

A cold fist gripped his heart. "Who's Ishamel Shavik?"

She closed her eyes, shook her head. "I'm sorry. I've already dragged you in far enough. I don't want you getting hurt."

Yeah, well, he'd already been skewered about a thousand times over the past few days. Just sitting here with her felt like an open wound. Yet he seemed to be addicted to this pain because he couldn't bring himself to snatch her, throw her over his shoulder, lock her in the truck, and call Senator Ramey.

Why had he prayed for the opportunity to bring her to justice all these years if he wasn't going to grab his chance with both burly hands? Maybe because she looked too . . . honest. Desperate. And the way she was gathering her composure and shutting him out before his eyes ignited all the suspicions he'd thought were in cinders. Was she innocent?

"Who is Ishmael Shavik?" he growled.

"I have to go to the restroom and brush my teeth." She produced a new brush and a traveler-size tube of Colgate. "I'll . . . talk to you when I get out—" she glanced around the café— "when we're away from here."

He swallowed a protest. Okay, yes, maybe it would be better to chat in the privacy of his truck. He nodded. "I'll be outside, calling Conner."

She slid out of the booth. "Thanks, Micah, for . . . breakfast." He watched her and couldn't help but feel the tug on his heart when her eyes glistened. Then she turned and marched off to the bathroom.

He paid the bill and strode outside, her words churning in his gut. Ishmael Shavik. Where had he heard that name before? He sat in his pickup, leaving the door open to let the fresh breeze shave off a few more vestiges of fatigue, and plugged his cell phone into the charger. He dialed Conner's cell.

The man picked it up on the third ring. "Hello?"

"Get out of bed. I need you to do some sleuthing for me."

"Good morning to you too, Tootsie. Where are you?"

Micah paused. "Kentucky. And I don't want to elaborate. I just need your help."

"Kentucky?" Conner groaned. "Micah, you didn't . . . do anything stupid, did you?"

"Maybe. Like I said, I don't want to elaborate, but I need you to see what you can find on a guy named Ishmael Shavik."

"Okay, stupid would be helping someone under arrest escape and then of course driving her across the country in search of her daughter. That's what this is about, right? Can you say 'aiding and abetting'? This will look great on your request for reinstatement."

"Ishmael Shavik. Try connecting him with the murder of John Montgomery."

"The guy from Kazakhstan? I thought you said his wife did it."

"Yeah. Maybe. But something she said—"

"So you *are* with her. Micah, you are so in trouble. Turn her in before you blow your career to smithereens."

"I'll call you in an hour. See what you can find."

"Micah—"

He clicked off. Clipped the telephone to his visor. The sun lit pools of water to gold and bedazzled the parking lot. An elderly couple emerged from an ancient Buick and ambled toward the café. The old man cupped his hand on the woman's elbow, helping her. What would it be like to grow old with Lacey, wake up each morning to her smile, race her on horse-back, or sit on the porch as the sun sank behind the green blue Kentucky hills?

Being with Lacey had surfaced regrets that he'd long buried. Regrets he'd rewritten as wisdom. Regrets that burned a hole in his heart, regardless of what they were named.

Ishmael Shavik. Yes, he'd heard the name before. Raising his eyes heavenward, he shot up a prayer for Conner. Truth was always on the side of righteousness, and for the first time, he wondered why he'd let himself so easily be duped into condemning Lacey. Maybe she *was* innocent, just as his heart wanted to believe. Maybe, in fact, she was the victim here. Maybe they even had a chance of resurrecting their friendship . . . and more.

Maybe this time he wouldn't let his feelings stick to his rib cage or catch in his throat. There was no John Montgomery to stand in his way, not anymore.

Micah put a hand to his chest. It burned, a strange mixture of hope and fear. Where was she, anyway? He got out of the truck and walked back inside the café. Maybe she'd returned to their booth.

But, no. The elderly couple had taken their places.

Micah flagged down Aunt Bee. "You know that blonde I came in here with? Did she leave?"

"Dunno," she said and brushed off.

He felt like an idiot as he shuffled back to the ladies' bathroom. He knocked on the flimsy door. "Lacey?" He heard water running. Boy, she was going to have clean teeth. "Lacey?"

Nothing.

Suddenly, his stomach rolled over, as if realization started in his gut and worked up to his brain. He knocked a final time, then called her name again. His loud voice felled the conversations in the café to silence. He heard only the roar of his foolishness, screaming indictment. *Idiot!* Ignoring the burn of a hundred eyes on him, he grabbed the doorknob and opened the door.

If he were a swearing man, he'd have let loose a barrage of frustration. As it were, he stood there, staring at the open window over the toilet and knew that everything he'd let himself believe over the past three hours—hope, forgiveness, redemption—had been ground to a pulp.

Lacey was still up to her old tricks. Deceit . . . and quite possibly, murder.

Definitely the murder of the last tendrils of mercy in his heart.

Chapter 10

OH, THE SWEET rewards of living in a small town. Lacey found an unlocked pickup three short steps from the bathroom window and dived in. She could hardly believe her good fortune when the keys dangled in the ignition. She turned it over, popped it into gear, and roared out without a backward glance.

Sorry, Micah.

She fought the burn in her throat. This was for his own good. She'd been stupid to let Shavik's name slip. To Jim Micah, master bloodhound, no less. If she hadn't called him on his cell phone nearly seven years ago and told him to stay away from her, he would have his own Syrian Doberman on his trail. Shavik took no prisoners.

Every suspicion she entertained that Shavik had only been the thug, the muscle and front man behind someone more sinister, had burst to life with the text message on her cell phone back in the hospital. Still, the identity of the kidnapper didn't really matter. Emily's life was in danger, and Lacey had every intention of sneaking onto the farm to her private office, swiping her most recent version of Ex-6, and bartering it for Em's life. Micah may know about the safe, but he knew nothing about the communications room she'd built in the cabin on the back half of the property, where she holed up after Emily's birth. Even then, she'd begun plotting Ex-6, hoping to find a way to make amends for John's death. If only she'd been smarter sooner. If only she'd listened to the voice of reason.

If only she'd listened to her heart. Then she would never have let Micah push her away and stride out of her life. She would have flung her arms around him and held on until he admitted all the things she'd seen in his eyes. Things she recognized too late.

She should have seen through that kiss to the emotions. Why had she waited for the right words?

Because she was idealistic. John wooed her with poetry and dreams, with the promise of glory and adventure. She should have paid attention, however, to action. Micah's actions.

She cut north on Guinn Lane and angled for the back road that ran behind the Galloway farm, which rolled over three hundred acres, spotted here and there with clumps of oak, maple, and cedar. She had no doubt that Micah had alerted the NSA to her destination. By now he was probably standing in the women's bathroom—she hadn't bothered to lock the door; he would have kicked it down anyway—full of fury.

She hadn't duped him, not really. She never said she'd let him tag along. But she felt his absence like a sucking chest wound. Despite his anger and misgivings, he was the only one on the planet whose opinion of her mattered. He'd been her best friend in her darkest hour. He alone had made her feel safe, and when she'd needed the right answer he'd delivered it.

For the first time since she'd met him, she couldn't swallow his faith. She refused to believe that God was in charge of the dark moments, that He could allow them. She'd made the wrong choices. God shouldn't have to pay for that. And if He'd somehow engineered them . . .

She eased up on the gas and turned onto the old rutted tractor path. She spotted Ernie Shold's house and approached slowly. The place felt abandoned. Broken windows, filthy curtains, a crumbled stone stoop. The taste of decay ringed the old farmhand's home in the overgrown tangle of fleabane.

She opened the doors to his garage and drove in. Then she sat in the dark and listened to her heart thunder. The place smelled of oil and dirt. She traced the path to her cabin in her mind—along the creek and up through the grove of maple. The hard part would be the stretch of fence line that ran between Ernie's pasture and Galloway's. Up the hill that overlooked the main house and into the secret entrance, Grave's Cave, then into the old Galloway mine. From there, no one but a practiced foot would find her secreted entrance to the cabin.

She exited the garage and pulled out the binoculars she'd pilfered from Micah's survival pack. That, his knife, a flashlight, and his nylon rope. If the NSA hoped to surveil her, they'd have to cover the back roads for miles.

She edged down to the creek, parted the blue-eyed grass, and emerged at the split of the fences, under a wide maple. Crouching for what felt like an hour, she saw nothing but two colts playing in the field. Their soft whinnies carried in the air. The mares would be in the other paddock. Recollections of happier times rushed back to her—when she'd speculated with her father on the value of the newest foals and when she stood in this very spot, heart racing, sopping wet from wrestling Micah in the creek.

As if reading her mind, the sun appeared from behind a cloud and warmed her face. Sweat trickled from under the confounded wig. The breeze had fragranced the day with the smells of fall, the lingering taste of summer. A catbird shrilled its mewing song.

The memories drew Lacey in. It had been here, under the canopy of this maple, that she'd first recognized her deepest longings. At least the one she'd wanted to grab on to with both hands.

It had been right after her mother's funeral the summer after her sophomore year. She'd known Micah nearly nine months, and despite the fact that she was dating John, Micah had become a friend. And, on the day they lowered her mother's body into the ground he'd become a soul mate.

Breast cancer had swept through Alicia Galloway's body and ravaged her in a matter of months. Lacey felt pretty sure that a part of her own heart had been scooped out and buried in that cold earth. She couldn't bear the reception, the somber tones, the faces of grief. She'd escaped to the creek, sunk down into the shadows of the maple, and let grief crash over her.

She didn't hear Micah approach, just looked up and saw him standing above her, pain in his eyes. Then he'd knelt and pulled her into those huge wide-receiver arms and held her. She hung on and sobbed.

John had already left for cadet camp at West Point. Micah, however, had ten glorious weeks before boot camp, and it seemed he spent every waking hour of those weeks either trying to divert her from her grief or helping her muscle through it. Watching him leave for camp had gouged out another huge chunk of her heart. She had leaned against his car, feeling herself shredding, and heard the catch in her own voice when she said, "Don't forget me."

He smiled, pure and sweet and dangerous. "How can I forget you? You're my lucky penny."

He must have seen her fears lurch up with the rest of her emotions—love, regret, friendship—for he'd reached out of the window and tugged one of her unruly curls. "I won't forget you. I promise."

Through letters and occasional visits, she'd continued to date John her junior and senior years, and she couldn't bear to question her motives. John was fun. Exhilarating. He embodied adventure and a bright future. Paralyzingly handsome, with his curly blond hair and scalawag smile, John knew how to tap into her desire to change the world and wrap it around his little finger. But sometimes, between the poetry and laughter, the games and heady dreams, she longed for something . . . more substantial.

And in the spring of her senior year, Mr. Substantial had come back to sprawl again under this maple tree, his arms crossed under his head, his eyes on her. Micah had returned to take Lacey to her senior prom in John's stead. Micah still looked devastatingly handsome in his faded Levi's and gray army T-shirt. Thick muscles betrayed his PT routine, and his dark hair had been shaved short, into a high and tight crew cut. Micah would be unbearably gorgeous in his dress blues tonight at the prom.

She could hardly take a full breath in his presence. John might be studying to be an officer, but his best friend, Jim Micah, was soldier to his marrow. Power. Righteousness. Duty. And tonight he was her date.

But today he was her friend. One who spent the afternoon riding and laughing with her. The way he looked at her . . . it sorta made a girl wonder if indeed, he'd missed her, just like he'd suggested between the lines in his weekly letters. And he smelled good. Too good. The perfect heady mix of masculinity and fresh air.

If Lacey didn't put some distance between them, she just might forget to which man she belonged.

"So you like Special Ops?" she asked. "I thought you had to be in the army for a couple years before they'd let you try out." She ran a piece of tall grass between her fingers, trying not to be jealous of the wind as it skimmed his hair.

"They have a special fast-track program. They're short on team members, and with the cold war breaking apart, Reagan wants to make sure we have the military specialists to take down any sudden eruptions for power."

The thought of him wielding an M-16 or, worse, being slain on some foreign war-rocked soil sent a shudder through her. "Is it hard work?"

He smiled, a lopsided, endearing grin of acquiescence. "The first time I jumped out of an airplane, I thought I was going to lose my stomach through my mouth. But . . . well, it's sort of exhilarating. Gotta watch how you land, however. You could break both your legs."

She made a face. He laughed. She felt it rumble through her, clear to the soles of her feet. How she'd missed him, his easy friendship, the way he seemed to know her thoughts. She thought of that as she watched him relax under the tree. If he were to die in some unnamed eastern European smudge on the map, she'd lose the last little still-beating piece of her heart.

"Why are you doing this, Micah? I mean, I understand John. He's after glory, driven by a weird mix of patriotism and idealism. And when he talks, I think he could inspire Gorbachev to become a patriot. But you're different. You've never told me why you're so dedicated. I mean, we haven't had a war for ten years. And hopefully we won't ever again. So why join the commandos?"

He touched a strand of her hair. "It always amazes me that no matter how hot it is, your hair always stays springy."

She batted away his hand. "That's because I'm cursed with Galloway curls."

"Blessed."

"Answer my question, Soldier Boy."

He grinned, a hundred-watt smile that made the balmy May day feel a billion times hotter. "Okay, but you have to swear, upon pain or death, that you won't reveal my secret." His eyes held tease, but she couldn't dismiss the hint of seriousness in his voice.

She held up her hand. "I swear."

"Upon pain or death."

She hit him, and he playfully protected himself. "Penny, I'm serious."

She rolled her eyes. "Upon pain or death."

His smile disappeared, his eyes fixed to hers. "Well, I always fancied that I'd been given a sort of sacred charge. Micah 6:8." His expression became very, very serious as he recited the Bible verse: "'The Lord has already told you what is good, and this is what he requires: to do what is right, to love mercy, and to walk humbly with your God.'"

He was giving her a glimpse beneath the mighty armor of Jim Micah, and it made her weak.

"Well, when I started looking and praying about my future, I kept coming back to military service." He sat up, braced himself on one arm. "Do you know that the Green Beret motto is Free the Oppressed?"

"No, I didn't."

He shrugged. "When the recruiter told me that, it was like fireworks shot off in my head. I'm going to be a Green Beret."

"That's really dangerous, isn't it?"

He didn't meet her eyes and instead leaned back, staring at the sky. "I'll be okay."

She reached out, palmed his chest, wanting suddenly to cry or even beg him not to go. She heard the catch in her voice and forced her tone to remain light. "You better be careful, Jim

Micah. Don't you dare die on me, or I'll come over there . . . and . . . and . . ." She couldn't conjure up a threat big enough to undo him, so she just shook her head.

He grinned, a teasing smile that made her a little dizzy. "Good." Then he ran his fingers over her cheek. His smoky green eyes were on hers, holding her, pulling her in.

In a desperate attempt for sanity, she tickled his nose with the blade of grass she still held. He sputtered, then roared with play and launched himself toward her. She took off, running through the creek. He tackled her halfway in, pulling her down into the cool water.

"Micah, stop!"

He laughed, then poured a handful of water down her back.

She arched away from the cold. "Stop it!"

"Okay, sorry."

When she looked at him, all play vanished. His smile dimmed, and heat pooled in his eyes. He stared at her, swallowed, and his gaze fell to her lips. She quivered with a strange sort of fear but didn't stop him as he touched her jaw and drew her close.

His kiss was soft. *Achingly* soft. Sweet. As if he was more afraid than she. He touched her upper lip, then both. His breath was light. "Lace," he whispered, drawing back. His gaze searched hers and suddenly she held nothing back. Everything she felt for him gathered in her eyes. *I think I love you, Jim Micah*.

He kissed her again. This time with surety. But just as perfectly. She closed her eyes and shut out everything but the feel of his lips on hers.

He curled his arm around her. "Lace," he repeated and deepened his kiss.

She felt a thousand private hopes take flight. Jim Micah. *In her arms.* This was what she'd secretly dreamed of for two years, even before she'd met John. Selfishly, after John had left for West Point, she'd hoped maybe they'd simply drift apart and Micah would become more than a friend. But John had kept calling, showing up at her doorstep during Christmas vacations, and well, Micah had never . . . really . . .

But now he had his strong arms around her, tasting of strength, of friendship, of her future. It knotted her throat, and she didn't dare breathe.

He broke away, breathing hard. "Lacey, stop . . . please. We . . . can't . . ."

She stared at his sickened expression, and horror drew over her like the cold lick of gooseflesh.

He looked away, as if he couldn't bear the sight of her. He even closed his eyes. "Oh, Lacey, I'm sorry. I shouldn't have. John is going to kill me."

He would have inflicted less pain if he'd kicked her in the heart. Instead he pushed her away and stood up. He blocked the sun, and water dripped off his now plastered T-shirt. His gaze landed on her and his expression looked terribly like regret. She clenched her jaw and held up her hand.

He pulled her up. "Let's get back to the farm." He didn't wait for her as he stalked toward the horses.

As he walked away, she knew. For a brief second, she'd seen his desires fill his eyes. And she knew they matched her own. He might not say it, but he loved her too.

But she was John's girl.

Now Lacey stood in the nook of the maples and let the breeze obliterate the echo of that memory. She *had* loved Jim Micah. And she thought he'd loved her. But she'd been wrong, and after that fateful night there had been no turning back.

It felt like she'd been running ever since.

Lacey scanned the horizon one last moment, saw nothing, and crouched to sprint for the hill.

A rustle of brush behind her made her freeze. She turned, then stifled a cry as a form launched toward her.

✦ ✦ ✦

The woman had the reflexes of a tiger. Micah rubbed his chin, feeling a welt growing where Lacey had kicked him, and glared at her.

"I suppose I should get used to you tracking me down, but please, Micah, believe me when I say you don't want to be here." She sat against the maple tree, breathing hard and massaging her shoulder.

He hadn't meant to take her down, aiming instead to clamp his hand over her mouth and keep her quiet. Obviously his stealth skills needed some polishing. "Why did you take off on me?"

She gave him a look that made him feel like a toddler.

"Okay, so maybe I deserved that. But, hello, I've mentioned more than once that I'm on your side. Do I have to tattoo it to my forehead?"

She closed her mouth, and for a second, he thought he saw her face crumple. But spy that she'd been, she recovered in a nanosecond. "Maybe you did say that. But frankly, I don't know who to trust. I'm sorry. I'm not turning myself in."

He opened his mouth to protest.

She held up her hand. "And I don't want you getting hurt."

Again he opened his mouth.

"I know, I know. You're already hurt." She pursed her lips and looked away. "I don't want you getting *killed*."

Oooh, that was new information. He stared at her, saw strain on her face that he hadn't seen before. "Who might kill me, Lacey?"

She said nothing.

"Okay, listen, like I keep saying, I'm a big boy. I've been around the block more than once, and obviously, you're still hurting from the accident. I see it on your face. So until I know what this is all about, let's just focus on Emily. She's lost, and you're in trouble. And I care."

She shot him a look of surprise, but he ignored it and kept on. "What's more important here is that you're not going to get into the stable without me. I drove around the main road. There are at least three NSA teams, one of which is comprised of sharpshooters. And they're in the house, having a little face-to-face with your brother."

Lacey grimaced. "I hope Sam is okay."

Micah shrugged. He couldn't help but wonder what kind of stories the NSA might be telling her little brother. Or what he already knew. When Micah had seen him in church a few weeks back, Sam hadn't breathed a word about Lacey. Micah assumed the guy hadn't seen her in years. "He doesn't know anything, does he?"

"What, like I'm a spy running from the government?" She smiled wryly as she worked her shoulder. "No, I managed to keep that tidbit of information to myself. Somehow. It's not like it is Thanksgiving dinner conversation."

"So your brother doesn't know about Emily?"

Her face darkened. "Yes, he does. As does Janie. Emily has lived with Janie most of her life."

Micah hadn't expected that. Although he hadn't really been able to wrap his mind around Lacey as a mother either. She'd jumped from young and innocent to sassy and tough and stayed there. There wasn't room for softness in that description. At least the kind that came with motherhood. Still, if he knew Lacey and her commitment to family and the way she grieved her own mother's death, she wouldn't easily hand over her motherhood reins to anyone. Even big sister Janie.

Lacey lifted the binoculars to her eyes and peered out. "I think we can go now. I don't see any movement."

"Don't think for a minute that I don't recognize my field glasses, by the way. I guess we can add thievery to your list of felonies."

"Yeah," she said, not taking the binoculars from her eyes. "I'm also pretty good at breaking and entering."

"That's not funny, Lacey. You're in so much trouble I think they'll probably deny your visitation privileges for the next two decades."

She glanced at him. No hint of a smile. "Not that anyone would visit me."

He felt punched. Even so, he could hardly believe it when he said softly, "I would."

She bit her lip before turning away. The wind swept that ridiculous blonde hair across her face, and the anger that had fueled him for the last two hours, the same anger that focused his thoughts and unwound her plan, evaporated at the expression of pain on her face.

"Emily was injured in my womb in Kazakhstan," she whispered, not looking at him. "She was born premature, with undeveloped lungs. Even now, she gets lung infections easily. Janie . . . helped me. She kept Emily for me while I tried to figure out who was on my tail."

"Someone was after you?" He edged toward her, wanting to ease the heaviness on her face, instead taking the binoculars from her hands. He swept the horizon with them.

SUSAN MAY WARREN

"Yeah. I think it was Shavik."

He drew the binoculars from his eyes, frowned at her. "Why?"

"It's such a long story. I don't know where to start."

"Try backing up to ten minutes before I found you in Kazakhstan holding a knife dripping with your husband's blood."

Micah got her attention, hoping to spark anger. Lacey might know how to play mind chess, but underneath the cool exterior, there was a woman who heated at his accusations. He hoped.

She licked her lips and stared at him with a cold look. "Shavik killed John." She took the binoculars from him, again put them to her eyes. "Sorta. He worked for a man named Frank Hillman. Who I think might still be on my tail."

"How would he know about Ex-6? I'm assuming that it's top secret."

She nodded. "Precisely."

He paused as realization sank in, sending a chill through him. "You think someone inside the NSA knows and is leaking information to Shavik."

"Or to Hillman." She crouched. "Ready?"

"Wait, who is Frank Hillman?"

Ignoring him, she pointed along the fence line. "Remember the old Galloway mine? Grave's Cave entrance is right up there."

He raised his eyebrows. "Um, you *do* remember that you, John, and I nearly got killed in that mine once, right?"

When she grinned, he saw the old Lacey, the one who lived for adventure, for challenge. "Uh-huh. Race ya."

She darted up the hill toward the cave entrance. He recognized the limestone boulders that concealed the entrance. If he

135

remembered correctly, it had also been their escape route when the abandoned Galloway mine caved in on them. He suppressed a shudder just thinking about the choking dust, the pitch-black that had poured into his eyes, his mouth. Lacey had been a quiet sophomore, showing off her parents' property to Micah and John. In the end, she'd saved their lives.

His lucky penny.

He ran behind her up the hill. She vanished behind the outlay of boulders, and he knew that five steps beyond was the cave opening. He was breathing hard when he met her inside.

She leaned against the wall of the cave. "You okay?"

"Good," he said between breaths, hating his vulnerabilities. Emily wasn't the only one missing a lung. He wiped a pricking of sweat off his temple. "Now where?"

"Inside. About fifty feet. Then the mine jags off from there. We follow it to the cabin."

"I thought we were going to the stables."

She grinned. "Yeah, you did, didn't you?"

He wanted to wring her neck as she started down the passageway. Her flashlight—no, *his* flashlight—striped the walls and lit their path as they angled into the darkness. The smell of bat guano and mustiness rushed him back to the Tennessee cave and Brian. He'd have to call Conner and see if the kid had been released from the hospital yet.

Conner. He'd forgotten to call him back. But maybe if he kept on Lacey's trail—something easier said than done apparently—he'd discover just who this Ishmael Shavik was without Conner's help.

And then what? Call Senator Ramey? Oh, sure, Micah rated high on the favorites list with this maneuver. Aiding and abetting. Well, if they weren't caught, no one would know . . . right?

His chest tightened. No, *he'd* know. The only way out of this mess was to turn Lacey in. Willingly . . . or kicking and screaming. Right after she got her Emily back. That's what drove him to follow her, despite common sense yelling in the back of his brain. He *did* care. About Emily—John's daughter. And about justice.

He hadn't been lying. Not . . . really.

He felt like a dog as he followed Lacey through the mine. She glanced back now and again and smiled at him. It only dug the guilt further into his chest. Yeah, some hero he was. He wasn't helping her. He was slowing her down. What was worse, he was going to arrest her.

But he would visit her in prison. Every day. Because, as much as he hated to admit it, she'd gotten under his skin. Like a virus. Or an old football injury.

What was more, the low simmer that had started three days ago in his gut, the one that had him questioning her guilt, had heated to full boil. *Shavik killed John?*

Of one thing he felt sure: Lacey Galloway Montgomery would die for her family. And John had been her man, as much as Micah hated that fact. He had no doubt that if she'd been given the choice she would have traded her life for John Montgomery's in Kazakhstan.

In betraying him, she would be betraying herself. No wonder her eyes looked empty.

No wonder she looked like a woman whose soul had died. So what had really happened in Kazakhstan?

Chapter 11

LACEY FOUND THE key to the cabin right where she'd left it, inside a plastic bag tacked to the upper side of a beam. Her light traced the outline of the door, its hinges webbed and rusted.

She heard Micah's labored breathing behind her, and a flint of worry pierced her concentration. "You okay?" she asked in a low tone.

"Yeah," he answered, but it sounded too fast, too easy.

She turned the lock, eased the door to the stairs open. The smell of cement and fresh air rushed at her, and dust filled her lungs. She stifled a cough as she angled her flashlight up the stairs, saw that the trapdoor was still locked. "Up here."

Micah moved in behind her as she climbed the stairs, unlatched the trapdoor, and pushed it open. The gray hues and cool air of a closed cabin signified safety. She held her breath and listened—no rushing feet to yank the door open, no sudden intake of breath as they waited to pounce.

She climbed into the cabin, flashlight in one hand, Micah's knife in the other.

The main room was empty. Sunlight cracked through the boarded-up windows. Dust twirled in the film of light and covered the sheets outlining the sofa and the rocker.

Micah climbed up behind her. "I thought this place had been abandoned."

"Yes. Sorta. I hid here for about a year after Emily was born."

"They didn't have you imprisoned at Langley?"

His question felt like a needle in her soul. "No." She bit back a retort, but it leaked out. "Not everyone believed I could kill my husband."

He looked at her, nonplussed. "I didn't mean that."

Sure he didn't. She gritted her teeth, cursing her feelings. She'd mingled memory with circumstance and come out with false intentions. Even if he had said he cared, she'd let herself read too much into his sudden appearance into her life. His cold words and stinging accusation blindsided her.

Lacey had no doubt he planned to arrest her the minute she found Ex-6. He cared about his country. The guy practically had the Stars and Stripes tattooed on his heart. There was no way he'd allow her to trade away national secrets. Even for Emily. Which meant he was a good guy . . . or bad guy?

She'd have to ditch him. She wanted to cringe but held it back. Just when she thought she might have a hero back in her life.

The little cabin had two rooms—a kitchen/main room and a back bedroom. She treaded to the bedroom and ran her light along the wardrobe, the saggy double bed, and the nightstand. Judging by the layer of dust, no one had even set foot in here to swirl the shadows, so no one knew that she stored the nation's most precious commodity in a room behind her grandmother's wardrobe.

She glanced at Micah, debating. Took a breath. "Can you go in the kitchen and get me a chair?"

He frowned, one eyebrow raised in suspicion.

"Please?"

She could just hold him at knifepoint, but somehow she couldn't bear to actually use the knife, which would make the act pointless. Unless, however, he believed she would use it, which he probably did. He still had the little prick on his neck where she'd ground the fork in. Emily was worth it.

He turned and she watched him go, feeling a little sick.

She waited until he was in the kitchen and then rushed to the bedside. She groped under the bed, up along the box spring. Yes! She wiggled the stun gun out from under the slats.

As she turned it on she truly hated herself. How could she do this to Micah? But he was like a hound on a rabbit and dead set on dragging her in to be hanged. Hadn't he said that on more than one occasion? Who knew but maybe he'd called the NSA and told them where to lie in wait for her?

She flattened herself against the wall and waited. When he entered the room, hands full of the chair, she aimed for his neck, gritted her teeth, and hoped he went down easily.

Maybe he should call. Give Lacey a pep talk. Nero stared at the clock, ran his glance back to Emily, who sat eating Froot Loops one at a time out of the box, her eyes glued to SpongeBob SquarePants.

If Lacey was cooperative, he'd let her listen to her daughter laugh. And then he'd remind the little spy who was in charge here.

He sat down at the computer and dialed his connection. Thankfully, Ishmael had set up the calls, sending them through a dozen servers, many of them dummies, across the world before connecting with Lacey's telephone. He typed in the text message, but before he hit send, he contemplated allowing Lacey to hear Emily's laughter.

No. Let her wonder. Let her feel the fear of not knowing, hoping against hope that the one she sacrificed for still breathed.

He had no doubt that Lacey would obey him. He hadn't watched her fight to protect Emily for the last six or so years without understanding the part the little girl would play in this moment. He'd wait, the taste of revenge filling his mouth.

If Jim Micah had somehow sniffed out her trail . . . well, wouldn't his death be that much sweeter? He'd waited nearly seven years to get the Green Beret back in his sights.

Nero took a deep breath, ran his hands over his empty stomach, feeling it knot. Despite his cravings, he'd have to wait. Jim Micah would die another day. Besides, being a smart man, surely he wouldn't believe a word Lacey said.

A smile tweaked one corner of Nero's mouth as he pushed send and imagined her receiving his message.

TIME'S UP.
TOMORROW, MIDNIGHT.
COWARD'S HOLLOW.
JUST YOU AND EX-6.

"What is wrong with you?" Micah turned, slapped Lacey's arm away from his neck. Whatever she'd held in her hand skittered across the floor. She didn't even glance at it while she punched him, knuckles first, in the chest. He gasped as the pain went deep. "Lacey, stop!"

She swept his feet out from him and he landed hard on his

back, knocking out his wind. She had the knife out and he decided from the look on her face to stay down. He mouthed the words *calm down* but felt a crushing weight on his chest.

Air, he needed air. He forced himself to take a breath, gasped, took another. "Stop," he managed in a rasp.

She was shaking, and if he could read her right she was just about in tears. "Turn over. Put your nose to the floor, lace your hands behind your head."

He blinked at her.

"Now!"

"All right. Okay." He turned over, grimacing as his chest burned. He was going to have a doozy of a bruise, right next to his scars. But it was nothing compared to the wounds she'd inflicted on his heart. And to think he'd actually begun to trust her, just a wee bit, not once but *twice*. Conner had been right. . . . This woman had a hold on him, one that made him a glutton for punishment.

She shoved her knee into his spine as she bound his hands above his head and then to the bed leg. With *his* rope.

"C'mon, Lacey, don't do this."

"You can't follow me anymore, Micah. I don't know what side you're on, but perhaps I need to say it again—this time in Russian or maybe Arabic?" She leaned close to his ear. "I'm not going to turn myself in, and you're not taking me in."

He swallowed. Okay, it freaked him out more than he wanted to admit how well she read his mind. She knew he wasn't just a goodwill ambassador, which probably meant she hadn't believed his declaration about caring either. "I'm just trying to help you."

"You can help me by forgetting my name," she said tightly. But he heard the strain in her voice. "I'm sorry."

She moved to the wardrobe and wheeled it back. Behind

it, a metal door told him that she'd done more than just hang out in this cabin and nurse her baby. She didn't glance at him as she pressed her hand to a security panel on the door, said her name, and stepped back.

"You built that?"

"Of course." After the panel clicked, she pulled the door open. Even from his less-than-advantageous position on the floor, he could make out a bank of computer and communications equipment. A soft buzz filled the otherwise silent bedroom.

That is, of course, if he ignored the sound of his breaking heart. Here he lay, hog-tied and helpless, watching the woman he'd once loved prove her betrayals in multitudes. What was he *supposed* to believe if she didn't give him a chance to trust her?

Micah ground his back teeth together. "You know my career is ruined, right?"

She didn't answer.

"I haven't told anyone where I am, but when the NSA finds me, they'll know we were together."

She popped her head out. Her voice shook. "When they find you like that, they'll know you're innocent."

"So, you're just going to call them and show them where your vault is? They'll bomb the doors off getting in there. And then what will happen to Emily?" He had her attention. "And even if I don't tell them, which you can't guarantee, they'll charge you with yet another crime. Assault. Kidnapping."

This snapped her out of her reverie, her eyes hard on his. "I don't care."

"You do care. I know you. You care so much that you're going to do anything to save Emily, even condemn yourself to execution. But more than anything you want to have your daughter. Don't you think I can see that?"

She tightened her jaw and turned.

"Do you know who wants this thing?"

She froze. "No."

"So it could be Iraq or Libya or Syria or even China."

She moved away.

"All right, listen, I know you're not a traitor."

"Oh, really?" Lacey snapped. She whirled and gave him a glare, one that should have turned his blood cold, expect he already felt pretty numb, especially as he mentally tallied his accusations against her. So maybe he deserved that glare. "I thought you'd be leading the posse to lynch me."

He felt the floor dig into his throbbing chest. "Listen, I was wrong, okay? I . . . should have known you better. I should have trusted you."

"Yeah, you should have." She frowned, and he watched her shoulders stoop. "But what could you do? You know what you saw. And what you saw was me covered in my husband's blood." She slid down to the floor, stared at him with red eyes. "But I couldn't tell you the truth. I just hoped that you'd believe me."

"I do," he said quietly, really embracing that thought for the first time. So he couldn't get his brain *completely* around that statement in a convincing clench, but he *wanted* to believe her. At least it felt better to be on the side of hope rather than despair. "Now, please, believe me when I say I am not going to turn you in."

Lacey suddenly looked exhausted and not a little beat-up emotionally. She held a rabbit's foot key chain in her hand. "When John and I were working overseas, we communicated with our handler via e-mail and telexes. Occasionally we'd have a dead drop. But the Middle East wasn't a friendly place, especially for Americans, and we had to watch our backs. We found it easier to e-mail our reports, encrypted, of course, and send them through about ten different servers. But even so, they were decryptable to the right hacker."

He watched her, twisting the rabbit fur between her fingers.

"We were tracking the sale of industrial secrets to a group in Kazakhstan. John had linked them to a Korean terrorist group named Chul-Moo. We were pretty sure that someone in the American oil refinery company we were embedded in, namely the company's CEO, Frank Hillman, was going to auction the ultra-gasification technology they'd developed to this group. The thing was, this process is illegal in most parts of the world because the refinery technology it uses to make syngas emitted ozone-destroying toxins and poisoned the air.

"We intercepted a communiqué about the buy and because of the urgency, John went in naked, posing as the buyer. Meanwhile, I was supposed to contact his handler. I couldn't reach him so I e-mailed him. Then I went to Kazakhstan to help John.

"John asked me to stay in the hotel. But you know me; I can't stand to be left behind." She closed her eyes, as Micah traced the scene in his head. "I followed John. Although I was careful, I disrupted his meeting with Ishmael Shavik. Shavik put a knife to my throat, told John that he knew he was CIA and that he was going to learn a lesson about double-crossing the Chul-Moo."

She took a breath, and her voice dropped. "I struggled and Shavik stabbed me. John went berserk. He jumped the guy, and I somehow ended up with the knife." Tears ran down her cheeks. "I knew I was hurt badly and he'd probably killed the baby, but I also knew that I couldn't let John die. I tried to get into the fight, but Shavik turned John around and shoved him into me."

She opened her eyes, and the agony in them shook Micah

to the bone. "So you see, I *did* kill John. I *am* a murderer. Therefore, I don't really care what happens to me. It's only Emily who matters now."

"How did Shavik know John was CIA?"

"I don't know. I've long suspected Frank Hillman. He was my boss . . . I mean, the boss for my alias. John and I both worked undercover as researchers for Hillman Oil. When I discovered that the gasification program Hillman had been developing was complete, I informed our handler and was told to keep my eyes on Hillman. He was acting very strangely, and I suspected him as the seller, although I never proved it. About three months after John was killed, I heard that Hillman had a daughter who had died right about that time. I can't dislodge the idea that his daughter had been taken and sacrificed because we disrupted Chul-Moo's buy."

"Which is why you think Hillman has it in for you."

She gave a halfhearted shrug.

Micah wanted to moan. No wonder she feared for her daughter's life. Revenge was a powerful motivator. "How did Hillman discover that John was CIA?"

She climbed to her feet. "I think my communication was intercepted." She sighed, ran a hand across her cheek. "Probably, if we had had secure communications, John would be alive today."

"You can't live with what-ifs, Lacey," Micah said, but his words screamed in his heart. He'd been taking hits from the merciless what-ifs for the last ten years.

She swallowed and her face tightened. "And I can't dodge them either." She blew out a breath. "Most of all, I can't live with the what-ifs if I lose you too."

He looked at her in horror, his throat raw. "You're not going to lose me."

She stared at him, looking painfully close to tears. Still, her voice came out clipped and hard. "You're right. I can't lose someone I never had."

He was debating how to respond when he heard a trill, like his cell phone. Only he'd left it charging in the pickup.

Lacey jumped, and he watched with wide eyes as she reached into her shirt and pulled out a Nokia. It trilled again. She didn't look at him when she slowly pushed the button and read the text message. Then she closed her eyes and put the phone to her chest. He could hear the despair in her voice. "I have to go, Micah. I'll call Sam in an hour and ask him to come and free you. Please don't follow me." She gave him a sad smile. "And thanks for letting me borrow your truck. I promise to return it if you don't call the cops."

She shut the wardrobe door and clipped the rabbit's foot onto her belt loop. She didn't turn around when he called her name.

The last thing he heard was the trapdoor closing.

Lacey felt sick. Bone sick. The kind of sick that made her want to curl into a ball and let the pain consume her whole.

She'd hurt, not just wounded, but seriously, bodily injured the one man she ached to trust. She missed him already, but if she didn't leave him there, trussed up, Emily would die.

Lacey sunk down to sit at the bottom of the cement steps leading up to the cabin, clutched her arms around her waist, and held in a wail.

She could hear Micah up there, thumping, grunting, yelling. He was probably cursing her name. Why had she told him about John? She'd been sworn to secrecy, and if the CIA ever found out, she'd be brought up on more charges—ones that were becoming harder to keep track of. But she'd had to tell Micah. Especially after he said he believed her. How she longed to hear that. But believing was different than forgiving, wasn't it?

Why did he keep following her? He was like a bulldog . . . but she should have known that before she called him. She'd only hoped he'd apply his bulldog tendencies to finding Emily.

Only wasn't that what he was doing? Her throat thickened. She'd dragged him into this mess, kicking and screaming, then beat him up when he actually started to care. Even if he had eviscerated her with the accusation, she saw concern in his eyes. Honest, authentic concern. The kind he'd showed her the day she buried her mother. And she'd just punched the breath out of him. Oh, she was a real gem.

Except that first message had said, *No Jim Micah.* The thought made her weak. The fact that Frank Hillman knew Micah's name only confirmed what she'd believed for years. He'd been watching from the shadows, watching her scream, watching John die. Watching her face light up with hope when Micah stormed into the warehouse, looking like a hero in war paint and his modern-day saber.

Maybe she could just check to see if he was okay. Thankfully, she'd installed an intercom system as a security precaution. She reached over and flicked it on. Yep. She could hear him plainly. Talking about her . . .

". . . and, Lord, I don't know what is going on with Lacey and her daughter, but she's in trouble, and she needs help. Give her wisdom . . ."

He was praying. *For her.* She held her breath.

". . . don't let her get hurt, please. If it's possible, please reveal these people who are after this Ex-6 thing. Bring them to justice. Most of all, look after Emily. Keep her safe and bring her home to her mother." He paused, and she could outline his face in her mind, his dark eyes, his set jaw, his expression of concern. "Lord, help her to see Your light in her dark world."

Lacey wrapped her arms around her waist and opened her mouth in a silent howl. Oh yeah, God was really here, wasn't He? If anyone proved that He wasn't in charge, it was Lacey Montgomery. She'd run her own life right into the ground. Her dad had been right. Letting John Montgomery woo her had brought her nothing but heartache.

She'd seen John call on God a few times . . . but never in prayer. He believed he could save the world on his own. John might have had the charisma of a spy, the makings of a world-class dealer, the passion to lead a small army into battle, and a smile that could melt her heart, but he misplaced the one thing that made him a good husband—faith. John had faith only in himself.

Micah had faith in God. Micah's hopes might be slightly sterile and void of John's passion, but they were firmly fixed in truth. Maybe that was the quality that emanated from Micah like a fresh breeze. Why she'd turned to him and not John when her mother died. Why his smiles of approval made her shine. Why she loved him deeper than—and before—John.

John was laughter and play.

Micah was solid. A man to build a life with.

And she'd tied him up like a Thanksgiving turkey. What if she couldn't get through to Sam? Or what if Sam was detained for hours or even days . . . or weeks? *Micah could die.*

Her throat constricted as she tromped back up the stairs. Of course, Micah was right where she left him, facedown, hands above his head. His wrists were red where he'd already begun to work the ropes. He would have rubbed them raw and gotten nowhere. She knew how to tie knots.

He looked up when she knelt beside him. She couldn't meet his eyes. "Do you promise not to turn me in until Emily is absolutely safe?"

"Lacey, more than that, I promise to help you clear your name. I'm in this with you."

She closed her eyes, willing back tears, his precious words reaching to the deepest places in her heart. "If there's one thing I know about you, it's that you keep your promises."

She met his eyes then, and he didn't blink. "Yes, I do."

She nodded, and the barest smile wheedled to the surface. "Okay, you can come with me. But I'm driving."

Then she took out his knife, sliced through the nylon cords, and freed him.

Chapter 12

MICAH SAID NOTHING while he followed Lacey through the tunnel. His silence felt like ice on her neck. Now that he was free, she still couldn't ignore the idea that he might have agreed to help her just so he could win her trust . . . and apprehend her. She tightened the hold on her knife, aware of his every step behind her as she scraped her light over the dirt walls, creaking beams, cobwebs, and rutted dirt floor.

When gray softened the inky black, she flicked off the light and slowed her pace. Micah came up silently behind her as she peered out into the pasture, down the fence line. The late-afternoon sunshine had turned the landscape to fire, lighting the fence aglow and darkening the grass. The horses had vanished, and the air was laden with the scent of decaying leaves. She edged out of the cave, then tucked herself behind the rocks. Micah crouched inside the lip. She felt his eyes on her. "It looks clear." She glanced at Micah.

His eyes were focused, his face grim. He nodded.

She bolted, running down the fence line, zeroing in on the stand of trees, the safety of the creek.

A gunshot made her jump, putting fire into her step. Another crack. Bark chipped from the maple in front of her.

"Run!" she yelled, hoping Micah was only a foot behind her. She dived into the grove of trees, behind the maple, turned, and gulped in a breath of horror.

Micah was still only halfway down the hill.

Another shot rang out.

"C'mon!" Lacey searched for the source and saw three men in one of her farm's four-wheelers. "Hurry!"

Micah's eyes were fixed on hers while he ran. A bullet embedded the tree one inch behind him as he lunged into the grove.

She grabbed him up by the arm, and he gulped in a ragged breath. "We can make it!"

She raced along the creek. Whoever was after them would have to negotiate the fence, either finding the nearest gate or getting off the four-wheeler and chasing on foot.

Lacey had always been a good runner. But when she glanced over her shoulder, dismay streaked through her. Micah was struggling. His face was white, his eyes wide, and he was sucking air like a drowning man.

"Go!" he shouted, and it came out a gasp.

She slowed, looking behind them. The four-wheeler had stopped at the fence, the men now straddling it.

"Go, start the truck!" Micah reached in his pocket, then tossed her the keys. "I'll be there!"

She frowned at him, but no words escaped before she turned and sprinted up the hill to the garage. Micah's truck was parked in the drive. She jumped in, fired up the engine.

Micah was just starting up the hill.

The shooters had cleared the trees.

Lacey threw the truck into gear and floored it into the field, straight at Micah. The truck hit a boulder and hurtled through the air. She muscled it steady and slammed the brakes when Micah reached for the door. As soon as he climbed in, she whipped a U-turn and stomped the accelerator. Weeds and grass spit out behind them while she roared up the hill. A shot pinged her door; another hit the bed of the truck.

"I don't suppose this thing is bulletproof."

Micah braced a hand on the roof, the other on the door, his feet spread wide on the floorboard. "Not yet!"

Another shot. The back window of the topper shattered. Micah ducked.

Lacey reached the rutted drive and punched the gas all the way to the mat. She didn't brake when she reached the road, slowing just enough to make the curve. She slammed into Micah, barely holding the wheel. He pushed her back, holding her steady while she righted the truck. Gravel spit out behind them. A shot landed in the tailgate.

They drove for a mile in silence, taking two side roads and finally pulling into a scenic lookout over some hiking trail. Lacey held the wheel, feeling the adrenaline surge through her in tremors. Her breath emerged in gasps. But she turned to Micah and grinned.

He was watching her with wide eyes, his face pale. "Are you having fun or something? Where did you learn to drive like that?" He smiled then, and it looked so much like admiration, she felt nearly buoyant.

"You taught me, remember? You took me out in your dad's pickup—"

"No, I didn't teach you how to keep your head with bullets flying at you." He looked back at his shattered window. "They're serious."

She touched his arm. "You okay? You don't look so good."

His mouth tugged up in a half smile. "Yeah. But the bad news is, I think they saw me."

She nodded. "With me. Which means you're in serious trouble, doesn't it?"

He looked away, his Adam's apple bobbing in his neck. "Where are we going?"

Her chest tightened. "I'm so sorry, Micah. I didn't want—"

His fingers touched her lips. "You can't say you didn't try." Sadness tinged his eyes. "I made my choice the second I hopped in the truck and floored it to Missouri."

She tingled where he'd touched her but backed away, afraid of the feelings that rushed over her. *Oh, Micah, please don't make me enjoy your friendship and believe in you. My heart can't take it.* "Because deep down you wanted to trust me?" Apparently, her mouth wasn't listening to her deepest fears. She might as well pluck out her heart and hold it there for him to take a good whack at.

Only he didn't. Instead, he nodded. "And now, Lucky Penny, we have to figure out a way to clear *both* our names."

She felt her throat thicken. Lucky Penny. How she longed to return to that moment when she could have chosen differently, when she had Micah right there in her arms in the creek and then pushed him away. She gritted her teeth to force back betraying tears and dredged up a smile. "We have to get to Coward's Hollow by midnight tomorrow night."

"Where's that?"

She smiled. "I was hoping you'd know."

He took a deep breath, coughed, and took another breath. No, he didn't look well at all. His skin was a little gray, and his chest rose and fell with exertion. Without thinking, she ran her finger along the scar on his chin.

He stilled, circled his fingers around her wrist. His beautiful eyes caught hers and held her gaze. "I know someone who might." He reached for his cell phone. She watched him as he dialed. Sweat beaded his forehead, and the scar on his jaw that he'd gotten during the Persian Gulf War stood out in stark white. He still had this devastating he-man, built-like-a-tank aura, but she couldn't deny the feeling that inside the muscled exterior, the man had been wounded.

Her mouth dried. He hadn't been wounded in battle, had he? All her nightmares rose with a howl. She always feared he'd die with a bullet in his chest in some refuse country, and she'd never know. The tears in her throat threatened to push out, and she blinked them back as he began to talk.

"Conner. It's me." He wore a grim expression, and she got a firsthand look at the trouble she'd caused him.

It wasn't like she hadn't tried to keep him safe. But maybe not hard enough. What if he had died as he stumbled down that hill? Her chest hurt, and she looked away from him.

"No, I'm still in Kentucky." He listened. "Thanks, I'm well aware of that. . . . Listen, I need your help. I need you to find out where Coward's Hollow is."

Micah tugged the wig off her head. Her hair had been piled into pantyhose, and this he wriggled off. Her hair fell in tangles, freed. As she watched his eyes, he brushed her sweaty hair back from her face.

"Are you sure? . . ." He glanced at his watch. "All right . . . yeah, we'll make it. . . . Also, I need—you're kidding?" He looked at Lacey and frowned. "You're sure?"

When he swallowed, she felt something akin to panic rise in her throat. No, they couldn't have found Emily's body. She started to tremble and reached out for the dashboard.

Micah watched her, concern rising in his eyes. "Right. Okay . . . well, listen, I need you to charge up the ELTs. We'll stop by the hotel."

Seeing the sympathy in his eyes, Lacey closed hers, felt her world closing in. *Please, no!*

He touched her arm. "Yeah, thanks." He clicked the phone shut.

Silence felt full and throbbing, embedded with pain. She couldn't look at him, didn't want to guess at his conversation. She forced her mouth shut, willing back the scream inside. No wonder she hadn't received a voice message with the call.

Was Emily dead? The thought scraped up a moan deep in her chest. It ripped its way through her until she was hunched over, her arms curled around her stomach.

"Lacey, are you okay?"

She shook her head, unable to find words to hurdle the pain. What if, at the end of the day, Emily *was* killed?

Like Frank Hillman's daughter.

"Penny, what's the matter?" Micah's voice, so gentle, felt like salt in her open wounds.

She reached for the door handle. She had to get out of here. She couldn't breathe.

The ground swayed beneath her feet as she stumbled out of the truck. She started to run, the air sweeping the vestiges of sweat from her face. She hurtled the guardrail and angled down toward the woods, through the tangles of shrubbery, tripping over the roots of elm and hickory. Her breath caught in her throat; tears glazed her eyes. She stopped short in the embrace of a huge tree and slid down into the hollow of the roots, her hands over her face, shaking.

Emily. How would she live without her smell, her embracing smile? The one thing that kept Lacey tethered to hope. *Oh, John, I'm sorry.* She covered her head with her arms and wept.

"Lace." Micah's sturdy, warm presence edged in on her

ululating grief. He knelt before her, then put his hands on . knees. "What's going on?"

She raised her gaze to him.

He touched her cheek, his eyes radiating fear. "You're scaring me."

She swallowed. "Emily . . . did they . . . find . . . ?" She closed her eyes.

"No."

She opened her eyes stared at him, feeling another hot rush of tears. What was wrong with her? She prided herself on keeping her emotions on ice, for facing danger with unflinching stoicism. And the mere thought of losing Emily had shredded her.

Micah held her jaw, thumbed away a tear. "Did you think I heard bad news about Emily?"

She licked her lips and looked away from him.

"Oh, Lace. No." He shook his head. "I asked Conner to check into something . . . I, uh . . . ." He blew out a breath.

"What?" she asked, her suspicions revving.

"Okay, here's how it is. I really want to believe you, and I thought I could help, so I asked Conner to find out who Ishmael Shavik was."

"Is."

"Yeah, well, he's dead. Was listed on the casualty list from the wreck," he said. "But he was listed on Interpol as an assassin."

She didn't respond.

"But you knew that."

"Of course. I told you."

"You did, didn't you?" His eyes searched hers, reaching out with questions, with fear. "There's a lot I don't know about you anymore."

"I think that goes both ways. Like . . . what's hurting you? You're . . . wounded or something. I saw how you were breathing when we were running from the cave. What happened to you, Micah?" She wondered if her worst fears showed in her eyes.

"I think we need to get going." He held out his hand.

She didn't take it. "Tell me what happened to you."

He seemed to consider this, his jaw tightening. "I'll tell you in the truck. Let's just go before our options are eliminated."

Right. Options. They still had them. Because Emily, as far as she knew, was *alive*. And she had to hang on to that belief if she hoped to get out of this nightmare, sanity intact. Adrenaline had found her soft spot and sent her into hysteria.

She took his hand and he helped her up. They hiked up to the truck without speaking and had only a short tussle for the driver's seat. He won.

Lacey sat in the passenger seat, waiting to understand the man she'd thought she knew better than herself. Or wanted to.

"I had cancer." It still hurt to say it aloud. Like it might be a weakness instead of an invasion. Micah had spent the first months feeling angry at himself for letting it happen. As if somehow he might have prevented the malignant cells from growing inside his stomach, spreading to his lung, to his liver. But as chemotherapy and radiation took hold, turned him inside out, writhed him with agony, he let himself be a victim. Let himself feel both pity and pain. At least, in the privacy of his home.

No one but his parents and his brother, Joey, knew the emotional hits he took. And saying it to Lacey now felt like taking a scalpel to his chest all over again. He even winced.

Her mouth cracked open. Then, "I'm sorry." And she sounded wounded for him.

It made him yearn for her more, as if he wasn't already longing to erase seven years of accusations, tunnel for the truth, and start all over again. If he hoped to start all over again, he'd have to go back in time to the night of her senior prom when he'd let fear manhandle him and sacrifice his heart. But yesterdays couldn't be recaptured. Not now, after the cancer had ravaged his future.

"I'm clean, at least I was at my last checkup. They took out a lung and part of my stomach and liver. But I beat it. I hope."

She touched his arm, and he flinched. "But you're going to be okay?"

Was he? Physically, perhaps. But emotionally, he still felt annihilated. Not by what had happened but by what he could never have. A child. The aggressive cancer treatment had stolen from him a legacy. The next generation. Someone in his likeness to love and cherish and be the kind of father his had been to him. There were times, especially in the past six months of living near Joe and his family, that this pain sliced so deep, he sometimes felt like curling into a ball and howling. "Yeah, I'm okay."

"I wish I'd known. I'd have figured out a way to see you."

He glanced at her, and the sorrow on her expression and in her radiant eyes made him believe her. "I probably would have liked that, even if I didn't tell you."

She chuckled. "Yeah, you might have cuffed me with your IV and screamed for security."

His smile dimmed. "Probably. And I would have been wrong." He touched her cheek. "I'm sorry I didn't believe you."

She shrugged, but his apology glistened in his eyes. "So, did you find out where Coward's Hollow is?"

"Mark Twain National Forest in southern Missouri."

She nodded, put her feet up on the dash, and leaned her head back. "We have a long drive ahead. Do you want to stop somewhere?"

He put both hands on the wheel, then looked at his speedometer. "No. We'll head to the hotel where my team is waiting. You're going to have Emily back in your arms by tomorrow night."

"If the NSA doesn't track me down first."

He said nothing. He still wasn't completely sure that giving themselves over to the greater powers wouldn't be in their favor, but after the shootout at the OK Corral, he wasn't sure that power was the NSA. Maybe he should call Senator Ramey after all. Or maybe . . .

"Lacey, in the glove compartment, you'll find my Bible. Can you grab it?"

She gave him a one-eyed frown, then took her feet off the dash and unearthed it. "You going to read as you drive?"

"No, you are. Open it to Psalm 107."

He saw her purse her lips as she turned to the psalm. "Okay. What verse?"

"Just read the whole thing. To yourself."

She gave him a look. "Listen, if you didn't get the message at breakfast, God and I aren't really on speaking terms."

"Yeah, I picked that up. And I want to know why."

She shook her head. "If you can't forgive me, how do you expect God to? I can't even forgive myself."

"But John's death was an accident, Lace. God knows that."

"Yeah, and He also knows about all the millions of compromises I've made, not counting the bad decisions based on greed or fame or whatever other sin He's warned against." Her voice sounded strained. "I've discovered that it's not the big

162

sins that dig at your soul, but the thousands of tiny, seemingly inconsequential ones that slowly gnaw away at any sense of hope." She looked at him. "I am not going into detail, but you of all people should believe me when I say I'm not a saint."

"Neither am I."

"You're different."

He gave her a hard look. "No, I'm not. Do you seriously believe that in my line of work I haven't made a few compromises? struggled with times when I've killed? fought my own fury for control?"

She clenched her jaw, and he could almost see her imagination run behind those pretty eyes. He didn't want to paint too dark a picture for her, but it seemed that she had some squeaky-clean, holier-than-thou vision of him and he wanted to dispel it here and now.

"Believe me, I'm no saint. I'm just . . . saved. And trying." Right now he was trying, with all his man-sized effort, to keep his hands on the steering wheel instead of driving into the ditch and pulling her into his arms.

Only that would defeat his prayer to cut her out of his heart. It wasn't lost on him that God was doing just about everything opposite to Micah's prayers. And instead of bringing her to justice, Micah was on the lam right beside her.

So much for being God's man.

Lacey sat beside him, obviously lost in her own thoughts, staring at the Bible.

"Read verse one aloud, Lace," Micah said, suddenly needing God's words like he needed his next breath. He had the passage memorized, had dissected it years ago.

"'Give thanks to the Lord, for he is good! His faithful love endures forever.'" She seemed to struggle with the words.

"Okay, now go down to verse ten, I think."

She traced her finger down the page. "'Some sat in darkness and deepest gloom, miserable prisoners in chains. They rebelled against the words of God, scorning the counsel of the Most High. That is why he broke them with hard labor; they fell, and no one helped them rise again. "Lord, help!" they cried in their trouble, and he saved them from their distress.'"

"Stop there."

But she continued: "'He led them from the darkness and deepest gloom; he snapped their chains. Let them praise the Lord for his great love and for all his wonderful deeds to them.'" Her voice broke on the last word. Micah glanced over at her, but her gaze was fixed on the Bible. "'For he broke down their prison gates of bronze; he cut apart their bars of iron.'"

She stopped, and silence filled the empty space.

Micah stared ahead, praying for wisdom. This faithless Lacey he hadn't expected. Maybe he thought she'd still be the woman who sparred with him over the gifts of the Spirit, who stood beside him, arms raised in worship at a summer revival meeting. Who took his hand and prayed for his safety at boot camp. He should have guessed that John's self-atonement theology would rub off on her. That years of grieving her mistakes might scalp her faith down to a nub. Still, he hadn't expected the anger, the despair, the cynicism. It hurt him worse than having her tie him up and leave him for the bad guys.

"'They rebelled against the words of God . . . ,'" he started.

"'That is why he broke them with hard labor,'" she finished. "You're trying to make a point here, aren't you? About God letting a person struggle, letting a person drown in darkness."

"I am. You're so sure that God can't be in control of your mistakes. But this verse says that yes, you can make mistakes— free will—and God does put you in chains. It's not about who does the shackling . . . it's about who does the *saving*. The people cried out to the Lord in their trouble, and He saved them from their distress. Whether we have free will or God has it all planned out, there is only one way to be saved."

She frowned, and he could nearly see her chewing his words in her intelligent mind. "Keep reading. The next passage is about people becoming fools and suffering because of their iniquities. And the next, God stirs the waters, causes the storms, then brings the people to safety. There is constantly the paradox of free will versus an all-sovereign God. And the only answer is—both are right."

"Both?"

"I know it's impossible for our brains to wrap around that. We like to think in linear patterns. Especially people like you and me. We want to solve problems, whittle down the scenarios, and egress without casualties. But we're not going to win this battle. Whenever our confusion and God's Word go toe to toe, God's Word will always win. Because it is from the mind of God. He is light and all knowledge. We see only darkly through the prism of ourselves and our experiences."

They turned off the country road and onto the highway. The sun had dropped below the horizon, and long shadows scraped the road.

"So you *and* John were right." There was something in her tone that made him smile. A sort of wonder.

He felt it too, a resonating peace knowing that John had a place of purpose in her life. What, Micah didn't want to speculate, but if God could use the last fifteen years and her marriage to John for good . . . "Yeah, I guess so," Micah agreed.

She closed the Bible, sat back. "I'm hungry."

He stifled a sigh, wishing that she'd allowed God's Word— the only thing that could save and restore her life—to dig deeper, shine light into her dark soul. "We'll stop at the next truck stop."

"Micah—" she touched his arm—"I know what you're trying to do. I . . . I miss God. I do. But I can't face Him. It hurts too much."

"He loves you, you know."

She went silent and backed away from him. His arm felt cold where her touch had been.

Chapter 13

MICAH FIDDLED WITH the radio, hitting Seek until he happened upon a country radio station. Lonestar's beat filled the car, and he turned it down, lest the sound awaken Lacey. He'd like to drive in silence, but fatigue pressed on him and he had to have the noise and the window cracked slightly to keep his reflexes sharp.

Good thing he'd helped her scarf down a bag of pork rinds. They tasted like cardboard—no, cardboard was probably better—but they were filling and just stomach-curdling enough to keep him uncomfortable and awake.

As for Lacey, she had curled up against the seat and fallen asleep, her penny red hair in tangles, her jean jacket over her. She looked breathtaking, especially in slumber. Finally, perhaps, at peace. Except every once in a while she let out a little whimper of pain or grief. He wondered if she'd ever truly sleep in peace.

He'd been fighting the nearly overpowering urge to pull over, wrap her in his arms, and let her sleep on his shoulder. Or in his embrace. Earlier, he'd nearly held her tight when he'd tracked her down the hill, through the bramble, and found her weeping at the base of a huge elm, as if her heart had shattered.

Lacey had some kind of magic power over him. Just being around her, he seemed to forget that she belonged to another man. Even if he was dead, John had been her husband and part of God's plan for her life. Micah had no right to her. He'd forfeited that on prom night of her senior year.

He glanced at her now, resisted the urge to touch her hair. He wondered if it was still as soft and silky. If, when she piled it on her head like she had that night, tendrils wisping around her face, she'd look like a teenager.

No, that night she'd looked pure princess. Ethereal. Regal. And off-limits.

He still remembered sitting outside her house in his car, staring at the lighted porch, sweating in his dress blues. He'd been posted out there for a good half hour, running over the afternoon's events in his mind. Focusing mainly, of course, on the kiss. The mind-blowing, heart-stopping, whoa-back-and-don't-let-your-emotions-show kiss. And that had been on his side. He hadn't expected the 110 percent response she'd given him. It scared him. Because since that moment, he'd dreamed, more times than he wanted to admit, of pulling her into the shadowed grounds behind the country club where they were holding prom and kissing her again. Just like he had in the creek.

Only he wasn't supposed to be holding her. At least not like that. She was John's girl and had been for nearly two years. But whose fault was that? He leaned his head on the steering wheel, feeling the cool leather against his hot brow. He'd introduced Lacey to John. Fool. *Fool!*

He'd been too stupid to say anything about his own feelings until it was too late. Almost overnight, she'd become John's girl. And then what could he do?

Somehow he summoned the courage to walk to her front steps. Ring the bell. Stand there until her father opened the door. Of course, her father trusted him. They'd attended the same church since he was a kid. Micah smiled, hoping Gerald Galloway couldn't see inside him to the desires he battled.

He knew he was a goner the second Lacey walked down the stairs. She wore a blue gown; he remembered that much because it turned her silver eyes the palest of blues. He could hardly breathe, let alone conjure up words as she took his hand and gazed into his eyes.

"You look . . . great," she said.

He licked his lips. Swallowed. "Yeah. You too." Oh, that didn't even begin to touch what he felt. She looked *incredible* and deserved to be told that. But tonight was about subduing all those feelings and running back to his army base, to his new world, as soon as he could extricate himself from this mission.

"I brought you a corsage." Micah held up the box, saw that the white roses had wilted, just a little. The carnage from his battle in the car.

She didn't hint that she noticed and held still as he pinned it on. He grimaced when his hands shook. He'd been shot at, dropped out of an airplane, hiked for days without decent food, and bested a man in hand-to-hand combat, and yet pinning on these flowers had him nearly unhinged.

"Thank you, Micah," she said. "They're beautiful."

"So are you, sis," said Janie, wearing a UT sweatshirt and holding the hand of her fiancé, Dan. "Mom would have been so proud."

Micah noticed tears in Lacey's eyes when she turned and hugged her older sister. "Thanks, Janie." Then she walked over to Micah and slipped her gloved hand through his arm.

"Don't they look great together?" Janie asked.

Gerald appeared with a camera. Lacey leaned into Micah as her father snapped the picture. "Now listen, you bring her home safely." Gerald shook Micah's hand, but caution edged his eyes. "She's my little girl and I want her to have a wonderful night."

Micah nodded and changed his mind, now dead sure that this man could see right through him. "Yes, sir."

Lacey held his arm as they walked out to the car. In her high heels, she stood nearly to his shoulder. But he felt a thousand feet tall while he helped her in the car.

The moon had risen, despite the early hour, and she pointed it out as they drove. He kept both hands on the steering wheel. She talked about others who would be at the prom, her sister's upcoming wedding, the dirt bike her brother Sam had purchased, and her favorite new foal.

He thought of John and prayed for self-control.

The country club was lit up with Christmas lights, the beat of a country music band thumping through the breeze. The rose garden had already bloomed, the fragrance perfuming the air. Laughter and the hum of voices spilled out from the veranda. Micah pulled up, glad he'd taken his father's Buick LeSabre rather than his on-its-last-legs VW Rabbit. He helped her out and then left to park.

As he approached her, needles of anger pricked at his guilt. John should be here. But the guy had chosen to go on a pretraining camp vacation with his college pals rather than take his gal to prom. So he'd called Micah, who played it cool and let John talk him into it instead of falling all over the idea like a desperate man.

John so didn't deserve this girl—no, *woman*. And she *had* blossomed into a full-grown woman, with a brain and courage. That afternoon she'd told him that she'd landed a scholarship to MIT. She took his breath away in so many ways.

She turned, apparently sensing his presence, and smiled.

His throat tightened. No, John didn't deserve her. But neither, probably, did he.

She took his arm and they entered the dance. A hundred eyes turned and Micah raised his chin, glad that the army had added tone to his bulky football muscle. When Lacey looked up at him with pride, it made his chest swell to three times its size.

He couldn't remember what he ate, if anything. His knotted stomach wouldn't handle it. And then they cleared the floor and the dance started.

He stood at the sidelines, paralyzed.

Lacey said nothing as the other partners took the floor, some line dancing, others two-stepping. He knew how to two-step, even knew a few Yankee twirls, but his polished shoes stuck to the floor.

Lacey's smile had vanished. She stared at the dancers, disappointment on her beautiful face.

Oh, what was he thinking, standing in for John? He was in big, big trouble. Still, he heard himself say, "Wanna dance?"

The world lit up with her smile. She nodded, and then they were on the dance floor, and he forgot all about John. Or feeling self-conscious in his uniform. Or even the fact that he was two years older than every other guy in the room and that the last time he'd been to a prom, it had been his senior prom and he'd sat in the corner, caught in a cloud of gloom as John twirled Lacey around the floor.

His turn.

They danced and laughed, and she felt perfect in his arms. She anticipated his moves, landed lightly in his arms, stepped smartly around him. They had rhythm and grace. During their final dance, he twirled her and she ended up in his arms in a last dip, her arms around his neck.

He knew then that they had to leave.

She didn't protest, simply grabbed her little purse from the table, hugged a couple of girlfriends good-bye, and left, hugging his arm.

The cool summer air whisked the sweat from his brow, snaked under his collar. He loosened it as he left her at the curb and walked out to the car. He would drive her straight home, say good night, and call it mission completed. Without casualties.

Only they ended up at Lover's Bluff, a ridge overlooking Ashleyville. The twinkle of lights and the moon overhead seemed to be blotting out all reasonable thought.

"Thank you, Micah, for taking me to the prom. It was . . . wonderful."

He sat with both hands clamped on the steering wheel, calling himself an idiot. Why hadn't he just taken her home?

Because, deep inside, he was still hoping that she might love *him*, be more than a friend. That she might choose him instead of John.

"It's a pretty night." She looked at him. "I wonder where John is right now."

He didn't want to think about John at the moment. "I dunno," he growled.

She frowned at him. "Well, I don't care. I had a magical night. You are a better date than he is." Her eyes widened and she put a hand over her mouth. "Sorry, that wasn't nice. I just remember that at your senior prom he danced with about ten other girls and then took me home early so he could go out with you."

That wasn't how Micah remembered it. In fact, he'd harbored some pretty dark ideas of just why John had left early with Lacey, and it was only Lacey's sweet innocence that following summer after John had left for boot camp that convinced Micah those musings couldn't be true. Now he wondered if they'd only been misplaced.

"Well, he missed out then," he said, feeling suddenly empowered. John didn't deserve this woman. He, Micah, would never deceive her like that.

She had a smile that, even without the moonlight, could turn his words to paste in this mouth. The added boost of heavenly radiance, the sound of cicadas, and the warm and summery breeze through the car, tangled all rational thought. He moved toward her, wrapped a hand around her neck, and kissed her.

Lacey touched his cheek, and he thought it might be to push him away. But she curled her gloved hand behind his neck, pulled him closer, and kissed him back. Her lips tasted of cherry punch, and her perfume reached out and obliterated the final shreds of common sense. He embraced her, fighting a rise of emotions.

He loved her. He loved her adventurous spirit, her smile, her laughter, and her intelligence. He loved the way she rode a horse with abandon, the way she trusted him, and the way she lit up when he walked into the room. He loved the fact that she made him feel alive, tugged cloistered emotions from his heart, and wasn't afraid to let her own feelings show. He loved her so much that when he lay in bivouac, staring at the stars during the hardest days of basic training, her pretty face had filled his brain and given him a smile before he fell into exhausted slumber. She didn't belong to John. She was Micah's. He deepened his kiss.

"Oh!"

He backed away, eyes wide, his breath caught.

She swallowed, but pain etched her face. "The corsage." She hunched her back to escape the needle piercing her skin.

With a contorted expression, she reached up and eased the pin out of the flower. It had blood on the end.

He stared at it in horror. What had he done? Like he'd been awakened out of an incredible dream by a reveille, he stared at her, his heart thumping. "Oh no, I did it again," he said with a groan.

"You did what?" She wore the same look she had at the creek. Shock. Fear.

Of *course* she was afraid. She was in love with John, and Micah had practically attacked her, not once but twice. He moved away, shaking. "I'm taking you home, Lacey." He started the car, then backed out.

"Micah, what's the matter?"

He glanced at her as he turned onto the road. "You know what the matter is. John. I'm his best friend. And you're his girl. I feel sick."

She gazed straight ahead, but he thought he saw tears crest over her eyes. Then she said so quietly he barely heard it, "But John's not here. You are."

He wanted to close his eyes, yell, or maybe just get out and run about thirty miles at a full sprint, just to feel anything but this fist squeezing his heart. John didn't deserve her, but Micah couldn't steal her. He wasn't that kind of guy—or at least he thought he wasn't that kind of guy until he'd gotten in the car and driven her purposely to a lovers' lookout. Some friend, some trustworthy pal he was.

He gritted his teeth, lest his emotions spill out and he tell her exactly how he felt about her dating the one guy who was headed for trouble. He knew John's dreams. CIA. Covert operator. Glory and adventure and changing the world one corner at a time. And he'd drag Lacey—smart, talented Lacey—right along with him. Probably get her killed.

Micah could barely see by the time he pulled up in front of her house.

She sat in the car without moving.

"I'm leaving in the morning, Lace. I'll write."

She wiped her face. "No, you won't. I won't see you again. You're going to get killed and then . . . it'll break my heart."

He looked at her, pretty sure that his own heart was about to leap into her arms. *Hold yourself together, buddy, just a minute longer.* "No, it won't. You'll have John. That's what you want, anyway."

She stared at him, a hard glint of anger in her eyes. She swallowed and her voice sounded cold. "Yeah, I guess you're right." Then she got out and slammed the door.

His throat was thick, his eyes burning by the time he got home. He packed a bag that night and was back at base by morning.

So much for completing his mission without casualty.

Now, twenty years later, watching her sleep, he knew his wounds were very much alive and bleeding profusely. *It hurts too much.*

He thought about her words from that night long ago, and suddenly something snapped inside him. Maybe she'd meant something else. Like . . . pointing out that Micah was the one who'd been there, the one she'd kissed . . . and he might be the one she . . . loved? Unfortunately, as a twenty-year-old, he saw only her ability to crush him. Yes, he'd been dangerously close to handing her his heart, but he blamed this impulse on the moonlight, the smell of her perfume, their easy friendship.

It had nearly killed him to walk away from her. But in the end, after he'd gathered his wits, he'd felt vindicated. She'd married the man she loved. If Micah had given her his heart on that starry night, he would have been decimated. A walking shell. Then again, that's pretty much how he felt most of the time.

He realized suddenly that rejection wasn't so much about how Lacey viewed him. It was about knowing how vulnerable and unworthy he was and how much he needed her love. Which was probably why Lacey looked hollowed out and on the fine edge of raw. She'd been hollowed out by grief and the crushing weight of her sins before a holy God. She'd had a sweet relationship with her Savior but had walked away from it one step at a time. Years later, she was crippled to the point where she couldn't face Him. She needed God's love more than she needed to breathe, and she knew it. Just like she knew the darkness buried in her soul.

And if anything happened to Emily . . .

Maybe God wasn't ignoring Micah's prayers. Maybe, in fact, He was answering the ones Micah had been too ashamed to voice.

He reached over and tugged Lacey over onto his chest. When she scooted closer and curled up, he felt something inside begin to heal.

"Okay, that's it. I need real food."

Lacey heard his masculine voice in that sweet place between dreaming and wakefulness, when it might be safe to just enjoy this warmth, this feeling of herself in someone's—John's?—arms.

She felt him move her off his shoulder, then the cool of the leather seat against her neck and cheek, heard the door click.

The click woke her. She opened her eyes. An overhead

light bathed the truck in orange luminescence. She pushed herself up, feeling lined and ugly. It took a moment for her to orient herself . . . she touched the dash, smelled the lingering scent of masculinity.

Jim Micah.

Had she been sleeping on his shoulder? She blinked and adjusted her eyes. They were parked facing a darkened, rumpled field. She glanced out of the back of the topper. A twenty-four-hour convenience store with two lonely gas pumps lit the night like a UFO. She rubbed her eyes, trying to remember the moment. They were on their way to Missouri to get Emily.

She should leave. *Right now.* Simply start the truck and back out, leaving Micah really angry . . . but very much alive. Because if he stayed with her, he would end up just as dead as John. She knew it in her heart. She swallowed hard and stared at the keys dangling in the ignition. Only, he was starting to believe her about Emily, about John. Believe that she couldn't be a cold-blooded murderer.

She touched the keys. They felt cold and jagged. Just like her future would be without Micah in her life.

But alive and angry were a billion times better than dead. *No Jim Micah.*

She scooted over into the driver's seat, turned the ignition over, and shifted into reverse.

Micah appeared in the rearview mirror, carrying a paper bag. She tore her gaze off him and hit the gas.

"No!"

She heard him yell and tensed. *Sorry, Micah.* She felt like a jerk, a kick-the-guy-in-the-teeth-while-he's-smiling jerk. But again, that was better than Micah ending up as a corpse. She braked, flung the truck into drive, punched the gas.

Micah reached her door as the pickup jerked forward. She

heard him shout and realized he'd grabbed the handle. "No, Micah!"

He was running beside the truck, banging on the window, yelling her name. She glanced over and wanted to scream. If he didn't let go, he'd be dragged behind. "Go away!"

"Open up! Don't do this, Penny!"

She gritted her teeth. *Don't call me that. I'm anything but lucky for you.* But the name made a direct hit. She slowed down, her breath gusting out. She lowered her head to the steering wheel, calling herself a coward. She didn't want to do this anymore. Not alone.

He opened the passenger door, slid in, and said nothing. He just sat there and stared at her, his chest rising and falling in heaves.

She couldn't look at him.

"When are you going to trust me?"

"It's not about me not trusting you. It's about you getting hurt. The text message said specifically, *No Jim Micah.*" She glanced at him and wondered if her fears showed in her eyes the way confusion showed in his.

He frowned and shook his head. "Who knows me?"

"I don't know. But they know enough about me to know that I'd call you."

He reached out, and she fought his sudden tenderness. Micah, her friend, had made a breath-stealing reappearance, and it was about all she could do not to be that gullible high school girl and forget everything but his hands in her hair, his touch on her lips.

She took a steadying breath. "Promise me when we get to the motel, you'll stay there with your friends." She tried on a look that shielded her fears and gave no room for options. "Promise me, and I won't kick you out of the truck."

He arched one eyebrow, and a slight smile lit his lips. "No."

"Micah, please. I know what I'm doing. I don't want your help. I can protect Emily on my own."

He narrowed his eyes at her. "You think you're pretty tough, don't you? Well, I'm sure you *can* handle it on your own. But you forget that we're in this together. I can't let anything happen to you if I want to stay out of the clink, remember?"

So maybe this wasn't about him being the friend he'd been.

"Besides, I want to help."

Okay, that comment thickened her throat. She shook her head. "You'll stay at the motel. Or this is the end of the line for us."

"You really think you're going to kick me out of *my* truck?"

She shrugged.

He smirked. "Don't answer that. How about this? . . . I promise to not promise to tag along until after we get to the motel and reassess."

Her brain knotted. She was way too tired for this. But— she rubbed her hand over her forehead—that sounded okay. Maybe. She agreed.

He laughed, and it felt so full and refreshing and right that she couldn't help but smile. "You're not easy to shake," she said.

"Penny, the feeling is completely mutual." Then he reached for the door. "You promise to stay here while I go retrieve my supper?"

She smiled slyly.

"What if I tell you I got a chili dog for you too?"

She made a face but nodded.

As if he didn't believe her, he hopped out and returned with the bag he'd dropped in less than ten seconds. "Are you driving?"

She put on her seat belt. "Yeah. Hand me my supper."

"As you wish." He dug in the bag and held out the chili dog. She took a bite, then handed it back to him and turned onto the street.

"Which way to the highway?"

"No, we're winding through the back hills. Take County 3, up at the next light."

Back hills. So they wouldn't be caught. A wave of remorse rushed over her. "I'm sorry I doubted you."

He took a bite of his own chili dog, then set it down and held hers out. "Again, the feeling is completely mutual."

His words, his voice, especially the way he helped her with her supper, felt like honey bathing her heart, warm and filling every crack with sweetness. She smiled and turned at the light. The dash light read 11:23 p.m. "How far are we from Poplar Bluff?"

"Maybe five hours. We've lost some time traversing the countryside." He finished off his chili dog.

"But we're safe. That's important."

"Yeah. You can bet, however, that Poplar Bluff will be flush with cops. I'm not sure whether we should go in by light of day, with traffic, or late . . . I'm leaning toward the light of day."

She nodded. "I still have my wig."

"And it's oh so cute too." He held out her chili dog, and she finished it.

"Can you hand me a napkin?" she asked and found one almost immediately in her hand. His attention to her needs felt so sweet. She fought to focus on the road. "Thanks."

"Well, the chili would make a great disguise too but not so attractive."

"Yeah, I'd look like Emily," she managed, then grinned at him.

He leaned back, crunched up his paper bag. "Tell me about her."

Lacey wasn't sure how to explain to him what it felt like to wear your heart on the outside of your body, to know joy in a baby's smile, to taste peace in the sweet embrace of a tiny arm. "She's blonde, like John, and she has his blue eyes. She has a great fighting spirit. She loves people and is constantly into mischief. But, of course, she can wiggle out of trouble with a smile."

"Just like John."

"Too much probably." Lacey smiled wryly as she accelerated to pass a hog-hauling truck. "Someday I want to teach her to ride, maybe on the farm or our own home. She loves Janie's farm, but Janie has five kids of her own, and I need to give Emily her own life. Her own space . . ." Her words trailed off as she heard the futility of that dream snicker and dig its claws into her soul. If she handed over her program to . . . whomever . . . she would be on the run for the rest of her life. A traitor to her country. "It's a nice dream."

Micah's gaze was on her, but she couldn't look at him. "What happened after she was born, Lace? You mentioned that she lives with Janie."

She tried not to flinch. "We stayed on the farm until she was about two. But that was the year my father was killed . . . and it seemed prudent to put her where she'd be safe and for me to keep moving."

Micah just frowned.

She concentrated on the road. "I always felt as if Ishmael Shavik—or maybe Frank Hillman—was on my tail. Little things told me, like a shadow behind me at the grocery store or knowing something had been moved while I was away. I received mysterious telephone calls. Like he was trying to remind me that he was going to repay me for having the audacity to live."

She felt tears prick her eyes. "When Dad was run off the road by an unknown driver, I knew that Hillman was sending me another message—he wanted revenge. I was already working on Ex-6 by then, and it drove me. I couldn't help but think that if our messages had been secure, John would be alive today. So I left Emily at Janie's house and hit the road, working on Ex-6 as I traveled. Three times a year I came into the NSA, tested my program with their hardware, then left. They wanted to put me in protective custody, but I couldn't bear the thought of . . . of . . ." *Of not ever seeing you again. Of dropping off the planet so completely that you'd never find me.*

"So you've been on the run for five years?"

She nodded, feeling her despair leak out. "I suppose with Shavik dead, I can stop running, but somehow I don't think it's as simple as that. Besides, when I hand over Ex-6, well, I'll be a marked woman, won't I?" She sighed. "Sometimes I just wish I could rewind time."

"What would you do differently?"

She didn't answer. A thousand what-ifs swirled in her head, but she couldn't voice them. Instead she shrugged. Dredging up a breezy voice she asked, "Do you still ride?"

He waited a moment before he answered. "Yeah. Deuce-and-a-halves, Black Hawks, and C-130 transports."

She laughed. "I can't believe you've been in Special Ops all this time." She shook her head. "I used to be so afraid you'd get killed overseas."

"I'll never forget when you came to Iraq after me. So many times I went back to that moment, to seeing you in that crazy gypsy outfit, greasepaint on your face. It made me think that someone cared."

She could feel his gaze on her, and suddenly the mission that she'd so neatly tucked into the don't-touch section of her brain leaped out and filled her throat. Oh yes, she cared. So much so that when she'd heard he'd been captured, she'd done the stupidest thing in history. She'd pulled strings, jumped the nearest airplane, and headed overseas thinking she could not only save him, but that he'd be glad to see her.

Sadly, he'd only gotten angry. John, on the other hand, had admired her so much that he proposed.

"John and I couldn't just let you die," she said simply, not giving in to the tug to explain her motives.

The sound of the wheels against the pavement filled the sudden silence, as if he too remembered their brief adventure—the way he'd held her, nearly trembling with shock—or relief—their wild flight on horseback, his anger at John. In the end, however, he'd had his chance to declare his feelings, to stop her from marrying John. Regardless of her feelings for Micah, John had been the one to offer her a future. Still, while she'd thrown herself into a life with John, her friendship with Micah and his job as a Green Beret had left the fragments of worry in her heart.

"I remember one night in Kuwait City," Lacey said. "I sat out on the balcony, staring at the sky—the stars sparkled against this incredibly black sky. And all I could think of was you, lying under the same patch of sky. I wondered how you were, hoping you were alive and well."

"You were married to John then."

"Yeah. I guess about two years. We had talked about having a family, but John informed me that he didn't want children, at least not until our current assignment was up." She remembered the one time she'd thought she'd might be pregnant . . . the white-hued panic on John's face had resonated nothing but dread. She swallowed against the image. "When I finally got pregnant, I didn't relish telling him about the baby.

That's probably why I kept it a secret. Since I tried to dress conservatively most of the time like the locals—I even wore a veil—it wasn't hard to hide. He was so busy; we never spent much time together. I counted it a miracle that I even got pregnant. He never noticed or maybe decided not to say anything."

"I'm sorry you felt that way. If it had been my child, I would have—" He cut off his words and looked away.

Lacey felt regret pulsing between them, the untended remains of what they'd started so many years before. She tightened her hands on the steering wheel, eyes glued to the road, but tears burned. If Emily had been Micah's child, maybe she wouldn't have been afraid to tell him. Wouldn't have felt like she was somehow destroying his life.

"Sorry," Micah said. "John was a good man and my friend. I didn't mean to say anything—"

"No, that's okay. I know." Lacey glanced at him, glad she'd corralled her emotions back in the paddock without incident. "He was a good man. Just . . . an idealist. Thought he could change the world."

Micah smiled. "And now you're doing it for him."

She frowned.

"Ex-6. You're saving America's secrets."

Hardly. She was about to barter them for her daughter's life. She closed her lips and stared at the road. If John's sacrifice and her mistakes could at all be atoned for, it was through Ex-6. But after tomorrow, there would be no redemption left. She shrugged, hoping to deflect his words.

"Lacey, you're not seriously considering giving the program away, are you? You do have some sort of backup master plan, right?"

She clenched her jaw.

"You *are* serious."

"Completely. What would you do if the person you loved was about to be killed? Emily is more than that to me. She's the air I breathe. She's my heart and my only reason for living. She's everything to me. And I'm not going to sit by and let her slip through my grip if I can do something about it."

Micah just stared, wide-eyed.

"Yeah, well, I guess you wouldn't know anything about feeling that kind of love, would you, Iceman?" She could hardly believe she'd said that. As the words left her she wanted to clamp her hand over her deceitful mouth. But they hung there, ugly and raw and pungent with hurt.

She half expected him to cold-shoulder her the entire way to Poplar Bluff. That would have been better, easier to handle than his soft words that followed. "Maybe you're right. Maybe I don't know how to love. Not that I didn't have a great example with my parents, but maybe I was just . . ." His voice caught, and his flash of anger yanked her gaze. "What was I supposed to do, Lacey? You were dating my best friend."

His dark eyes held hers and suddenly every hurt, every grief, every tendril of love for him she had stomped down inside her heart rushed to the surface. Years of longing and fighting the memory of what could have been filled her.

"What, Lacey?" he asked again, this time even softer, with an edge of desperation.

She considered her words, unsure exactly—

He suddenly lunged forward. "Lacey!"

Bright lights filled the cab. She jerked the wheel. The tires screeched as they swerved away from the oncoming lights. The pickup hurtled toward the black mesh of forest with a gut-rending squeal.

Chapter 14

MICAH GRABBED THE wheel just as the truck hurtled into the ditch. Lacey slammed on the brakes. The pickup bounced in the grass, skimmed a tree. Lacey banged against the steering wheel. A blinding pain spiked up her arm to her shoulder. She cried out as the vehicle jolted to a stop.

Micah had hit the windshield. Glass webbing the front panel, a trickle of blood, and an ugly bump evidenced a skull-jarring smack. He still had one hand on the wheel, but his eyes were closed and he was breathing hard.

"Are you okay?" she asked on a fine wisp of voice.

He took a deep breath. "Yeah. But I'm driving." He opened his eyes. She expected fury. Instead, concern radiated out in waves. "You scared me."

"I scared myself. Sorry."

His gaze was so intense it raised the little hairs on her neck. He swallowed, searched her face. Then he curled his hand around her neck and kissed her.

She froze, scrambling to keep up. But his very muscled arm was around her shoulders, his hand touched her cheek, and his lips—strong, salty and so very, very familiar—were on hers, moving almost hungrily.

As if she *had* scared him. She closed her eyes. And without a thought kissed him back. *Micah, oh, Micah.* She wound her arms around his waist. She felt his heart thumping wildly and didn't know if it was because of her or the accident. But she didn't care. Micah, back in her arms. She pulled him closer, drank in his kiss, forgetting the space of time and hurt.

Forgetting everything but the way she loved him. When she'd walked down the aisle with John, she'd stomped her love for Micah into a hard ball and shoved it into the back of her heart. She had loved John, and she kept that thought forefront and center until finally her feelings for Micah had whimpered defeat and crawled away into hiding. Hidden— and perhaps small—but not entirely forgotten. Like one never forgets their first love, she could no sooner forget him than stop breathing.

He touched his forehead to hers. He was shaking, just a little, and that fact rattled her. "Lacey," he said, his voice roughened, "you scare me so much sometimes I think my heart can't take it."

Then he kissed her again. Not at all hungry this time, but soft, achingly sweet. Perfect.

Micah.

When he pulled away, she saw in his eyes the same feelings she'd seen in the creek, at prom on the dance floor, and especially at Lover's Bluff. Even in Iraq, behind all that anger.

He loved her.

She ached for him to say it, but he just stared at her, studying her face. She wanted to move toward him, but something—maybe their painful tomorrows—made her scoot back.

He made no move to follow her. And then, sorrow filled his face. "I gotta figure out a way to clear your name."

She blinked at him, emptied.

"Because I'm not sure how I'm going to let you walk out of my life if I don't."

Something inside her broke open and wailed. "I told you I was trouble," she said thinly.

He just looked at her. Then he opened his door.

She got out and walked around to the passenger seat. The sooner they got to Poplar Bluff the better, because every minute she spent with Jim Micah only dug her longings in deeper.

And leaving him might be like tearing herself in half.

It took nearly a half hour to dig the pickup out of the bramble and grass and maneuver it back onto the road. Micah drove for the next three hours, adrenaline wringing out his muscles before fatigue burrowed deep. Lacey was asleep against the door when he pulled over into a rest area, rearranged her against his chest, and tried to stretch out.

But the needed sleep wouldn't come any easier with her curled up against him, a hand over his chest, her hair tumbled down over her face. She smelled sweet, with a hint of femininity and fierceness, and it wound around his heart and tugged.

Yes, he had to figure out a way to disentangle her from this mess. He bulleted the facts in his mind, trying to sort truth from fiction:

Seven years ago, his best friend and her husband, John, had been killed in Kazakhstan. The point man for the double cross—Ishmael Shavik, international assassin.

Lacey had a baby, born prematurely in that attack, which she'd kept secret. That thought tightened his chest.

For the past seven years, Lacey had been developing an

encryption/decryption program for the NSA, one that was finished enough to sell . . . or steal.

Three days ago, Ishmael Shavik had been spotted on the train. Why was he there? To kill Lacey? Why hadn't he done it years earlier if he'd been tailing her for so long?

The NSA's appointed bodyguard—with or without Lacey's knowledge—had been killed, perhaps by Lacey, during the train accident.

The NSA had arrested—or only detained?—Lacey and ordered her to release Ex-6.

Emily went missing.

While Micah had been tromping around in the woods, Lacey had discovered that Emily wasn't missing . . . but had been snatched.

He frowned. How had she found out? And what had she said about a text message? Carefully, he reached inside her jean-jacket pocket as he muddled out the rest. Lacey had sprung herself from NSA custody and hightailed it back to her farm in Kentucky, where she'd . . . picked up a copy of Ex-6? And now, she was headed to Coward's Hollow—if he could trust her information—to exchange the program for her daughter's life.

He found her cell phone and pulled it out. She sighed, then burrowed deeper into his embrace. He felt like a thief as he raised the phone, pushed the text-message-retrieval button. When he read the first message, his heart dropped like lead in his chest.

```
HELLO, LACEY. I HAVE EMILY.
WILL EXCHANGE FOR EX-6.
NO TRICKS, NO NSA.
NO JIM MICAH.
WILL CONTACT IN 24 HOURS.
```

Anger flared. Whoever had Emily had better be ready for him. No Jim Micah—yeah, they'd wish they'd never met him. He scrolled to the next message. Crazy relief rushed over him when he saw she'd been telling him the truth. Midnight at Coward's Hollow. He swallowed, feeling idiotic tears prick his eyes. What a fool he'd been to doubt her. She'd been right— deep inside, he knew she could never have done the things she was accused of.

Why had the CIA let the charges against her stand? They must have had a good reason for sealing her case. Perhaps the real killer behind Ishmael Shavik was still at large—the killer who had burned John and set up his wife to take the fall. Lacey had mentioned Frank Hillman. Micah slipped the cell phone back into her pocket, feeling the overpowering urge to shake the truth out of Mr. Hillman.

The biggest questions throbbed in his mind—which by now was so far from sleep that he might as well drive: Who wanted Ex-6 and why?

Lacey would have to bind and gag him if she thought he wasn't going with her to Coward's Hollow. Especially after kissing her . . . and feeling how she kissed him back. He touched her hair, then let it fall between his fingers. Yep, silky. Soft. The feelings that washed over him threatened to consume him.

If he didn't figure out a way to rescue Emily and keep Lacey from trading American secrets, then he'd be running too, his life destroyed. Because he wasn't letting Lacey walk out of his life again. No matter how many times she tried to ditch him.

He knew she wasn't the girl he'd left behind in Ashleyville, but she'd become so much more than he'd imagined. Brave and adventurous, smart and feisty. She was also loyal and true and generous and breathtaking. She knew how to dig under the hard crust of his heart and till his feelings. Over the past two days, something alive and wild had sprouted in his heart. The magnitude of it nearly choked him.

He stroked her hair, closed his eyes, his emotions thick as he whispered, "Lord, we are in way over our heads here. But You know that, and You know the way out. Please help me find it. Help us get Emily back without trading Ex-6. Give me wisdom. And please, Lord, help me be the man Lacey needs me to be. Finally."

He listened to her soft breathing, felt her body rise and fall against him, and a feeling of peace, so unlike anything he'd ever experienced, rushed over him. Almost as if she belonged there.

Gently he pushed her away. He sat up, resettled her on his chest, and started the pickup.

Two hours to Poplar Bluff. He'd sleep after Emily was safely home. He hoped that was sooner rather than never.

The sun had just cut the horizon with a swath of pale gold when Micah drove through the outskirt neighborhoods of Poplar Bluff. He wove through morning traffic, hunting for tails or surveillance, and finally, feeling safe, drove to the Tree-Line Motel.

When he emerged from the truck, the air felt warm and soggy, still fighting the wake of the summer storm. He took in his surroundings before he woke Lacey.

She startled awake; it took a moment for her to orient herself. Being the operator she was, she adapted in a blink, grabbed the wig and the backpack, and slid out of the driver's side.

"C'mon," he said quietly. He glanced at Conner's truck, saw he'd activated his external security, then lightly gripped Lacey's elbow and led her toward the motel, up the stairs to a second-story room near the middle of the walkway.

Conner opened the door when Micah rapped. The guy's

golden blond hair, long and curly, nested his head, and he looked like he hadn't slept in about three days. Either that or he'd been freshly yanked from bed and had slept bare-chested in a pair of old fatigues.

Micah imagined he might not look much better. "Hey ya," he said. "Conner, you probably don't remember, but this is Lacey Montgomery. Lacey, Conner Young." He turned to Conner. "Where are the girls staying?"

Conner barely blinked at his quick intro. "Dannette's next door; Andee and Sarah are down the hall." Stepping out into the hall, Conner knocked on the next door.

A moment later, Dannette answered. She was already dressed in a pair of blue track pants and jacket, her eyes clear. As usual, one step ahead of them. She was probably on her way to walk Sherlock. Her gaze passed Conner to Micah. "Welcome back."

"I brought a friend. Can she use your bathroom and maybe your extra bed?"

She looked at Lacey, who had straightened. "Absolutely." Dannette held the door open.

Lacey glanced at Micah, and for a second he saw questions race through her eyes. "It'll be okay," he said softly. "Dannette is a friend. She helped me look for your daughter."

Dannette appeared startled. She had received sketchy information at best, and he didn't blame her for her confusion as she shut the door.

Conner, however, did not hold back his opinion. "You're in over your head here, pal."

Micah entered Conner's room. "You have no idea." He pulled off his jacket, sank onto the bed, and flopped back. Exhaustion washed over him like a tsunami. FOX News droned quietly in the background. "Her daughter's been kidnapped."

The silence from his friend across the room made Micah open one eye. Conner leaned against the table, arms folded over his chest. "Why aren't the cops handling this?"

Micah tossed his arm over his eyes, shielding his brain from the looming realities. But Lacey's face and the feeling of her in his arms, kissing him with a very yes-I-want-you-in-my-life response filled his mind. He turned onto his side, grabbed a pillow, and crammed it under his head.

"What can I do, Micah?"

"I dunno. She always seems to be outflanking me, or worse, trying to leave me in the dust. Maybe just make sure she isn't ditching me right now."

"Ditching you?"

"I don't want to talk about it." He closed his eyes, felt slumber tug at him. "Did you find out any more about Ishmael Shavik?"

"He had ties with Hayata."

"Oh, beautiful." *Hayata*, loosely translated from an ancient middle Asian dialect, meant "life" and was the user name of a freelance terrorist group that had anything but life on their agenda. With ties to nearly every known terrorist group from Syria to North Korea, Hayata had one priority—cash. Micah had run into Hayata thugs in various no-name countries in Eastern Europe and Asia, and the memory left him with a burning hole in his gut. The worst part—their leadership was a shadow, someone who knew how to disappear. Suddenly the acquisition of Ex-6 made perfect, bone-chilling sense. "So Shavik could have been working with any number of terrorist factions."

"Do you know why her daughter was kidnapped?" Conner asked, obviously not intending to let Micah sleep.

Micah sighed, opened his eyes. "Lacey's designed an encryption/decryption program contracted by the NSA. It's nearly finished."

Conner looked impressed. "Government encryption. No wonder Senator Ramey called me, hunting you."

Micah froze. "Ramey called?"

Conner nodded. "You'd better check your messages. I left three for you."

Micah groaned and pulled his cell out of his pocket. The battery had died, obviously the victim of Micah's wandering mind. He tossed it to Conner. "Can you charge it up for me?"

"You going to call Ramey back?" Conner dug around in his bag for a cord.

Micah winced. "I don't know. I ran into Deputy Director Berg. I have a feeling Ramey's not calling to cheer on my little sideline adventure."

Conner plugged in Micah's telephone, then stood and stared at him. Amazing how one look could say so much.

"What am I supposed to do?" Micah asked. "This guy has Lacey's daughter and Ex-6 is her only bartering chip. She's going to trade it for Emily."

"Ouch. I'm thinking that's a big N-O. You know what could happen if such a program got into the wrong hands."

"Yes, we had that discussion. She's got a midnight meeting. Until then, I have to keep her in pocket. Which—" he hit the pillow again—"can be a fairly painful, if not impossible, process."

Conner walked over to grab a sweatshirt. "I can see that. Is that a welt on your jaw? Don't tell me she kicked you."

"More than once."

"I'm going to say this one more time because I'm your friend. Are you sure you want to do this? If Ramey finds out . . . well, he probably already has." Conner let out a breath. "You're so cooked, pal. You might as well kiss those bars good-bye."

Micah just wanted to put his hands over his ears and wish

himself far away, maybe back in time to that sweltering prom night, where he could reset his future, and this time fill it with hope. "She needs . . . help."

"Have you ever heard of 911?" Conner raised one eyebrow, his look like a punch in the chest.

Yeah, okay . . . moment of truth. "She needs *me.*"

"Captain Jim and the Enterprise to the rescue." Conner sighed and held up his hand before Micah could argue. "You get some shut-eye. I'll take a shift. Anything I should know?"

Micah closed his eyes, too tired to argue. "She likes to climb out of bathroom windows. And she's got a wicked left hook."

"That pretty thing?"

Micah opened his eyes and glared at him. "Listen, Mr. Smooth Operator, she's off limits, okay?"

Conner smirked. "Finally made your move, huh?"

Micah grimaced, thinking back to his grab-and-kiss. Yeah, he was a real charmer. "No. Well . . . maybe. I don't know."

"Which means . . . ?"

Micah sighed "I kissed her. I was hoping that would broadcast my feelings." Which at the moment he wasn't even sure about. Okay, yes, he loved her. He wasn't so stupid as to deny the feeling that boiled in his chest. But was he ready to marry her, to shoulder her burdens, to love her despite her mistakes?

He swallowed against a lump of grief. What about her lack of faith? How could he marry a woman who bristled every time he brought up God, the most important part of his life?

Conner must have seen his debate. He frowned. "So you haven't told her how you feel. Do *you* even know?"

"I love her. But she's . . . she's got a black hole in her heart where her faith was. She used to be this woman who loved God with abandon. Her passion for God stirred my own." He thought of her anger in the café and later her apathy in the truck. "I almost don't recognize this person,"

Conner sat on the bed. "You see a prisoner, Micah. Someone trapped in the darkness. You see who she was and what she could be. If I understand her sketchy history at all, I'm guessing Lacey hasn't had a lot to thank God for—at least from her perspective. Her problem is, she can't see God in her life. She can't see how He might be reaching out to her through the darkness."

Listening, Micah propped himself up on one elbow.

Conner snorted. "Don't you think it's interesting that in her darkest moment, she might call for a person who walks in the light? The one person who knows the dark paths she's taken? Didn't you say she murdered your best friend?"

"That was an accident." Micah was amazed at how easily he jumped to Lacey's defense.

"All the more reason for God to use you, pal, to help her see His love. You're right; she *does* need you."

"I don't deny that I think God is at work here, Sparks." He rubbed his forehead. "But I can't declare my love for her until I can ask her to marry me."

Conner's mouth opened, just enough to declare shock. "Marry? Whoa, okay, so something did happen in the last forty-eight hours. You should have been ready to do that when you kissed her."

Micah made a wry face. "The truth is, I should have asked her about thirteen years ago when she showed up in Iraq." Or maybe even before that. Like prom night, her senior year. "But I was . . . afraid. I loved her so much, but I couldn't squeeze the words out of my mouth."

Conner steepled his fingers, grinning. "Ah, a classic case of the Gideon complex."

Micah stared at him, completely baffled.

"You wanted her to prove to you that she wouldn't hurt you before you declared your love for her. You wanted a wet fleece."

Micah remembered Lacey's hollow, broken expression after their kiss on Lover's Bluff and her words about John not being there to kiss her . . . suggesting that Micah was, and that was okay. And then her soft voice in the truck last night, unveiling the truths in her heart . . . *it hurts too much*. He had wanted proof that she was worth fighting for. That in the end she wouldn't turn toward John and away from Micah. No, John hadn't deserved her . . . but neither had he.

"You have no choice," Conner continued. "You have to take the Romans 5:8 route."

"Conner, I'm tired—"

"You gotta tell her you love her, not expecting anything back. You need to lay your heart out there, even if it's going to get squashed. God did that for us. And He expects us to do it for each other."

Micah let out a long breath. "That's gonna hurt."

"Anyone can give her a kiss. Even me—"

"Try it. I guarantee you'll lose a kneecap."

Conner laughed. "You need to do something that really . . . makes her do a double take . . . maybe . . . a poem?"

"Oh, who are you, Cyrano de Bergerac?"

Maybe it was the morning light threading through the curtain, but he thought he saw Conner blush. "I dunno. Maybe you're right. I'm a lot of talk. But I'm thinking that if you're trying to show her what it means to be loved by God, you can only model it yourself."

Micah blinked and sat up. "If she's unavailable to hand over Ex-6, then she can't be charged."

Conner frowned at him.

"Can you make me a copy of her program if I get it to you?"

Conner nodded, his expression wary.

Micah pushed to his feet. "Fire up your gizmos, Sparks. And get me a topo map of Coward's Hollow. She's not going to make the exchange . . . I am."

Lacey stood in the shower, letting the water wash off the smell of the hospital, the vestiges of fatigue, even the sweet scent of Micah's coat.

Now that she was back in Poplar Bluff, she had to figure out a way to shake Micah. She shouldn't have told him about Coward's Hollow. But if she enlisted Dannette, perhaps—and what exactly was his relationship with the tall blonde, anyway? Lacey hadn't missed the worry in the woman's eyes, which made her wonder just how well she knew Micah.

Dannette knew, for example, that he wasn't in tip-top shape. The fact that she phoned someone named Sarah and asked her to go over and check on Micah meant he had told them about the cancer.

That others knew Micah better than she did shouldn't surprise her. But she couldn't help the spurt of jealousy. Stupid, stupid woman. Micah would be wise to hook up with a gal like Dannette. Or anyone else whose future didn't include being a fugitive from the U.S. government. She braced her arms against the wall and lifted her face into the shower, trying to wipe the image of Micah holding someone else—like Dannette—in his arms.

She shouldn't have surrendered to his embrace. Again, she was about to get her heart ripped out. Just when she thought she'd scarred over for good. But, no, he'd held her, then politely stepped out of her life. Just like he had fifteen years ago. Only he didn't know that she'd seen how hard that had been for him.

Lacey plugged the tub, and the water pooled around her. She closed her eyes, letting memory be her friend.

Once she'd said yes to John's proposal, life moved faster than she could breathe. Suddenly, she was walking down the aisle on a warm June day in her tiny hometown church toward the man who would be her future. A man who made her feel important and beautiful. Lilies and roses fragranced the sanctuary, and ahead of her stood her groom—handsome, built, adventurous John, his blue eyes full of mischief and delight. He looked stunning in his tuxedo, and she barely noticed the man standing next to him, staring at his polished shoes . . . Jim Micah.

She spoke words, she was sure of it, because the ceremony ended with applause and the pronouncement of husband and wife.

And then John swept her away in a limousine. "You're so beautiful," he said as he took her face in his hands and kissed her gently.

She'd be happy—she knew it. John Montgomery, for all his sparkle and charisma, had chosen her, loved *her*. And she loved him back, with the part of her that longed for something more than the life her mother had. She wouldn't be a farmwife, stuck in a small town waiting for her man to return home from his overseas adventures.

She'd be by his side wherever he went. In fact, she'd be the best thing that ever happened to Lt. John Montgomery. And the fact that being with him offered a life of adventure, a noble purpose . . . wasn't that what she'd always wanted? She smiled, kissed him back, putting passion into her touch.

"Wow," John said, pulling back. "I hope there's more of that."

"Of course," she said and settled into his embrace.

Two hours later, the cake had been cut, the toasts made, the dancing had begun. Occasionally, she'd spotted Micah, mostly chatting with his parents, his brother. He never glanced at her once. Still, she noticed when he left, and the tendrils of their former friendship tugged at her heart. "John, I need some fresh air," she said when he pulled her close for yet another love song.

He looked at her, frowning. "Are you okay?"

She smiled. "Of course. I'm just . . . overwhelmed."

"Okay. Do you want me to come with you?"

She said no and felt relief when John didn't argue.

The cool air, redolent of roses from the nearby garden, stirred the worry in her heart as she walked out into the night. The stars shone with a brilliance unequalled. She cut away from the club, followed the path down to the pond.

The sound of quick breaths stopped her. She hid behind a willow tree and peered through the night toward the pond. Jim Micah sat on a bench, elbows on his knees, head in his hands. His shoulders shook.

Lacey watched, realizing he was . . . crying. Her mouth dried. Big, powerful Micah, dissolving before her eyes. Broken. Weeping in some private agony. Her throat thickened. Why would he be crying?

She turned and crept away, back to the reception. But she buried the image in her heart, taking it out now and again to ponder it. To hope, perhaps, that he'd been crying for her. For the *them* that had never been.

Now tears burned her eyes, and under the cover of running water, she let sobs rack her body. Weeping, just like Micah, for the *them* that would never be.

Chapter 15

MICAH OBVIOUSLY DIDN'T trust her as far as he could throw her, which must not be very far, because his friend—what was his name again? Conrad? Conway?—stood outside the motel door when Lacey emerged wearing a pair of Dannette's track pants and a sweatshirt.

She recognized a pit bull when she saw one, even one as cute as Conway, with his curly, burnt blond hair and mischievous smile. He had his arms crossed over his chest—now clothed in a black knit shirt and red down vest. "We're waiting for you down at the café. Want some breakfast?"

"We?" She slung the backpack, bulging with her yellow wig and dirty clothes, over her shoulder. They might come in handy at the next stop. The rabbit's foot key chain she'd clipped to the waistband ties of the pants. If she could have found duct tape, she would have taped it to her body.

"Yeah, me and the rest of Team Hope," Pit Bull Conway answered. He shoved his hands in his pockets and walked casually ahead of her, but she had no doubt that should she bolt, he'd tackle her like a halfback. The guy had military written all over him despite his nonchalant grin. They appeared to be two friends, but his undercurrent of suspicion could power a small town.

"Who's Team Hope?" she asked, scanning the parking lot below as she trailed behind him. She counted seven cars in the lot, three with Missouri plates. None looked government issue. Across the street at the gas station, a man in an orange baseball cap fueled his pickup, his back to her, and another on a motorcycle kicked up his stand and motored off without glancing in her direction. Cars rolled by, splashing at the curb. Overhead, the sun beamed from a cirrus-filled sky, the clouds deflated of ammunition. Sparrows chirruped. So maybe she could relax and allow herself a couple of deep breaths.

"Oh, just a bunch of friends," her bodyguard replied. "We hang out together and sometimes do search-and-rescue ops. Micah pulled us in to search for Emily."

At her daughter's name, Lacey's throat thickened. *Emily, please be safe.* How she suddenly longed, as she once had, to kneel and find comfort in handing over her fears, her pain, into God's hands. But there was no going back now. Despite Micah's words about God breaking her free of captivity.

"They cried out to the Lord in their trouble and he saved them from their distress."

The thought caught her, and she couldn't deny the way her heart spasmed. But the idea of returning to God, knowing that she'd turned her back on Him—willfully—no, she didn't have the right to ask for His help now.

"What was your name again?" she asked as they descended the stairs.

"Conner Young."

When he smiled at her, she felt a tug toward friendship. Conner, not Conway. And he did seem like a Conner—sorta honorable. Polite. Possibly . . . kind? Maybe she'd been too rough on the guy. Just because he had been sent to keep an eye on her didn't mean he wasn't on her side.

In fact, he looked almost . . . familiar. "Have we met before? What did Micah say yesterday about you remembering me?"

Conner cut her a glance, and she thought she saw chagrin on his face. "Yeah. We met in Iraq. I was . . . with Micah."

Oh yeah. One of Micah's roughed-up Green Berets she and John had helped free. She grimaced. "You were wounded."

He looked away. "I never thanked you for coming in after us. You were gone by the time they discharged me from the hospital in Germany."

She recalled the young man with the matted, bloodied hair, the leg wound, and pained eyes. Mostly, she remembered she'd been young, foolish, and idealistic.

"What a beautiful day, huh?" Conner said, as if wanting to yank them out of painful memories. "Yesterday the sky was groaning, pouring itself out. Today nothing but blue skies and sunshine. As if God washed the landscape clean."

Lacey nodded, not sure how to respond. She felt like she was talking to Micah, Mr. Faith. The desire to figure out a way to save Ex-6 and Emily and to start again rushed over her. Micah *had* kissed her. . . .

No, fatigue had eaten away at her common sense. Micah may have kissed her, but it had been nothing but a heart-rending panic reflex, a physical expression of relief after she'd nearly killed them both. And she wasn't going to do anything that might get another man she loved killed.

"Yes. It's a great day." She heard the despair in her voice.

Conner said nothing as they crossed to the tiny café in the front of the motel. He opened the door and out spilled the sound of chatter, the stomach-grabbing smell of bacon frying, and the taste of small-town friendship. He pointed at a small group crammed into a corner.

Lacey approached with a smile while she searched the

room. Two elderly ladies in a booth along the front window; a single man, dressed in a business suit, reading today's news and sipping coffee at a middle table. No NSA duos. Still, her stomach knotted.

Conner pulled up a chair and motioned for her to sit while he slid in next to Dannette.

"You look nice," Dannette said. "Glad the duds fit."

"Thanks for the loaners." Lacey felt slightly ill that she'd have to boost them. She'd figure out a way to send her a check.

"Lacey, this is Andee MacLeod," Conner said, gesturing to a young woman with light mocha skin and black hair. "And this is my cousin Sarah Nation. She's from New *Yark* City." He reached over and grabbed Sarah's cup of coffee. "Where's your shadow, New York?"

Sarah made a face at him. She had blonde hair, and it was tucked back into a baseball cap, the long mane bundled in a ponytail, and eyes that looked like they could sting from ten paces. At least until she smiled at Lacey. Lacey felt their warmth to her bones. "Glad to meet you. I'm an EMT with the New York Fire Department. And Andee here is a part-time everything—trail guide, helicopter pilot, mountain goat. She lives in Alaska in the summertime, hangs in the Lower Forty-Eight during the winter."

"Glad to meet you," Lacey said. "Where's Micah?"

"He's snoozing," Conner said and snatched a menu from Andee. "What'll ya have, Lacey? It's on me."

Lacey wasn't sure how she should react to this generosity from Micah's cronies. Did they know who she was? More importantly, did they know her history with Micah?

"So, where's your little shadow, Sarah?" Conner asked again, peeking over the menu.

Sarah scowled. "Far away from me, I hope."

Conner grinned. "Or he's lurking in the next booth, hoping to hear your sweet voice. Again." He glanced over her shoulder. "Uh-oh, I think I see him!"

Sarah turned, and Lacey didn't miss the flush on her face.

Conner laughed. "I knew it. You like him." He leaned over to Lacey, his tone conspiratorial. "We bumped heads with this forest ranger when we were looking for your daughter, and he caught Sarah in a . . . vulnerable moment. Anyway, he was here twice yesterday, asking us how we were, like he cares *I'm* alive." He waggled his eyebrows. "Nope, he was checking on old Fanny Crosby here."

Sarah hit him with her menu. She wasn't smiling when she looked at Lacey. "I sing when I'm tense."

Sarah shot daggers at Conner while the waitress appeared and took their orders. Lacey glanced at Conner, and when he nodded, she ordered an omelette and a side of French toast. And orange juice. Then sausage, just for good measure. And a cinnamon roll to go.

Conner had his eyebrows raised when she finished.

She tucked her backpack between her feet and leaned into the table. "So, Micah is sleeping?" Well, he had been up all night. Still, she missed him, and in the back of her mind hoped she'd get a chance to say good-bye. Right before she locked him in the bathroom. He and the polite Pit Bull Conner.

"So, Lacey, where are you from?" Dannette asked.

Lacey surveyed her a moment before answering. The woman seemed to be the serious one and gave Lacey a reserved smile. "Ashleyville. I grew up with Micah."

Andee nodded. "You were in the train wreck, right? How are you?"

In pain from head to toe and inside out. "Good. Thanks. I dislocated my shoulder."

Andee laced her hands on the table. "I'm sorry we didn't find your daughter. Micah says you know where she is."

Lacey shot a look at Conner, but his face betrayed nothing. "Yes," she said, feeling like a liar.

"Good." Relief washed through Andee's brown eyes.

Dannette smiled and grabbed her coffee cup. Sarah glared at Conner, who was trying to balance a saltshaker on a mound of salt.

"Was your husband in the crash?" Andee asked.

Lacey saw a shadow cross Conner's face. Obviously Micah had told him something. Lacey smiled. "No, he wasn't." She glanced at Conner. "Actually, I'm a widow."

Sarah touched her arm. "I'm sorry. Andee didn't mean to pry."

Lacey shook her head, realizing how few times she'd actually called herself that. As opposed to *murderer.* "He died a number of years ago actually. I'm used to being on my own."

"I'm sure it's hard to raise a daughter by yourself," Andee commented.

Dannette watched Lacey with solemn eyes.

Lacey made a wry face, nodded, but inside she felt like a hypocrite. No, she'd let Janie do the raising. She had shown up only for the high moments—and even then, seemed to miss them more often than hit them. Still, Emily loved her with abandon that made Lacey ache. *Please, God, can't You make this better?* Her unbidden prayer caught her by surprise, and she forced through a wave of guilt.

"So you and Micah grew up together. I'll bet you knew him in his football days then, huh?" Sarah set the saltshaker on the pile, and it balanced perfectly on one edge. She gave Conner a smug look.

"Yeah. He was a running back."

"Did you keep in touch over the years?" Dannette asked.

Lacey felt herself prickle. "No . . . I mean, sort of. My late husband and Micah were best friends. He was in our wedding. But I lost touch over the years."

"He sure rushed to your aid the minute you called. We returned from the 7-Eleven in time to catch him roaring out of the parking lot of our motel like he was on fire." Andee grinned, then leaned back to receive her plate of pancakes.

After the waitress delivered their orders, Lacey dived into the omelette and French toast. It hit her stomach like a long-lost friend.

"I'd say he seemed like a man who never forgot his first love," Conner said, spooning his oatmeal.

Lacey nearly choked on her coffee. "Sorry, what?"

Conner grinned at her, then at the rest of the group. "Oh, sorry. I just meant that you must have meant a lot to him. Hey—" his blue eyes lit up—"if you went to the same high school, you must know his friend Penny. He used to tell us stories about her horse farm and this mine that he nearly got trapped in once. They must have been really good friends because he wrote her letter after letter, even when we were in country. He'd store them in his duffel bag and wait until we were EVACed. Then he'd send the entire wad of letters. Evidently, she was some sort of computer genius, working in . . ." His voice trailed off, and he wore a funny look. "Never mind."

Lacey's throat tightened. "Yeah, I knew her," she said lightly. "They were really good friends."

Conner stared at her, unblinking. "Good friends are hard to forget."

Lacey's appetite was gone, but she forced herself to eat each bite, telling herself that this meal might be her last for a while.

"Conner, do you think Micah will be reinstated?" Andee asked softly.

"I don't know. He's got a senator pulling for him, but unless he passes the PT test—" Conner stared at his bowl of oatmeal—"I'm thinking no."

Lacey searched their faces. "Reinstated? You mean to active duty? He's not current?"

Andee glanced at her, then at her food, and the conversation died.

"I know about . . . his sickness," Lacey said, "but I didn't know he wasn't on duty."

"Medical leave," Conner said. "He's going up for review in a couple of weeks."

"And then he'll head back to his unit . . . where?"

Conner shrugged. "Eastern Europe or maybe one of the Stans. He's a born leader, and the teams could use him. They called him Iceman, you know."

Oh, how she knew. That nickname haunted her.

"It was because he just turned his emotions off when we were under attack. He's mechanical and will take it on the chin without flinching. Knew what to do every time. A tactical genius." Conner turned his coffee cup slowly, methodically. "The only time I saw him come apart was on a mission in Bosnia. This little girl walked into the middle of a gun battle between two street factions and was mowed down. Micah ran into the middle of the fight, scooped her up, and fled, full tilt, all the way to the field hospital. Like he didn't think of anything but getting her there. I thought he'd lost his mind.

"When he came back, he nearly single-handedly took out each one of those killers, rounded up the survivors, and dragged them into camp. I think they're still sitting in prison." Conner shook his head, remorse on his face. "Iceman might have steel in his veins, but he loves kids. What a shame he'll never have any."

Lacey felt cut off at the heart. Micah would *never* have kids? "Oh."

Dannette glared at Conner. "He'll love you for that one."

Conner looked sheepish. "Sorry. I thought he told you."

Lacey shook her head. "That's okay. I won't mention it." She wanted to hit something until her body hurt as much as her heart. How utterly unfair that Jim Micah, who just might be a stellar father—she nearly gasped, remembering his comment in the truck about if he'd known she was pregnant. . . .

What must it feel like to be searching for your best friend's daughter, knowing you'd never have one? No wonder he was dedicated. And in big trouble because of her. If he wanted to be reinstated to his Green Beret unit, he'd have to distance himself from her—and pronto. Now wasn't soon enough to lock him in the bathroom and flee for the hills. Maybe she wouldn't even stop to lock him in the bathroom or say good-bye.

"I'll be right back," she said and pushed her plate away. She ignored Conner's frown as she got up from the table and gripped the backpack.

See if Conner the cheery pit bull would follow her into the bathroom.

"She's in Poplar Bluff." The voice at the other end of the cell phone put a smile on Nero's face.

"Great. Keep her in sight, but keep your distance. I want to see if she has what we're looking for."

Nero closed the telephone and stalked over to the hotel window. From here, he had a sweeping view of a mall and two pizza joints. How Missouri had changed over twenty-five years. He remembered when this town had nothing more than a Dairy Queen and a strip mall. From the way it was expanding, it wouldn't be long before the forest was completely obliterated. Thankfully, his parents' old homestead still stood, poised at the edge of Mark Twain National Forest.

He had suffered a momentary fear that Lacey wouldn't know where to find Coward's Hollow, had even debated sending her another message. But she was smart. He knew how smart. He'd watched her in Kuwait, her intelligent eyes taking in her surroundings. She missed nothing. She'd figure out how to meet him.

His insurance sat on the bed, playing with a McDonald's Happy Meal toy. She didn't look at him as he let the drapery fall. The scene felt oh so familiar. Childlike trust purchased with a toy and a bag of French fries. She was even somewhat cute, with her blonde hair, her blue eyes. She looked so much like her father. She might be difficult to sacrifice. But sometimes duty cost lives. Especially when they got in the way.

Lacey had certainly gotten in the way. He couldn't wait for the past to flash through her eyes tonight when he dangled her daughter's life before her. Seven years seemed way too long to wait for payback.

He sat down on the end of the bed and picked up the doll. "Can I play too?" he asked, then smiled.

"I caught her climbing out of the bathroom window," Conner said by way of explanation as he hauled Lacey into the motel room by the arm. He had the makings of a shiner. "And you were right about the left hook."

"Let me go," Lacey hissed, then yanked out of Conner's grip.

Micah couldn't help but smile. He set the map down and closed the door behind them. "Hi, Lacey."

"Don't hi me. You had him tailing me." My, she looked cute with her hair down, still slightly wet, her eyes blazing.

"Of course I did, Penny. I'm not stupid."

She clenched her jaw, obviously fighting a retort. "I thought you were supposed to be sleeping."

"Calm down. I'm on your side, if you remember."

"Sorta." She swung the backpack off her shoulder, flopped into an armchair. "But I don't need your help. Not anymore."

"That's what you think. Coward's Hollow is a fifty-six-acre portion of Mark Twain National Forest. It has caves, a twenty-foot waterfall, and enough forest for you to be lost in for a couple of decades. Tell me, when you were at the farm training in weapons and hand-to-hand combat, did you go to survival school too?"

She glared at him.

"Just what I thought. Listen, I've lived in the woods for the better part of my life. If anyone should be sneaking around trying to get a fix on your kidnapper, it's me."

"No. Not if you hope to have any sort of career beyond this moment. Traitors don't get their M-16s back."

He frowned at Conner. "Thanks a lot."

Conner held his hands up. "That was Andee's doing, not mine." He glanced at Lacey. "I made other mistakes."

"Lock the door and chain it, Conner." Micah motioned to Lacey. "C'mere. I want to show you my plan."

Lacey rose and moved toward him. She smelled fresh but emanated such fury he braced himself. She leaned over the map. "What's this, a topo map?"

"Yeah, and as you can see there are only two service roads into the area. Which means your kidnapper, if he isn't on a four-wheeler, will have to take one of those two roads in to meet you. Did he say where in Coward's Hollow?" He hated asking. . . . The potential for her to lie wavered before him.

When she answered no, he felt a wash of relief. Again proving that she wasn't the liar he'd called her a billion times over. "So he'll have to call you with coordinates."

"At least for the drop," she said.

"When the call comes in, we'll connect the dots. Conner will surveil one road, Sarah and Andee the other. Dannette and you will be on standby with her bloodhound in case things go south. I'll head in and make the drop, get Emily, and we're home free." He pointed to Conner, who picked up Lacey's backpack.

She turned. "Hey!"

"Where is it?" Conner started to open her bag.

Lacey crossed the room in two strides and swiped it out of his hands.

"Conner is going to make a copy of the program," Micah said. "Where is it?"

"No." She gripped the backpack tightly. "I can't let you do this."

"Yes." Micah touched her arm. "We'll make a copy, and then Conner will corrupt the one we hand over."

"He'll know. I'm sure he'll test it. Then he'll shoot Emily and you." Lacey's fear shone in her eyes. She reached into her waistband, held out her cell phone. Her hands shook as she dropped the bag and fiddled with the telephone. A moment later, a shriek and a keening cry filled the room, "Mommy!" Lacey held the phone up and played it again.

Micah watched her fight a bevy of emotions as she stared

at him. He tightened his jaw, but that wail had gouged a hole in him too. No wonder Lacey was scared.

"I can't risk losing her." Lacey still trembled as she put the telephone back in her waistband. Her voice fell to a ragged whisper. "Or you."

Micah wasn't about to lose her either. Not again. If Conner hadn't been standing there, he just might have taken the two steps to her and crushed her inside his embrace. "Okay, then, you corrupt the program. Make it undetectable."

He could nearly see her brain whirring. She frowned and asked Conner, "What kind of computer do you have?"

"It has dual four-gig Iridium processors, hyperthreading technology, one gigahertz FSB, two gigs RAM, scuzzy hard drives, eight USB ports, four FireWire ports, and a HD plasma display."

"That should do." She turned to Micah, not noticing Conner's deflated expression. He lived for his computer acronyms. "But I'm bringing the program in. I don't care if you're part wood elf. Emily is *my* daughter."

Ouch, *that* hurt. "Yeah, I know."

She stared at him, and he saw a strange, unidentified emotion run through her eyes. "We'll talk about it when I get back," she said.

"Only if you promise not to bushwhack Conner—no, better yet I'll go with you." He began rolling up the map.

"I promise I won't bushwhack him."

"Or jump him and leave him hog-tied in the back of his pickup. Or steal my car or try and sneak out of the bathroom." *Or break my heart again into a thousand pieces.*

She cracked a small grin. "Okay."

He nodded to Conner, who opened the door. "Kindly step out to my office, milady," Conner offered.

Lacey glanced at Micah, a frown on her pretty face.

"Just you wait, Penny. You're going to be green at his sweet setup."

She followed Conner outside, and Micah stood at the motel-room door, watching as they descended the stairs and crossed to his pickup.

Conner opened the camper end of his truck and they piled in. Micah suppressed the urge to run over and padlock the door. But she'd promised.

Right?

Chapter 16

AS LACEY TYPED at Conner's computer keyboard, she feared how badly she wanted Micah's plan to work. She stood up, loaded the program onto a CD-ROM, and extracted it from the drive.

"Finished?" Conner sat on the bed, waiting. To his credit, he'd actually closed his eyes and feigned a snooze, as if he weren't keeping an eagle eye on her every move. She didn't buy it for a second.

She nodded. "I think I'll go back to the hotel, try and get a nap."

"Okay." He rose, obviously intending to accompany her.

"Alone."

He smirked. "Right. I wasn't going to . . ." He looked away and—wasn't that sorta sweet?—blushed. "I'll just sit outside your door."

She rolled her eyes and snatched her backpack. The sunshine made her blink, and she felt another ripple of exhaustion. If she went to sleep she might snooze through the next decade. More likely, instead of sleeping, she'd stare at the ceiling, her daughter's face filling every nook and cranny until she went insane with worry.

She took the stairs two a time. Conner wasn't more than three steps behind. She tried to ignore him as she opened the door. Dannette sat on her bed, reading an SAR magazine. Her dog Sherlock lounged next to her, relishing the absentminded attention of Dannette running her hand behind his floppy ears.

"Do you have a pair of tennis shoes I could borrow?" Lacey asked.

Dannette looked up, obviously startled. Then, "Uh . . . yeah." She gestured with her magazine. "By the bathroom."

Lacey strode over to pick them up. "Thanks."

"Help yourself to anything in the suitcase." Dannette gave another hint of a smile.

Lacey nodded. "Thanks."

Conner was outside, leaning against the rail, his designated perch. Surprise washed his face when Lacey returned.

She said nothing as she turned down the corridor, then descended the stairs and ducked around the back of the motel.

"Where are you going?"

She didn't slow. "To work out. I need something to refresh my brain." She opened the door to the motel's exercise room.

Her heart did a double flip and took off in a sprint. Micah was at the weight machine, looking buff and powerful in a T-shirt and sweat shorts. No wasted skin on *his* body. His teeth gritted, his face glistened with sweat as he sat, feet planted, and worked his beach muscles. As if they needed any assistance.

She dragged her attention off him and stood there, debating the wisdom of sticking around. Then again, she certainly wasn't going to fall into Micah's arms. She'd been kicked in the teeth once before, thank you. She had to keep her distance if she had any hope of escaping with her heart semi-intact. Besides, Conner was here.

She sat, pulled off her boots, and tied on Dannette's shoes.

She heard the weights on the machine grind, then fall into position.

Silence.

When she looked up, Micah was staring at her, an odd look on his face. Half smile, half intrigue. "Howdy."

"Hi." She stood up, stretching, painfully aware that both men were watching her as if they'd never seen a woman work out before. "Sorry to bother you. I just need to run a bit."

"No bother. Help yourself."

She heard him suck in a breath, then exhale as he lifted another round of reps.

Conner studied both of them. "Okay, I'm not staying. Aside from the fact that it smells like a year's worth of sweaty socks in here, I think you'll be safe, Lacey."

She looked at him, eyebrows up. Safe felt relative with Micah in the room, and frankly, she wasn't all that anxious for Conner to leave, but the door closed behind him before she could respond.

"How far do you run?"

Lacey turned. A trail of sweat tracked down Micah's temple. His black hair stood up in spikes, and whiskers layered his chin. He looked way, way too capable, painfully disarming. Safe, *oh sure*. She fought the memory of his arms around her and beelined for the treadmill. "Five miles." She set the speed and began at a warm-up pace.

Micah watched her a moment, then changed positions on the machine and began to work his biceps.

Lacey upped her speed, falling into a comfortable pace. Sweat beaded on her temple, and it felt somehow cleansing. "Conner seems nice. So do the rest of your friends. They were really kind to me at breakfast. Did you threaten them or something?"

Micah laughed, and the sound of it radiated warmth right to her bones. "No. They're just a great group. Dannette, Andee, and Sarah were all roommates at one time or another. Conner and Sarah are cousins, and the three of us were climbing buddies. Over the years we just added more. The fact that we all love Jesus seems to bind us together."

Lacey nodded, feeling like an outsider. She used to understand how it felt to share fellowship like Micah had with his friends. The memory threatened to turn her inside out. She pumped up her speed, deciding to push herself.

"You do this a lot?" Micah stood and grabbed a towel, rubbed it over his face.

"Run?" Her breath came out in bursts.

"Yeah."

"Every day if I can. It clears my head." Okay, so maybe this was too fast. She clicked the speed down.

He smiled. "Me too. I remember you used to ride to clear your head."

"Yeah, well, it's hard to take a horse on the road. Doesn't fit into the hotel room."

His smile dimmed, and he had a pained look in his eyes. "It hasn't been easy, has it?"

She shook her head, fearing the sudden threat of tears. She upped her pace and fought the surge of emotions. "I made my choices. I can't look back."

"It doesn't have to be this way," he said softly.

She focused on the whir of the machine and slap of her feet.

He sighed. "I thought about you, you know. When you were in Kuwait. I was in Bosnia most of that time, and just like you, sometimes at night I'd stare at the stars and think of you. Somehow knowing you were out there, doing your part to change the world . . . it felt comforting."

"You give me too much credit. I didn't do anything like you did." Conner's story whooshed back to her—along with the image of Micah carrying a bloodied little girl to a hospital. "I wish I'd been about saving lives."

"You were. It might have felt about money, but technology is the new arena of warfare and you were on the right side. The Ex-6 program could save hundreds of thousands of American lives, not to mention soldiers who count on secrecy."

"I'm sorry," she said, remembering his brush with betrayed information. The images that came to mind made her wince.

"Yeah, well, we knew we had a job to do. But it's never easy to lose a friend or a man under your command." He walked over to the mat, sat down, and laced his hands behind his head. "You keep going. You don't look back. If you second-guess every move, you become paralyzed. Sometimes it's simply taking one breath after another. You look to that breath, then the next, and you live on the hope that maybe your mission means something in the great scheme of things."

She suddenly burned to ask him. One breath after another—was that how he survived after her wedding? Because now that she thought about it, that was how she'd kept living the lies, long after the glitter of spy life had worn off. She'd focused on smiling, on believing that someday she and John might have a real life, a real family. Only now, her regrets had her by the throat, and she couldn't seem to even breathe, let alone live.

Sweat dripped off her chin as she topped three miles. She shook out her hands. "What will you do if you can't go back to your Green Beret team?"

Micah's eyes widened, and for a second she thought she saw something spark in them. "I don't know . . ." He stood, walked over to her. "Do you ever think about going home?"

Only every waking moment. She kept running, but he

turned down the speed. She braced her arms on the handles before she stumbled. "Why did you ask me that?"

"You need to come home to Ashleyville. With me."

She stared at him. "Micah, have you lost your marbles? I'm going to be a fugitive!"

"No, you won't. You'll give the kidnapper the corrupted program and report it to the NSA. Then you'll be free." He didn't say it, but she saw the hope in his eyes. *Free to be with me.* She felt suddenly weak and stepped off the treadmill, trembling.

It rattled her how badly she wanted the life she saw in Micah's eyes. He must have sensed it because he reached over and tucked her hair behind her ear. "Think about it."

Oh, how she wanted to come home to this man, to wake up each morning in his arms, to see him throw Emily in the air and love her like a father loved a daughter. He'd love her little girl; she knew it. She could envision Emily with her skinny arms wrapped around Micah's neck, could hear her call him Daddy. She turned away before her eyes filled.

Micah came up behind her. She stiffened. "We can start over. You can bury those demons. Find your spiritual footing again. Square what you know in your heart about God's faithfulness with the doubts you have in your brain. You've given in too long to Satan's lies, Penny. God loves you and wants you to come home."

"There was a time, Micah, when I would have agreed with you. I am not without dreams. I wanted Emily to have the life my parents gave me—a home, horses, green grass, and blue sky. Once I even tried to talk John into it." She faced Micah. "He told me that we could never go back. We knew too much about the world, about evil, to ever sit on our hands in Ashleyville."

She shook her head. "And I know too much about myself to believe God would let me go home. I'm not a fool. I read the newspapers too, and they weren't kind."

She saw Micah blink.

"'Local Woman Suspected in Slaying of Husband.'" She raised her eyebrows, remembering the headline on the AP wire. "Don't think for a second that it's going to be forgotten."

"I don't care," Micah said.

"Yeah, well, you should. If you really hope for a life beyond this moment, you should make sure you stay far away from me."

Micah felt ill at the broken look on Lacey's face. He reached out to her, but she jerked away. Her eyes swam with unshed tears, and she clenched her jaw.

How can I hope for any kind of life without you? He wanted to scream the words, but they wouldn't leave his locked chest. "Then we'll go somewhere else."

Her face twisted. "Yeah. You to Leavenworth and me to the gas chamber."

"You're being overdramatic."

"Am I?" She picked up a towel and scrubbed it over her face. "Well, maybe I am, but I'm telling you, I'm trouble."

"And I said I'm not afraid of trouble."

Her eyes sparked. She touched his jaw where she'd kicked him. "Really? Because I'm thinking that we both felt a little sick when I did this."

He swallowed hard, took her hand, and leaned into it. "I forgive you."

Her eyes glistened as she yanked her hand away. "Don't forgive me. Just forget me."

He saw the fight in her face, and her words came back to him: *"You're so cerebral, Micah."* Yeah, he'd spent the last fifteen years shoving his feelings into compartments, eating tactics, breathing duty because he knew that if he ever let his feelings out of the box, they might devour him. But . . . maybe it was time to open the box.

"I could easier forget to breathe," he said softly.

Her vulnerable expression decimated the last of his defenses. He cupped his hand around her neck and drew her close. He kissed her gently, fighting the desperation that seemed to well up inside him. Keeping her body away from him, she put her hands on his chest, her touch hesitant.

Oh, how I love her, Lord. Can't You fix this? When she made a small sound of acquiescence, something inside him gave way. *Oh, Lace.* She tasted of salt and sweet surrender; she fisted his shirt and stepped closer.

He put his arms around her, then pulled her into his embrace, not caring that they were both sticky with sweat. She laid her head against him, and he felt her relax. For sure she could hear his racing heart, feel him tremble.

"Besides, I promised not to forget you—ever. Remember?" he said.

She shuddered. "I'm so afraid you're going to get killed, just like John," she said in a voice nearly inaudible.

He groaned. "I'm not John."

She said nothing.

"We'll figure out a way to bring you and Emily home, Lucky Penny. I promise." *Please, Lord, let my words be true. Show me how to finally be the man Lacey needs.*

As Micah held her, feeling her hands dig into his shirt, he thought he heard a soft voice deep in his heart whisper, *Be still, and know that I am God.*

But he'd been still and silent for so many years. Wasn't it time for action?

Chapter 17

THIS WAS A bad idea. Lacey knew it in her gut. Yet the tugging to let Micah help shoulder her burden had wrapped around her heart until she felt nearly undone.

He hadn't forgotten her.

So Lacey stood among Micah's friends, listening to him describe the plan, watching his finger trace the outline of the map, check the ELT scanner, and clip it to his belt. Conner paced the room. Dannette sat on the bed, petting her bloodhound. Andee leaned against one wall, arms crossed over her petite frame.

Lacey could hear Sarah and Hank Billings arguing outside about his wanting to join them on their search, and it wasn't pretty. The tall forest ranger had appeared sometime in the late afternoon, carrying an armful of detailed topographical maps. He offered not only to help search but to let Micah use his four-wheeler, now loaded on a trailer behind a forest-service pickup.

Micah declined both offers but had invited the guy for coffee. Obviously, much to Sarah's chagrin.

Lacey knew how she felt. Micah wore his commando face and seemed to be bullying everyone around at the moment. She turned over the CD case, knowing her world was contained in this little padded square. She hoped the virus she'd implanted worked. As soon as whoever took Ex-6 downloaded the program, it would launch a worm that would slowly eat through the files, corrupting them more the longer he used them. She just hoped he wouldn't catch on until after Emily was safely secured. She could use a blip of hope right about now.

"Any word yet, Lacey?"

Lacey shook her head. She'd hoped to receive a message from the kidnapper soon about where to meet Emily, but it was already 10 p.m. "I'm going on record as saying that I think this is a bad idea. The more people involved, the greater chance for discovery. Micah, you could be leading your team into an ambush. We don't know how many people this guy has out there, and if he was working with Shavik, you know they play for keeps. They're not going to be armed with BB guns and jackknives."

"If Micah isn't seeing reality here, you should," she said to Conner. After surveying Conner's electronic setup—something Bill Gates and the NSA would envy—she'd discovered that he had spent much of the last decade working against groups like the Taliban, Hezbollah, Chul-Moo, and Hayata. She didn't know why Conner had left the commandos, but she counted on his inside knowledge to make Micah see the folly of diving into this situation with his brave but unarmed team. "Please listen to me."

Micah gave her a hard look. "Don't tempt me to lock you in the bathroom."

She opened her mouth, closed it. Fury had her by the throat.

"Okay, then I think we need to leave soon," Micah said. "But first I'm going to pray."

Conner opened the door and called out to Sarah. She

stomped in, shut the door on Hank. Lacey caught a glimpse of his baffled expression.

The group huddled up like a basketball team. Micah even knelt. The sight of Captain Jim Micah on his knees, humble before God, sent a strange spasm of warmth through her.

Lacey stood slightly away from the rest and locked her hands together, her eyes open, trying to set her heart to stone. It was getting more and more difficult to deny that God hadn't heard her feeble, foxhole prayers and sent in the A-team. *A* as in angels.

"Lord, You promise in Isaiah that You will be with us when we pass through difficult times. That You won't let them sweep us away. We need You now. You tell us that we are precious in Your sight. And we know Emily is. Because You love us, please act on our behalf. Deliver Emily from this situation and our secrets from terrorists' hands. If possible please deliver Lacey from this person who wants to destroy her life."

Lacey's throat thickened. That was like asking God to deliver her from herself. She'd been her own destroyer. Made her own choices. Shackled herself to evil.

"Lord, we call upon You for mercy, for wisdom, for power. Grant us a clear path tonight and hedge us in on all sides with Your protection. In Jesus' name . . ."

Amen, thought Lacey as she wiped a tear away. So much for her stonewalled heart.

Micah stood. "Let's roll."

Lacey rode between Dannette and Micah, squished like a prisoner. Conner, Andee, and Sarah followed, and behind them came Hank in his truck, hauling the four-wheeler. Lacey remembered Sarah specifically telling him he wasn't invited. Obviously Sarah had as much trouble getting Hank to take her seriously as Lacey did with Micah.

Micah's presence beside Lacey felt warm and solid,

despite the dread that radiated cold through her bones. They said little as they drove. Micah gave Dannette directions as she drove and asked Lacey three times if she'd gotten a call.

When they reached Service Road 20, Dannette cut north on a thin track between trees. Conner and his crew stayed on the road. "I hope you can get a signal here," Micah said.

Lacey took out the telephone, prompted by a sudden spurt of fear. The signal was faint but strong enough to receive a message.

They tracked farther into the tangle of woods. The moon had risen, cutting a silvery swath before them, beyond Dannette's headlights. The darkness that pressed in against the windows sent a shiver down to Lacey's toes. Emily was out there. Cold. Afraid. Alone.

Lacey knew exactly how she felt.

"Stop the truck," Micah said. Dannette rolled to a stop. "Okay, according to the map, this is the edge of Coward's Hollow." He folded the map, shoved it into a pocket in his black sweater. He had smeared black paint on his face, and he looked like a scary black-ops soldier.

Or maybe like the man who'd saved her life in Kazakhstan.

He strapped on a thick watch, a neck mic, and an earpiece, then shoved the transmitter inside another pocket in his sweater. "You contact me the minute he calls," he told Lacey and handed her another transmitter. "It's already 11:45, so it shouldn't be long. Where's the package?"

Lacey held out Ex-6 and barely let go when he grabbed it. "Micah," she said, knowing her emotions filled her eyes, "please be careful."

The stony look he'd given her since climbing into the truck softened. Just enough for her to glimpse the man she loved inside all that black paint and warrior exterior.

"Stay here. Please." He must have seen her fear for he touched her face with his gloved hand. "Lacey, remember the widow of Nain. God cares." She held his hand to her face, aching to believe him. "I'll bring back your daughter."

She nodded.

Then he slipped out into the night. He vanished into the bramble in a second.

She closed her eyes, reciting in her head the prayer he'd spoken: *"Grant us a clear path tonight and hedge us in on all sides with Your protection."*

Her telephone jangled. When she picked up, a voice emerged from the other end. "Mommy?"

Her heart stopped.

"Mommy, are you there?"

"Emily! Honey, are you okay?"

"Mommy!" her daughter screamed.

Lacey heard scuffling, then a slightly accented voice said, "Now you know she's alive. You have fifteen minutes to get to Swallows Cave. Drop Ex-6. Return to the truck. If it works, you'll get another call from me in thirty minutes telling you where to pick up your daughter."

What? *No.* "I want her now. You won't get Ex-6 until she's in my arms."

"Then say good-bye now."

She heard more scuffling. "Mommy!"

"Okay!" Lacey's throat closed, so she forced her voice through it. "Okay. Yes. It'll be there."

"Good. And don't bring company. I'll be watching and I want to see your pretty face as you betray your country."

Lacey glanced at Dannette. "Okay."

The line went dead. Lacey stared at the phone, her pulse nearly deafening.

"What did he say?" Dannette asked.

Lacey looked at her. "I gotta go. I'm sorry, Dannette, but Micah is only going to get us killed."

"No. Trust him. He knows what he's doing."

"Tell him to come back in. I'll meet you back at the truck." Lacey handed Dannette the receiver. "I also know what I'm doing."

But inside, her scream, the one that began years ago, revived and echoed through her empty soul.

Micah didn't have to go far to realize that Lacey was going to defy him. He hadn't really believed she would stay in the truck, but watching her stalk out into the night ripped a hole through his chest.

Was this how John felt when he saw Lacey appear in the warehouse, knowing that the woman he loved was about to sacrifice herself for him? Or had John even thought that far? John had been so much about himself, his own glory. Micah saw that clearly now.

Micah stole silently behind Lacey as she tracked north, using a flashlight, a topo map, and a compass. So maybe she *had* taken a survival training class. She moved like a cat through the woods, stepping over trees, around brush, tracking mostly by the light of the moon.

She finally crouched behind a downed tree length and checked her map. Then she tucked it away and pulled out a package.

The rabbit's foot? He frowned. There was no way he was going to let her become a traitor without duking it out with her. He scrambled toward her and leaped to tackle her when she sprang out from behind a tree.

Lacey whirled, then aimed a kick at his shoulder. He dodged and pinned her, breathing hard. She pushed against him. "Leave me, Micah. Please."

"Never," he hissed. "What are you up to?"

She shoved him away. "Promise you'll stay here?"

He shook his head.

Frustration flashed across her face. "If you care about me or Emily at all, you'll stay here." She got up and tucked the rabbit's foot into her pocket. "Give me the CD case."

He fished it out of his belt pouch and handed it to her. "I have eyes on you at all times. You get into trouble, I'm not staying put. That's my promise."

She swallowed, and he thought he saw a flicker of pain in her eyes. "Don't get us killed."

Then she turned and sprinted for a chert, a slice of limestone in the folds of a long ridge known as Swallows Cave. She crouched at the entrance, looked around, and dropped the CD case. She spun around, as if to sprint back.

A shot chipped off the rock right above her head.

Lacey dived into the darkness.

Micah was on his feet, pulse roaring. It was a trap. Whoever was after Lacey's program had no intention of letting her live.

Another shot.

Micah searched for the shooter, but he didn't have his night visions or even a shotgun to scope through. "Get out of there!" he yelled toward Lacey.

A barrage of shots flaked off wood over his head. He hit the ground, army-crawled toward the cave entrance. "Lacey, are you okay?"

Nothing.

His heart climbed into his throat. Why hadn't she stayed

in the truck? He was poised to leap into the cave when another shot clipped the air. His shoulder burned, a pain so sharp it swiped his breath, his every thought. He went down, not sure where he was hit, fighting through the folds of shadow and gulping in air.

"Mommy!"

He pushed himself to his elbows, clenching his teeth against agony.

Emily had stepped out of the cave, her face white. *No, Lacey!* But he couldn't push the words out through the pain. Micah's gaze fixed on a light, then on the silhouette of a little girl holding a teddy bear.

Mommy!" she screamed again.

Lacey stepped away from the cave entrance, hands up. Like a sacrificial offering. Her face was stoic and she spoke calmly. "Mommy's here, honey. Don't cry."

"I thought you were told not to bring anyone with you," came a voice from the shadows. An accent-laden voice.

Lacey didn't flinch. "He followed me. I didn't invite him."

That much was true. Micah crawled out of his position, got to his knees, and struggled to flank the speaker. The pain had released him, adrenaline cutting off the nerves to his brain and reducing the wound to a gnawing burn. He picked up speed.

"Do you have Ex-6?"

Micah heard Lacey say, "It's in the entrance to the cave."

"Good. Go back to your truck."

Micah glanced at her. She was barely outlined by the moonlight, but her expression could stop a small army. "Not without my daughter."

"If you want her to live, you'll leave."

Micah could see the shadow now. His blood went cold in

his veins when it cocked a handgun and pressed it against the little girl's head.

Lacey was right; Emily looked just like John. Blonde hair, cute, pug nose. He shoved his feelings into a hard ball to deal with later and forced himself to move behind the man.

"Please, I've given you what you want. Let her go."

A bitter laugh came from beyond the shadow, and it razed Micah's nerves. "Should I trust you? Like John did?"

Micah eased closer.

"Go home, Lacey. Or I'll deliver your daughter in a body bag."

Micah leaped. He tackled the shooter as Emily ran, screaming. A shot, and Micah heard Lacey yell. The shooter turned, cuffed him across the forehead. The blow made him see white.

Another shot, and this time Micah felt it in his leg—wet and hot. He groaned but held on to the struggling figure. "Run, Lacey!" He felt something rake his head and blinked against the pain.

"Don't let her get away!" The man under Micah yelled to his partner and threw him off.

Micah faced the sky and saw the buttstock of a Colt Commando assault rifle arrow toward his face. He rolled. It landed in the dirt. His assailant swore when Micah grabbed his ankle. He tried to rise, but his leg wasn't working, and the butt came down on his wounded shoulder. He howled in agony. *Run, Lacey!*

The last thing Micah saw was a foot aiming for his head.

Lacey scooped up Emily, put her on her hip, turned, and sprinted. She heard Micah howling in the background, but her legs churned as she put distance between herself and the Korean on her tail.

The same large Korean who'd brought her the cell phone in the hospital. And on the train.

Idiot, idiot! She couldn't believe she'd not processed these info bytes before now.

"Mommy!" Emily screamed. Her arms and legs wrapped around Lacey's body in a death clench.

Lacey tucked Emily's head in close, protecting her from the slap of brush. She felt a trickle of blood on her chin as a branch caught her mouth, but she'd memorized her path and ran with surety. The sound of crashing behind her diminished. Along with Micah's howl.

She ran faster, hoping to outrun her grief. She reached the truck and piled in. "Go, Go!"

Dannette stared at her. "Where's Micah?"

"Go!" Lacey crushed Emily's body close, every nerve rippling. In a couple seconds she was going to unravel.

"We'll wait for him."

Lacey reached over and put the truck into drive. "Go. Micah's dead." She grabbed the wheel with one hand and crunched the gas pedal. They shot up the path.

Dannette pushed Lacey's arm away, then kicked her leg. She was visibly shaken. But when a shot pinged her truck, she floored it. In the container in back, her dog let out a barrage of barks and growls.

They careened through the forest in silence until they hit Service Road 20. Conner was there, his lights bathing the road. Dannette slammed on the brakes, breathing hard. Tears glazed her eyes as she stared at Lacey. "Dead?"

Lacey could barely speak past her heart jammed in her throat. "He took the shooter out so Em and I could get away."

She'd wanted to scream when she saw him go down, but going after him without protecting Emily first would destroy everything he'd sacrificed his life for. She put her daughter away from her, held her face in her hands, and examined her. "Are you okay, honey?"

Emily sobbed. Lacey gathered her in as Conner and Sarah approached. Andee remained in the pickup talking into the radio, her big brown eyes on Lacey. If she was trying to raise Micah, she'd only get static. Lacey had seen someone shoot him at least once. If not twice.

Lacey closed her eyes and fought the darkness closing in on her.

Chapter 18

"DANNETTE, YOU TAKE Sherlock and see if you can pick up Micah's trail. Andee, you track with Dannette and take the first-aid kit." Conner had suddenly morphed from goofball to general.

Lacey watched, nearly numb, as Conner moved into action, barking orders like Micah or perhaps the officer he'd been. "Sarah, check out Emily. Lacey, I need you to tell me everything. Leave nothing out."

Lacey felt the devastation and tried to find words that might explain Micah's death.

Sarah took Emily from her arms, and Lacey couldn't bear to meet her eyes. But there was compassion on her face. "He'll be okay, Lacey. He's a fighter."

Lacey didn't argue, even though she knew the kind of men Ishmael Shavik had worked for. Horror speared her soul. She should have never, ever called Micah. Her selfishness had cost another man his life. She wrapped her arms around herself, holding back the urge to writhe from the inside out.

Conner crouched before her and put his hands on his knees. "What happened?"

She shook her head. "I should have said no. What was I thinking? I should have never called him—"

"Calm down," Conner interrupted. "Micah's no dummy. He's a Special Forces captain with years of training. Now, if we want to find him, we need you to get past your guilt and focus on hope. Take a deep breath."

Lacey concentrated on his eyes. When she saw no indictment in them, it nourished the wounded places inside. "Okay."

"Tell me what happened."

"I don't know. I left the package where he instructed, and suddenly someone started shooting. As if it were an ambush. Micah yelled and I think he was shot. Then I saw Emily." She laced her shaking hands together. Some operator she was. Falling apart on the spot. She glanced at her daughter, who was draped in a blanket and being soothed by Sarah's gentle touch.

"The kidnapper told me he was going to shoot Emily, so I thought if I could just get him to shoot me instead maybe she'd run, or Micah could grab her. Somehow I thought Micah would read my mind and he'd move around behind him. And I think that's what he did. Only . . . Emily ran to me, and Micah tackled him. And . . . he . . ." She closed her eyes. "Micah told me to run. . . ."

Conner touched her cheek. "Okay, listen. You did the right thing. Emily matters first. Micah walked in there of his own choosing. We'll find him." He stood. "Dannette, you ready?"

Dannette stood by the truck, holding her keys. "Yes. I'm driving back up to the LKP. I'll give Sherlock the scent there."

"I'm going with you." Lacey walked over to the pickup.

"Hardly. I know what I'm doing." Dannette's eyes flashed anger. "Thanks, but you've done enough damage."

Lacey froze. The accusation speared her. Maybe she'd been right in guessing that Dannette and Micah had a relationship. She forced an even tone, pushing past the guilt. "Yes, I have. But I know where we were, and if you want Sherlock to pick up Micah's trail, that's a good place to start. Micah may still be there."

Lacey saw sadness flicker across Dannette's face, but she ignored the twist in her heart. If Micah made it out of here alive, he deserved to have someone like Dannette who could love him and never endanger his life.

"Get in," Dannette said.

Lacey nodded. Then she turned and ran to Emily, who was sitting on Sarah's lap. Fat tears ran down her face. "Emily, Mommy is going to look for a brave man who tried to help us. I will be *right back*. Sarah will take care of you, okay?"

Emily's lower lip shook. "No, Mommy."

Lacey touched her daughter's cheek. "Yes. I promise I'll come back. *I promise*."

Emily's big eyes traced hers. "Okay."

Sarah cuddled her. "I'll take good care of her," she said to Lacey.

Lacey could hardly speak when she climbed in the truck between Andee and Dannette. They drove up the service road in silence. She'd have a hard time cutting the tension in the truck with a chain saw.

"Stop here," Lacey suddenly ordered.

"No, we were farther," Dannette argued.

Lacey shook her head. "See that indentation in the ground and the scrape of dirt? Those are your tire tracks."

Dannette stopped the pickup. "I'll get Sherlock. There are flashlights in the back. And a first-aid kit."

A first-aid kit wouldn't begin to touch Micah's injuries. Still, Lacey couldn't help but feel hope as they quickly filled the pack and grabbed flashlights. "Follow me," she said and marched into the forest.

The light transected the darkness and showed a few

broken branches where either she or her tail had parted the wilderness. She followed her trail and found the place where Micah had lain as she crept to the chert in the rock.

She crouched and her pulse filled her ears when she saw blood soaked into the leaves.

Andee pulled up beside her and said nothing.

Dannette let Sherlock take a whiff. "He can start tracking from here."

Lacey climbed over the log, eased up to Swallows Cave, painfully aware that whoever had ambushed her could still be lurking. Nothing happened as she scanned her light over the cave entrance.

But the CD case was gone.

She stood at the entrance. "They were over here," she said, shining her light toward the place where she'd seen Emily illuminated, her eyes big, her little body trembling.

The urge to find the kidnapper and do something very, very painful to him clutched her. No one should be allowed to scare a child. *Ever.* Lacey closed her eyes, fighting a surge of rage.

Find Micah. His howl of agony rang in her mind. She opened her eyes and ran toward his last known position.

Dannette met her there. Sherlock was off his leash, wearing his shabrack, and sniffing.

"See the broken branches and the matted dirt?" Dannette said. "Micah was here."

Lacey flicked her flashlight over the forest. Dark splatters on the leaves and a trail of damp ground. "And he was bleeding badly."

Sherlock alerted, two short barks.

"He's found the trail," said Dannette. "Find!" she yelled to the dog.

Sherlock took off through the forest.

Dannette followed, then Andee and Lacey. Lacey heard the ladies cutting through the bramble ahead of her, but she'd gone numb. Micah wasn't here. Which meant, if he was still alive, he might be in the hands of . . . whom?

They emerged to another road. Andee ran her flashlight over her map. "This one isn't marked on the map."

"It looks like an old logging road, from the grass cover and deep ruts." Dannette pointed her light on the strip of grass where Sherlock ran to and fro, his nose down.

"What's he doing?" Lacey asked.

"Trying to reacquire the scent. My air-tracking dog might be able to locate Micah if he was on a vehicle, but even then the smell of exhaust would decay the human scent." Dannette crouched to study the grass. "Looks like a four-wheeler. These tracks aren't wide enough for a pickup."

Lacey watched the dog for another minute. She keyed her radio. "Search to Base."

Sarah's voice responded. "Base. Come in Search."

"Your buddy Hank still around, Sarah?"

Static. Then, "He's not my buddy. But yeah."

"Tell him to follow the service road we took. It should intersect with an old logging road. And tell him to bring the GPS. Micah has an ELS on him. If he's still alive, he'll have activated it." Her voice faltered on "if he's still alive." She closed her eyes. *Please, God.*

But despite her inklings that God had sent Micah, there was no way He was going to listen to her now. She'd messed things up and let her impulses grab ahold of common sense by giving in to the small, compelling urge to let Micah come to her rescue. She just hoped they could find him before whoever took Ex-6 discovered the virus.

She had no doubt that Micah's life—if he still lived—was a ticking clock.

Dannette called her dog and rubbed her hand over his head. "Good job, buddy. We'll find him."

"Copy that, Search," Sarah said, affirming Lacey's plan. "Base out."

Lacey tapped the receiver against her knee. "Please, Micah, stay alive."

✦ ✦ ✦

Micah felt like a deer carcass, strapped to the back of the four-wheeler as it roared through the forest. His wrists burned against taped bonds, and he fought the blindfold that cut into his eyes. Every jolt speared him anew; every rut that sent them into the air threatened to drive his teeth through his skull. It took all his focus to muscle through the fog of darkness and pain to stay conscious.

At least all this pain meant he was alive. And the one thought that saved him was the gut feeling that Emily was safe.

Emily *and* Lacey.

The four-wheeler hit a bump, screamed through the air. When they landed, Micah's head banged on the fender. He saw white light and gritted his teeth. *Focus on staying awake.*

They skidded to a halt. Rough hands yanked him to a sitting position. "On your feet."

Micah didn't even have the strength to lash out at the voice so he let himself be shoved over to a pickup. He was thrown into the back, and the tailgate was closed. The smell of dirt and oil curdled his nose, making his misery acute. He curled into a ball and let the pain suck him under.

He awoke—or thought he awoke—to darkness. He tried to

open his eyes, but they seemed glued shut. Panic rose inside and he fought it, centered on his heartbeat, and took an assessment. He was still bound: his hands behind his back, his ankles together, tape over his eyes. His leg burned, but he could move it, so it wasn't broken. He lay on his side, his wounded shoulder facing up, and when he took a breath, the pain was so sharp he had to stifle a gasp. He strained to hear past his racing pulse and made out two voices, one barking orders. They were talking about . . . Ex-6?

"It doesn't work." The voice was accented.

"Why?" This voice sounded familiar, and it nudged a memory—one he couldn't quite grasp.

"Everything I've tried to decode has returned corrupted. She double-crossed you."

Micah heard swearing, shattering glass.

Then his skin prickled when a breath cascaded over his ear. "You're so pitiful, you know that? If only you knew the woman you risked your life for." The contempt in the voice raised another flint of recollection. *Who?*

Micah swallowed a retort.

"Oh, so you're awake, huh?" A short laugh, no—a burst of satisfaction. "You know she planned this, don't you? I hope you don't think your little agent girlfriend is trustworthy."

"She won't give you what you want," Micah snarled. Would she? Or would she abandon him to his fate? She had warned him, practically begged him not to follow her. He deserved what he got, right?

"Yes, she will. Because it's all part of the plan. And she'll tell your friends that she doesn't want to cause the death of another man."

"That was an accident," Micah growled.

"Oh, was it? Were you there? Did you see her try and trade John's life for a profit?"

Micah was silent, furious at himself.

"Oh yes, she knew we'd double-cross John. She wanted a piece of the action."

"She was trying to save John."

"Then why did she let him go in the first place? She met him at the hotel before our meeting. If she told him he was compromised, why did he go? Do you think he didn't know we'd have him killed?"

Micah tried to close his ears, but questions churned in the deep places, where he'd buried them over the past three days.

"Have you ever considered that Mrs. Lacey Montgomery *wanted* her husband to be killed? That maybe she had a better offer? One we've been waiting to cash in on for years? Oh yes, pal, we had this planned from day one. She and I. She knew the money we'd make, hand over fist, with the gasification process, and when it went south it was your Lacey who hatched the new plan . . . the one involving Ex-6.

"She was the one who told us where she'd be traveling; she was the one who set up the plan for a kidnapping. She was the one who wanted to barter her daughter for Ex-6 because if she got caught, she'd have a credible defense. And she was the one who decided to call you since we were never sure if you saw me or not back in that warehouse in Kazakhstan, and we didn't want any loose ends."

"I don't believe you. The text message said 'No Jim Micah.'"

"That was her idea. She knew the one way to get you involved was to keep you shut out. Tell me, how did you find out? Did she tell you, or did you sneak the information off her?"

Micah remembered that moment in the truck. To her stirring just as he took the cell phone out of her pocket. To her stillness as he read the messages. No, she wouldn't have . . .

except, if she had the same training he had, she would have jostled with the first nudge in her pocket. More than that, she wouldn't have kept such a valuable piece of equipment in her pocket, where it could be easily lifted. Truth felt like a sword dissecting his heart.

"She's been neck deep in this the entire time. And she'll act like she's bargaining for your life. When, in truth, she's just playing a part. Delivery girl. And in turn, she'll end up with a wad of cash in her offshore account, a new identity, and the gratitude of North Korea."

Micah felt kicked right in the heart. No, she hadn't used him. Couldn't have faked her feelings in the pickup, the way she'd kissed him, or her tears over her daughter.

Only she was a career spy. Someone trained in deception. He fought a rush of hot fury—at himself for believing her and at her for using his own heart as a weapon against him.

"If you think she cares if you live or die . . . well, you're more gullible than John Montgomery was. He might have been a two-timing snake of a husband, but he married a black widow."

✛ ✛ ✛

Dawn bruised the sky as Lacey tracked back on the four-wheeler to Service Road 20. She'd been up and down every logging road, every dent in the forest. No Jim Micah.

Which meant that he was either dead and didn't hear her or had been taken by the people who had taken Emily.

She felt emptied and hollow as she pulled up to the huddle of vehicles. Conner leaned against his truck, his arms folded across his chest, pushing the dirt with his foot. Dannette held Sherlock's lead. Sarah and Emily were sleeping in the cab of Conner's truck.

Hank strode up to her. "Anything?"

She shook her head.

"You're tired. Maybe I should have a go."

Lacey got off the four-wheeler. "No. He's gone. They took him; I feel it in my bones."

Andee climbed out of Dannette's truck, then slammed the door. The noise frightened a flock of crows to flight. A chilly, early morning breeze stirred the trees. "What should we do now?" Fatigue lined her pretty face. She'd tied her hair back with a bandanna, and the effect had made her look even more petite. More pretty. Lacey had a hard time believing this woman could muscle a helicopter into submission.

"I don't know." Lacey scrubbed her hands down her face. "If they have Ex-6, it won't take them long to figure out it doesn't work. And then I don't know what they'll do to Micah."

"We're going back to Poplar Bluff," Conner said. "You still have the cell phone, right?"

Lacey felt for it in her pocket. Just to confirm, she checked. No new messages.

"Why don't you ride with me, okay?" Conner didn't elaborate as he walked around to the passenger side, but Lacey had a sick feeling it had to do with Dannette and the fact that Lacey had led the man Dannette loved into danger.

And here she'd been thinking she and Micah might have had a future. Fool. Fool! That's what happened when she'd started to listen to Micah's words of faith with her heart instead of her head.

She felt brittle as Conner lifted a sleeping Emily out of Sarah's arms.

"I have an older model truck. No air bags. Emily can sit in the front seat," Conner said when Lacey peeked in, glancing for a backseat.

Sarah awoke and shot a questioning look at Conner. He shook his head, and her face fell. "Sarah, would you mind riding with Hank or Dannette?"

Lacey wasn't surprised when she opted for the lady's truck. Conner slid Emily into the middle of his cab and buckled her in. Lacey climbed in beside her, holding her close. When Conner pulled away, leading the caravan, she stared into the dark forest and felt her worst fears unhinge.

She'd killed Jim Micah.

She pulled her daughter tight and closed her eyes. Conner said nothing. Lacey didn't know whether his silence stemmed from fury or a desire to protect her.

As if she deserved protection.

The ride to Poplar Bluff seemed like a blink. They arrived just as sunlight emblazoned the store windows. Lacey cradled Emily in her arms and trudged up to the motel room.

Dannette said nothing as she opened the door to the women's room and let them inside. After Lacey tucked Emily into one of the double beds, she sat at the end and hung her head in her hands. She felt empty. Like a hole had been scooped out of her chest where her heart had once been. She began to shake, forced herself to settle down, and walked over to the sink. She splashed water on her face, then scrubbed it hard with a towel.

She heard Dannette leave, quietly shutting the door behind her.

Lacey slid down into a ball, knees up, and buried her head in her arms. *I'm so, so sorry, Micah. I told you; didn't I tell you?* Her eyes burned.

From across the room, her cell phone trilled.

She leaped for it, crawling then finding her feet and digging it out on the third ring.

TEN TONIGHT.

TUNNEL BLUFF CAVE.

NO COMPANY.

BRING THE REAL EX-6.

OR JIM MICAH DIES.

She stared at the message with a mixture of euphoria and disbelief. Micah was still alive, right? Hope felt too raw, but she closed her eyes and held on anyway. *Please, God, don't let Micah pay for my mistakes.* This time she didn't care if she didn't deserve to throw her requests at God. Micah deserved it.

She got up, checked her daughter, then headed for the door. Conner was leaning against the outside rail, talking to Dannette in low tones. Their conversation must have been serious because they stopped talking, and Conner straightened, frowning. "What?"

"He's alive. And they want the real Ex-6. Or they're going to kill him."

"That's not an option."

"I know." She looked down at the text message. "I'm not going to let them kill Micah."

"I mean, giving them the real Ex-6." Conner crossed his arms. "I can't let you do that. Micah and I had a chitchat before we left. He told me that under no circumstances was I to let you hand over Ex-6. Ever."

Lacey stared at him, seeing the soldier he'd once been.

"Micah swore to protect his country with his life. And he'll do that. He would die before he'd let another country tap into America's secrets." Conner narrowed his eyes. "I would think you took the same oath."

Lacey glanced at Dannette, who wore a half frown. "I did. But I can't let them kill Micah . . . I love him."

"You have a fine way of showing it," Dannette said.

"Excuse me, but do you know anything about this? Do you know that I tried to leave him three times, that I practically begged him not to come along?"

"If you know anything about Jim, he doesn't take no for an answer. A better option would have been not to drag him into this at all. You don't put a person's life in danger if you love him."

Lacey clenched her jaw, but she couldn't help noticing pain and guilt roaming in Dannette's eyes. She might love Micah, but Lacey had a low, gut feeling that there was something more behind the way Dannette's eyes filmed over. Dannette held her shaking hand to her mouth and turned away.

"She's just . . . well, Dannette knows what it is to lose someone," Conner said.

Dannette turned back, and tears furrowed her cheeks. "I'm sorry, Lacey. I shouldn't have yelled at you. I'm just afraid for Micah. But inside I know he would be so overjoyed that you have Emily back. That would be enough for him." She put her hand to her mouth again. "Forgive me."

Words left Lacey. How could Dannette even consider apologizing to Lacey when she was the one who had made the mistakes? Dannette was right. If she loved Micah, why had she called him? "I . . . uh, of course." She frowned, watching Dannette shuffle along the deck to the stairs.

Conner watched her go. "You can't hand over Ex-6."

Lacey folded her arms, leaned against the railing. "What am I going to do, Conner?" She heard the despair in her voice but didn't care. "I'm trapped. I've loved Micah so long he's embedded in my heart. I can't let him die. John's death tore me apart. Micah's would destroy me."

Conner touched her arm, and something in his expression

felt like Micah. Strong. Wise. "There has to be an answer. And maybe God led you to us to help you find it."

She studied him. A young man, maybe in his early thirties. He had lines of stress around his eyes, betraying that maybe he'd seen too much in his life. Sarah too wore the expression of strain. And Dannette seemed acquainted with grief. Again, she considered that yes, maybe God had sent her to Micah's Team Hope. Proving that . . . what? God still cared? The idea left her mouth dry.

Lacey licked her lips and nodded. "Okay. I have an idea."

Chapter 19

"WHY DO THEY call you Sparks?" Lacey was bent over Conner's keyboard, typing.

"Oh, just a wee bit of magic I did while in training at Robin Sage," Conner answered from his perch on his bunk in the back of his truck. "We were trying to get a sat link, but our equipment was damaged. We snuck into the terrorist's camp, and I snatched their shortwave. But while I was soldering wires to the board, I sort of . . . started a small fire that turned into a major conflagration that ended with us getting caught."

When she glanced at him, he shrugged but wore a grin. "Anyway, the name stuck. I'm pretty good at communications though."

"I see that." She pulled the rabbit's foot off her track pants and snapped it apart.

"Is that one of those micro hard drives?"

"Yeah. A USB pendant. It's got the Ex-6 program on it." She plugged it into his USB port.

"Why did you give the kidnapper the CD-ROM?"

"Because it can get lost . . . or damaged, right?" She smirked. "Now the other little gem." She extracted a small compact from her bag.

"Is that what I think it is?" Conner reached over, as if mesmerized.

"Don't touch. It's a prototype. PCMCIA card, aka the Ex-6 hardware. It attaches to your external plug-in port." She found the fitting for the PCMCIA slot, then plugged in the card. "Voilà, instant enigma machine." The program loaded, and she plugged her telephone via a cable into another USB port.

"Why didn't you give the guy that?"

"He didn't ask for it." Again, she smiled.

"Micah should have trusted you," Conner said starkly.

Lacey's heart dropped an inch. "Yeah, well, he had his reasons. Besides, I'm fully planning to give them what they asked for, so don't forgive me too fast."

"But what I don't get is if you do, doesn't the NSA have a copy of the program, rendering the copy you give these guys useless?"

"No. Not if their purpose in sending the information is to see who's watching," Lacey answered. "Even if the NSA did use their copy of Ex-6 to pull apart the messages, the sender would know that the message had been compromised. And this would be enough to keep the sender out of NSA's sights or whoever else might be trailing them."

"So the value is more in the fact that they can assess who is watching and take appropriate precautions."

"Virtually making whoever is using it impossible to find."

"Especially if the whoever is already a rogue and a deadly terrorist group like Hayata."

"Which makes the fact that Ishmael Shavik tailed me all these years downright chilling." Lacey finished downloading her messages from the telephone onto Ex-6.

"But you're still giving them Ex-6?" Conner's eyes glinted.

Lacey couldn't look at him. "I have no choice."

He took a deep breath. "Okay, let's just assume for a second that I'm going to let you do that. What's your brilliant plan?"

"I'm hoping to use the Ex-6 decryption program to uncover the source code from these text messages and maybe trace it back to its original IP. It might lead to some answers, some way to outflank them."

"If the messages were sent from a computer."

"If they were sent from a cell phone, we'll get the originating number. From there, we can trace it to the right owner." She drummed her fingers on the desk. "Quite the setup you have here."

"Digital television, wireless connections. I keep improving it."

"Why did you leave the commandos? Micah said you were one of his best men."

A shadow crossed Conner's face. He looked away, and for the second time she saw a facet of Conner that wasn't dead serious or all games. Grief. It nearly consumed his expression. She swallowed, recognizing the hues.

"My brother was murdered a year ago. I came home to settle his affairs on leave and decided not to re-up."

Lacey frowned, knowing there was more but deciding not to pry. Again, it niggled at her that God may have picked this group—one comprised of members who had their own secrets—for a reason. But digging for that reason might take more time and energy than she could muster with Micah fighting for his life because of her. "Did they catch the person who did it?"

Conner stared at his feet, his lips pursed. "I don't know if they ever will. The case is pretty cold. They think it was a drug shooting, but I don't think so."

"I'm sorry."

"Yeah, me too." He gave her a slight smile. "Micah told me about Kazakhstan. About John."

Lacey studied the keyboard. "I figured he did. Your expression all but blared it in the café. Did Micah also tell you I was accused of murdering my husband?"

"Yeah. Micah looked into it for a while, he said. But then he got a call telling him you were guilty and to keep out of it."

Lacey nodded. "I called him."

Conner went very, very still.

"I knew he was getting too close. John believed that there was someone inside the company we were working for who was compromising our agents. There were two killed the month before John in an operation very similar to ours where industrial secrets were sold. I admit, my suspicions ran more toward the man we supposedly worked for, but either way, I didn't want Micah ending up a casualty too. Especially if I was wrong. I was afraid if Micah got in too deep, he'd start making that someone mad."

"And get killed." Conner searched her eyes.

She nodded, and her throat felt thick. "So much for my good intentions."

"Micah also said you have a black hole where your faith was."

She flinched. "That was especially nice of him."

Conner gave her a half grin. "Well, he was trying to show you he loved you by going in your place to the cave. But, well, I guess that backfired."

Lacey just stared at him, blinking. Micah loved her? "Why didn't he tell me?"

"I don't know, Lacey. Maybe he thought actions were better than words."

"The sad part is that I knew that. Deep in my heart, I knew he loved me. But I accused him of being an ice man—void of feelings."

"He's got feelings. Just has a hard time vocalizing them."

Her throat prickled. "I don't deserve him. I've made so many mistakes. Since the day Micah walked away from me at my senior prom, I've been trying to get his attention, prove my life was better without him. I've only made a mess of it. And now I'm trapped. Even if he gets out of this, I still have shadows. Secrets. I'm shackled to my mistakes."

The look of pity on Conner's face made her want to cringe. "I know. That's the thing, Lacey—we all do. That's what being a sinner is all about. We can't help but make mistakes. And we wind up shackled to them, paying the price. But Jesus unlocks those prisons. Isaiah 61 says that Jesus came to release us from darkness. It's more than just salvation—it's restoration. I think of a dungeon. There we are, sitting in our filth, wasting away, and Jesus flings open that door, comes into our prison, despite our stench, lifts us up, and carries us up the stairs to the sunlight."

She pictured it, how it might feel to be picked up and carried out. She flinched when she saw her wounds, her filth, her stench revealed, nearly overpowering, as she reached the daylight.

"It doesn't end there," Conner continued. He leaned forward, his hands clasped. "Isaiah says that God gives us beauty for ashes, joy instead of mourning, praise instead of despair. It's not just salvation; it's transformation. It's God redeeming our reputation, giving us overflowing mirth in our hearts, clothing us with a countenance of rejoicing instead of grief. We are not merely set free; we're washed and given an entire new body, an entire new life.

"That's what Jesus meant when He said, 'I—yes, I alone—am the one who blots out your sins for my own sake and will never think of them again.' You are completely new in His eyes because of His amazing love for you."

Completely new. Lacey swallowed the burning ache to believe Conner's words, to cry out like Micah said.

"You can't solve this by yourself. But God can. That's what hope is all about. Letting God do what seems impossible."

There were so many impossibilities here, she didn't know where to start asking. Or even if she should. As Lacey debated, she saw a dialog box appear on her screen. "We're in."

Thankful to extricate herself from the feelings that threatened to swamp her, she typed in the keystrokes that would unlock the code. She'd designed the system to reveal both the transmission path, or source code, and the message. In this case, the message was decoded. But the source code scanned down two pages. Lacey scrolled to the bottom. "This is from a government server."

"What?"

"Yeah. Whoever sent this routed it through a government IP. I recognize the subnet address."

"You think it's someone in . . . what? The Department of Defense? The NSA?"

Lacey shook her head. "I've thought of that more than once. Like, why didn't the kidnapper ask for the prototype? Anyone who knows anything about quantum encryption knows you need software *and* hardware." That omission had been bothering her for more than three days. Ex-6 was useless without the prototype, which the NSA didn't know she had. She'd developed her own in the NSA lab and given them a copy, while smuggling out the original. Gut-instinct insurance.

"Is it operational?" Director Berg had asked her in the

hospital. She'd answered yes. And after that she had received the kidnapping call. . . .

She opened up a new page. Her fingers hovered above the keyboard as she considered obliterating her last wall of defense. Once she went online, she would trigger a NSA trace—one that could lead Roland Berg right to her doorstep. She had no illusions that this time the NSA wouldn't stop with flimsy handcuffs and a don't-worry-we'll-be-nice speech.

Lacey took a deep breath, then logged on to the Internet, typed in the keystrokes, and accessed an online data-storage cache. "In the early days, I did some of my work at NSA HQ and learned how the government server cycles its passwords. I wrote a program to assess them."

She watched Conner's computer download a program from the cache. "It'll get us in the server, and I can take a look around."

Conner stared at her with a look of pure wonder. "Okay, who are you?"

Lacey grinned. "I have a PhD in a couple subjects. That helps. But in your world, I'm a hacker. A good one."

"I knew I liked you." He stood behind her, one hand on the back of her chair.

The program opened, and two minutes later Lacy was inside the server. "Every message has a message ID. And those identities are stored in an ID log." She scrolled down the list of message ID numbers, looking for her message. "Here." She pointed to the screen. A few keystrokes later, she read the user ID: *FHillman.*

Frank Hillman. She fought her quickening breath.

"Who is F. Hillman?" Conner asked, unaware that her world was sliding out from under her feet. She *knew* it. In the pit of her stomach, she knew she'd been correct.

"More importantly," Lacey said in a quiet voice, "why would Frank Hillman have an IP address inside a NSA server?"

"And Frank Hillman is . . . ?"

"He was my boss in Kuwait. I thought he was a businessman, but in my heart I knew he was an international thief and a murderer. I think he framed me for John's murder."

She noted Conner's grim expression. "Let's see what kind of mail he's been sending, shall we?"

She sorted the list according to user ID and discovered only three text messages. The ones he'd sent her. Frank Hillman obviously didn't use this address for normal business correspondence.

"Wait." Conner tapped his finger on the screen. "Hillman Oil. The newspaper said the rig that caused the train wreck was from Hillman Oil."

Lacey paused. "Okay, let's search Hillman Oil." She googled the name. A listing came back. She scrolled down it and opened a few pages of information. "His company's grown. I thought it was destroyed after the Kazakhstan incident. It's worldwide now."

"Pakistan. Afghanistan. Kazakhstan."

She glanced at Conner. "A Korean man chased me through the woods. . . ."

"Look at this one." Conner gestured to a link on the screen.

Lacey opened it and read: *Hillman named to EPA Congressional Committee for consideration of gasification laws.* She closed her eyes, pinched her nose with her fingers. "It can't be."

"What?"

She shook her head. "This is unthinkable."

"What?" Conner's voice undulated with frustration.

"He's doing the same thing he did in Kuwait. Why?"

Conner leaned back, his face contorted. "I am so not following you here at all, Lacey. Please clue me in."

"Here's the rundown. Hillman Oil is a mining and refinery company, meaning it does both the extracting and refining of the crude. Refining is the process of breaking oil into usable parts. The problem is that there's a lot of waste, even in the most advanced processes. Frank Hillman's company designed a system—on paper—called gasification that would use that waste, plus regular household waste, to create syngas. Syngas is the building block of many types of fuel. In theory, a great way to recycle waste, right?"

Conner shrugged, and she had the feeling she'd lost him. "Imagine that you had a plant in town where you could take all your waste, then turn it into gasoline. No more wars with Iraq and Iran or deals with Arabia. No more posturing for control of the oil-producing regions or tankers dumping oil into our oceans. Gas created out of nothing but our own household waste. Of course, we're talking all waste—from cans to paper to plastic, so forget about recycling, but still, gasoline for our cars, right?"

Conner's eyes lit up. "Okay, now I'm tracking."

"The trade-off is this: your breathable air, your potable water. We didn't know it at the time, but studies over the past seven years in Kuwait showed that the toxicity levels of the by-products of this process—ash and smoke—were more than just dumping the waste into the ground. They created a toxic water source and that made the days under the toxic cloud dark as night. The only thing good gasification does is make lots of money for the ones at the helm." She motioned to Hillman's name.

"Hillman was going to sell this process to Chul-Moo, a North Korean mafia group. I always thought he had been behind the double cross in Kazakhstan, but I never proved it. I mentioned it in my report, and since that time, I've had someone following me. But I could never make the link." She went back to the press release. "Says here the committee is researching the option of relaxing some EPA rules in certain areas to test the syngas option. What do you bet those areas are under Hillman control?"

"But why would Hillman want Ex-6? It has nothing to do with this, does it?"

Lacey sat back, crossed her arms, and ran the past few days over in her mind. She leaned forward and typed in another search—*Hillman Oil + Korea*. "I have a hunch."

One hit appeared. From the AP wire news. *Two Hillman Oil Employees Found Murdered.*

Lacey read the article, scanning down with her finger.

"Says they were North Koreans and victims of a random mugging in Almaty. Just says they worked for Hillman Oil," Conner summed up.

"Almaty is in Kazakhstan."

"I'm completely baffled," said Conner.

Lacey logged off, exited her program, and removed the pendant and PCMCIA card from the slot. She packed it away in her pocket.

"What are you doing?" For a guy who had probably faced down a few terrorists and rogue-nation creeps, he looked downright terrified.

"I'm going to find out what's going on and free the man I love."

Micah felt like he'd been drop-kicked. Every muscle shrieked, his shoulder gnawed at him in nearly consuming pain, and his head pounded where his brain tried to escape through his skull. Most of all, his heart felt freshly shredded. Lacey was a spy, a double-crossing thief. A traitor.

He was such a fool. *Of course* she'd murdered John. John had never been faithful to her. Micah knew that. He should have warned Lacey from the first moment he suspected. But it would only have sounded petty and desperate.

Well, he *had* been desperate. And he had to believe that she had been too. Right. Oh, please, let it have been desperation that drove her to sell out her country. He ached to believe her, to take the accusations that saturated his thoughts and spew them out, but they made too much sense.

He groaned and heard laughter.

"Does it hurt, Micah?"

He frowned at the mention of his name.

"Good. Because it should. She doesn't love you. She never did. She loves no one but herself."

No, that wasn't true. Micah centered himself on the look on Lacey's face when she played him the message from her daughter. Stark horror. Grief. And she had gone out in front of a bullet for Emily. Only they'd swung the rifle at him, hadn't they?

His mind felt knotted. *Lord, help me see wisdom.*

It probably wouldn't matter anyway. Either way, he'd die as soon as they got Ex-6. Either Lacey was a Benedict Arnold—which would rip his heart right between his ribs—or she was going to sacrifice her freedom and her life for him. Neither option seemed acceptable.

"How do you know so much about me?" Micah asked the air.

"She told me about you. Many times. She told me about this man who had been her best friend in Ashleyville. A little homework and a trip to Kentucky did the rest. Her father was very illuminating right before he died."

Micah sucked a breath, reaped agony.

"He thought I was a lawyer on assignment to clear her name. Really I just wanted her attention. Her undivided focus on finishing our plans. She is so easily distracted, Lacey is."

Micah disagreed. The woman he knew was 100 percent devoted, especially to the ones she loved. But then again, that was the woman he knew. What about Lacey the spy? *Lord . . . wisdom. Help me see the truth.*

The Lacey he knew had broken out of the hospital in her bare feet to figure out a way to free her daughter.

Or was it to get Ex-6?

No.

The woman he knew had let him go after tying him up at her cabin.

Or was that to earn his trust?

No.

The woman he knew had surrendered in his arms, her feelings spilling out of her in a kiss. Now that hadn't been faked . . . had it?

The woman he loved had tried to get him to go back to the truck. She hadn't faked her sweeping kick either.

In fact, if she wanted to give away Ex-6, she could have dropped him right there in the woods, delivered the real Ex-6, and escaped with her daughter.

Conner's words returned to him, an echo of hope inside his head: *"You gotta tell her you love her, not expecting anything back."* And then he recalled Romans 5:8: *"God showed his great love for us by sending Christ to die for us while we were still sinners."* That meant loving Lacey even if she was still a liar, a thief, a murderer. That meant loving Lacey despite her apparent deceit. The love example from 1 Corinthians suddenly felt painfully applicable: *"Love never gives up, never loses faith, is always hopeful, and endures though every circumstance."*

I say I love her, Lord, but I haven't, not really. I believed the worst about her for years. Please forgive me. Please help me to see the truth now and love her regardless of what it is, just like You love us.

Like a light shining down into his darkness, illuminating the truth, he remembered Lacey barreling down the hill in his truck, churning up grass in her wake and shouting, "Get in!" Heard her soft breath, lost in slumber as she cuddled against him in the truck. Smelled her from across the motel room, freshly bathed and leaning into his plans with hope. She was a seasoned spy. She could have ditched him—truly ditched him—with Ex-6 at any time.

Yet she'd tried to save his life. Over and over and *over*. He knew, without a doubt, she'd do it again. And probably die trying.

"Be still, and know that I am God." He let Psalm 46:10 fill his mind. He'd been so busy trying to figure out a way to pry Lacey out of this mess, he hadn't spent more than two minutes on his knees, praying. But hog-tied, blindfolded, and helpless seemed like a pretty good time to get busy, seriously busy, with God.

Lord, help me see the truth. I believe that You brought Lacey back into my life for a reason. But I have totally blown it. I wanted to be the man she needed—and now I see I just made it worse. I wanted to bring her to justice, but what she needs is mercy and a huge dose of love in her life. Your love.

He nearly choked, thinking of the despairing hole where her faith had been. *"You're so cerebral, Micah,"* Lacey had said. And maybe he was. Maybe he hadn't let his knowledge of

Christ travel the eighteen inches down to his heart. Suddenly he ached for the void in her soul.

But true love always hopes.

If it's in Your plan to get me out of this mess, Lord, teach me to love her—and You—how You intended. Please move me past the fear of vulnerability to a new place with Lacey. And with You.

For the first time in his thirty-eight years, he felt a rumble, a live pulsing in his heart, something that felt both frightening and compelling. More than desperation. More than hope.

Immanuel?

Micah couldn't dodge the image of God inclining His ear toward him, reaching out, and drawing him into His embrace. A wild tingle possessed his bruised body, something new and definitely not cerebral. It emboldened him, adding fervency to his prayer.

And please, Lord, even if You don't mean to save me . . . protect Lacey and little Emily. Bring them home.

Chapter 20

"THIS ISN'T GOING to work, Conner. Who wears jewelry to a drop?" Lacey touched the wireless video feed fitted into the choker at her neck. "He'll see right through this."

"Keep your collar up and don't let him get that close. You just talk. I'll pick up the rest, then feed it into my computer. Senator Ramey has already agreed to listen in. So either way, the truth will be exposed. If something should go south, this little gem is equipped with GPS. We'll be able to find you."

Lacey looked at him, not sure what he meant.

Conner smiled. "The world will know that you aren't capable of murder or treason despite what happens."

"That's assuming Hillman or whoever will be there, and that I can somehow make him confess." She raised her eyebrows. "You're assuming a lot from me."

"Well, actually, I'm trusting in God more than you, but I do have high hopes. You can thank Micah for convincing me of your persuasive powers." He smiled again, but this time it was touched with melancholy.

"If I hand over Ex-6, the government will know I'm a traitor. The senator won't miss that."

"Then don't hand it over before you get your information. And trust us to back you up."

She knew she didn't deserve his kindness or that of Dannette and the rest of Micah's team. Nevertheless, the support pumped courage into her veins.

"Let's go over this map one more time." Hank Billings stepped up, holding a marked topo of the Tunnel Bluff Cave area. He spread it out on the table and leaned over it.

Lacey couldn't help but notice how Sarah leaned against the wall, arms crossed, disapproval on her face. Obviously Hank hadn't done anything to endear himself to the feisty EMT over the past twenty-four hours. Maybe it was his constant humming. Or the way he'd announced that should the situation disintegrate, he was calling in the Poplar Bluff Sheriff's Department . . . or the NSA.

Lacey tried to focus on Hank's words. "Take FS Road 3225. It cuts right through the Tunnel Bluff area. There's an entrance to the Tunnel Bluff Cave here—" he pointed to a higher area—"and a twenty-foot waterfall here, another exit. This is the official entrance, so I'm thinking that's your drop point. The cave is intertwined with tunnels and nooks, so don't go too far inside; you'll be lost forever." He gestured to another high area, a quarter of a mile from the falls. "You can take the Forest Service road to the trail entrance, then take my four-wheeler up the trail. I'm thinking we'll follow you as far as the FS road, right?"

Sarah's eyebrows raised. "We?"

Hank ignored her, his attention on Conner, who nodded. "It'll be good to have someone there who knows the area," Hank said.

Sarah shook her head, said nothing.

"There's only one glitch in this plan," Conner said. "The

GPS is line of sight. If you go underground, Lacey, we can't track you. And the video feed has a quarter-mile radius. You should be fine, but just so you know that if you are intercepted and taken somewhere, we'll lose contact. It's important you get face-to-face with whoever has Micah and not let him extract you from that location."

Lacey nodded, filing the information. She knew Frank Hillman was on the other end of this nightmare just as he'd been in Kazakhstan. Despite the knots in her stomach, she couldn't wait to yank off his mask. And if he'd hurt Micah . . .

Then again, Micah was already horribly wounded. She took a deep breath. And just think how he'd feel about her after she turned over the key to her country's secrets.

Once Hillman got the program, even if she had made another copy, it wouldn't matter. The government didn't have anything stronger than Ex-6. It was like knowing the enemy could read your thoughts, despite the fact you could read theirs.

"Let's go," she said and buttoned her jean jacket.

"Not yet." Conner motioned to the group. "We have to pray."

Lacey sighed and braced herself.

"Lord, we're aware that You are still at the helm, even though we're in this dark place. We ask for Your light to shine. Reveal the one who is behind this nightmare. Guide Lacey's steps. Bring Micah home safely. And, Lord, please protect Ex-6. In spite of Lacey's intentions, we also know her desire is not to betray. Protect us, O Lord."

"Amen," Lacey whispered, feeling unexpectedly shaken by Conner's words. It unnerved her how she ached for them to see fruition.

Lacey gathered her sleeping daughter in her arms a final moment and kissed her on her forehead. "I love you, Em."

Andee touched Lacey's shoulder. "I promise to take good care of her."

Lacey nodded, feeling once again like a poor excuse for a mother.

As night pushed through the trees, they wound through the lower Ozarks of Mark Twain National Forest. Lacey went with Conner, Dannette and Sarah rode together, and Hank drove alone, pulling his four-wheeler. They made a lonely procession, their lights scraping the dark and foreboding forest. Lacey held on to the armrest, feeling her nerves strum in the silence. She fought an overwhelming urge to pray as Conner's words echoed in her head.

They rolled up to the trail entrance, Conner's lights pushing back the grip of forest. Conner checked her equipment, tested the GPS and the video feed. "Remember, line of sight. Don't go into the cave unless you have to. And don't let him take you anywhere."

Lacey nodded and tightened her grip on her cell phone. She'd checked the signal, saw that it had weakened to a blip.

When Hank handed her a tiny mag light he said nothing, but his eyes spoke concern. She liked him—despite his teasing of Sarah. The fact that he'd befriended them and made them feel like he could be an ally, regardless of his role as forest protector, made her wonder what his future might be with this team. He'd even purchased the round of pizzas they'd inhaled for dinner.

Lacey checked her pocket. The rabbit's foot sat snugly inside, clipped to an inner ring. Hopefully it would be enough to barter for Micah's life. When it was over, she'd ditch the GPS and take off. Her heart ached at the emptiness that threatened to consume it. She'd left instructions to deliver Emily back to Janie and written her daughter a letter of apology.

Maybe . . . when Emily had grown up, she'd understand why her mother couldn't face life in Leavenworth. Then again, her future felt like a dungeon.

She climbed on the four-wheeler and gunned it up a wide hiking trail through the forest. The waning moon filtered through the trees, slivered the path with fractured light.

Andee had marked the map with red marks and packed it in a Ziploc. Lacey took it out, shined the light over it. She remembered Hank's words. If she took another entrance, she might be able to sneak up on . . .

Yeah, and wasn't that what happened in Kazakhstan? She hadn't stayed behind, like John had asked. She'd tried to sneak up on the meeting and surveil it for evidence, hoping to fortify John's suspicions and keep him safe. She'd only gotten nabbed. And her husband killed.

Perhaps she should just stick to the plan. After all, if Micah had been able to drop off the fake Ex-6 the first time around, maybe he wouldn't be wounded and traded like cash.

No, he'd be dead. And Emily would still be in Hillman's claws. Lacey had no doubt it was Micah's quick thinking and sacrifice that had won her back her daughter. She owed it to him to save his life. If she could.

Lacey stopped the four-wheeler, got off, and cut off the path into the forest. Ten minutes later, she found the chert entrance. Drawing her breath for courage, she glanced at her watch: 9:45.

She ducked and entered the cave, hoping that it would lead to truth. She ignored the fear radiating at the back of her chest and strode into the cleft of rock. The crack in the earth opened just enough for her to walk upright. Even then, she had to dodge outcroppings. Above her, the crack converged, tightened. It didn't escape her that the farther she walked, the tighter the opening became. Hank's words hung in her mind like a cobweb: *"The cave is intertwined with tunnels and nooks."* She'd taken that to mean it would intersect with her destination.

Had it not been for her flashlight, the darkness would have suffocated her. She felt it close in, held at bay by only the thin swath of luminescence. She took out her compass to compare it with the topo map. The smell of must and the cold emanating from the limestone surface prickled her skin as she confirmed her direction. Yes, the tunnel should connect with the main entrance. Well, maybe.

As the tunnel closed around her like a cocoon, she wondered if she'd traded cunning for common sense.

For Micah's life.

She dropped to her knees as the tunnel suddenly plunged to knee height. The tunnel ran five or so feet, then opened. She scrambled through, layering her hands and her legs with filth.

She flicked off her light when she emerged into a cavern. Climbing to her feet, she listened but heard nothing, and in the absolute night she saw nothing. She turned on her flashlight and ran it over the void. Stalactites plunged from breathtaking heights; the smell of standing water pinched her nose; and a stilled, mildewed breath, frozen in time, filled the space. She heard her thundering heartbeat and staggered under the immensity of the room that could house the Astrodome. She felt tiny. Insignificant. Overwhelmed.

Sweat trickled down her neck. She fought her racing breath. This was a bad idea. Again, her impulses would cost the man she loved his life, like they had in Kazakhstan. She reached out as her legs went weak. She felt something move beneath her hand and pulled back. Some sort of reptile scurried under a rock in the beam of the flashlight.

She shivered as she pulled out her map. Choices lay before her. Picking her way through the cavern, hoping to find an entrance on the other side. Or following the wall and veering east at the first possible tunnel.

She ran her hand over the rock while she moved along the edge, her heart leading the way. Suddenly the wisdom behind the kidnapper's choice as a drop point made perfect sense. If he killed her—or Micah—in the caves, their bodies would decay before anyone found them—if ever. It made for a convenient and easy burial ground. Especially these wild caves that might never be explored. The thought strengthened her step. Surprise was her only ally.

She found an entrance behind a rockfall, had to drop to her knees to follow it. Holding her flashlight in her mouth, she scampered through the wormhole, pulling herself through the last five feet on her stomach.

The sound of soft voices made her pause. Holding her breath, she heard the static of a radio, an answering call. She checked her watch: 10:03. Had it been only eighteen agonizing minutes? She flicked off the light, stuck it in her pants, then crawled forward.

She emerged in the gray dusk produced by the sphere of a radiant lithium light in a small cavern. Lacey crept up behind a rock and peered over.

Micah was propped against one wall. Tape covered his eyes and lashed his hands behind his back. He was badly hurt, but she saw anger in the set of his jaw.

Probably because the man across from him was laughing. "She's left you to die, just like she did her husband."

Micah faced straight ahead, but a muscle twitched in his jaw.

Lacey felt sick. She closed her hand over the rabbit's foot in her pocket, suddenly believing in luck.

No. Something more than luck.

Help me, Lord, she thought, trying not to flinch. *For Micah's sake.*

"She's late. You'd better hope she's not trying to double-cross me. Because, ploy or not, I have no trouble killing you. Just to remind her that I don't leave a trail."

Lacey's heart raced in shock. Roland Berg! John's handler. She crept back, and her foot sent a flurry of stones skittering along the cave floor.

Roland turned and flashed his light toward her.

She ducked but her heartbeat thudded, betraying her in her ears.

"You're there, aren't you, little lucky penny? I knew you'd come. Just like you came for John."

Lacey held her breath.

Footsteps. Then the *cha-ching* of a handgun chambering a round. "Come here, Penny. Or the great Jim Micah dies."

Micah felt as if he'd been drilled about thirty times in the chest. He fought through a web of pain as he imagined Lacey rising from whatever hiding place she'd secured, raising her arms, and glaring at his captor.

"Somehow I should have guessed that you were behind this," Lacey said, her voice hard. "You've been feeding Hillman my information for years, haven't you?"

"Lacey, you have debts to pay. Yes, Hillman Oil needs your Ex-6 system, but Frank doesn't have the brains to see the big picture. This is about more than just decoding secrets."

Micah raced to grasp the meaning of the words and identify the speaker. Again, the familiarity of the voice throbbed in the back of his mind. Where had he heard it before?

"I think it's time for the truth, Berg."

Berg? As in *Roland* Berg? NSA deputy director? Micah felt ice rush down his spine. Lacey had been dead-on to suspect the NSA. Except why did Roland kidnap her daughter? Unless this wasn't NSA business.

Micah felt the blunt end of the pistol dig into his temple. He heard Lacey's breath catch, the shuffle of feet, before she spoke. "I have what you want. Don't hurt him."

"Funny, we've been here before, haven't we? And again, I caught you before you could tape my meeting and turn me in." He made a *tsk*ing noise, then paused. "Come here." His voice turned hard. "Closer."

Micah tensed, hearing Lacey's feet move against the rocky floor.

"Raise your arms."

"Keep your hands off me," Lacey said, but Micah heard her quick intake of breath and felt ill at the scenes that played in his imagination.

"You still can't follow the rules, can you?" A sharp slap made Micah jump.

Micah heard something tinny drop to the cave floor, then the crunch of metal.

"Who's listening to our conversation, Lacey?"

"No one. That was a gift from a friend."

Micah heard the static of the radio, then Berg's voice. "Come back, Shin. She's here."

"And here I thought you worked for Hillman," Lacey continued. "Turns out he works for you."

"Everyone works for me, honey."

Micah heard Lacey's voice sharpen with accusation. "My

e-mail wasn't intercepted by Ishmael Shavik back in Kuwait. You sent him."

"John was always too cocky for his own good—and yours. I'm surprised that you didn't catch on to him years before. You really don't believe all those out-of-country trips were on company business, do you?"

Micah gritted his teeth, seeing behind his blindfolded eyes the pain flashing in Lacey's eyes, but her voice was surprisingly calm. "John loved me in his own way."

Director Berg laughed. "Well, you may be foolish at love, but at least you've got brains where it counts. Where's Ex-6?"

Micah leaned back against the wall, felt for a sharp rock, and began sawing at the tape binding his wrists.

"No wonder you squashed the investigation on Hillman. You knew he wasn't at the helm." She gasped. "You killed his daughter, didn't you?"

"Hillman didn't take me seriously. He set fire to his business, thinking I might believe that all the gasification plans were destroyed. But I'm not that stupid. Hillman is a visionary, and even if he can't implement the plans in America, there are plenty of other countries who will overlook environmental havoc for hard cash. I knew Hillman would re-create his program. The money was just too enticing. You see, nothing escapes my vision."

"John trusted you."

"Yes, and that made his death that much more painful. It is so much easier to manipulate those who trust. But you aren't that easily fooled. That's why you tried to surveil my meeting, right?"

"I was trying to save John's life and catch a traitor." Her acrid tone echoed in the chamber.

Micah freed his hands and slowly turned them, ripping off the tape.

"I'm no traitor. I'm a patriot—loyal to my own interests." Berg gave a huff of scorn. "You should know better than anyone that you have to look out for yourself or you'll get burned. I learned that too well after my daughter died. She languished for months in agony while I tried to save the very people who refused to let me rush to her bedside. She died without seeing her daddy. He was off fighting an unseen war, so that Americans could keep their fists on their cash." Micah heard a flint of pain in his voice. "The only real patriots are those protecting their own skin."

"No. There are people willing to fight for the things they believe. People like our soldiers overseas, standing in the gap for freedom. People like Micah and his friends, the ones who risk their lives for others."

"Ah, see, Lacey, I knew that about you. You've always looked to be a part of something greater than yourself. I'm your greatest fan, don't you see? I'm the one who convinced Director Morgenstern that you could build Ex-6. I kept funds funneling in your direction. I'm the one who made sure no one interfered, even when Ishmael could taste blood. I'm even the one who found little Emily and kept her safe. I'm your savior, because I believed in your big dreams. And now you're going to save me." Micah heard another slap and winced. Berg's voice hardened. "Where's Ex-6?"

"No wonder you don't need the prototype," Lacey said softly. "You already have the copy I made you."

He chuckled. "Copy? I thought we had the original. I should have known you'd double-cross the NSA. I guess I'll need your Ex-6 hardware also, Mrs. Montgomery."

Micah ripped the tape off his eyes. Although dimly lit, the room blinded him with color and distorted shadows.

Lacey was sitting on the cave floor, glaring at Deputy

Director Roland Berg. When Micah focused, he saw a trickle of blood run from her lip. He had the uncontrollable urge to murder Roland Berg slowly with both hands around his neck. So much for being an iceman. If anything turned him to fire, it was seeing Lacey wounded.

Lacey didn't so much as glance at Micah, but he saw her shift her weight. "Why do you want it?" she asked Berg.

He laughed. "I'm a broker. Nothing more, nothing less. I find what people want and connect the dots—for a very nice price. The North Koreans have a need; you have a product. Secrets, Lacey. I've been selling them for years. And poor Frank . . . well, he doesn't know that the men he hired actually work for me.

"Unfortunately, my contacts in North Korea ran into a bit of trouble with the researchers we sent in. Evidently the researchers made the mistake of trying to bargain their freedom for the code to unlock the gasification program they developed. What they didn't know is that we had you and your Ex-6. How ironic that the very refinery program you went to Kazakhstan to save is the one you now will be handing to the Koreans by giving them Ex-6. Frank doesn't know his windfall appointment to the Energy Commission is really my ticket to the helm of Hillman Oil. Or that he's about to make me and my associates very, very rich. I can't wait to tell him."

Berg must have smiled because Lacey looked nearly sick. "I'm almost glad you disrupted our plans seven years ago. Think of the money I would have lost."

Lacey glared at him. "You won't get away with selling the secrets, you know. I have other copies."

He shrugged. "It doesn't matter. In the end, I'll be very rich and living somewhere off the grid—"

"Don't bet on it. I activated Ex-6. As you know, the second

I went online, the NSA started tracking me. They're probably outside right now, waiting for you."

"And who do you think they'll call first? C'mon, Lacey, don't be stupid. I'll just show them your dead body and tell them that Mr. Micah here caught you betraying your country. You shot each other in a fit of rage."

Lacey looked at Micah. "I'd never do that," she said quietly.

Berg shook his head in disgust.

She turned her attention back to Berg. "I'll find you. Even if you get away, I will too, and I'll follow you to the far end of the ocean. You know I will."

He shook his head. "You know, that is one thing I do believe." He held the gun to her head. She didn't even blink.

Micah went cold.

Berg sighed. "It's time to retire, don't you think?"

Lacey lifted her chin to stare at Berg with icy eyes. "I agree. I'm tired of running too." She sprung up, kicked his arm. A shot chipped at the cave wall. She whirled and landed the next kick on his jaw. He hit the ground on his knees as the gun skittered away.

Lacey leaped toward the gun. Berg swept it up and squeezed off a shot toward Lacey. She didn't even flinch when the shot whizzed past her head.

Micah fought with the bonds around his ankles.

Lacey landed on Berg and straddled his chest. Berg clipped her across the face, sending her flying. Berg launched toward her, rage in his eyes.

Micah ripped the tape. "Lacey!" He bounded to his feet.

Lacey's eyes connected with his. "Run!"

Micah lunged for Berg, but his leg buckled.

Berg grabbed Lacey by the hair and shoved the gun against her neck. "I should have done this myself seven years ago."

With a roar of fury, Micah tackled Berg.

Another shot, this time behind him. Out of his peripheral vision, he saw Lacey running full out toward another attacker.

Berg's fist connected with Micah's jaw and pain exploded in his head. Then Berg pointed the gun at his chest. Micah strong-armed the gun away. Another shot pinged the cave ceiling. Stones showered around them. Micah's heartbeat swished in his ears; sweat pooled on his neck.

Another shot. Then footsteps, running. He caught sight of Lacey just as she sprinted after the other shooter into a darkened tunnel.

No! Panic shaved his concentration, and Berg wrenched the gun from Micah's grasp. Micah saw the barrel flash. He blinked as darkness strobed in his eyes. Then he was falling.

He heard the last sound of pain echoing through the cave chamber, the mournful cry of defeat.

Chapter 21

LACEY BACKPEDALED HER arms, stopping short of pitching into the yawn of air ahead of her. The mournful cry of the Korean raised gooseflesh as he descended into some great gulf. Her heartbeat filled her ears. She whipped out her flashlight, panned it across the darkness. Nothing but black.

A shot echoed behind her. She jumped and the flashlight tumbled from her grip, bounced, and fell into the hole.

Micah!

Lacey grabbed the rock, catching herself before she too pitched over the edge. *Okay, don't panic. Just turn around.* She gulped in a steady breath, turned, and braced her hand on the wall.

She focused on the illuminating truth as she stumbled back toward the cavern, forcing her thoughts on facts, not on the very ugly image of Jim Micah lying in a pool of his own blood.

She felt ill. She could hardly believe she'd played into Roland Berg's games for so many years. Was this what John meant when he'd told her to stay behind and to trust no one?

Except Micah. She should have trusted Micah.

She ran ahead and jarred into a rock wall. What? Where was the cavern?

Frustrated, she stood in the pitch-black surroundings, straining to see. The darkness invaded her pores, her eyes, her mouth. The smell of mold and the chill of the cavern crept up her pants, her shirt. The cold tightened a fist around her hope.

Please don't let Micah be gasping his last breath while I wander the corridors of the underworld!

She wanted to scream, remembering him bound, wounded. She could hardly believe he'd somehow worked himself free, only to pounce on Berg just as the traitor was about to drill a bullet into her skull.

She reached out, found another wall, and picked up her pace. She strained to hear footsteps, the sound of scuffling, anything besides her own shuffling footsteps melting into the dark.

Nothing.

Lacey had no illusions that Berg wouldn't kill Micah or her. Frank Hillman hadn't been behind Ishmael Shavik after all. In fact, maybe he'd been a victim. One whom she had blamed for years.

Roland Berg had set up the buy in Kazakhstan—after she had told John that the gasification program Frank's company had developed was nearly completed. Maybe Berg had recruited Frank for his plan, or maybe he'd simply blackmailed him. Obviously Ishmael Shavik had been sent to warn Hillman—and catch John.

Only she'd disrupted the buy. So who had called in Micah's unit?

Roland Berg? Of course. To clear himself of implication.

Without Micah's sacrifice, she would have never known the truth, never unlocked the secrets behind John's death.

Lacey heard the trickle of water, like the clinking of champagne glasses, rending the fabric of silence.

She stopped. Darkness played tricks with her; light

peppered her eyes. Or maybe it was just the memory of light. "Micah?"

Nothing but the sounds of her heartbeat and her breath whooshing loudly in her lungs.

She tensed. Had she heard water before?

Turning, she continued, slower, listening. When the wall curved, she followed it and bashed into another dead end.

Her heart leaped to her throat. Feeling the wall with both hands, she knelt, found an opening at her feet. Would it take her back to the chamber? Obviously she had taken a wrong turn or maybe two. And how long had she been walking? She turned on the light on her watch. It showed 11:30. She stood, turned, and started back in what she hoped was the right direction.

The sound of water grew, along with the rush of her pulse. The darkness felt suffocating. She fought to break free, like she might in a pool of quicksand. But the harder she struggled, the farther it engulfed her.

She sat down, folded her arms across her chest. Breathed in . . . out. She put a hand to her neck. The transmitter was gone—torn off in Berg's rage.

"Help, Conner," she said softly into the swaddle of night, as if she still had it. "I'm lost."

✦ ✦ ✦

"Micah, just hold still." Sarah pushed hard against his reopened shoulder wound. His eyes nearly crossed, and he gritted his teeth.

It made the pain only slightly more bearable to see Conner straddling Deputy Director Berg and tying him up with nylon climbing rope.

"Where's Lacey?" Micah asked. He'd barely unraveled the night's most recent events. Lacey jumping the other shooter—a Korean. Conner nearly getting his head blown off as he kicked the gun out of Berg's hands and inadvertently connecting with Micah's shoulder. Sarah catching Micah a second before he hit the floor. Hank following Lacey into the black hole.

"Does he know what he's doing?" Micah asked. "I'd better go after him."

"Sit down. He's been hanging around us for three days. It's time he earned his keep."

Micah closed his eyes against another rush of pain. "Okay, that's good, Sarah."

"You need a doctor and now."

"Not until we find Lacey. I heard screaming before." Long before. A breath-stealing pain wrenched his chest. *Please, Lord, no. Please let Lacey be okay. Bring her out of this safely.* He struggled to his feet. "How did you find us?"

Conner stood up, and by the look on his face, the old adrenaline still ran through his veins. Micah had no doubt that Conner would miss the Green Berets as years drew out.

"I had a hunch," Conner said. "I remembered what you said about Lacey being one step ahead of you all the time, and I guessed that she would try and outwit whoever had you. I didn't seriously think she was going to just hand over Ex-6, so Hank and I tracked her. When she veered off the trail, Hank figured out where she was going, and we decided to loop around to the opening. We saw the big Korean guy take off inside and ran to catch up." He gave a one-sided, sardonic grin. "Sorry we were late."

Micah shook his head. "Do you know who this is?"

"No. We had Lacey wired but lost the transmission shortly before we entered the cave."

"You're sitting on NSA Deputy Director Roland Berg. From the gist of their conversation, he's been a double agent for years. At least a freelancer, working as a mole in the NSA. He set up John and framed Lacey. I knew she was innocent." That felt good to say . . . way too good when the woman he loved was stumbling around in the dark. In so many ways.

"I gotta find her." Micah stalked toward the tunnel entrance. "Billings!"

The sound echoed down the chamber into the folds of the cave.

"I'm here." Hank appeared a moment later, flushed. "I can't find her."

Micah stared into the darkness. "How big is this cave?"

"Miles. It runs under this entire section of Mark Twain National Forest."

Micah closed his eyes, braced a hand on the wall. "I'll need water, rope, my helmet, extra lithium batteries, and a space blanket."

He opened his eyes and saw Sarah's gaze on him, hard and dark. "No."

He frowned. Took a deep breath. "I'll be fine."

"No . . . I mean . . . you should have said *we*."

Conner hauled Berg to his feet. "I'll get Dannette."

Hank stopped on his way out of the chamber. "I'm calling the sheriff's department. This cave is known to swallow people alive."

Micah remained silent, feeling like it already had.

Lacey crawled toward the sound of water, painfully aware that she was digging crustaceans and dirt into her hands. Her eyes played tricks on her—light jagged against the rock, giving illumination to her imagination. She saw stalactites and stalagmites, bearing down upon her like teeth. Felt salamanders and spiders run up her arms, squish between her hands and fingers. The chill of the yawning cavern seeped into her pores. When her hand splashed into water she nearly screamed.

It was just a cave. And someone would find her. Soon. Right?

She hesitated to drink the water. What amoeba could be floating in a cupful of supposed nourishment? Still, it was flowing. Survival school had taught her that flowing water washed away impurities. Especially if she could scoop water from below the surface.

She trailed her hand along the water, came to a wall or outcropping, and leaned against it.

Surely Micah would find her. Unless, of course, he was dead.

She closed her eyes and let herself shake. She'd seen the look in Micah's eyes—compassion and sheer trust when she said she'd never shoot him. As if he believed her, *truly* believed her.

No, as if he loved her.

Conner said that Micah had tried to help her in order to prove his love for her. In fact, she wondered if that wasn't why he'd shown up in Missouri in the first place.

He loved her despite the fact that she'd done her dead-level best to kick him out of her life. Loved her despite the suspicions, the lies, the mistakes. He loved her when she couldn't even love herself.

She put her arms around herself, seeing his gray green eyes searching hers. "Oh, Micah, I'm sorry."

Berg had destroyed the transmitter. Now it was just her

words against . . . the NSA deputy director's. She'd never see daylight again even if she made it out of the cave.

Perhaps it would be better to simply sit in the darkness and let the cold close its fist around her. She already felt frozen most of the time anyway.

She rested her head against the rock, trying to dispel the freak-night images that flashed in her mind. Insects. Animals. The thought of her skeletal remains being dragged out by dogs.

Maybe she shouldn't wait for help.

She stood up, ignoring the commonsense screaming in the back of her brain, and started walking through the darkness. She tripped and caught herself on her hands, but her face hit a rock. Blood warmed her lip. She pushed her hand against the flow, turned, and leaned back against the rock.

She had as much chance of getting out of here on her own as she had of figuring out how to escape the tangle of her life and live happily ever after with Jim Micah and Emily.

She put her face on her knees and let despair wash over her. At least she still had Ex-6. But as soon as they found her—*if* they found her—Roland would have her arrested. Which would bring her full circle from three days ago. Only this time, she'd be accused of selling national secrets.

Then again, was that so different from being accused of betraying her husband?

"God takes your reputation and makes it new."

Conner's soft voice played in her mind. She slowed her heartbeat, tried to find the conversation in the snarl of memories. *"It's not just salvation; it's transformation. It's God redeeming our reputation, giving us overflowing mirth in our hearts, clothing us with a countenance of rejoicing instead of grief. We are not merely set free; we're washed and given an entire new body. You are completely new in His eyes because of His amazing love for you."*

His amazing love. She blinked, suddenly remembering the song Sarah had been humming yesterday as they'd prepared for the first drop. It had tugged at memories, so long suppressed, but now the words rushed through her like the freshwater from an underground spring.

Amazing love! how can it be
That Thou, my God shouldst die for me?

Lacey fought a sudden onslaught of grief, seeing her mother—frail, unable to stand, but gripping her hymnal as she sang. . . .

Long my imprisoned spirit lay
Fast bound in sin and nature's night.
Thine eye diffused a quick'ning ray;
I woke—the dungeon flamed with light!
My chains fell off, my heart was free.
I rose, went forth, and followed Thee.

They'd played it at the funeral at her mother's request. Lacey remembered thinking of her mother, freed from her broken, cancer-ridden body, springing forth into life.

Set free.

Like . . . being carried out of a cave . . . into the light.

Lacey knew all about living in darkness. She pressed her lip, feeling it throb. She'd built a dungeon for herself, closing the door behind her in self-incrimination. Except, unlike her mother, she deserved her pain.

She put a hand to her mouth, heard her own groan. She whispered the words of Scripture Micah had given her:

"'Some sat in darkness and deepest gloom, miserable prisoners in chains. They rebelled against the words of God, scorning the counsel of the Most High. That is why he broke them with hard labor; they fell and no one helped them rise again. "Lord, help!" they cried in their trouble, and he saved them from their distress—'"

Her own voice, and it threatened to mock her. Cry out to God?

She didn't deserve to cry out to God. Not when she'd turned her back on Him. Not when she'd deliberately married a man who led her away from truth. Not after she'd made mistakes that cost lives. She couldn't forgive herself. How could God forgive her?

"Remember the widow of Nain." Micah's voice—soft, gentle, patient—filled the hard corners of her mind. Why had he said that?

The widow of Nain? She closed her eyes and in the silence and darkness dredged up the story. A widow. Her only son dead. A funeral procession. Luke 7.

Oh yeah, now she remembered. Micah, sitting beside her at the creek in the early days after her mother's death. The wind playing with her hair, his eyes kind as he spoke. "'Jesus went with his disciples to the village of Nain. . . . A funeral procession was coming out as he approached the village gate. The boy who had died was the only son of a widow. . . . When the Lord saw her, his heart overflowed with compassion. "Don't cry!" he said. Then he walked over to the coffin and touched it. . . . "Young man," he said, "get up." Then the dead boy sat up.'"

Lacey had been drawn in nearly as much by the passion in Micah's face as his words.

"You know what I love about this passage?" He had picked up a leaf and brushed it between his strong fingers. "I love the way Jesus is moved by our pain. Do you know what the word *touched* means? It means 'to connect or bind.' He bound

Himself to the new life of the dead boy. But the antonym of that word really sheds light on His actions. It means self-control. So when Jesus touched that boy, He threw off His self-restraint and did what He most longs to do."

Lacey remembered frowning at Micah. "I don't understand."

"You know what I think? Jesus wanted to show mercy to every single person He met. He wanted to sweep them up and embrace them with His love. But because of His eternal plans for goodness, He can't always do that. I don't know why, but I believe He has a greater good than healing our temporary pain. Still, the picture of the widow of Nain shows me that Jesus longs to heal, to reach out and touch our hurts. His nature is to show mercy to the hurting. On the grieving. On the lost."

"Really?"

"Yeah." Micah had tossed the leaf into the creek, and Lacey watched it float away. "God's very character is mercy. He yearns to show it to us. That's what the Bible is all about—God showing us mercy in the sacrifice of His Son. It's not about us deserving it—we never will. It's about His giving it just because of His love. We don't get to turn our back on God—because the suffering of Christ demands we confront this mercy. Turning away would be like a wounded person slapping away the nurse's hands."

Or a prisoner refusing redemption.

Lacey rubbed her eyes with the palms of her hands. White light streaked behind her eyes. What she wouldn't do for light right about now. Showing her the way . . . home . . .

In a flash of memory that should have been accompanied by angelic singing, she saw herself praying to the hospital ceiling three days ago, asking for help.

Could it be that God had heard that prayer after all? That

He'd sent the one man from her past who could help her find her way . . . not back to Ashleyville . . . but back to faith?

Could it be that God had been showing her mercy all this time? Yes, she'd rebelled against Him by marrying John. But even in that, He'd given her Emily. Flesh-and-blood proof of His love. Of His mercy. And He'd kept Emily alive, despite the desperate odds. He'd given her daughter a home and love, while Lacey tried to uncover the truth.

He'd revealed John's killer. Even if it was only to Micah. The one person to whom her innocence mattered.

Maybe God had been showing her traces of His mercy for years. She'd just been stumbling through darkness and too blind to see it. Afraid that if she turned to the light, He'd see her scars, her mistakes, her filth.

"He yearns to show us His mercy." Could it be that in turning toward Him, she'd only see God's heart? His desire to reach out and heal her wounds?

No, she didn't deserve forgiveness. But maybe it wasn't about deserving it. Like Micah, stepping in to show her he loved her even though she attempted to kick him out of her life. God giving her mercy, touching her life because . . . He longed to show her He loved her? Just like He longed to raise the son of the widow of Nain, release the captives, and open the prison doors. And give her beauty for ashes and joy instead of mourning.

She'd been running from the one Savior who could offer her true, unflinching, unbridled redemption, not because He didn't want to give it but because she felt too repulsive.

"Lord," she said and heard fear in her voice. She closed her eyes. "I know I don't deserve Your forgiveness. I've made mistakes. And I've willfully sinned." She licked her lips, realizing how parched she felt, inside and out. "I . . . am sorry. So . . .

sorry. Please, please forgive me, because of Your great mercy. Please cleanse me and create a new person out of me. Give me praise instead of despair."

She covered her face with her hands, suddenly shaking with the feeling of warmth that emanated inside. It trickled through her, renewing, like sunshine on weary, cracked bones. She gasped, drank it in, let the feeling settle into every inch of her fear and hopelessness. "Oh, Lord, You—and only You—are my Savior. And You alone can redeem me. Not Micah. Not myself. Not Emily. You."

She gulped deeply the sudden wash of peace, the feeling that her life was fully known and healed. God, invading her pores, reminding her of Conner's prayer: *"We ask for Your light to shine."*

God's light wasn't harsh and brutal. It was merciful and healing. Lacey wiped her face with her hands, pulled her knees up to her chest, and leaned on them, speaking to the inhabited darkness. "Lord, please save Micah. Thank You for using him to show me that I don't have to run. And if it's possible—" she swallowed hard, pushing against a rush of tears—"figure out a way for me to go home."

Chapter 22

MICAH GRABBED A water bottle, downed its contents, then turned back toward the cave entrance. The sun threaded rose and gold through the trees, hinting at hope, but Micah's spirit felt nothing but dark despair weighing heavier with each passing hour. Lacey could easily be dying of hypothermia.

"You aren't going back in, are you?" Sarah sat on a rock, her shoulders sagging, filth covering her from her face to her toes.

Micah stared at her. "Of course."

They'd spent the better part of the night crawling through the labyrinth, down alleyways, up cliffs, into wormholes. Hank was right—the cave had swallowed Lacey whole. He was mustering his SAR forces at the moment, and Micah couldn't deny he hoped the ranger hurried.

The cavern felt like a Sub-Zero freezer the deeper they went, and they were no closer to finding Lacey than they had been when she'd gone after their assailant into the bowels of the earth. Two hours ago, Micah had crawled out and submitted to medical aid, hoping for a fresh map and a sunny update. He should have stayed underground.

He'd gotten a few stitches in his leg and packing for his

shoulder wound. In the wan hours of daylight and under Sarah's scrutiny, the flesh wound seemed well bandaged and even healing. Sarah gave him a shot of Demerol and he felt 75 percent better. Except for the gaping hole where his heart had been.

He filled the water bottle, snatched a handful of granola bars, a fresh lithium battery for his helmet, and a dry pair of gloves. "My radio isn't picking you up, Conner."

Conner wore a grim look. "I'm going with you."

Micah shook his head. "No. Not until the NSA gets here. I want you on hand to testify to what I heard."

"You stay; I'll go."

"Yeah, and then how am I going to explain how their deputy director lost all his teeth?"

Conner quirked a smile. "Right. Okay. Dannette is packing up Sherlock. Maybe she'll head back in with you." Without something to identify Lacey, Sherlock had been unable to trail her. Defeat hung on Dannette's countenance and in her body language. Micah had a feeling that behind her stoic Scandinavian demeanor, her heart of compassion was bleeding with frustration.

"I don't want to wait. It's getting colder. I just hope she's staying put, not moving around."

Conner raised his eyebrows. "You're talking about Lacey?"

"Exactly my point, Einstein." Micah ignored Sarah's and Conner's protests as he hiked back into the black hole.

They'd sketched a rough map of the cave while they searched, and Hank had promised to bring back a detailed map. Micah entered the dark tunnel again, trying to think like Lacey. She'd been running after the Korean. Fast. They'd found the rock lip where he'd gone over, and Micah's light picked up a broken and unmoving body at the bottom. Micah had endured a moment of crushing pain until he deduced that it wasn't Lacey.

Her route from there got hazy. There were three tunnels, leading to dozens of other routes. He turned around. She would have returned, so he tried to imagine what she would do. He closed his eyes, trying to imagine her. She was smart. She would have tried to retrace her path. He brailled the rock, took ten steps, found that it wound around in a half circle, cutting off to the north and away from the cavern where he'd struggled with Berg.

He followed, still brailling the cave. When he came to a rock formation, instead of climbing up, which felt logical, he reached out with his other hand, found the wall on the other side, and continued. The rock narrowed, and he aimed the light down to a small tunnel. He knelt before it, trying to imagine Lacey crawling through.

No. She would have sensed folly in that. He stood and continued tunneling through the darkness, his eyes half closed. *Please, Lord, give me vision beyond the obvious.*

The fact that God had heard his prayers and unveiled John's killer—the real killer—had sprouted something hot and alive in Micah. It only grew when he followed the tunnel left as it veered away from the entrance tunnel. He heard the faint trickle of water running over rock.

He whirled toward the sound. Lacey's survival skills would have told her that water meant life. And possibly an outlet.

He stopped in a cavern and scanned his light across the room. Stalactites hung from the ceiling like giant drips, and a crystal-clear lake mirrored the jagged ceiling. On the other side, aragonitic bushes, magical in their whiteness and crystalline shape, bloomed like wildflowers in the eternal night. He took a deep breath, somehow feeling that she'd been here. "Lacey?"

He held his breath. Heard nothing. *Please, Lucky Penny, stay put. Let me find you!*

Micah walked to the water's edge. Something—mottled water near the edge and disturbed silt—caught his attention. As if the water had been stirred. He walked along the edge of the lake, then flicked his light into the tunnel where the water flowed . . . out?

He stepped into the water. The cold stabbed him, yanked out his breath. If she'd tried to follow the current, she wouldn't last long, not in this water.

He waded forward, feeling common sense calling his name and warning him away. But something, perhaps the burning in his chest, tugged him toward the passageway. He called out, heard her name echo. The current seemed stronger, and his legs started to numb.

He moved into the darkness, noticing that the tunnel had begun to close. This was folly. Still . . . he disregarded his breath, his thundering heartbeat. Listened.

Splashing.

He drove forward, pushing his light ahead. "Lacey?"

The sound echoed. The splashing stopped. He waded forward. The water rose to his hips, his waist. The tunnel narrowed, and he ducked under a rough mouth of rock that made him dip at the waist. Scooping up a mouthful of water, he choked and coughed. The rock ate the sound in a single gulp.

Then the mouth abruptly opened, and Micah stopped, mesmerized. He'd entered a cavern the size of a baseball field, where the stream slushed out to a small lake. The surface mirrored the centuries-old stalactites and columns and the limestone boulders the size of Volkswagen Bugs dislodged from an ancient earthquake. The stillness of the cavern pressed his ears.

"Lacey?" His voice sounded tinny and small in the great expanse.

He heard the splatter of rock. He flicked his light in the direction. Lacey stood, sopping wet, gripping a fist-sized boulder. "Micah!"

"You gonna throw that at my head?"

She stared at her weapon, paled, and dropped it. "No. I—" Then she looked up at him. "Micah. You're—" she shook her head and her face crumpled—"you're alive."

He gave a slow smile as he waded toward shore. "Yeah. But more importantly, so are you. What are you doing in here?"

"I remembered the map, that a waterfall exits in the caves. I was following it downstream." She shivered.

His throat tightened. He had no idea how far the river traversed the cave, but in the pit of his stomach he knew she wouldn't have surfaced alive.

He climbed out of the water, and in two steps had her in his arms.

She hung on tight, her arms around his waist. "You found me. I can't believe you found me." Her voice sounded shallow, rushed. So utterly not Lacey.

"Are you okay?" Relief betrayed him in his racing heartbeat.

She felt so small, so suddenly frail. Where was the trained agent he'd seen kick Roland Berg in the teeth? "Honey, you're scaring me," he said.

"I'm okay," she whispered but tightened her embrace.

His light illuminated the crystals stacked in the stones behind her, and they shone like diamonds.

"What's the matter, Lacey?"

"I just thought . . . I mean, I thought you were shot, and then I thought it might be easier to live in this cave for eternity than face . . . that . . ."

He closed his eyes, letting her words burrow deep into the crevasses and tunnels of his heart. "Oh, Lucky Penny, I knew I'd find you." He cupped her jaw and ran a thumb along its edge. "Shh."

"Micah, I'm so sorry. I'm sorry I never trusted you. I'm sorry I married John. I'm sorry I spent so many years trying to make you pay for . . ."

"For not saying I loved you?"

She looked up, and her beautiful eyes glistened. "You didn't have to say it. I knew it. I saw it so many times."

"I *do* need to say it." He searched her face, seeing in her expression everything he'd remembered and more. He leaned closer and touched her lips with his.

Her arms moved up around his neck; she clung to him and kissed him back.

Then he realized why he felt whole and alive and real when she was with him. Why he'd spent his life trying to free the oppressed and find the lost. Because it was only with her that he felt both freed and found. Felt alive and as if he'd come home. Lacey belonged in his arms—just like she had when she'd fallen off the bleachers so long ago. And he was supposed to be the man to catch her.

"Lacey—" he wove his fingers into her hair, pushing past his sandbagged emotions—"I love you so much that it makes me ache. I can't find the words—"

"That works." She looked up at him, smiled, and tears ran down her cheeks. "I know I don't deserve your love, Micah, but I'm so thankful for it."

He rubbed her tears away with his thumb. "Don't deserve it? I'm the one who should be dropping to my knees in repentance and angst. I've spent the last fifteen years furious with you and the last seven promising to send you to prison, if it was the last thing I did."

"It's not about deserving though, is it?"

He searched her twinkling eyes. "What are you talking about?"

She shrugged. When she smiled, he saw something alive. Something that hadn't been there three days ago. Something he remembered from long ago.

"You know, God just might be using you, Jim Micah, to bring prodigals home."

He wanted to leap or maybe sing at the top of his lungs. Still, he could barely find his voice. "Really?"

"Yeah. I'm just sorry it took me so long to figure out that if I turned toward the light, I wasn't going to get burned. But God showed me that His light was mercy and healing. Not horror." Her quavering smile held the facets of grace. It made her . . . stunning.

Micah had always held an intellectual view of salvation. He knew he was saved because he applied Romans 10:9 to his life. But seeing redemption in Lacey's eyes welled up a feeling so thick it made his eyes burn. It took on living color, sounds of hallelujah, made him want to dance. So this was how it felt to rejoice.

"I wish we'd been able to transmit Berg's confession. He's going to burn me the second he gets on the line to the NSA," Lacey said.

Micah shook his head. "Oh, don't worry about him. Conner popped him good, and he's awaiting the NSA regulars in his pickup. I think that after I give my testimony and we dig up the North Korean lying at the bottom of the gorge, you'll be a free woman."

"Your testimony?"

He grinned. "Yeah, well, you forget I'm a decorated officer. I think they'll put some stock into my statement. . . ."

"You'd do that for me?"

He frowned. "Do you not get it? I can't wait to stand up for you. After the way I treated you I'm surprised you don't slap me and run for the hills."

"Oh, I'm hardly going to wallop the man who rescued me." She ran her hand down his whiskered face.

"Hello? Not all these bruises are from Berg, you know." He grinned.

Her smile dimmed. "We have a lot of ground to make up for, don't we?"

He leaned his forehead against hers. "Yeah. But I like the sound of that." Then he kissed her again, and this time he poured his emotions into the touch. She wove her hands into his hair and returned his kiss, completely obliterating any idea that John Montgomery still had her heart.

Micah backed away before she turned his knees weak and crumbled years of self-control and resolve. He was a healthy male, after all, and she had the power to turn his best intentions to cooked grits. The only time he planned to throw off his self-restraint was on their wedding night. Which, he hoped, wasn't too far away.

"I'm in love with you, you know," he said. "That feels so good to finally say."

"Then say it again."

"I'm madly, deeply, wildly in love with you, Lacey Galloway."

She grinned and he saw in her eyes the mischief that had always made him feel just a little bit afraid and very, very alive. "It's about time."

Then she kissed him again, and he forgot all about being

cold or the fact that they'd have to walk back through the murky water and the dank cave. He saw only the sunshine waiting at the end.

"Ready to go home?" he asked, breathing just a little harder than he should, as she pulled away.

She swallowed hard, and something like pain ranged across her face.

"What is it?"

She sighed, stepped away. His arms already felt cold and empty. "It's Emily. She's John's daughter."

"And?"

"Will that be a problem for you? I mean . . . I know you can't have children. Will it hurt too much to have Em in your life?"

He blinked at her, his mouth opening. So that's what Conner meant about giving away his secrets. Only this time hearing the truth didn't rip open his heart. In fact . . .

Micah reached out and took her hand. "You know, God answers our prayers in mysterious ways. I guess He just knew that I needed to be Emily's dad."

Emily's dad.

As they stared at each other, Micah's throat grew thick and prickly.

"You're going to be such a stellar father," Lacey said, and tears crested down her grimy cheeks.

"I hope I'm an even better husband," he said softly.

She smiled. "That, I'm looking forward to."

He cupped her face in his hands, thumbed away her tears. "Me too."

Slowly, she nodded, her eyes telling him everything he'd forced her to bury inside her heart for years. "Now, Jim Micah, please take me home."

Epilogue

"LACEY, HURRY UP! The burgers are nearly finished!"

Lacey waved at Conner, who wore a crazy chef's hat and apron over his turtleneck and jacket, as she cantered her horse through the yard. The smell of grilling hamburgers had her stomach doing cartwheels.

"Race ya!" Micah yelled from over her shoulder.

She turned, smiled at him, and shouted, "Yah!"

The cool late-autumn wind licked through her hair while she stood in the stirrups and galloped toward the barn. The sky smiled down on them today, a light blue with wispy cirrus, the smells of decaying loam and the last of the wildflowers in the air. "I'm winning!"

"Never!" Micah nudged up beside her. His shoulder had healed well, and even his leg seemed to be holding out. Then again, he could be bleeding from both ears and he'd still say he was fine.

She urged her horse forward, breathing hard, her thighs screaming. It felt like heaven to be riding again. She pulled the animal up just as they reached the trail to the paddock. She laughed, feeling full and alive. Whole. "I won."

Micah rode up beside her. The wind had tousled his

hair—now that he'd been discharged from military service, he'd let it grow out and it curled deliciously around his ears. His beautiful eyes took her in with one sweep, and the smile on his face did dangerous things to her heart. She wondered if the fact that she was going to marry this man as soon as she could put together a wedding would ever cause her *not* to gasp, *not* to feel overwhelmed.

God had brought her home. Back to Micah's arms. Yes, there were times when she was wrapped in his embrace, beating him in Scrabble, or even debating him over theology, that she could hardly believe she was the same person.

Then again, she wasn't. She'd been transformed. And this new Lacey, the one who could stay home and be a mom . . . well, the idea still knocked her off balance.

"Yeah, but I haven't been on a horse for twenty years. Give me a month. You'll owe me a chocolate malt." Micah dismounted, grinning.

"I don't know, old guy. I think you're past your prime." She giggled at his openmouthed shock.

"Hardly. I'll show you prime. C'mere." He reached for her, hooked his hand around her neck, and kissed her.

It was all she could do not to step closer, wrap her arms around his waist, and forget that they were supposed to be attending their engagement party. She wanted to lose herself in the cool afternoon, the warm protection of his embrace, the sweetness of his touch.

He must have wrestled with his own temptation for he backed away, leaned his forehead against hers. "Okay, that's enough."

"Point taken, Soldier Boy." She took a deep breath and forced herself away, started walking out Sugah. "Have you decided what you're going to do?" Micah had spent more than a few hours wandering the hills of her brother, Sam's, farm over the last month, and she had her suspicions that his hikes gave motion to his inner sortings.

"I dunno. I always thought I would be in the army. That the Green Berets were my calling. But maybe it's not the calling that God changes. It's the task."

She glanced at him. The wind raked back his hair and lifted one corner of his jacket.

"Remember my life verse?"

"Micah 6:8, yeah. Something about doing justice and loving mercy."

"And walking humbly with God. I thought by joining the commandos, I was living out that verse. And by resigning . . . well, I was failing God or something."

Oh, Micah. Sometimes his honor amazed her. Why, oh why, hadn't she seen that years ago, instead of letting John sweep her into his adventures?

Except maybe Micah wasn't ready for her then. Maybe God had His own work to do in him. And in her. Neither, perhaps, had been ready for the life God wanted for them.

This life. That thought quickened her heart as they unlocked the paddock and loosed the horses. Sugah ran in a circle, her age betrayed in her gait.

"I was thinking, however, that God hasn't changed my calling. I am still supposed to live out Micah 6:8. Only maybe He's changed the how." Micah braced his arms against the rail, watching the horses. "I'm thinking about asking the others if they want to make our rescue team official. Perhaps go free-lance."

Lacey studied him. He wore such vulnerability on his face; she realized he'd just opened up his heart for her to get a good look at his dreams. Just like he had on that hot Saturday so many summers ago. "I love that idea," she said. *Nearly as much as I love you.*

He smiled slowly, and like warm honey it filled her every pore. He held out his hand. "I think we have a party to attend?"

Sarah was sitting on a lounge chair on the flagstone patio, Emily on her lap, waging a thumb war, when they climbed up the steps. "Mommy!" Emily bounced off Sarah and ran to Lacey. Lacey swung her up, and Emily wrapped her legs and arms around her.

This 200 percent sold-out affection her daughter gave her with nary a blink still took some getting used to. Lacey tucked her head against Emily's downy hair and inhaled.

"Andee's helping your brother set the table," Conner said, gesturing with his spatula. "Dannette just called. Said she was sorry she couldn't make it. But she sent her congratulations and says for you to e-mail her with a full description of your ring." He rolled his eyes before he turned back to the burgers, which spit and sizzled.

Lacey put Emily down, who turned and took Micah's hand. He glanced at her and at Lacey, a smile tipping his mouth.

Lacey smiled back, then lifted her hand and stared again at the carat diamond-and-ruby setting Micah had taken from her old engagement ring and turned into his own creation. It seemed somehow fitting that John be in the symbol of her new life. Not only would Emily always have her father's blood running through her veins, even if she took the name Micah, but God had used John to show Lacey the meaning of mercy. John had been a part of her life that she'd had to live in order to discover the fullness of God's love. At least she decided to look at it that way.

"Oh," Conner said, turning the burgers, "that guy Hillman called."

Lacey frowned, looked at Conner, then back to Micah. "What did he want?"

"Dunno. Said to call him back. He left a number."

Lacey swallowed hard. She'd blamed Frank Hillman for murdering her husband, for tracking her for years, for kidnapping Emily. And he'd been innocent. In fact, the NSA had analyzed Micah's statement, then detained, question, and locked up Roland Berg. NSA Director Morgenstern had pulled her aside and revealed the extent of Berg's terrorism. Evidently, she hadn't been the only one stalked by Roland Berg. He'd killed CIA agents, sold industrial secrets he'd been sworn to protect, and extorted money from expats working around the globe. The CIA had strong suspicions that Berg might even be linked to the upper levels of Hayata, Shavik's terrorist group.

She'd also been correct about Hillman's daughter's death being a revenge killing. She had no doubt that Micah had saved Emily's life by tackling Berg and his North Korean accomplice. Nor did she doubt for a millisecond that Berg would have killed Micah and her as soon as he grabbed Ex-6. Once she pieced together time and circumstance, it hadn't been hard to realize that Berg's motivation in keeping Micah away wasn't to stop him from interfering . . . but rather because Berg knew if Micah aligned with Lacey he might use his stubbornness and high-level political relationships to dig to the truth. Micah might, in fact, have discovered that Berg had engineered the double cross in Kazakhstan and covered it up by calling in Micah's commando team.

Micah had saved her life in so many ways, but most of all he refused to let her flee the secrets of her dark night.

He had looked downright resplendent the day of Berg's hearing, dressed for the last time in his dress blues. She'd waited for him outside Morgenstern's office at Langley. As

Micah pulled her into his arms and kissed her right there in front of everyone who had heard the stories of the spy who murdered her husband, he swept from her heart the last vestiges of doubt and fear that they couldn't start over.

Micah may have thought he was supposed to bring her to justice . . . but God had sent Micah to set her free.

That fact came fully to breast a week later when Janie brought Emily to the farm. Home. Forever.

"I'll call Hillman," Lacey said and started for the kitchen. Micah touched her arm, gave her a sympathetic look. "It's the least I can do," she said.

She stole a French fry from the pan on the stove, picked up the number, and greeted Andee as she passed through to her bedroom. Sam had graciously allowed her to move into the house until her wedding. She closed the door behind her and sat on her bed, still amazed that she could walk into a room without looking over her shoulder and jumping at every sound.

She dialed Hillman's number.

"Hello?"

With a halting voice, she identified herself. Then quietly she apologized for suspecting him of murder. She had acted just like Micah, believing something without proof, wanting to place blame to assuage her grief. "I'm so sorry," she said, trying to keep her voice steady.

"No, it's me who should apologize. If I'd had the courage to tell the CIA what had happened, maybe you wouldn't have been blamed for your husband's death. Maybe Roland Berg wouldn't have had the opportunity to terrorize another family." His voice, with the slightest Southern accent, broke.

"You can't live with what-ifs, Mr. Hillman," Lacey said. "But you can live with hope. I've found that Jesus offers us second chances. More than that, He offers us new life. And . . . peace."

His silence told her that he still wrestled with remorse, the same emotion that had held her prisoner for so long.

"Jesus opens prison doors. He heals and restores. I'll be praying for you, Mr. Hillman."

"I'm glad you're okay, Lacey," he said.

The dial tone droned in her ear. Lacey took a deep breath, feeling sorrow line her throat. She understood the urge to cling to grief, to regret, despite the fact that it gnawed away at a person's soul. She set the phone in the cradle.

"Everything okay?" Micah stood in her doorway. Emily was in his arms, hers around his neck.

Lacey smiled. "One day at a time, right?"

He nodded, a slow smile on his face. "I love you, you know."

She padded over to him, put her arms around them both. He felt powerful, so very capable of helping her heal, despite the scars from his cancer. He put an arm around her and pulled her tight.

"I know," she whispered.

"Emily and I have a question."

"Yes?" Lacey ran her fingers down her daughter's chubby cheek. They'd put Emily into counseling, and over the past month, her nightmares had lessened. Lacey believed that in time they'd vanish completely. Especially in the embrace of Micah's love.

Emily gave a saucy, six-year-old grin. "Can . . . Daddy take me riding?"

Daddy?

Lacey glanced at Micah, saw his widened eyes, the fear and hope on his beautiful, rugged face. "What did you call me?" he asked, a soft catch in his voice.

Emily giggled. "I never had a daddy."

Lacey fought the urge to argue that point, but the delight, the raw hope on her little girl's face obliterated words. What was it about children that enabled them to wear their heart on the outside of their bodies without fear? Lacey touched her daughter's shoulder, aching to protect her.

It wasn't necessary.

"I'll be your daddy," Micah said, his eyes glistening.

Lacey felt her own fill.

"Can we go, Mommy, please?" Emily clasped her little hands together and, all dramatics, leaned down as if begging.

"Lunch is almost ready," Lacey said and quickly swiped away her tears.

"It'll be quick." Micah bounced Emily up to sit on his shoulders. "I promise." The look of joy on his face made her want to give him the moon and stars.

"Not too quick." Lacey held up a warning finger.

Micah laughed. "Okay, not too quick." He grabbed Emily's ankles as he turned away. "Have you ever been on a horse before?"

Leaning against the doorjamb, Lacey watched them go, her heart feeling like it might burst.

"No," Emily said. "Don't let me fall, okay?"

Micah's voice faded out. "I won't, honey. Daddy won't let you fall. I promise."

Lacey smiled.

Jim Micah always kept his promises.

A Note from the Author

SECOND CHANCES. A fresh start. New beginnings. These words fragranced my mind as our family began a new life in America this past year. We built our first house, started attending new schools and a new church. Suddenly we had a clean slate, free from the expectations and boundaries that had defined our lives as missionaries.

It was during these first steps that I came across Isaiah 61. It's the same passage Jesus Christ quotes in Luke 4:18-19. "The Spirit of the Lord is on me, because he has anointed me to preach good news to the poor. He has sent me to proclaim freedom for the prisoners and recovery of sight for the blind, to release the oppressed, to proclaim the year of the Lord's favor."

Isaiah 61 continues with: "To bestow on them a crown of beauty instead of ashes, the oil of gladness instead of mourning, and a garment of praise instead of a spirit of despair. They will be called oaks of righteousness, a planting of the Lord for the display of his splendor."

These verses intrigued me. Probably because leaving Russia felt in many ways like walking out of a dungeon. Yes, we'd loved ministry there. Yes, I'd chosen that life. But Russia can be a dark, oppressive place, where you have to search for light and hope. More than that, I felt boxed in by expectations, unable to envision a different future. As we settled into our new community, I felt able to take a free, full breath for the first time in years. Slowly the fear and tension began to slough off me, and I saw a change taking place in my heart and my countenance.

I began to dig through Isaiah 61, to study the meanings of the words, and salvation took on new shades. I've been a Christian for over two decades, but seeing from a new viewpoint the depth of the transformation Christ has performed in my life through the years overwhelmed me. You see, I'd been a girl longing to change my world. In doing so, however, I found myself in my own sort of "prison."

Christ, however, is about changing me, *through* my world, as well as His Word. And in bringing me home, He's opened a new chapter of understanding who He is. God cares not only for the lost masses, but for the needs of Susan May Warren and her family.

In many ways, I am walking free for the first time. It makes me long to become that "planting of the Lord for the display of his splendor."

Lacey is a woman who wanted to change her world. Because of that, she chose a man who embodied adventure. She found out that life wasn't the world she had dreamed of, despite the fact that God had used it to mold her into the woman she would someday be. Sadly, Lacey felt she'd walked so far away from God, there was no return. More than that, she felt imprisoned by her choices.

We often create prisons for ourselves through high expectations, idealism, even the belief that God can't—or shouldn't—redeem our poor choices.

The good news is that Christ came to set us free. He's the

author of fresh starts, and He changes us from the inside out—
our situation, our attitudes, even our appearance. Complete
transformation.

The more I think about it, the more it takes my breath
away.

> *They cried to the Lord in their trouble, and he saved them*
> *from their distress. He brought them out of darkness and the*
> *deepest gloom and broke away their chains. Let them give*
> *thanks to the Lord for his unfailing love* (Psalm 107:13-15).

Thank you for reading *Flee the Night*. I look forward to
sharing other Team Hope adventures with you. Most of all, I
pray that you would find a fresh start today with the Savior
who's come to set you free.

In His grace,

Susan May Warren

About the Author

Susan May Warren recently returned home after serving for eight years with her husband and four children as missionaries in Khabarovsk, Far East Russia. Now writing full-time as her husband runs a lodge on Lake Superior in northern Minnesota, she and her family enjoy hiking and canoeing and being involved in their local church.

Susan holds a BA in mass communications from the University of Minnesota and is a multipublished author of novellas and novels with Tyndale, including *Happily Ever After*, the American Christian Romance Writers' 2003 Book of the Year and a 2003 Christy Award finalist. Other books in the series include *Tying the Knot* and *The Perfect Match*. *Flee the Night* is her first book in her new romantic adventure search and rescue series with Tyndale.

Susan invites you to visit her Web site at www.susanmaywarren.com. She also welcomes letters by e-mail at susan@susanmaywarren.com.

Turn the page for an
exciting preview of book 2
in Susan May Warren's
Team Hope series

Escape to Morning

Escape to Morning

TODAY, MORE THAN any other, reporter Will Masterson prayed his lies saved lives. Starting with his partner, Homeland Security Agent Simon Rouss, aka Haviz Tarkan. *Please, God, be on my side today.* Will raced down the two-lane rutted forest service road, cursing his stupidity as well as a few new souvenir bruises. He smelled rain in the air as the wind shivered the trees with a late-season breeze. His nose felt thick and caked with clots.

He should have known that his sympathetic commentaries in the *Moose Bend Journal* toward the recent immigrants flooding over the Canadian border would have drawn blood with the locals. Blood that would hopefully protect Homeland Security Agent Simon Rouss while he embedded deeper into the terrorist cell in the hills.

Because Will knew that the men who'd hijacked him and hauled him into the forest to beat the tar out of him over his recent op-ed piece weren't actually disgruntled rednecks, but rather international terrorists.

The lie that had just saved Will Masterson's hide—the lie perpetuated by the boys toting .30-06s and wearing work boots—was the only thing keeping Simon from being brutally murdered.

Which would only be the first in a hundred—maybe a thousand—murders by the Hayata terrorist cell hiding in the northern Minnesota woods.

If only Will hadn't been ambushed by the double-edged sword sitting in his PO box. A letter from Bonnie. He'd opened it, and the words knifed him through the chest.

> *Bonnie Strong and Paul Moore invite you to a celebration of life and love in our Lord Jesus Christ.*

He should have dropped the invitation to his floorboard and crushed it under his foot. Instead, he'd let the memories, the grief, the failure rush over him and blind him to the three hillbillies lying in wait like a nest of South Dakotan rattlers. A year of undercover work, of slinking around this hick town, praying for a way to destroy the Hayata cell, and it all had to come to a head the same day his mistakes rose from the past to haunt him.

Sorry, Lew.

"Tell Bonnie and the girls I love them." Lew's dying words, hovering in the back of Will's mind, could still turn his throat raw. If Simon bought it, Will would be sending yet another letter home to the wife and loved ones.

Soldiers had no business getting married.

Will's breath felt like a razor inside his lungs. A branch clipped him, and blood pooled inside his mouth. Ruts and stone bit into his cowboy boots as he ran, and sweat lined his spine. Overhead, the sky mirrored his despair in the pallor of gray, the clouds heavy with tears. How long had he been unconscious after they'd thrown him off the four-wheeler?

Better question—how much did they guess about his alliance with Simon? Obviously, the good ol' boys who snatched him as he'd sat in his truck, waiting for his contact and regretting Bonnie's choices, knew Will's habits. *Simon's* habits. They'd found them, despite the fact that he and Simon had picked the backwoods gravel pit for its remoteness. But please—*please*—let them believe Will's lies . . . which would mean maybe Simon's cover hadn't been blown.

Maybe there wouldn't be another unnamed star embedded in the wall of honor at Langley.

Thunder rolled overhead just as Will burst from the road onto the gravel pit. Yes, thank you, the thugs/terrorists/angry readers hadn't damaged his wheels. Probably, however, they thought his 1984 Chevy wasn't worth their time.

What they didn't know was that reporter Will Masterson didn't just spend his time penning controversial editorials and writing the crime beat for the local weekly. Under the hood of this baby, he had a 350 Hemi with a high-lift cam and a four-barrel Edelbrock Thunder carb.

They didn't call him Wild for nothing. Okay, yes, he'd earned that nickname for different reasons, during a different life. But sometimes the moniker still meant something. Like now, as he hopped in and slammed all three hundred and fifty horses to the floor, spitting gravel behind him as he raced to the Howlin' Wolf.

Plan B.

Please, Simon, be there. Or, if Simon had been forced to make a fast exit, let him have taped his latest intel under Will's favorite table.

After a year of undercover work, they had one chance, one click in time to get it right. One opportunity to avenge the thousands of victims who had died at the hands of terrorists around the globe. Victims like Lew.

Please, Simon, be there.

✦ ✦ ✦

The late-afternoon drizzle seemed a fitting backdrop to the painful truth that Dannette might have to voice to the crowd of soggy search-and-rescue personnel combing Eagle Mountain.

Fern Humphrey—dementia patient, age eighty-six, grandmother of seven, great-grandmother of fourteen, and recent escapee from the High Pines Rest Center—would return to her family in a body bag.

Please, Lord, don't let her die alone.

Dannette crouched beside Missy—her half-shepherd, half-retriever mix—and ran a hand behind the dog's floppy ear. Missy's respirations came one on top of another, her stacked breathing a natural alert for the smell of something near or already dead. Although trained in search and rescue, Missy and Dannette had recovered more than their share of casualties, and Dannette read the diminishing potential for success in her animal's demeanor.

Twilight threaded gray fingers around the trees, through the brambled forest and around shaggy pines and spindly poplars. A crisp, postwinter breeze, dredged up from the still-soaked earth, whistled against Dannette's Gore-tex jacket hood. She felt chapped, hungry, and worn birch-bark thin. With night encroaching, hope had dwindled with the sunshine to a meager shadow.

She drew out a water bottle, set down a collapsible bowl, and filled it. Missy rose and lapped greedily.

Fifty feet away, she heard the echo of Kelly's call to her dog, Kirby. The younger SAR shepherd, out on his first real trial, probably hadn't yet picked up the scent cone or Kelly would be radioing Dannette for advice.

The overpowering smell of death scared most dogs.

Then again, it didn't exactly warm Dannette's insides with a happy feeling.

Dannette rose and let Missy finish her water. Maybe Missy was wrong. She wasn't Super Dog, although Dannette had to admit that following Missy's instincts often led them to crannies and hideouts unthinkable even to the most keen SAR personnel. And Missy was an air-scent dog, which meant she followed the smells left by the scraping of skin on rocks, trees, and bushes. Sadly, Missy's abilities decreased as the day worsened.

If only it hadn't taken the nursing-home staff an hour after Fern turned up missing at morning breakfast to call the sheriff's office and two more hours and the urging of the mayor—Fern's desperate son—to finally call Kelly, their nearly certified K-9 handler. Not only had a late-morning shower diffused the scent cone left by Mrs. Humphrey, but the variable winds and temperatures had scattered the scent and confused Missy. They'd walked the perimeter in a hasty search for two more hours before Missy caught the scent and alerted to Mrs. Humphrey's trail.

As usual, Dannette found that the dementia patient didn't stick to the deer trails or clearings. Mrs. Humphrey had pushed through honeysuckle and raspberry bushes, climbed over downed birch, crossed a stream, and ascended a hill that should have put her in traction. Even dementia patients who struggled to move in ordinary circumstances proved they still had gumption when some errant impulse revved up their synapses. But Mrs. Humphrey had lived a stout life, ran a farm until her husband's death a few years ago, and would probably be still milking her Jersey if her mind hadn't decided to betray her. The woman could easily be a mile from here or sitting atop Eagle Mountain.

Or injured.

Or, if Dannette read her dog correctly, dead.

Missy sat on her haunches and licked her lips. Water dripped off her jowls.

Dannette emptied the bowl and shoved it back into her backpack. "Okay, ready?"

Missy tilted her head.

"I know, sweetheart. But if it makes you feel any better, I'm glad you're here. You handle death so much better than Sherlock. He'd have his hackles up and be cowering under that white pine." She stepped away from Missy, changed her tone. "Find."

They'd been working on a free search all afternoon, after Missy's first alert. With Kelly and Kirby twenty-five feet to the west, Dannette let Missy run twenty-five feet or more ahead, quartering the wind for scent debris. Dannette checked her GPS with her map, pinpointed her position, and radioed the incident commander.

"10-4, Search 1," replied Sheriff Fadden. Dannette pictured the guy as she'd left him, wearing his black, lined Windbreaker, his stomach rebelling against the snaps, using a blow horn to direct traffic. Just what Fern Humphrey's loved ones needed while they watched the chaos.

And to add to their pain, Dannette had seen two news reporters from the local rags already lurking, smelling blood.

The leeches.

"Just heard from Search 2," Fadden continued. "Kirby alerted to scent and Kelly is tracking north, toward Eagle Cliff." He had a flattened Midwestern accent, although nothing else about him could be labeled flat. Including his ego. One month of working with or around him with the local SAR crew told her that she'd have better luck trying to reason with a bull moose.

Dannette held no doubts that if Fadden could get away with it, he'd drop-kick her and her SAR dog into the next state.

But he needed her, and they both knew it. On hand to help Kelly and her K-9 Kirby pass their SAR K-9 certification, Dannette and Missy were the only K-9 unit within two states with the teaching hours and credits to certify the team. Said certification would qualify the sheriff's department for a healthy government grant for rural SAR, an end goal that Fadden never failed to keep in the forefront of Dannette's purpose in Moose Bend. Sadly, in his mind, that goal didn't warrant tapping his force for live-victim-search training or scooping from the currently dwindling county SAR fund for K-9 training scents and devices.

The Fadden types in the world didn't put stock in the successes of the canine SAR community, and in fact they stirred up false hopes with their unrealistic, all-or-nothing attitudes. One failure and the entire SAR K-9 reputation suffered. One success and they were heralded as heroes.

It left little room for the long, dark afternoons that defined SAR K-9 work. If she and Kelly failed to locate Mrs. Humphrey, Dannette knew Sheriff Fadden would push what buttons he could to shut down her K-9 training course and send her back to Iowa. Which meant more people, like Mrs. Humphrey and five-year-old Ashley Lundeen, would perish, alone and afraid.

This is not about Ashley. Dannette's thoughts recoiled against the familiar stampede of memories, and she shook herself back to the search at hand. "10-4," Dannette said as she checked her topo map, noted Kelly's sector and direction. She frowned, checked again. "Search 1 to Search 2, please confirm location."

Kelly's voice came over the line, young and just breathless

enough to indicate she was following Kirby at a fast clip. "Crossing Devil's Creek, about one hundred yards from Eagle Cliff."

"10-4," Dannette acknowledged, her heart thumping. If Kirby had *also* alerted, perhaps Mrs. Humphrey still lived and had simply holed up in a location that emitted a putrid odor, a cave with guano or even the remains of a dead animal. Dannette folded up the map, her heart lightening.

She plowed into the fractured shadows of the forest, watching Missy work the scent. The dog stopped, circled, her nose high, turned, and looked at Dannette. Dannette used her clicker to urge the dog forward. The handheld device gave instant encouragement without having to rely on verbal cues.

The rain drizzled down into her jacket and she shivered—hungry, cold, tired. But she refused to think of the hot shower waiting. Not until she found Mrs. Humphrey.

No one deserved to die alone. Without family.

The thought roughened her throat as she steadied herself on a skinny poplar and climbed over a downed, softened birch.

Without family. No, Dannette had a family—her dogs, Sherlock and Missy. Probably the only real family she'd ever had, except for Jim Micah and the other members of Team Hope. Yeah, they felt like family. At least as far as she'd let them inside her heart.

It just wasn't wise to let people that close. Because getting close also meant getting a glimpse of the nightmares she still hadn't shaken.

This is not about Ashley. Dannette told herself that twice as she watched Missy run back, the hair on her neck bristled. Breathing rapidly, Missy sat, a passive alert to the target scent.

"Good dog," Dannette said. "Refind."

The dog bounded off, far enough ahead to keep the scent

but not so far that Dannette couldn't see her. *Please, Lord, have her on the trail of something real and alive.* She could still hear little Robby—Fern's grandson—pleading in the back of her mind. *Please, find her*, moaned another voice, one buried in her heart.

She pushed through a netting of branches and flinched for only a second when one backhanded her. The smell of decay and loam stirred up from the melting snow and foraging animals clung to the night air. Darkness drifted like fine particles of snow through the forest, so gradual as to nearly not recognize its accumulation. A cool breeze carried the echo of barking, a faint tugging on Dannette's ears as she pushed aside tree limbs and plowed through bramble. Hopefully Kirby and Kelly weren't far behind.

Missy waited at the base of a large rooted trio of birch. She looked at Dannette, her ears pricked forward. Dannette put a hand on her back. "Find."

She fought to keep Missy in her sight. They'd have to quit soon, and that thought made her want to weep.

Please, Lord, let them find Mrs. Humphrey. Alive.

Missy barked, an active alert that she'd uncovered something. Dannette marked a tree with a reflector, then plunged through the brush after the dog. Missy stood, outlined in a hover of pine.

"Search 2 to Search 1." Kelly's voice broke over the radio.

Dannette keyed her radio while she tried to get a fix on her canine. "Search 1 here." The deepening twilight turned the forest into a black-and-white, low-budget horror movie, complete with escaping birds and the rustle of ominous wind. Dannette reached for her flashlight, flicked it on.

Froze.

Missy stood over a form, a body for sure, dressed in dark

pants and a blue Windbreaker, crumpled in the fetal position, its back to her.

Mrs. Humphrey?

Her heart banging against her ribs, Dannette held her breath and approached. Missy danced around the form, animated, her breaths fast.

Dannette's chest clogged, and a tiny, panicked voice inside told her to turn and *run*. The dark memories lurked on the fringes of this moment to snare her and suck her down, to drown her.

Dannette held back a gasp and reached for her dog.

The form wore a black bag over its head. The smell of death didn't permeate the air, but the fine hairs on Dannette's neck prickled as she inched away. "Good dog," she whispered.

Static proceeded Kelly's voice, punctuating the moment, frazzling Dannette's tightly strung nerves. "I found her! Mrs. Humphrey is alive!"

Dannette's knees gave out, a weakness borne from part relief, part horror. And maybe a little from the ringing in her ears.

Who exactly had *she* found?

THE DEEP HAVEN SERIES BY SUSAN MAY WARREN

Happily Ever After

Mona thought her hero was just
a fairy tale. . . .

ISBN 0-8423-8117-1

Tying the Knot

Anne was at the end of her rope
. . . until her hero came along.

ISBN 0-8423-8118-X

The Perfect Match

Ellie's life was under control . . .
until he set her heart on fire.

ISBN 0-8423-8119-8

Visit **www.heartquest.com** today!

WELCOME TO **HEARTQUEST**

HEART QUEST

Visit

www.heartquest.com

and get the inside scoop.

You'll find first chapters,

newsletters, contests,

author interviews, and more!